To Want for Nothing

Book One of the Urban Warlocks

M.B. Kelly

Dedication

This book has been in the making for some five odd years in one way or another. I dedicate this book to Kimmi, Jon, and the many who have supported me along the way.

And for kicking my butt (metaphorically) when I was tempted to give up.

This book would not have been summoned without the bravery I gained from Gail & Piper.

Thank you.

Contents

1

Spring Cleaning

R YAN CLEARS HIS THROAT and says aloud to the empty air under the light of a full moon:

> *"From this realm to the next,*
> *I seek demon aid for trade.*
> *For this night I bring you forth,*
> *Until a bargain is made,*
> *You're mine for the stay."*

It's the stupidest thing he's ever read, and he feels even more ridiculous as he says it, but as the last word leaves his mouth there's a strange tingle along his skin. It's almost like the feeling the air gets before a lightning storm, but the skies have been clear all day.

Frowning, Ryan repeats the words. As he completes the final line, the strange sensation returns, but it's stronger than before. Like the hairs on the back of his arm are about to stand on end.

Heart racing, he repeats the chant a final time. And this time, the air on the rooftop seems to shift like it's being displaced.

***

Two Weeks Earlier

"We've got this, Mom," Ryan insists as his mother hovers over Justin's shoulder while he tries to uncover a rather large chest hidden beneath piles of boxes. Her once dark hair is now more salt than pepper, cut in a bob with thick-rimmed glasses perched atop her head.

She frowns and puts her hands on her hips as she turns her attention to him. "Well, can you blame me for wanting to spend time with my only son? It's been six months since you last came to visit!"

Ryan swallows down the protest that he's been busy. It's an old argument with her and not one he wants to waste time re-hashing. "The faster we can get this done, the sooner we can come downstairs and visit," he counters, running his fingers through his unruly, tawny hair. They've barely started, but he's already working up a sweat in the stuffy attic.

"Very well, I'll go get some lemonade and snacks ready. We can order your pizzas when you're done. Just let me know if you need anything," she says, agreeing to go downstairs with their reassurances.

"Your mom is really nice," Justin points out once she's gone. "I think she's just a little lonely. If you need a ride to come visit more, just let me know."

Guilt twists in Ryan's stomach making him feel even more uncomfortable. "Maybe. Let's just get this over with."

It's a rather mundane day in early spring when unremarkable Ryan Smith finally cons his best friend, Justin Perez, into helping clean out his mother's attic. She's been harassing him to do it for years since his father passed, but he has finally run out of excuses to put it off. He is currently between work projects and is well enough off due to his frugal living to be able to spare the day to bum a ride out of the city and across the bay with his friend Justin. Justin is easy to persuade with the promise of pizza in exchange for a ride and some manual labor. Whether Justin agrees because he is a good friend or simply a self-employed photographer in his mid-twenties with nothing better to do is hard to tell.

No, the most difficult part is insisting that Ryan's mother leave the work to them and stop micro-managing. The task itself feels overwhelming, probably because he has been putting it off for so long. The attic is cluttered with old furniture, dilapidated boxes, and garbage bags filled with old toys and clothes. Most of which could have been donated years ago, the normal kind of mess that accumulates after generations of a family lives in one house.

A single bare bulb in the rafters lights the space well enough to see the clouds of dust that are created whenever anything is picked up, shifted, or opened. Ryan and Justin have donned gloves and face masks as they set to the task ahead of them.

Now that Justin has the freedom to move about without potentially knocking over Ryan's mother, he lifts a large crate from atop the trunk with ease. Ryan envies the man's longer, darker hair that he's able to pull back into a small ponytail to keep out of the way. Ryan's hair has never been that long: he doesn't think he can pull off that look. Instead, as they kick up dust, Ryan's hair just plasters itself to his head. Working together they manage to sort the items into into three piles: keep, donate, or trash.

As Ryan debates over how to categorize some of the more keepsake-like items, Justin goes through and wipes down the furniture to determine if it's in good repair. Despite living in the attic for over a decade, Ryan's mom may want to keep some of the nicer pieces, but he may try to convince her to sell them.

Time seems frozen in the attic like the decades have been thrown together haphazardly. The only natural light comes through a small window near the roof, slowly dimming as the day turns to evening. The only other light is a single bare lightbulb dangling from the rafters.

"I think we've done as much as we're going to get to today," he admits, wiping a mix of grime and sweat from his brow with the back of his arm.

Justin stands up and stretches his arms over his head, giving a long groan in the process. "I think we've hit most of it," he admits. "There's just this trunk that is the last thing to be sorted, and we may actually need your mom to go through those items."

Ryan sighs and shuffles over to look down at the large piece of furniture. "Is there even anything in it?" he asks.

"I think it's full." Justin proves his point by trying to lift the large chest, but he barely gets it to budge. It's solidly built, but there has to be something inside.

Ryan runs his hand over the latch, brushing away the dust to read the letters etched into the front: T.A.S. "Maybe it's just more clothes?"

"Clothes wouldn't weigh *that* much. Only one way to tell," Justin says and crouches down to open the trunk.

The latch sticks, but with some brute force Justin is able to force it open. Ryan has to admit to himself there is a benefit to going to the gym, but he just doesn't have the interest.

Lifting the heavy lid, they find the trunk does contain some clothes. There is a nicely folded gray suit and some spare bedding, but beneath that are several thick books. No wonder the damn thing is so heavy. There are old textbooks on biology and natural sciences that look like they've been around since the middle of the last century.

Ryan pulls out a book bound in burgundy leather and, opening the cover, finds it's a family bible. It obviously hasn't been touched in a long time since the family tree inside the cover seems to end with his dad's generation. The name at the top of the spreading branches is Thomas Andrew Smith, identifying him as Ryan's great-great-grandfather.

"T.A.S?" Justin asks, pointing out the name. The initials do match the latch.

"Probably," Ryan has to admit. "Other than the bible and maybe some of the bedding, I don't think much else is worth keeping. These textbooks have to be horribly out of date."

Justin shrugs. "Some people collect stuff like that," he comments as he shuffles through the books. "Oh!" He pulls out a large bound book with a scrolling knot-work design along the spine. "This looks neat!"

Ryan eyes the tome with mild interest. "What is it?" he asks.

As Justin flips through the pages, Ryan's interest dissipates while he glances at the headings over Justin's shoulder. Things like *Wards to Trap Mischievous Spirits* and *Building a Basic Apothecary* mark the sections of the book.

"It looks like some sort of fantasy novel," Justin comments, his own excitement still evident.

Ryan sighs and turns back to the trunk. "It's probably just junk," he mutters, his attention turning to the suit as he eyes it curiously.

"Do you think your mom will let me keep it then?" Justin shuts the book and holds it up to the light inspecting it more closely. "The binding on it is pretty neat! It could make a cool prop, at least." Justin is constantly on the lookout for interesting looking things in his line of work. The man has gone home on more than one occasion with something Ryan thought was just junk and he made something spectacular out of by using it in an uncommon way.

"You can ask," Ryan says. "Let's head downstairs and let her know everything is ready for her inspection. Besides, I could definitely use some food."

Justin helps Ryan carry the small collection of items from the trunk down the rickety steps out of the attic for his mother's perusal.

As he guessed, his mother is most excited by the bible. "I think I remember your grandmother looking for this when you were born," she comments. "She probably wanted to add your name to it, but by then it had been misplaced."

After looking over the clothes, she holds up the suit jacket to Ryan's back and insists he takes it home with him. "You need a nice suit," she comments, even though the thing is far from being in style. Rather than argue with her, Ryan chooses the path of least resistance and accepts the hand-me-down. It may actually fit, which the last suit he bought for his high school graduation definitely doesn't anymore.

"Do you know what this is, Mrs. Smith?" Justin holds out the old tome he wants.

His mom's interest in the book seems to be on par with Ryan's. "I have no idea," she admits as she takes the book and flips through the pages. "Maybe it's one of those home remedy books?"

Justin just hums and nods. Then he goes in for the kill and shoots her a big, innocent smile. A grown man has no business being that adorable and Ryan almost scoffs at how thickly he's laying it on. "Can I take it? I think it has a really cool binding."

Ryan's mom is as much a sucker for Justin's charm as anyone else, and she happily agrees. "You've been such a great help, of course! Now, go clean up and I'll order some food."

While his mother orders the pizzas, Ryan and Justin peel off their work gloves and masks to wash the dirt and dust from their arms and face. Justin then carries around the old book, continuing to flip through it while Ryan quietly stashes the suit with his book bag so he won't forget it.

For his mom's sake, of course.

After dinner, his mom surveys their work in the attic. They carry down the bags for donation, leaving the furniture for either storage or a junk removal service depending on the state it's in. She agrees that the textbooks are probably just junk, but insists he takes them anyway. His other friend Ethan (and truly he only has one or two more friends other than Justin) has a bookstore in the city. He'll either take it or dispose of it depending on his judgment.

Ryan is glad they were able to get the work done in a single day. As Justin drives them back into the city with the moon high over the bay, Ryan lets the lull of the car's motion rock him gently into dozing. Now he'll have Sunday to do what he wants most with his free time: sleep and nothing.

The two best things.

Justin drops Ryan off at home with his old second-hand suit and collection of outdated textbooks. Both take up residence in the back of Ryan's closet and become a future-Ryan's problem. Justin seems happy with his heavy book as he heads home for the evening.

And, like with most things in his life, all things from that afternoon become out of sight, out of mind. He doesn't even give the old book Justin made off with a second thought.

Ryan is lying in bed, scrolling through social media on his phone late at night a few weeks later when a pounding comes from his front door. He has half a mind to ignore it, but it's not like he's sleeping anyway. Rolling out of bed, he shuffles through his dark apartment in his boxers and an oversized t-shirt to a new round of door pounding.

"What?" Ryan says, exasperated, as he pulls open the door.

There, on his stoop, is Justin, his eyes wide and his long dark hair pulled back into a messy manbun. He's dressed in workout gear: shorts, a hoodie, and sneakers. In one hand is the bigass book he got from Ryan's mom's attic.

"Ryan!" He grabs his friend's shoulder with his free hand. "I think I summoned a demon."

Not amused, Ryan blinks up at his friend. "And this prank of yours couldn't have been done over the phone?" he asks.

As if being reminded of something, Justin glances around. "Fuck, no, I think I left my phone in my work studio. But I'm serious!" He pushes past Ryan, flipping through the pages of the book as he lets himself into the apartment.

Sighing, Ryan hits a light switch, illuminating the living room and lets the door swing shut in his friend's wake. He trails after Justin and plops down on the old second-hand couch that has moved with him from place to place since his college dorm days, watching his friend pace back and forth as he searches the pages of the giant tome.

"Here!" Justin stops his pacing and comes over to hold the book out to Ryan. Begrudgingly, he accepts it and looks at the open pages. The heading reads *To Summon a Demon*. He looks from the scrawling script and intricate circle drawn upon the page and up to his friend.

"This is what you're going with?" he asks, skeptical.

"I'm serious," Justin insists. "I drew the circle thingy, and I chanted the words right there, and POOF! A man with horns appeared in my studio! I swear!"

"Ah," Ryan nods. "Horns? Very original."

"I swear! In a ball of flame! He appeared out of nowhere and offered to grant me a wish!"

Ryan rolls his eyes. "Was it a demon or a genie? Did you have to guess his name? Or perhaps he had a creepy monkey paw for sale?"

"Damn it, I'm not joking," Justin cries, throwing his hands up and pacing the tiny living space.

If this is a joke, Justin is taking it just a little too far. Ryan frowns and looks down at the open book sitting in his lap. "Maybe you fell asleep in your studio," he offers. "Perhaps you had a bad dream?"

Justin stops his pacing and spins to face him, brown eyes narrowing as he considers the explanation. "If that was a dream, it was the realest damn dream I've ever had."

"Come on," Ryan complains, shutting the book and putting it on the cushion beside him. "Isn't this a little far-fetched? Demons?"

For the first time since he barged in, a bit of doubt enters Justin's eyes. "Maybe you're right," he says slowly. "Do you really think I could have imagined the whole thing?"

Ryan nods, crossing his arms over his chest and relaxing back into his couch. "It makes the most sense," he points out.

"I'm not so sure," Justin says shaking his head. "Will you take a look at it, please?"

Sighing Ryan nods. "Sure, buddy. But why don't you head home and get some sleep first? I'm sure things will seem more reasonable in the morning."

Justin's eyebrows pinch together. "Yeah," he says slowly. "Yeah, maybe. Um, I'm sorry for barging in like this."

Ryan stands up and takes the few steps to close the distance between them. He puts a hand on his friend's shoulder. "It's okay," he reassures him. "It sounds like a pretty wild dream."

"I don't think it was a dream," Justin repeats, but he lets Ryan slowly lead him back out.

"It's okay," Ryan pats his back. "We'll talk tomorrow. Okay? Get home safe."

Justin frowns, his shoulders slumping. "Yeah, okay. Goodnight, Ryan."

"Goodnight," he says and opens the door for Justin. His friend, looking defeated and a bit shaken, slumps out of his apartment again. Ryan would feel a little bad, but he's not entirely convinced this isn't just a giant prank. Alone once more, he shuts off the lights and heads to bed.

When he wakes up the next morning, he has almost forgotten about the entire incident from the night before except the book is still on his couch as evidence. He gives it a curious glance before grabbing his work bag and heading out the door in his usual casual clothes: a black hoodie and black jeans that are a bit too faded even by stylish standards.

Ryan could work from home since he is a remote data entry clerk, but he doesn't have good WiFi in the basement apartment. For a change of pace he makes his way to a nearby coffee shop for the day. As he plugs away drinking far more coffee than a human being should and moving numbers from place to place, Justin's wild eyes and even wilder claims stick with him.

When he finally comes home that evening, the book is just where he left it, but this time it feels like it's mocking him. He feels silly even considering Justin's claims and his plea for Ryan to look into it.

Rather than letting the sensations linger and pester at the back of his brain, Ryan drops his work bag by the door and goes to settle on the couch. He picks up the hefty book and sets it in his lap to start flipping through the pages.

The beginning of the book feels almost like the opening of a cookbook. There are basics of components, recipes, and measurements, but Ryan has no context for what the words on the page are even referencing. Like the book is written by someone using the same language, but somehow a completely different lexicon.

As he flips through the pages, he finds each section has a very similar makeup: a specific purpose or intention followed by a list of components. Things like specific woods, herbs, or stones. The objects seem totally random and completely arbitrary to Ryan. Then each section usually has some sort of drawing: either a circle or strange-looking scribbles.

He continues to flip past each section until he gets to the one Justin showed him the night before: demon summoning. It looks very similar to all the other sections. The purpose? To summon a demon and request aid. The components: nothing. Then a large elaborate circle with delicate drawings along the edge. Ryan can almost guess that if Justin had opted to mess around, he would have picked this one for the look of the circle alone. Maybe that there were no components helped as well – no last-minute dash to the market for some uncommon ingredient.

He can't believe he's actually considering this, but honestly? Ryan has nothing better to do tonight. He can try out the stupid summoning and prove Justin is either messing with him or had a bad dream. It's not going to hurt anyone, and maybe it'll even help put Justin's mind at ease.

Glancing around his tiny apartment, Ryan figures there isn't really a clear space large enough for the circle. Besides, what would he draw it on?

Sighing, he gets off the couch, tucking the book under one arm and going into his desk. He finds a stray piece of chalk that had come with a little blackboard that he had hung on his dorm room door to tell people to go away once upon a time. Then he heads out of his apartment and straight for the steps to the roof.

He lives in the basement unit of a rather basic four-story building, the underground apartment being cheaper than anything else, but there is a communal roof space for the building. No one ever uses it except for the occasional party, so he figures it'll be private enough for his silly experiment.

With each step up the stairs that wind back on themselves, Ryan feels a little sillier. Each groan of the metal staircase as he makes his way higher is like a warning to go no further. By the time he reaches the roof he considers turning back, but he's already come this far. He flicks a switch at the top of the landing and a row of party lights left up year-round along the edge of the rooftop come alive. It's colorful, if not very bright. Just enough light to see by as the sun disappears behind the city skyline, giving the night over to a bright, full moon.

Ryan sets the book on the roof's surface, and opens it to the strange circle to start copying it onto the gray concrete of the rooftop. His lines are messy because he's half-assing it as he goes. He makes the circle large enough that doing the details of the design isn't tiny, impossible work with the piece of chalk. In the end, he ends up with a circle that probably has an eight-foot diameter.

When he's finally done, he tucks the mostly depleted piece of chalk into his hoodie pocket and slaps his hands together to get rid of the excess dust. Then, grabbing up the book, he sits on the outside edge of the circle, his back to the stairs he came up. All that's left to do is read the silly chant.

Ryan clears his throat and says aloud to the empty air:

> *"From this realm to the next,*
>
> *I seek demon aid for trade.*
>
> *For this night I bring you forth,*
>
> *Until a bargain is made,*
>
> *You're mine for the stay."*

It's the stupidest thing he's ever read, and he feels even more ridiculous as he says it, but as the last word leaves his mouth there's a strange tingle along his skin. It's almost like the feeling the air gets before a lightning storm, but the skies have been clear all day.

Frowning, Ryan repeats the words. As he completes the final line, the strange sensation returns, but it's stronger than before. Like the hairs on the back of his arm are about to stand on end.

Heart racing, he repeats the chant a final time. And this time, the air on the rooftop seems to shift like it's being displaced.

2

Well, That's New

SKYLAR IS HANGING OUT with her best friend, Kris, when she feels the familiar pull. She'd promised to help Kris get his horns buffed this evening, like doing mani-pedis on a girl's night. They are both relaxing in their comfy lounge clothes, just getting started when the tug behind her belly button starts.

Kris is sitting on a stool in the middle of Skylar's kitchen, the container of horn shine on the counter and a towel wrapped around his shoulders. "He wasn't terrible," Kris is saying about the last warlock to summon him to the mortal realm. "Total muscle bunny, you know? Big arms, tiny waist, long dark hair. It totally worked for him."

"Lucky." Skylar is about to complain about the crusty old men who keep summoning her and asking for wealth or power or the downfall of their rivals. Blah, boring. "And here we go again. Sorry, Kris. Looks like I'm off to fulfill the completely predictable desires of another loser."

Kris sighs. "It's okay. I just really wanted to spend some time with you, is all. Besides, you never know! This warlock could be like my muscle bunny."

"Doubt it," she says as she recaps the horn shine.

"Well, I guess I'm *his* demon technically." Kris stands up, stretching his arms over his head with a satisfied groan. He shoots a sly smile at Skylar. "But yeah, he's my new warlock."

Skylar blinks at him. "Wait, you didn't fulfill his deal yet? How are you here?"

"I was going to tell you, but I guess it'll have to wait. Good luck!" Kris looks entirely too smug and Skylar wants to insist further, but her situation is getting more urgent. The pull is getting stronger and the longer Skylar ignores it, the worse it'll get. From an annoying tug to a pull so strong she feels like she's about to be turned inside out.

"Fine, keep your secrets," she pokes at his side where she knows the man is ticklish. "I promise I'll do your horns next time." She reaches up and presses the tip of a finger to the end of a horn that sweeps forward and up from Kris's temples, the base hidden behind the taller demon's fluffy, curly hair. "Maybe we can sharpen them, too."

Kris waves her off. "I just want them to look shiny and pretty right now."

"For your bunny?" Skylar smirks.

"Just go!" Kris laughs and gently shoves her shoulder. "Message me when you get back."

Skylar laughs, pulling Kris into a side hug. "Fine! Talk to you soon, I hope."

Kris pats Skyler on her back, just below the junction of her wings and gives her a quick kiss on the forehead. "I believe in you. You'll be back in no time."

Just then another tug comes that causes some actual pain. Skylar grimaces and gives a nod to her friend. She shuts her eyes and lets the metaphysical string that is pulling her drag her from the demon realm to the mortal one. It is like standing with her feet solid on the ground before being yanked by an incredibly strong bungee cord.

When her feet meet solid ground again, she conjures up a giant cloud of smoke to obscure her incredibly off-putting sudden appearance. She even makes it smell like brimstone, since that's what the humans seem to expect. If she gives the summoner what they want, she can usually go home faster.

So, in that vein, she stands tall (or as tall as her five feet and then some will allow her) and waits for the smoke to clear. She holds her black-feathered wings up and back, not sure how big the space she is being summoned to will allow. She rests her hands on her hips, crossing one leg in front of the other, and tries not to squint through the smoke. She wants to seem impressive and disinterested at the same time. Her dark blue hair is swept back and she stands with her chin up. Gone are her comfy joggers and loose T-shirt and she makes sure to appear in her tightest black leather pants and a silky black button-up shirt tucked in at the front.

Slowly the smoke clears, but she doesn't see anyone standing before her as she expected. She pouts and is about to say something when the smoke near the floor shifts away and she sees a human low to the ground outside the summoning circle. He is sitting cross-legged with a large book in his lap and eyes round in surprise. It's dark enough that she can only tell that they are a light color: blue or green perhaps. The man's hair is a tousled mess of sandy strands, and he looks a bit pale as if all the color has been drained from his face.

He looks absolutely gob-smacked.

Skylar can't say she doesn't like the way this is shaping up. With the human on the ground, she towers over him. It gives her the ability to look down on the warlock with disdain, which is a rare opportunity. This human is dressed in all black, which isn't unusual, but there are no ceremonial robes or funny artifacts. Just an oversized black hoodie and jeans. She has to give it to Kris: so far this is nothing like she expected.

Especially since once the smoke clears it is obvious they are on someone's roof terrace. The moon shines brightly overhead and there are party lights strung up around the railing that marks the edges of the roof. She can't help but quirk an eyebrow as her gaze drops back to the warlock.

The man hasn't moved. He is sitting perfectly still, even once the smoke has all but completely dissipated, his mouth hanging open slightly. Skylar waits an extra-long beat before deciding to take the initiative.

She steps forward, sweeping her arms and wings wide to perform a low bow from the waist. She drops her head to look at the toes of her boots for a second before raising her gaze to meet the warlock's once more from her bowed position. "What does the warlock wish of me?" she asks in a low, silky voice.

Finally, the warlock blinks. Then he shuts his mouth before it can catch any flies. Skylar stands back up and waits for the silly human to start making demands. Instead, the human scrambles to his feet, turns on his heel, and starts to speed away.

"Hey," Skylar calls after him in her normal voice, dropping the affectation. "Wait! Where are you going?"

The warlock walks across the roof towards what looks like the stairs heading down.

"Stop!" Skylar shouts with an edge of desperation. "Warlock? Wait!"

That doesn't work. The human makes it to the stair landing and starts to disappear out of view as he makes his way down.

"Hey asshole!" Skylar screams after him. "I can't leave this stupid circle if you just walk away!" But the human is already out of her line of sight.

Skylar drops her wings and lets her arms fall to her sides. She looks around the roughly sketched circle. This warlock is either extremely messy or completely inept. She is surprised the stupid thing had managed to summon her at all.

She tries to puzzle through how she got here in an effort to figure out how to get back. Skylar runs her fingers through her hair and turns in a circle. The moon is still fairly high in the sky. Maybe if she waits until sunrise the magic that brought her here will break? She doesn't know. She's never been summoned out in the open before, let alone abandoned in the summoning circle. What were the chances another human would happen to wander by on this rooftop and break the circle for her? It didn't seem likely if the warlock had chosen this spot to do the summoning.

Skylar is about to cry out in frustration when the mop of messy hair reappears from the stairwell.

"You're really stuck in there?" calls out a voice, low but hesitant.

"No," Skylar growls. "I'm standing here spinning in circles for fun! Of course I'm trapped. Your circle may look like shit, but the magic that binds me here isn't."

The warlock slowly makes his way back up to the landing and steps onto the roof, but he doesn't move any closer. He just stares at Skylar, clutching the tome he is carrying to his chest like a shield.

Skylar stares back at him. "Well?" she calls out across the distance. "What is it that you want so we can get this over with?"

"What do I want?" The warlock seems truly confused. "You're really going to grant me a wish?"

Skylar sighs and feels her shoulders slump. "I'm not a freaking kapre with a magical white stone, but that's kind of the deal. You summoned me, you get to make a request. So, what is it that you want?"

"I don't want anything," is the warlock's immediate response as he shakes his head.

"Then why did you summon me?" Skylar throws her hands out to gesture at the summoning circle.

The warlock shrugs but takes a few careful steps closer. "I didn't think it would work."

Skylar slaps her hand on her forehead and groans. She knows humans were more skeptical of magic now than ever, but a warlock who doesn't believe his magic would work is something new. If he didn't think it *could* work, honestly, it shouldn't have. "You must have believed a little. The proof is that I'm here."

"I didn't expect it to work," the warlock seems to correct himself.

"Well, *Warlock*," Skylar crosses her arms across her chest and levels her gaze back at him. "It did work. Congratulations. If you didn't think it was going to work, why did you do it?"

The warlock shrugs. "My friend said he did it, so I did it, too. To call his bluff."

"That's the most ridiculous thing I've ever heard," Skylar says flatly. "But, now that I'm here, what can I do for you?"

The warlock frowns at her. "You're not very nice, are you?"

The entire situation is so ridiculous Skylar can't help but laugh. "Oh, I can be *very* nice," she smirks at the warlock. "I can grant you riches. Or fame. Or admiration. Tell me: what do you desire?"

The warlock is wandering closer. "And what do you get in return?"

Skylar blinks at him. No one has ever asked her that before. "What do I get? I get to go home, I suppose."

"Why did you come?" The warlock is only an arm's length away from the circle if Skylar could reach out of the circle at all. Which she can't.

"Luck of the draw, I suppose. I didn't really have a choice," she responds curtly. "Do you really not know how this works?"

The warlock shakes his head. "Not really. So, what's your name?"

Skylar takes a step back from the warlock, surprised by the sudden question. "Why?"

"I'm Ryan," the warlock offers instead. "I'm sorry if I inconvenienced you, Ms. Demon."

"Well, Warlock Ryan," Skylar says, and she can see the warlock visibly cringe at the title. "If you're so reticent you could just let me go."

"How?"

"Either let me grant you your desire, or you can dismiss me from the human realm. Though, to be honest, no one has ever really done that to me before." She shrugs.

"Why not?" Ryan opens the book he's holding. "I didn't see anything about that in here."

"Well, probably because everyone who summoned me wants something from me." Skylar begins ticking off the reasons on her fingers. "Money, fame, revenge."

Ryan looks up from the pages of his book. "So, why won't you tell me your name?"

Skylar shifts, uncomfortable under the weight of the warlock's gaze. Why is this human so off-putting? He is incredibly dense, and it makes Skylar wonder: if this hapless human had managed to summon someone or something dangerous would he still be alive?

"Because my name would give you power over me," she finally answers.

"Don't I have power over you already?" Ryan challenges, a little more sass in his tone than plain open curiosity.

Skylar scoffs. "Not really. This circle has more power over me than you do right now."

Ryan frowns as he shuts the book and tosses it to the ground at his feet. He shoves his hands in his hoodie pocket and looks at Skylar. Now that he's standing so close, she is forced to look up to meet his gaze. "But I really don't want anything."

"Nothing?" she asks, shocked.

"Nothing I can think of."

"You're a funny one, aren't you?" Skylar narrows her eyes, trying to figure out what game he is trying to play. "Well, what about your friend? Did he tell you how he got rid of the demon he summoned?"

The warlock shifts his weight from one foot to the other. "Not really. If he made a wish, I don't know what it was."

Skylar groans. She really just wants out of this entire disaster of a summoning. "Okay, tell you what. I'll tell you my name so you can cash in your wish at a future date if you promise to *never ever* try to do this again. You may not get someone as nice as me next time."

Ryan licks his lips and looks Skylar up and down. "And if I want to get you again?"

Skylar blinks, shocked by the question. Is this guy *flirting* with her? "Then you'll have my name, won't you?"

The warlock seems to consider Skylar again before he nods. Whatever hint of playfulness she had glimpsed is gone. "Fine, I won't summon a different demon if you give me your name. And I'll only summon you back if I can think of something that I want. Is that a fair deal?"

Skylar puts her hands in her pockets and walks as close to the edge of the circle as she can. "Since when do mortals care about fair deals? They summon demons to take what they want and can't get on their own."

"I don't want anything," Ryan points out.

"Ugh, fine!" Skylar throws her hands up. "My name is Skylar."

Ryan smiles. "Nice to meet you, Skylar. I guess it's time to send you home."

"Sure," Skylar says, skeptical. "Thank you, *Warlock*."

The warlock cringes again. "Please don't call me that. It doesn't make me feel very good: like spiders crawling over my skin."

Skylar cocks her hip and appraises the warlock once more. He doesn't look like much, though his power is evident in his ability to summon her there without the faith it would work. And with a circle that looks like it was drawn by a third grader. "It's not spiders," Skylar says. "That's the power you control. Or at least you would if you learned how to use it properly."

"Yeah, right," Ryan says dismissively. "And who could teach me?"

"Maybe your other warlock friend who summoned a demon?" she suggests. Then after a beat. "Or me."

Ryan runs his fingers through his hair. It doesn't make the tousled mess any neater. "I'll think about it. But for tonight, let's just send you home. Shall we?"

Skylar stands up straight and moves back to the center of the circle, her wings shaking as if to settle ruffled feathers. "At your will, Warlock Ryan."

"Gah," Ryan shivers again. "Please don't call me that again."

"I won't, if you send me away." Skylar gestures for him to continue, tickled by how the tables have turned.

"Brat," Ryan mutters. "Fine. Skylar, I release you from the mortal realm to return home until I summon you again. Just don't call me a warlock, again."

And just like that Skylar feels the bungee cord that keeps her there snap. It is like she is free-falling, and it ends only when she reappears back in her kitchen. Since she is home, she doesn't bother with the theatrics. She just suddenly exists where she hadn't been before.

Kris is still in her kitchen, raiding her cabinets. He has an apple stuck in his mouth as he rummages through the shelves, but he pauses to look back at Skylar in surprise. He opens his mouth, arms still frozen over his head, and the apple drops to the countertop with a dull thud. "You're back!"

"You're still here," Skylar returns, looking at her friend in surprise.

"Yeah," Kris grins bashfully. He lowers his arms and turns to face Skylar. "I was kinda hungry and was looking for a snack."

Skylar waves away his explanation. "It's fine. You're welcome to stay. You know that."

"Thanks!" Kris picks the apple back up and takes a big bite. Then, with a mouth full of apple chunks asks: "How'd it go? That was pretty fast."

Skylar sits down on the stool that has been abandoned when buffing Kris's horns got put on hold. "To be honest, I'm not sure."

"What did the warlock want?" Kris takes another bite of the apple and leans against the fridge.

"Nothing," Skylar answers. "He wanted absolutely nothing."

Kris smirks. "I guess it's time to tell you about my bunny."

"Fine," Skylar sighs. She hops off the stool and pats the empty seat. "May as well buff your horns while we chat."

Kris picks the towel back up from the counter where he'd tossed it and puts it back around his shoulders before settling onto the stool. "So," he says around another mouthful of apple. "It was last night, and I got summoned."

Skylar slips on pair of gloves before uncapping the horn shine again. "Like one does," she comments.

"Yup," Kris crunches into the apple.

Skylar takes the opportunity to pick up the rag she had pulled out earlier that day and scoops up a decent amount of horn shine. She closes the distance between them to begin rubbing it across the other demon's horns.

Kris chews and swallows the bite of apple. "I did the whole 'fire and brimstone' routine. You know? Create the illusion of fire and rise up from the flames to the smell of brimstone."

"Fire looks good on you," Skylar hums in acknowledgment. "I prefer just smoke."

Kris beams. "Thank you! So yeah, I did the whole fire thing and the next thing I know I'm getting blasted with a fire extinguisher!"

"No way," Skylar gasps and stops what she's doing to look Kris in the eye. When Kris meets her gaze and nods, they both burst into laughter. Shaking her head, Skylar goes back to shining the horn. "That's got to be a first."

"It was," Kris says before crunching into the apple again. Once he swallows he continues his story. "Anyway, I'm coughing and trying to tell the guy to stop. When I could finally breathe again I was completely blown away. There stood this guy in black gym shorts, one of those dark muscle shirts, and sneakers. Tattoos up one arm. Hair long enough to pull into a bun on the top of his head. Total gym bunny, you know?"

Skylar is holding Kris's curly hair out of the way so she can get down around the base of the horn. "That's different for a warlock," she as to admit. "Even my guy tonight looked different. Not the usual ceremonial robes. Just a normal guy off the street kind of look."

"If this is a new trend for warlocks, then I approve," Kris jokes before finishing off the apple and tossing the core into Skylar's sink. "So my whole spiel is ruined, right? How can I be all 'What mortal summons me?' in my big booming voice when I've just finished choking on chemicals?" Skylar just nods as she moves onto the other horn. "Instead, I just look at the guy and go: *really*? Like he was just standing there ready to spray the first demon that showed up?

"Next thing I know he's dropped the extinguisher and is apologizing to me! 'I'm sorry, Mr. Demon. Please don't smite me.' Ha! As if I could from inside a protective circle."

Skylar shakes her head. "I swear, warlocks today don't know shit. The one who summoned me tried to just up and walk away!"

"That may actually be worse," Kris has to admit through his laughter. "Long story short: the guy didn't know what he wanted. Like yours, I guess.

He said he wanted to prove he could do it, because he was under the impression it wasn't real."

"What are they teaching warlocks these days?" Skylar commiserated.

"Right? I tried to offer him stuff, you know? Riches. Fame. Sex appeal, not that he really needed it. I felt kind of bad for the guy, so I told him I'd take a rain check on it. Honestly, we spent the rest of the time talking and I was actually enjoying myself. He's into photography, too! So we discussed that for like an hour."

"Kris!" Skylar scolded. "Summonses aren't dates! Can you imagine what the higher-level demons would say if they heard you talking like this?"

"Look, I'm just saying: if warlocks are changing, maybe we should, too? Not every demon has to be trying to fit some bullshit image of demons. Maybe some of the elder demons are scary and mean, but there's so few of them! I don't think that applies to us. Do you feel evil?"

Skylar shakes her head. She and Kris had both been born this way. They couldn't help what they became. "You're not evil," Skylar admits.

"And neither are you." Kris grabs Skylar's wrists and pulls her hands into his own. "It's just a role we play, but wouldn't it be nice if we could just be us?"

Skylar frowns and thinks about Kris's words. Normally she doesn't care if the warlocks that summon her think she is evil, because they are just projecting themselves onto her. They are evil, greedy, and lustful. Skylar is just a tool they use to get what they want, but what if a warlock isn't any of those things? If they don't project those negative things onto her, then what would Skylar be to them? Could she be herself?

"You've still got shine on your horns, I'm almost done." Skylar tugs her hands free to finish buffing Kris's horns.

"You're the best," Kris beams up at her.

3

Questions Upon Questions

AND JUST AS SUDDENLY as she'd arrived, the world shifts ever so slightly and the stunning woman is gone. Ryan finds himself alone on the rooftop, gaping at the center of the now empty circle where just a moment before stood a beautiful and terrifyingly real winged demon. His mind reels as it tries to make sense of this new reality. He's not sure if wings are any better than horns, but that seems secondary to: *Oh my god, demons are real!*

"Holy shit," he whispers to himself. He really didn't think that would work. Even as he'd gone through the steps to actually summon a demon, he had been 99.9% certain Justin was just messing with him.

A cool breeze kicks up on the roof, making the twinkling party lights sway and pulling him from his thoughts. Quickly, he looks around as he tries to figure out what happens next. The next time there's a rainbow, will Ryan be able to find a leprechaun at the end? If demons are real, then what else is out there?

He bends down and picks the book back up, glancing around and looking for what his immediate next step is. The clumsily drawn circle is the only evidence left of what transpired this evening. And if he can summon a demon using it, does that mean anyone can? Nervous about the drawing being discovered, Ryan starts scuffing his shoe over the chalk lines blurring them until they are unrecognizable as anything other than smudgy marks on the rooftop.

Clutching the book to his chest, Ryan scurries back down the stairs all the way to the street level before ducking down another small staircase to his own basement apartment. Darting inside, he makes sure to lock the door behind himself before heading directly to his bedroom. He throws open his closet and tosses the tome in, causing the stack of old textbooks to topple over, before slamming the door shut again.

There's only one other person he can talk to about this! He sits on the edge of his bed and pulls out his cellphone. He immediately has a message window open to text Justin, but pauses before he even starts. Is it safe to talk about something like this in text messages? Can it be used as evidence that he's lost contact with reality?

No, better to discuss the whole matter in person.

Ryan holds the phone with both hands, waiting for Justin to respond.

The text sits unread. And with each passing minute Ryan feels a knot of anxiety twisting tighter in his gut. He needs to do something to release it, but what?

Tossing the phone aside, Ryan goes over to his desk and pulls out a spiral notebook. He flips past the first couple of pages of scribbled work notes to a fresh page and picks up a pen to start immediately jotting down the details from tonight. Suddenly he's worried that if he forgets anything, he won't be able to repeat the summons.

-Drew the circle to the specifications

-Read the chant

-Time passed – how much? Minutes?

-Puff of smoke & smell of rotten eggs (?) signaled demon's arrival

-Demon: dark blue hair, brown or black eyes, large black wings, unearthly beauty

-Name: Skylar

-Can grant a wish and until the wish is fulfilled is somehow tied to summoner?

-Cannot leave the circle

-Why do they have to grant wishes?

> -Where are they summoned from?
> -Why did my family have this book? Look for more information on Thomas Andrew Smith?
> -Are demons trustworthy?

That last question leaves Ryan frowning at his own tiny, scrawled writing. Demons aren't trustworthy. Right? Isn't that what it means to be a demon? And who is he supposed to ask to find out? The whole thing is starting to give him a headache.

He gives up trying to make heads or tails of the entire situation and pushes himself up from the desk. He kicks off his shoes before he strips off his hoodie and jeans. In just his shirt and boxers he crawls into bed, even though it's not even that late. He keeps his phone next to his pillow in case Justin gets back to him soon.

Sleep, which usually comes easily to Ryan, is elusive tonight. He tosses and turns, thinking of black feathers, cutting words, and the tome tossed in his closet. His mind keeps churning over all this new information, making twisted dreams of possible scenarios when sleep finally comes.

His text alert goes off rapid fire pulling him from a fitful dream. Groaning, he blindly reaches out to search for his phone. Peering at the screen with one eye, he sees Justin has finally gotten back to him.

Justin

Your treat? Any time!

Well, except before 5 tonight.

I have a photo shoot with a client until then.

Ryan

That's fine.

Text me when you're done and we can figure things out from there.

Perfect! See you tonight!

A quick check of the time tells Ryan that he has at least ten hours to figure out what he's going to tell Justin. The idea of just stewing in his dark apartment all day does not sound appealing. What better way to distract himself than with work? He typically doesn't like to work on Saturdays if he doesn't have an impending deadline, but the idea of doing nothing seems worse for once.

He shuffles out of bed and starts getting ready for the day. Once he's dressed and refreshed, the events of last night seem further removed from reality. He opens his closet to get a fresh hoodie and his eyes fall to the large tome sitting atop the messy pile of textbooks.

A creeping uneasiness gives Ryan pause. Is it safe to leave a book like that lying around? If he can summon a demon, then anyone can. No, best to keep the book with him, even if he doesn't like the idea of carrying such a heavy weight around.

Having made up his mind, Ryan grabs his work bag and shoves the giant volume inside. Along with his laptop and work essentials, the added book makes his bag look like it's going to burst at the seams, but it'll have to do for today.

That leaves the pile of neglected textbooks and Ryan decides *fuck it*. He grabs a delivery box and fills it with the books. He's been avoiding Ethan's store for weeks now and he might as well just bite the bullet and take these in. Besides, he does miss his friend and feels like having him nearby may be a comfort today.

So, laden with old books and an overtaxed work bag, Ryan makes his way out into the world. The spring season is in full swing, so the mornings are still chilly as Ryan makes his way through the bustling city streets. Cars crawl by, the people on the sidewalk moving faster in some areas as everyone tries to get where they are going. He's sure some of the poor fools are off to work like him, while everyone else is out to enjoy their weekend.

The walk to Ethan's bookstore, *Much Loved Books,* isn't far, but feels a hundred times farther with Ryan's increased load. He's sweating and struggling to maintain his grip on the box by the time he shoulders his way through the front door. The bell that hangs over the entrance tinkles as Ryan rushes the last few steps to put the heavy box down on the checkout counter. In his effort to not drop the damn thing, he knocks over a small pile of books, and a bookmark display goes crashing to the ground.

"Hello, welcome to—," comes Ethan's baritone voice as his head peeks around a corner. As soon as his dark eyes land on Ryan, he drops the customer service spiel. "Oh, hey, stranger." He smirks as he comes around the row of shelves and walks towards the front counter.

"Sorry for the mess," Ryan apologizes, dropping to a knee to gather up the bookmarks that fell to the ground.

"No worries," Ethan reassures him as he steps behind the counter and collects the tumble of fallen books. "At least it was you making the mess this time instead of me. Did you bring me something fun?"

As Ryan sets the bookmark display back on the edge of the counter, he gives the taller man a shrug. "Not really. Last month I finally caved and went up to my mom's place to empty her attic. She had a bunch of these textbooks sitting in a trunk, but we weren't sure they'd be worth anything."

Ethan hums as he reaches into the box and pulls out a few of the books in question. "They're in pretty decent shape," he comments, turning them over before setting one down to flip through another. "You'd think science and biology textbooks would be good for a long time, but a lot has changed since these were published back in—" He pauses to check the copyright date in the front of one of the books. "—1942."

"So they're worthless?" Ryan guesses.

"Every book has worth," Ethan counters. "I just don't know if I can get much money for them anymore, but I'll take them off your hands. I can get them recycled at least."

"Thanks," Ryan gives the man a grateful smile. "How have things been around here lately?"

Ethan puts the textbooks back in the box and lifts it with an ease Ryan finds wholly unfair. "Not bad," he says, setting the box on a table behind the counter. "Without my loiterer hanging around, things have been pretty boring."

"I buy coffee," Ryan protests.

"I don't sell coffee," the bookstore owner laughs. "It's okay, man. I'm just teasing since I haven't seen you in so long. I was starting to think you'd finally fallen into a sleeping beauty-like slumber and were never coming back again."

"Ha ha," Ryan deadpans. "Just say you missed me, and we can call it good." He adjusts the bulky work bag on his shoulder.

"Your presence was missed," Ethan admits. "Welcome back. Your favorite table is empty, as usual. I'm pretty sure the padding in that seat is officially molded to your ass at this point."

"Thanks." Ryan lingers by the front counter as Ethan starts sorting through the box of textbooks. "Um, I'll be around if you need any help." In exchange for using the store's WiFi and space, Ryan sometimes helps when it gets busy. And Saturday is more likely for that to happen.

Ethan glances over his shoulder, raising a dark eyebrow. "If you're working, it's fine. Thanks for offering."

Ryan just nods and goes off to find his favorite spot. There's a table in the back corner of the store for people to sit and read, but he usually co-opts it for his workspace since there's an outlet nearby. The bag makes a heavy *thud* as he sets it on the table thanks to the extra cargo it's carrying today. Ryan settles into his chair sinking into the comfy cushion. Its position puts his back to the history section, but allows him a clear view of anyone coming in through the front door. He likes to people-watch when his eyes need a break from staring at his computer screen.

The rest of the morning flies by as Ryan works on sorting the data from a survey for this company to input into a findings report. The next thing he knows, there's an ache between his shoulder blades from being immobile for too long, and Ethan is sitting down across from him.

"Lunch time," Ethan announces, placing a wrapped sub by Ryan's mouse pad. "Take a break and eat with me."

Ryan quickly saves his work and shuts the laptop. "Thanks," he says, giving his friend a smile as he pushes the laptop to the side in exchange for the sandwich. "Things been slow today?"

Ethan, who is unwrapping his own sandwich, gives out a laugh. "No, actually. It's been pretty busy. You've just been too tunneled in on your laptop to notice."

"Oh," Ryan blinks. "Sorry."

"It's fine. Is what you're working on that riveting?" Ethan takes a bite of his sandwich and watches Ryan expectantly.

"Not really," he has to admit. "Just really tedious data organizing." As he unwraps his own sub, Ryan's stomach gives a pang at the aroma of deli meat and cheese. Bits of shredded lettuce escape from the sandwich as he picks it up.

"Must be pretty important if you're working here on a Saturday." Ethan is digging into his own sandwich from his favorite deli down the street.

"Maybe I just missed hanging out here," Ryan teases and takes a bite. Food is exactly what he needed. "Besides," he says after he swallows, "I'm waiting for my friend to get done with a client. What better place to kill time than here?"

Ethan laughs and just shakes his head. Their lunch repast is cut short when an elderly couple comes in asking for help finding a graduation gift for the granddaughter. Ethan folds the last half of his sandwich back into the wrapping and excuses himself.

Before reopening his laptop, Ryan texts Justin that when he's done with work he should just come by the bookstore. He works for another couple of hours and finally shuts his laptop. It feels wrong to be working any longer than he has to on a Saturday. He packs up his work stuff and stashes his bag behind the front counter where Ethan is ringing up a couple of teens and their stack of yaoi manga.

"Have a good day," the clerk tells the girls as they hook their arms together and leave giggling.

Ryan smirks and glances at him. "Have you been hiding your yaoi section from me all this time?"

"Not at all," Ethan laughs as he picks up a stack of books. "I actually get a lot donated, but they never stay on the shelves long. Are you done with work for the day?"

"Yeah," Ryan says. "Anything I can help you with before my body freezes in a hunched-over position?"

Ethan pauses, the stack of books resting against his chest as he considers Ryan's request. "What are your feelings about dusting?"

And that's how Ryan spend the rest of his afternoon: dusting the shelves and tops of displays while chatting with Ethan and the occasional customer. It's actually really relaxing, interrupted only occasionally by a moment of panic to check that the book is still safely in his bag behind the counter.

At about a quarter after five, Justin strolls into the bookstore. The man is dressed like he just came from a photo shoot where he was the model instead of the photographer: black leather jacket, blue jeans, crisp white shirt. He smiles when Ethan comes around the counter to greet him. Justin has been by the shop a couple of times to meet Ryan in the past.

Ryan goes to put the dust rag away and grab his bag as the two catch up. "Thanks for letting me chill here today," he says to Ethan as he steps out from behind the counter.

"Any time, you know that. Have a good evening, you two." Ethan waves them off as they head out of the shop.

"So," Ryan says as they start walking down the street. "What did you want to eat?"

Justin laughs. "Do I even need to say?" he teases. There is a small hole in the wall taqueria near *Much Loved Books* that is their usual go-to, so honestly Ryan probably didn't even have to ask.

"Just making sure," he says. Ryan has done such a good job of *not* thinking about this today that he doesn't even know where to start, so he keeps things light. "How'd the shoot go today?"

"Today was pretty cool, actually," Justin says, the excitement for his work bleeding into his words. "The client was this sixteen-year-old girl who de-signed an awesome futuristic-fantasy elf cosplay. We hit up the park and a couple of the statues in the city to take some shots. Her parents paid for the whole thing. Can you imagine having parents that supportive of your passions? I'm actually kind of bummed that we finished early, but it let me get over here that much faster."

"Yeah, cool," Ryan mutters, distracted. To be fair, he isn't sure what a futuristic-fantasy elf would look like.

He's spared from having to come up with a new topic of conversation when they enter the taqueria. Not waiting for Ryan, Justin walks up to the woman and starts ordering their meal. Other than some basic Spanish, Ryan isn't able to keep up as the two banter back and forth. He just waits for the total to come up and hands over his card, thanking the woman for her help.

While Justin waits for the food, Ryan nabs a table in the back. There are only five tables in the tiny restaurant, but he purposefully chooses one that's away from the front windows, even if that's where Justin usually likes to sit. This table at least offers the illusion of some privacy for their conversation. The work bag feels particularly heavy as he places it on the floor between his feet.

A few minutes later Justin walks up with a tray covered in food: tacos on corn tortillas, rice, beans, a massive burrito, chips and salsa. He sets the tray down and smiles at Ryan. "This is mine. Where's yours?" he jokes.

"Rude," Ryan says and reaches for one of the tacos.

"So," Justin says as he cuts the burrito in half, "have you looked into that book anymore?"

Ryan freezes, taco almost to his mouth. There is no more stalling, so he lowers it once more. "Maybe," he says cautiously.

"And what do you think? Do you believe me?" Justin pushes, even as he picks up half the burrito and takes a bite.

Ryan sighs and puts the taco back on the plate, his appetite gone in the wake of nerves that he's actually about to admit this. "Yeah, Justin. I believe you."

Justin blinks and stares at him with wide eyes. "Wait, really?"

"Yes, really," Ryan repeats.

The blank stare continues. "Why did you change your mind?"

Ryan squirms under Justin's scrutiny. "I have my reasons."

A light seems to spark behind Justin's surprised stare and his mouth drops open. "You did it, didn't you!" His accusation is a little too loud for Ryan's comfort.

"Lower you voice," he hisses as his eyes dart towards the ladies who operate the restaurant. They aren't paying them any mind, but it still makes him twitchy. "I didn't say that."

Justin puts the burrito down and leans closer over the table. "That's the only thing that would make you change your mind."

"Fine," Ryan huffs. "I did it. And it worked. Happy?"

Justin sits back in his seat, but he seems less proud of himself than Ryan expects. "Yeah, I guess. Did..." His sentence trails off.

Ryan picks the taco back up and takes a bite, waiting for Justin to continue. When Justin remains silent, he asks. "Did what?"

"Did you talk to Kris?" Justin asks and Ryan can't quite read the emotion behind the question. Was it hope or dread?

"Who is Kris?" he asks, confused by the shift in the topic.

"You know," Justin whispers. "The demon."

Realization dawns on Ryan as he chokes on a piece of shredded lettuce he'd been attempt to swallow. Maybe eating is too dangerous at the moment. He drinks some water to help clear his throat. "What? No, I didn't. And should you be telling me their name? Doesn't that give you some kind of power over them?"

"Does it?" Justin gasps and slaps his hand over his mouth. "Shit, forget I said that."

Ryan rolls his eyes. "I guess asking you any of the questions I have after last night is kind of pointless."

"Sorry," Justin mumbles. "But I left you the book. Why didn't you just look it up?"

"I really can't make sense of a lot of what's in the book," Ryan has to admit. "The language is kind of archaic."

Justin perks up in his seat. "Maybe we can try to figure it out together?"

"I'm sure as hell not going to ask anybody else," Ryan says. "I think we should also try to look up my relative Thomas Andrew Smith. Maybe he has some sort of connection to the book?"

Justin swallows another bite of burrito and nods. "Maybe your mom knows something?"

"I don't know. I guess I could shoot her an email and ask,," he thinks aloud.

"Totally," Justin continues to nod. "And we can comb through the book and see if we can figure anything out together."

As much as Ryan appreciates Justin's offer, he isn't sure what the two of them can figure out that they couldn't have done alone. In addition, he is deeply reticent to involve him in this. But what other option does he have? Maybe he will have to summon Skylar back to answer his questions, but he really wants to save that until there is no other possible source of information.

4

When A Demon Is Born

Skylar

2008

WHEN PEOPLE WARNED SKYLAR that puberty isn't easy, they really undersold it in her opinion. Her mother does her best giving Skylar a book about what kind of changes to expect to her body and answering her questions. Now that she's thirteen and still hasn't had her first period, her mother is starting to worry, even though her pediatrician assures them it's normal.

What her mother can't help her with is the strange itching between her shoulders. It started out as just a nuisance, like a bug bite, but the sensation has spread like a rash. She asks her mom and her little sister to check from time to time, but both of them say there's nothing there to see.

"Except for where you're scratching yourself," her mother scolds her. "Leave it alone and it'll get better."

Skylar wakes up one night from a fitful rest because the itching has become a burning sensation. She sits upright in bed on the verge of tears, shoving away the covers to get some relief. It feels as if a red-hot poker is trying to pierce between her shoulder blades and Skylar lets out a painful scream.

She catches her reflection in the vanity mirror through the haze of tears. Wisps of dark hair have escaped from her messy ponytail as a small, scared girl in a sleep tank top sobs. Suddenly, as if her back has torn itself open, two large wings with feathers as dark as midnight sprout and flare out behind her. Before she can even take a full breath to scream again, it feels as if the bed has fallen out from beneath her and she is falling.

When she lands, her knees hit something soft that cries out in surprise. She falls onto her butt, trying to make sense of what is happening. The room is dark and she can't see anything in front of her for a long moment. A light turns on and she blinks at the sudden brightness, but hears a voice yelling.

"Really? It's the middle of the night!"

Skylar finds herself sitting at the foot of a large bed in front of a man who is scrambling to untangle himself from the sheets. The stranger's light brown hair is disheveled from sleep and he's dressed like the dad in an old television sitcom with a button-up pajama top. He could have been considered handsome, but his skin is covered in scales that run up his neck and over his jawline. There are also scales that come down in a peak from his hairline. He turns yellow eyes with vertical slits, like the pupils of a serpent, upon Skylar.

"Your timing leaves something to be desired," he sighs and runs his fingers through his hair.

"W-w-where am I?" Skylar stutters.

With a put-upon huff, the stranger throws his hands out to gesture to the room. "Welcome to the demon realm," he announces. "Specifically, my bedroom. Which you cannot stay in, but no worries. We'll get you settled for the night. You can call me Warren, and it seems I will be your demon mentor."

Skylar's lip trembles. Demon? "Am I in Hell?" she whimpers.

"It's too early in the morning for this," Warren groans mostly to himself. He rubs his face before looking back to Skylar. "No. Heaven? Hell? That's all bullshit made up by humans to make themselves feel better about death while simultaneously feeling superior to the next pitiful human. Think of this as more like a pocket dimension. One that you cannot leave unless you're specifically summoned out."

Skylar feels completely overwhelmed with tears streaming down her round cheeks. "You mean I'll never see my family again?" Images of her mom and dad flash before her eyes. Thoughts of never seeing her younger siblings make her heart ache. What about her aunts and uncles and cousins?

"Seriously, this is conversation best saved for when the sun is up." Warren's cutting tone is gone and he truly seems sympathetic. "I know it'll be hard to achieve, but a good night's sleep will really be what's best for you."

Maybe she's still dreaming? Skylar holds onto that hope as she lets the strange man lead her to another room. Nothing looks familiar as they move through the, what? Is it a house? An apartment? It's a place she's never been before. The moon shines bright outside the window and seems closer than it ever has before, shedding light on a city skyline that seems as foreign as a Martian landscape.

"You can use this room for the time being," Warren says, opening the door to another bedroom. It's larger than Skylar's living room at home with a four-poster bed standing in the center. She tentatively steps inside, and looks around with wide eyes. "Trust me," the man says. "Sleep will do you a world of good." And with that, he leaves, gently shutting the door behind him.

Still in her sleep shorts and tank top, Skylar dives onto the bed, hoping that when she wakes up again she'll be back in her own room. It's hard to figure out how to sleep with the large wings on her back. She ends up curling into a ball with the sheets pulled up to her shoulders and tucked under her chin, but with her back exposed to the unfamiliar room.

Somehow between the pain in her back dissipating and being completely overwhelmed, Skylar does fall into a dreamless sleep.

The next morning, Warren seems to be in a better mood. He gives Skylar a change of clothes that happen to fit her, even with the wings: a pair of slacks and a loose top that droops in the back. Why does a man in his thirties have clothing for a teenage girl? It feels like the least of her concerns.

Then he feeds her and, while he doesn't try to comfort Skylar with false platitudes, he does give her space to herself. At least until breakfast is over and his mentorship seems to begin.

Warren sits Skylar down in a private library at a table across from himself. She sits with her hands clasped in her lap and her wings twitching nervously. Her shoulders are hunched as if she can make herself smaller than she already is. Any other time, she'd love being in a library. Skylar of yesterday would have delighted in roaming the shelves and touching the books.

"What's your name?" Warren asks gently.

She blinks. Unsure why, she assumed he would know it. "Skylar Valera," she responds quietly.

"Well, Skylar, I'm here to help you adjust to your life as a demon. I'm guessing this isn't something you were expecting?" Skylar shakes her head and Warren continues. "Every demon who is born as such is recalled to the demon realm when their demonic traits manifest during puberty."

"How can I be 'recalled' if I've never been here before?" Skylar asks, perplexed. A spark of anger born from frustration burns in her chest.

Warren sighs. "It's a turn of phrase."

"So, I was born this way?" she asks, confused.

Warren nods. "Whenever a demon and a mortal create progeny, that child is always a demon."

Skylar finds herself struggling to understand. The words make sense, but they don't feel like they apply to her. "So, my mom or my dad is also a demon?"

"Yes," Warren nods and then freezes "Did you live with both a mom and a dad?" Skylar nods. "Then I hate to break it to you: one or both of them are not your biological parent. Demons cannot live in the mortal realm."

And once again Skylar finds her lip trembling and tears threatening to spill over. It isn't the last time in the weeks to come.

Warren is true to his word and takes Skylar under his wing (so to speak) to teach her what she needs to know about how her life has changed. As her mentor, he answers any question she has about being a demon.

"So, I can do magic?" Skylar asks as they sit in their usual seats in the library. She has a notebook with some scribbled notes. Warren didn't provide it for her. She'd ask for the pages herself, finding the act of taking notes soothing.

Warren nods as he sits across from her. He's dressed in a burgundy robe with patterns and symbols stitched into the trim. It is something he puts on whenever Skylar is having a formal lesson or he is meeting with other demons in an official capacity. "You *are* magic now. Mortals who want to do magic have access to it, but they have to use trappings in order to direct it. Spells, rituals, potions, or even demons. Mortals are extremely limited in their magical abilities. Some have more power. Others have less. All demons have unlimited power. We are limited only by outside forces and certain laws of the universe. For example: in the human realm we can't make something out of nothing. It has to come from somewhere."

"Like my clothes or this notebeook?" He nods and Skylar frowns as she scribbles down her notes. "Outside forces?" she asks, peering up through a piece of loose hair that has fallen from her ponytail.

"Yes. One of the most common restrictions mortal magic users – warlocks – use against us is the protection circle they use for summoning. We are trapped within the circle unless released and cannot harm the summoner. However, there's a less obvious structure in place even though it's everywhere. Can you guess what it is?"

Skylar pouts as she considers Warren's question. Sometimes he does this, and she thinks it's to make sure she's paying attention. Her eyes roam over the shelves of books, then the large window that looks out at the city. She sees tall buildings along the skyline with other demons going about their daily lives. No one works, but there is a built-in hierarchy that Skylar has yet to really understand. Anything a demon needs or wants, they can create in the demon realm. Food, clothes, possessions, entertainment. The only thing they can't do is leave.

"Is it the demon ream itself?" Skylar asks.

Warren smiles at her and he looks a little proud. "So clever," he comments. "Yes. The demon realm was created by warlocks to trap demons. Think of it like a storage container. It is a place they send us until they want to use us. We can do whatever we want here because it does not affect the mortal realm."

That seems strange to Skylar. She feels like she's missing something. "The warlocks created this place for us? We don't have to work. We don't get sick. We can do whatever we want. That doesn't seem like a bad thing."

Warren leans forward and looks Skylar in the eyes. The yellow irises become less unnerving every day. "It's very important you remember this one thing, Skylar: a prison is a prison, no matter how nice it may seem."

Skylar blinks, trying to understand. "But why is it a prison?"

"That's a story for another time," Warrens says with a frown set upon his face. He leans back and a forked tongue licks along his lips to wet them before he continues. "The important thing to remember is that the demon realm was created so that the warlocks could control us."

"How did warlocks trap the first demons into the demon realm?" Skylar feels thirsty for information now that they seem to be getting to a topic Warren doesn't want to explain.

"The two were actually created at the same time: the first demon and the demon realm." Warren starts to pick at his nails and becomes more distant.

Skylar feels the connections forming in her mind. "So, the first demon wasn't born a demon?" Warren just nods even though this is a revelation to Skylar. She'd assumed all demons were born, but that makes sense. This isn't a chicken or the egg kind of question. "Were *you* born a demon?"

Warren's hand comes down on the tabletop with a thunderous smack. "We're done for today."

Quickly, Skylar learns Warren never wants to talk about himself. Well, not entirely. He loves to talk about himself as far as his position or wealth of knowledge, but not anything personal.

Eventually, Warren gives Skylar leave to go and explore the demon realm on her own. According to him, the entire realm is a smaller version of the mortal realm. There are only hundreds of demons as opposed to billions of humans, but as the human realm changes, so does the demon realm. Technology advances and becomes available, even if demons don't need things like cars to get around or cellphones to communicate. It does get them things like modern buildings and comforts, though.

Skylar is on one of her excursions when she walks by a horned demon trying to get a picture of a flower in the park. He seems to be struggling as she pauses to watch the demon shift minutely from side to side as he points an older-looking camera around. He looks young, maybe about her age, but it's hard to tell with demons. When the demon finally lets out a frustrated huff, she clears her throat. "What's wrong?"

Startled, the demon looks up from where he's crouching. He blinks warm brown eyes, and his hair is a nest of tousled curls around the horns. "It's these horns," he groans and flicks a finger against the bony extrusion. "They block the light and cast a shadow."

"Well, let me see if I can help," Skylar offers as she steps off the park path to crouch in the grass beside the other demon. She tucks a strand of her hair, which she has turned from black to a rich dark blue, behind her ear. "Get in the position you want to take the photo and let's see."

The demon holds up the camera to look through the lens and frame the photo. "See what I mean?" he grumbles, and she can. The angle of the sun hits in such a way that the demon's horn casts a shadow across the colorful petals.

Skylar holds up her hand so that her palm is hovering just above the problematic horn. Sure, it cast more of a shadow until she mutters: *luminos*. Then, with just her thoughts, she adjusts a glowing orb in her hand until the light cast upon the flower is indistinguishable from the sun. Immediately, the demon snaps a picture and lowers the camera to smile at her.

"I still forget we can do magic," he admits with a laugh. "I'm Kris."

And just like that Skylar makes her first friend in the demon realm. They become nearly inseparable. If they aren't with their mentors, Kris and Skylar are with one another. Kris has only been in the demon realm about six months longer than her and they are able to help each other cope with the loss of their families in a way that their mentors simply can't.

2014

Mentorship, as it turns out, typically lasts about five years before the demon is released from the care of their mentor. Then, through a drawing of lots, they are given their own residences and left to their own devices. Skylar is out of Warren's apartment and on her own before she ever gets her first summons.

She's been living on her own for a few months when the first one happens. She is sitting in her living room listening to music and reading a book when an uncomfortable tug appears in her belly. At first, she thinks maybe she's just hungry and is planning to take a break after the chapter she's reading. Then the tug comes back, but a little stronger.

Frowning, Skylar puts the book on her coffee table. It's too early to be that time of the month. When she stands up to head to the kitchen, a third, stronger tug comes. The force of it is so unexpected she doubles over and nearly falls to her knees.

Dread crawls up her throat when she realizes what must be happening. Skylar isn't ready for this. For months, she seriously hasn't even thought about what to do in this scenario. Warren has done everything he can to prepare Skylar, but now those lessons fly right out of her mind. She looks down at the lounge pants and oversized shirt she's wearing and just knows that it isn't demon-appropriate attire.

"Shit," Skylar curses aloud.

She closes her eyes and tries to calm her racing heart. She's undergone years of tutelage, she can do this. She takes two deep breaths and tries to focus on what she imagines a demon should look like before she lets the tugging take her. Once she has an image in her head, she lets the final painful tug pull her from the demon realm and back to the mortal one. For the first time since she was recalled, she feels the ground fall out beneath her as she is pulled through whatever space exists between the two dimensions. As much as anyone can tell her what to expect, it's nothing like experiencing it first-hand.

When she finally hits the ground again, she is forced down to one knee to keep from toppling onto her face. She has conjured up black leather pants and a fitted matching bodice. Instinctively she throws her wings out to help catch her balance, but it mostly only adds to the effect of her appearance. Hopefully she looks more like a fallen angel than a disoriented teenager. She is left staring down at her toes on the bare concrete floor and regrets not thinking of shoes to protect herself from the discomfort of the cold floor.

"Demon," a male voice intones. "I am your warlock: Magus Pallando. Rise and do my bidding."

Skylar is thankful she is looking down because she can't help the eye roll she gives at that greeting. Slowly she rises and finds himself staring eye-to-eye with a middle-aged man in elaborate gaudy crimson robes trimmed in gold fringe. If this guy's real name is Pallando, Skylar will eat her wings. He looks more like a John in the middle of a mid-life crisis:

balding gray hair, potbellied, and jowly. Suddenly she is no longer nervous, because the entire situation seems too ridiculous. Skylar struggles to school her expression.

"Warlock," she says with a sweeping bow only to help hide the smirk she is failing to fight off. "How may I be of service to you?" She keeps her gaze lowered as her eyes skim over the outline of the protective circle she is summoned into.

"You're a pretty one," the warlock comments and it makes Skylar's flesh crawl knowing those eyes are on her.

"My warlock flatters me," she chokes out before standing up once more. "What is your will?"

The warlock (Skylar refuses to think of him as Pallando) straightens his shoulders and does his best to look down on her though he is only a few inches taller than her. "I demand you grant me unparalleled handsomeness."

Skylar blinks at the warlock and waits for him to say something else, but that appears to be it. She has to bite the inside of her cheek to keep from laughing out loud. Instead, she bows her head and says: "As my warlock wishes."

The glamour is an easy one and Skylar can't believe how lucky she is that this warlock's vanity is the only thing he cares about. She raises her hand, and with the snap of her fingers the glamour settles into place over the warlock. Like a sheet being draped over a piece of aged furniture, the glamour shifts the warlock's image. Skylar takes a step back to admire her handiwork. It is all an illusion, but one that should hold up to any mortal's inspection.

The warlock turns away from the circle and steps to a nearby wall. Only then does Skylar really take in the rest of the room. It looks like a basement or cellar of some sort—windowless and dark except for the dozens upon dozens of candles on every available surface. It seems unnecessary since there are fluorescent lights on the ceiling, but those probably ruin the aesthetic the warlock seems to be going for. The walls are lined with short bookcases and shelves filled with books, jars, and trinkets. A worktable of some sort is covered with scattered pages. A tall candlestick holder sits along one wall next to a full-length mirror.

The mirror is where the warlock gazes at his new reflection. His hairline has filled in with lush, sandy-brown hair. The man's jaw is now cut and the softness beneath his robes is gone, replaced with hard planes and lines. Skylar watches from within the protective circle as the warlock becomes engrossed with his own reflection.

Time passes and Skylar stands in the circle seemingly forgotten. It is the first moment she has to think about the fact that she is back in the mortal realm since she was thirteen years old. She suddenly wonders where her parents are. Do they miss her? Or has her entire childhood disappeared like a reflection from a puddle that has dried? Thoughts she has kept buried in the back of her mind come bubbling to the surface with a sense of possibility.

Her eyes drop to the thin chalk lines that mark the floor. Those markings are the only thing keeping her trapped in place. Otherwise, she could merely imagine herself back to her childhood home. Reappear just like she had disappeared all those years ago. Would they even recognize her anymore? She is taller and basically an adult now. If she could grant her own wish, it would be to see her parents just one more time and ask them if they knew she'd become *this*.

Skylar bites her tongue to distract herself from the tears threatening to spill. It's been so long since she thought about her family and suddenly she feels like that young, scared girl who was first recalled to the demon realm. Thankfully, the warlock is too distracted with his own reflection to notice as her demon facade slips momentarily.

Abruptly, Skylar wants to be back in the demon realm. Back where she can't even hope to see her family again. Warren always calls the demon realm a prison, but in some ways, it feels safer there. Easier to not have to deal with messy things like *feelings* and *memories*.

Once she is sure her confident look is back in place, Skylar clears her throat. "Is my warlock happy with his wish?"

The warlock jumps as if startled by the voice of someone other than himself. He obviously forgot Skylar was still there, trapped within the circle. "Your work is impeccable," the warlock admits.

"Thank you," Skylar says calmly. She doesn't want to point out that while the man may look young and healthy, he isn't actually younger. And while he may look like a strapping young man, that won't keep him from dying of old age. That doesn't seem to be a concern for the warlock at the moment.

"Pallando" has yet to look away from his own reflection, but apparently he doesn't need to do so to send Skylar away. "Demon, I release you back to the demon realm. Return."

And, just like that, the pact is complete. The magic that binds Skylar to the mortal realm breaks and she is sent hurtling back. She reappears back in her apartment. Skylar collapses back onto her couch and all the tears she fought back suddenly break through the dam she's built. For her first summons, it doesn't leave her feeling the way she expected.

Skylar sobs herself to sleep that evening.

5

Magic Studies 101

IT'S A COUPLE OF days before Justin has an opening in his schedule to come over. The beauty of Ryan's work is that he can do it whenever he wants as long as he meets his deadlines. And while he doesn't prefer to wake up before eight in the morning if he can avoid it, he does so this Tuesday to accommodate Justin's schedule.

There's a pot of coffee on the coffee maker and Ryan has already moved their research materials to the tiny table in his cramped, but hardly used kitchen. He has the book, of course, but also printouts of the information his mom sent him. When he'd emailed her about wanting to know about Thomas Andrew Smith, his mother was happy to send over the genealogy work Ryan's father had done before he passed. He's also put out a couple of notepads and pens for taking notes.

Just as he is pouring himself the first cup of coffee, there's a knock at the door. "Come in," he calls from the kitchen.

A few moments later, Justin comes in dressed in gym shorts, a tank top, and sneakers, his hair damp and unruly. "Morning," he says cheerfully as he puts a gym bag down on the floor under the table.

"Did you work out this morning?" Ryan asks, disgusted by the idea of having the energy to do that.

"Yeah," Justin says, quirking his head to the side before taking a seat at the table.

"Hmm," Ryan shakes his head. "Want some coffee?"

"Nah, I'm good for now. Where do you want to start?" Justin claps his hands together, rubbing them as his eyes look over the contents laid out before him.

Ryan, still dressed in his sleep pants and a baggy shirt, brings his coffee over to the table and sits across from him. "I've been *trying* to look over the book, but I'm not getting anywhere with it. Why don't you take a stab at it, and I'll start with the stuff my mom sent me about Thomas Andrew Smith."

"Sounds good to me." Justin slides the giant book over to himself. Ryan pushes a pen and notepad toward him before grabbing his own supplies and the stack of printouts.

Taking a sip of coffee, Ryan starts looking over the information his mother had on hand. First there is a picture of the family tree from inside the bible they'd found. He doesn't find it particularly helpful for what they are researching, but he looks over it anyway.

Thomas Andrew Smith is obviously his great-great-grandfather on his father's side of the family. According to the dates in the heirloom, the man died when he was forty-two years old and left behind two sons and a daughter. Not sure what good any of that information is, Ryan jots down the dates in his notebook and moves on.

His mother has also sent along fuzzy pictures of Thomas Andrew Smith's birth announcement, wedding announcement, and the birth announcements of his kids. They aren't particularly the cleanest photocopies, but from that long ago it's better than Ryan is expecting.

The most interesting among the pages is Thomas Andrew Smith's obituary. It features a photograph and Ryan can't deny the family resemblance. Thomas Andrew Smith looks a lot like Ryan's father (and Ryan himself): lighter hair, round eyes, and a permanent frown on his face. He reads through the obituary, eyebrows climbing higher with each passing word.

"I don't know if this is relevant," Ryan says, breaking the silence between himself and Justin, "but Thomas Andrew Smith was murdered."

"Really?" Justin gasps and looks up from his own scribbles, dropping his pen. He leans closer to look at the page Ryan is holding. "Does it say he was killed by demons?"

Ryan rolls his eyes. "No. The obituary just mentions it in passing, no details. 'Thomas Andrew Smith was killed by a colleague in his organization.' That's the only thing it says."

"Does it say what the organization was?" Justin asks.

"No." Ryan shakes his head, skimming the article again. "It's probably just a really unfortunate coincidence though, right? Maybe that book has nothing to do with Thomas Andrew Smith and it just happened to end up inside his trunk?"

Justin's shoulders slump and he hums. "Maybe."

Ryan drains the rest of his coffee and pushes the stack of printed pages aside. "Any luck with the book?" He gets out of his seat to refresh his coffee cup.

"Not really," Justin admits. "It feels like the book expects the reader to have a basic knowledge that we just don't have. Maybe if the thing had a glossary? A beginner's guide? I don't know."

"Did you make a list of words to look up?" Ryan asks when he returns to the table with a full cup. "I can try looking them up while you keep going."

Justin tears a page from the notebook and hands it over. Taking the list, Ryan pulls out his phone and starts to look up the terms while they continue to work in silence. The words themselves seem to be scientific terms for roots, or wood, or crystals. He also learned that *overmorrow* could mean *the day after tomorrow*. It's interesting, but not particularly helpful.

After Ryan has looked up over two dozen words, Justin throws his hands up in the air. "I give up for today! I can't do this anymore right now. My brain is about to melt out of my ears. I feel like we haven't really gotten anywhere in the four hours I've been here."

Ryan can't deny it. "Let's give it a break for today. Maybe we can look at it with fresh eyes another time?"

"Maybe," Justin agrees, but he doesn't seem very confident. "How about lunch?"

They agree to go hit up a ramen place down the street to get away from the research. Justin watches as Ryan throws the tome and their notes into his work bag.

"Why are you bringing those with you?" he asks as Ryan goes to slip on his shoes, not bothering to change out of his lounge clothes.

Ryan points at Justin, then at himself. "You summoned a demon. I summoned a demon. Probably means anyone could summon a demon, right? I'd rather not just leave this laying around."

Justin shrugs, picking up his gym bag. "I see your point. Food. Now. Please?"

They didn't get back to research again that day. Justin went off to work on photo editing and Ryan determined a nap was in order. Ryan now finds himself carrying the tome with him everywhere he goes. It's starting to create an ache in his back from lugging the thing all over the city. He is sitting in *Much Loved Books* with his work computer open in front of him contemplating how much a safe would cost so the damn book could at least be locked up.

He finally opens a new tab to research what a small safe would run him when Ethan comes over to the table. "Hey," he says. "You cool with some company while I take a break?" He holds up a small take-out container and his travel tea infuser.

Ryan gestures to the otherwise empty table. "Have a seat," he offers. "I'm not getting much work done anyway." Then he turns his attention back to the prices of safes. The best ones are, of course, prohibitively expensive. He thinks maybe he can afford at least one of those little lock boxes that are meant for protecting documents against a fire.

What Ryan doesn't notice while he continues to scroll is that Ethan has slid over the table to settle next to him to eat. He puts his lunch down and pulls out the chair, but finds the seat occupied by Ryan's bag. Innocently enough, he picks it up to make room for himself, but as he does the zipper bursts open and spills the bag's contents to the ground.

"Shit, I'm sorry," Ethan apologizes. Immediately he reaches down to pick up the items that have scattered onto the ground.

"Huh?" Ryan glances up from his computer. He notices the newly emptied bag in one of Ethan's hands as he is reaching for the book with the other. "No! Ethan! It's fine!" Ryan pushes away his laptop to try and intercept, but he's too late. Ethan is already turning the book over in his hand.

"What's this?" he asks, placing the empty bag on the table and opening the book.

Ryan scoops the pages of research from the floor. "Oh, that? That's nothing. Just a book I found at my mom's." He forces a laugh trying to make it seem trivial, but also to cover his own panic. "It doesn't even really make any sense."

"Oh, like those textbooks you brought in earlier?" Ethan hums as he flips through the pages. Ryan fights the urge to rip the book out of Ethan's hands, but he's sure that will seem even more suspicious. He isn't even a hundred percent sure why he is nervous, but his heart is pounding in his chest.

"I didn't know you were into magic," Ethan comments casually.

Ryan pauses trying to shove the pages back into the torn bag and blinks at him. "Wait, you recognize that stuff?"

Ethan chuckles. "Yeah, it's an interest of mine. I know enough to know that I'm not particularly inclined towards being a magic-user," he admits.

"An interest of yours?" Ryan is too dumbstruck to do more than repeat Ethan's words. How can Ethan be talking about something like magic so casually?

"Yeah. I found this guy who runs a website for descendants of warlocks. Or at least that's what he claimed. I came across the site in my research. Turns out not that not everyone can use magic," Ethan explains as he continues to flip through the pages. "The guy called me a 'dud.' It's not the nicest word, but I've heard worse. I don't know what it is that makes one person able to do it over another. I suspect it's hereditary, though."

Ryan blinks at Ethan in surprise. "So, you're saying you believe this kind of stuff."

"Why not?" Ethan finally looks up from the pages of the tome to meet Ryan's gaze. "Practicing magic was something that used to be widely accepted, even just a century or so ago. With the sudden advancements of technology came a decline in magic practitioners. Perhaps they had less access to the things they used magic for? Or just became more secretive? I don't know, but either way it's fascinating to learn about."

"So, does this book make any sense to you?" Ryan nods his head towards the open book in Ethan's hands.

"Well, kind of. It seems way more advanced than anything I've come across before." Ethan's eyes drop back to the book as he continues to flip through the pages. "Most of the stuff I'm interested in is plant magic, you know? Helping things grow and the use of plants and herbs for medicine. Just little stuff I could try at home to keep my bonsai healthy."

"When you put it that way, it actually makes total sense." Ryan scoots his chair closer to look over Ethan's shoulder. "So, do you think you can help me make sense of the stuff in this book?"

Ethan's eyes light up. "You want to learn, too?"

"Maybe?" Ryan answers, less certain.

"I'd be happy to help." Ethan is beaming at Ryan and in that moment he can't imagine anything bad could ever happen. Ethan is just too decent of a person to want to use magic for anything nefarious. Besides, this is a way Ryan can possibly get answers without having to summon Skylar again. Maybe, with Ethan's help, Ryan can determine if it's safe to bring the demon back. If Skylar can be trusted.

"Remember my friend Justin?" Ryan asks.

"Yeah," Ethan nods. "The good-looking guy who takes pictures?"

"That's him," Ryan confirms. "He's been helping me with this project. Do you think you can walk us both through some stuff?"

Ethan shuts the book and hands it back to Ryan. "Sure. I'll get back to you with my schedule for the next week and we can figure something out."

"Thanks." Ryan stuffs the book back into the broken bag, even if it won't zip shut again. "I guess I need a new bag," he mutters.

Ethan rubs the back of his neck. "Sorry about that."

"It's not your fault." Ryan shakes his head as he tucks the bag under his seat. "I've been carrying around this stuff for a while now and it was probably just a matter of time until it burst through the seams or something."

"I have a tendency to have things just fall apart in my hands, so I assumed it was my fault," Ethan gave a self-depreciating chuckle as he reached for his snack.

It's almost another week before the three of them are able to get their schedules to align. Ethan gets his part time employee, Nadia, to run the shop for the afternoon. Ryan is lugging the book and their notes across the city in a grocery tote to Justin's place since he has more space, and his roommate will be out of town. Ryan still isn't positive Thomas Andrew Smith has anything to do with the magic book, but it's easier to just keep everything together for now.

The other upside to Justin's place is that his apartment is a lot more modern and well maintained than Ryan's own. He's able to take an elevator up to the fourth floor rather than having to lug his heavy bag up multiple flights of stairs. The benefit of having a roommate: better accommodations.

Ryan feels like his shoulder is about to collapse under the weight of his bag by the time he is knocking on Justin's door. To his complete and utter amazement, it's Justin's roommate who answers.

"Ryan, hey. You're late, it seems. Everyone is waiting for you in the living room." The roommate, Ashe, holds the door open for Ryan to enter as he gapes at the man like a fish out of water. Ashe is a bit taller than Ryan and looks unfairly good in a casual pair of khakis and a loose sweatshirt.

"I'm on time," he grumbles. "It's not my fault Ethan is early to everything." Ryan shuffles in and finds a large suitcase in the vestibule. He looks at it, then back to Ashe. "Justin mentioned you'd be gone. Are you going on a trip?"

Ashe gives a chuckle. "Yeah, I've got an out-of-town modeling gig. I'm really looking forward to it since it's a fashion show I haven't done before. It helps that my girlfriend is going to be there. It's a great chance to spend an extra day with her before I come back, and she heads over to New York."

Of course Justin rooms with a model, but the two have been best friends since high school. And Ryan actually does like the guy. He's just nervous about exposing anyone else to what they are here to discuss this evening.

"Well, have a good trip," Ryan offers.

"Thanks," Ashe smiles. "You actually caught me on the way out. You guys have a good afternoon."

Ryan shuffles into the living room as Ashe throws on a jacket to head out the front door, luggage in tow. Ethan is sitting on the couch with a small stack of books on the coffee table in front of him.

Justin is being a good host and is coming in with bottles of water. "Hey, Ryan," he says as he sets down the bottles, Ethan thanking him.

"Ryan," Ethan greets him. "Justin and I have already ordered food. He said he knew what you'd want."

Ryan sets the heavy bag on the table next to Ethan's pile of books and flops down in the armchair, leaving Justin the other spot on the couch. "Yeah, he does. He also knows if you guys order before I get here, I won't be able to insist on paying."

"True," Justin gives a smirk. He leaves a bottle for Ryan on the table in front of him before uncapping his own bottle. "So, we've got the place to ourselves for the rest of the day. Where should we start?"

"Well, I brought some of my starter books," Ethan gestures towards the stack.

"May I?" Ryan asks and grabs the top book off the stack when Ethan nods. He sits back and flips through it. "I brought the tome in the shopping bag, along with our other notes. Feel free to look through it."

Eagerly, Ethan reaches for the shopping bag and pulls out the book.

Justin sits back on the couch and sips his water. "So, how much did you tell Ethan?"

"I told him we found the book at my mom's," Ryan shrugs. "That's all." Ryan is nervous about telling Ethan too much. He's not sure if the man would want to try summoning a demon for himself or think they were stupid for doing it. Or, perhaps worst of all, would think they were lying.

Instead, Ryan skims the book in his hand. It seems more like a handbook for some sort of organization rather than a spell book like his tome. He flips back to the cover to read the title: *The Order of the Knowing Well*. He arches an eyebrow at the title and goes back to where he'd bookmarked the page with his finger.

> Membership to the Order is limited to those with proven magical abilities and their descendants (regardless of magical ability). Exceptions will be made for scholars of exemplary achievement and will be judged by the Council of Elders.

> All members are required to adhere to the code of conduct (page 13). Failure to comply with the code can lead to ex-com-

munication and – in most extreme circumstances – banishment. The Council of Elders will lead any tribunal to judge accusations of non-compliance.

Ryan flips to page thirteen. "What is this book?" he wonders aloud.

Ethan glances up from Ryan's book. "I came across that at an estate sale, actually. Printed in 1911, it looks like a guide to being in a group called The Order of the Knowing Well."

"What's that?" Justin asks from where he's slowly curling up on the couch.

"From what I've been be to piece together, it's an organization for warlocks," Ethan explains. "After I found that handbook, I was able to find some vague information about it on the internet. It's where I found that guy who called me a 'dud.' As far as I've been able to determine, it's an order that was established around the 1800s, but I never got an exact year. Membership has always been pretty hush-hush."

Ryan hums in interest. "Really? It says members could be ex-communicated. It seems pretty unlikely that people kicked out wouldn't ever talk about it."

"I thought that, too," Ethan adds, looking excited. "However, I haven't found any account of ex-members. So, either they rarely excommunicate anyone, or—"

"—they aren't real to begin with," Ryan finishes for him.

Justin hums and shuffles closer to Ethan to peek at what he's reading. Ryan look back down to the book in his hands.

<u>Code of Conduct</u>
1. Details of the Order are not to be shared with those outside its membership.
2. The membership roster is never to be shared with outsiders.
3. Magic should never be used against the Order or its members.
4. Magic should never be used to mettle in mundane politics.
5. Magics forbidden by the Council of Elders are never to be performed.

6. Killing a member of the Order through magic or mundane
means will result in banishment.

"A lot of these rules are really specific about magic," Ryan comments.

Ethan nods without looking up from the tome in his lap. "I mean, if your organization is based on magic, why wouldn't it be?"

"Have you come across any other magic organizations?" Justin asks.

"Nothing as structured as The Order of the Knowing Well," he admits. "But it's not like I spend all my time doing this. It's a hobby. I've never seen anything like this book." He holds up Ryan's tome. "I don't know if other books like it don't exist, or if they are just really well protected, but it's a lot more elaborate than any of my books."

Justin tucks a leg under himself so he can face Ethan more directly. "What do you mean by 'elaborate'?"

Ethan hums as if he's considering his response. "I mean: most of the books I have are magic primers. Things like how to determine if you have magic powers. The basics of magic for every day use. Mythology around magic. I can't even be sure if what I've found is completely legit or not. This book, however, is like going from a primary math book to calculus."

Suddenly Ethan pauses. Quickly he flips to the back of the book to skim a few pages before going back to the front of the book.

Ryan puts the handbook he's holding aside and watches Ethan. "What are you looking for?"

"All books printed by a publishing house have information about their publishing, like copyright date and the city. Something like this doesn't seem like it would be mass produced. So I was looking to see if it has anything to say where it came from." Ethan holds open the book on the page after the title page. "Something like this!"

Ryan slips out of the arm chair to perch on the arm of the couch as Justin leans closer.

There's a list of names on the page, much like it would be for contributing authors. Ethan is pointing to the bottom of the page where, in stylized script, are the words: The Order of the Knowing Well.

However, there is a name on the list that catches Ryan's attention. He glances over to Justin to see if he has caught it, too. Their eyes meet.

"Thomas Andrew Smith," they say simultaneously.

"Who?" Ethan asks, glancing between the two of them.

Just then the doorbell rings and Ryan startles.

"Food!" Justin exclaims as he jumps up. "Probably best to put the books aside for now. Pizza can get greasy." He bounds out of the room to get the order, which leaves Ethan looking at Ryan with a befuddled expression.

"Take a look at some of the loose pages I brought," Ryan offers, picking up the stuff his mother sent him. He sits back in the armchair. "I don't care if this gets pizza on it."

They switch the book for the printed pages. As Ethan scans the printouts, Ryan clears the books off the table, slipping them into his shopping bag under the table for safe keeping.

"Wait," Ethan says, looking up from the pages. "Thomas Andrew Smith is a relative of yours?"

Ryan nods. "That's how we got our hands on the book in the first place. This is all the information I could get from my mom about him. I wasn't even sure he was connected to the book until now."

"Why did you think he might have been?"

"The trunk we found the book in had his initials on it," Ryan explains. "But it also had a bunch of random stuff, so we weren't sure."

Justin comes in with two large pizza boxes and a 2-liter of soda tucked under his arm. He sets the items down with some napkins and paper plates before announcing he's going to go get cups.

Ethan seems more interested in the printout of the obituary than the food in front of them. "Do you think he may have been killed by the Order?"

Ryan's eyes widen. "I hadn't until right now!"

"Makes sense," Justin adds as he comes back in with disposable cups. "Maybe he was either killed by a member of the Order, or he is an example of why no one knows about the Order."

"Maybe we're getting into something dangerous," Ryan frowns.

Ethan puts the pages down on the arm of the couch and reaches for a paper plate. "All knowledge is worth having," he states, loading some pizza onto the plate. That seems to be the cue for everyone to start eating. As they do, Ethan continues his story. "I'd come across a book in the library donations when I was in college, and it sparked my interest. At first, I thought it was part of a fantasy series, but the more I researched the more I began to suspect it was based on something more historical."

"When did you start believing?" Justin asks around a mouthful of pizza.

"I met a practitioner when I was trying to find authentic sources. She gave me a couple of lessons, which is when I started to realize I couldn't really do any of it myself. Still, I saw enough that I started to believe."

"Do you know what a 'warlock' is?" Ryan asks, remembering the strange sensation whenever Skylar called him that.

Ethan shrugs. "It's just a word for a magic user – anyone who uses tools to harness and practice magic."

"Tools?" Justin asks.

"Yeah," Ethan nods. "People need things like wands and magic circles in order to do their magic. I guess it's like a focus? Or a lightning rod, but for magic?"

Justin leans closer. "So, what do you know about summoning?"

Ryan chokes on his bite of pizza and gulps some soda to clear his throat. "Justin," he hisses, trying to catch his breath.

"Depends on what you're summoning," Ethan says slowly, glancing between Ryan and Justin. "I've read spells for summoning nature spirits, or good luck, or wealth."

Right away Justin reaches for the napkins and wipes off his hands. "What do you make of this?" he asks and grabs the bag of books. He pulls out the tome and flips through the pages to the summoning circle.

Ryan is left watching wide-eyed as Justin hands the book over to Ethan. He scrutinizes the page as he studies it, brow furrowed. Ryan's heart feels like it's about to pound out of his chest as Ethan studies the spell. Fear that he would give them an appalled look shoots through him.

"This isn't like anything I've ever seen before," Ethan finally says. "It looks like a ritual for summoning beings from another dimension. Most of the stuff I've read was about stuff that already exists on our plane of reality."

"Have you ever read about anything that lives in another dimension?" Ryan hesitantly asks.

Ethan rubs his chin. "Maybe? It isn't my particular interest, so not in any depth."

"The tome calls them demons," Justin interrupts. "You don't think they mean like devils, do you?"

"I doubt it," Ethan shrugs. "That has very religious trappings. Let me check my collection." He reaches for the bag and pulls out a book called *Glossary of Magical Terms*. He flips through the pages before settling on one in particular.

Aloud, Ethan reads: "Demon: a magical being that exists in the demon realm. Can be summoned to use magical powers beyond a warlock's capability. Not for inexperienced practitioners. "

"Well, that's vague," Justin comments.

Without looking up from the book, Ethan waves his hand. "There's another entry for demon realm. Demon realm: a pocket dimension created by warlocks to house demons." He stops reading.

After a beat Justin clears his throat. "Is that it?"

"Yeah," Ethan frowns.

"So, nothing about whether or not they are good or evil?" Ryan asks, not sure if he's hopeful for an answer or not.

Ethan blinks at Ryan. "No, but the book says summoning demons isn't for beginners." He narrows his gaze and shifts it between Ryan and Justin. "Why?" The single word is laced with suspicion.

Ryan frowns. There isn't anything screaming "evil creatures from Hell" in the book, but the definitions aren't entirely reassuring. "I think Justin and I may have gotten in over our heads," he admits.

"You mean you can do magic?" Ethan asks, but his tone is more excited than reprimanding.

Justin just smirks. "Hell yes, we can."

6

Distractions

WEEKS GO BY AND Skylar hasn't been summoned by Ryan again. She isn't comfortable with the idea that there's a warlock out there who knows her name and has power over her. Ryan will continue to have influence over her until they complete the deal. Every time she feels a summons coming Skylar hopes it will be him, but it never is.

The few summonses she does get are the usual mundane requests. Like the warlock who wishes to curse his work rival so that every time they try to talk with clients they have disgustingly bad breath. Then there is the warlock who wants to write a best-selling novel. That one was particularly easy: Skylar enchanted his words so they would be irresistible to read. Another warlock wished to have her daughter accepted into a prestigious university.

People never consider the consequences of their wishes, which Skylar always finds amusing. Like the warlock who wished for the best-selling books didn't ask for them to be any good. They are going to sell well and will get horrible reviews. The daughter accepted to the university will get to go to the school, but there is no guarantee she'll succeed. And in the end, none of that is Skylar's problem. She did what was asked of her, it was not her fault that the mortals were short-sighted. It would be amusing if it weren't so fucking frustrating.

Skylar is on her way over to Kris's for their midweek movie marathon. For some reason, Wednesdays are slow nights for demons. Maybe because it's the middle of the week and mortals are busy? Who knows, but it's the perfect night to get together and watch the latest blockbuster movies.

She arrives at Kris's apartment and knocks, but there's no answer. It's of little consequence since Skylar can just let herself in. Locks aren't really a thing in the demon realm. If you want to keep demons out of your space, you just ward it. Skylar and Kris have given each other free access to each of their apartments, so she just opens the door.

"Kris, you home?" she calls into the apartment, but gets no answer.

Shrugging, she shifts out of her jeans and t-shirt into a comfy pair of sweats and a tank top before settling onto Kris's couch. She picks up a remote and starts flipping through channels on the large flat screen on the wall, looking for something to watch as she waits. Kris will come back, she's confident. She drapes her wings over the back of the couch and settles in.

She is an episode and a half into a new drama about a time-traveling doctor trying to hunt down his evil twin who gave the woman he loved amnesia so he can restore her memory in the past when Kris finally arrives. Her friend strolls in from the bedroom dressed in a Gucci t-shirt tucked into skinny black jeans. His hair is combed up and back with his horns up over the style.

"You look very dapper," Skylar comments as she mutes the television.

Kris smiles at her and instantly changes into a pair of blue and white striped pajamas with little hearts before he collapses on the couch next to her. "Sorry I'm late," he says as he throws an arm around her shoulders. The smell of brimstone lingers around him.

Skylar raises an eyebrow. "You had a Wednesday night summons?" she balks.

With a smirk on his lips, Kris nods. "Maybe I did."

"Then why do you look so happy?" she asks, confused. Most of the time either of them usually comes back from a summons with an exasperated sigh.

Kris taps his fingers along Skylar's bare shoulder. "Maybe it's because I was summoned by my bunny."

That just makes Skylar pout before she can really examine why. "Really? Did he decide what he wants?"

"Kind of." Kris takes his arm back to recline on the couch and rest his head in Skylar's lap. She starts carding her fingers through his curls around the base of his horns like she always does. "He just wanted to ask me some questions. Then we played some video games for a little while."

Skylar's hand pauses, her fingers still buried in Kris's thick hair. "Wait, what? Where are you getting summoned that there's video games?"

Kris shrugs and taps her hand as a subtle gesture to keep going. She starts scratching his scalp. "It looks like an office of some sort? Bunny has a large sheet of paper with the summoning circle drawn on it. It looks like he rolls it up and stores it between uses."

"And that works?" Skylar gasps. She's only ever seen circles drawn onto the ground or, in the most extreme cases, carved into the stone or wood.

Kris smiles smugly. "He may not be the most powerful warlock I've ever met, but he's really smart."

"Oh, is he?" Skylar is worried about her friend's infatuation with the warlock. What if he is being duped? "What kind of questions did he have to ask you then?"

"Not much really. He asked if demons are evil. If we drag people to Hell. If we want to take over the mortal realm. If I know something about a well of knowledge."

Skylar withdraws her hand from Kris's hair, and he frowns. "Those are some very aggressive questions," she points out.

Kris waves his hand as if waving away her concern. "Yeah, but I reassured him none of that was true. Then we played a racing game and talked about our days."

"Kris!" Skylar gives his pectoral a sharp smack. "What did I say? Summons are not dates! The warlock is literally sticking you in a smaller cage to use you before sending you back to a bigger one."

"Warren made you paranoid," Kris complains. "My mentor never framed anything as being a prison. If anything, being here makes us free of the mortal realm's responsibilities! We're really *free* here!"

This is a conversation Kris and Skylar used to have all the time. It became very apparent that the viewpoints of their demon mentors were very different, therefore they were taught very different perspectives about the existence of demons. Not wanting to get into the argument again, Skylar drops it.

"I just worry about you and this warlock. He seems different, but that doesn't mean it's a good kind of different." She bends forward to press a kiss to Kris's forehead before she goes back to threading her fingers through his hair.

Kris grabs Skylar's other hand and rests it on his chest in both of his. "Trust me, Sky. Bunny isn't a bad guy. Now! What should we watch tonight?"

Already comfy on the couch, Kris conjures a bowl of popcorn that appears on his stomach so they can both snack. They pick a movie and relax into their usual routine. It's too easy to let go of conversation from before, and Kris seems perfectly content to do so. The giddy smile from seeing his warlock plays across his lips as they watch the latest superhero movie.

Skylar, on the other hand, is too distracted to really pay attention. Not just by this bunny warlock, but that's how it starts. Her thoughts drift to wondering if Ryan is ever going to summon her again. And if he does, what will he ask of her? Will he become predictable and ask for fame or riches even though he claims he doesn't want those things? Or will he be like Kris's new warlock: friendly, unassuming, and curious? Skylar doesn't dare to hope that Ryan will surprise her again like he did that first night. No, she decides before the movie is over. Either she will never see Ryan again or, when she does, the warlock won't fail to disappoint her with the usual litany of greedy requests.

As the movie credits roll, Skylar glances down to Kris who is still curled up with his head in her lap. He'd dozed off towards the end and is sleeping peacefully. A small smile plays on his lips as he dreams, and Skylar is happy her friend is so relaxed. She leans forward to press another gentle kiss to the sleeping demon's temple.

In an effort to not wake her friend, Skylar gently lifts Kris's head and slips out from under him replacing her lap with one of the couch pillows. She takes the empty bowl of popcorn to the kitchen and ditches it in the sink. Listlessly, she opens the fridge and snags a beer. She's been too much in her own head and needs to relax.

After a long pull from the beer, Skylar paces back into the living room where Kris is still peacefully dozing. She fights the urge to wake the other demon and demand a distraction.

Instead, she leaves a note for him: *Hey bestie. Sleep well! I'm going out for the evening. ~ Sky*

Skylar downs the rest of her beer and changes her outfit. Gone are the comfortable lounge clothes. Now she's wearing a leather mini skirt and a black mesh top with a sparkly silver bra underneath. She slicks back her hair as she leaves Kris's apartment. There's a club called *Dante's* open down the block and that's her new target. She opts to walk off her nervous energy, heeled boots clicking along the pavement as she strides towards the club. Skylar chooses to interpret the buzzing in her chest as excitement and not anxiety as she approaches *Dante's* front doors.

There is an ever-present line of people waiting to get in, but it is an illusion. It's just random people standing in a queue that never moves so that demons can feel superior as they walk right past them and into the club. Skylar doesn't understand the appeal, but enough demons apparently like it so the illusion is refreshed each night.

The illusory crowd lines up along the front of the building and winds around the corner. Beautiful people smoke, leaning against the cool brick exterior of the building, or kill time on their phones as they wait. Skylar doesn't pay them any mind since they aren't real anyway. She strides right past the line and into the building.

Booming music greets her as she enters the darkness of the club. Strobe lights randomly flicker over the writhing crowd that fills the dance floor. Demons in various states of undress mix with those wearing the most expensive and stylish clothes from every era. Skylar feels downright tame by comparison, but the night is young.

The thrumming beat is luring her out to the dance floor, but she really wants something more to drink first. Skylar pivots towards the long bar where a small crowd is lounging. Sure, none of them need to order drinks when they can just make them materialize, but the charade is part of the atmosphere of the place. And some demons really enjoy mixing drinks and playing bartender. Tonight, that's not the case.

Skylar plants herself on an empty stool between demons who are too busy talking to their companions to pay her any mind. A highball glass filled with her favorite cocktail, Tequila Sunrise, appears at her elbow before she reaches down to pick it up. She takes a long drink and lets her eyes roam over the demons gathered. There are so few demons in the demon realm that she recognizes just about everyone, even if she doesn't know many of them very well. On top of that, the usual demons seem to frequent the club most often.

Wednesdays are often the club's busiest nights, which is why she and Kris usually choose to spend their evenings at home.

There are side rooms off the main floor for more debauched activities. Skylar rarely visits those rooms since she mostly just comes to the club to dance. That's not to say she hasn't had her fair share of sexual activities in one room or another when the mood strikes her. Very often, though, there are other things going on that she is less involved in - activities more rooted in violence than sex.

The demons talking on the stools to her right drift off towards the dance floor. It takes only a moment before the space is filled with a friendly face. Omar, who Skylar only really socializes with in the club scene, sidles up next to her. His biceps flex as he rests an elbow on the bar and leans toward her. The wolf-like ears, covered in black fur much like the hair atop his head, swivel toward her to show Skylar that she has his full attention.

"Been a while," he says with a big, toothy grin. Skylar catches other demon's eyes looking her up and down. "How are you?"

Skylar shrugs. "Same old, same old." She takes another drink from her glass. "Anything new with you?"

"Not too much," Omar admits with a nod. His long, wolfish tail covered in the same dark fur, wags behind him. "Derek and I moved in together."

"That's a big move." Skylar feels her eyebrows rise at the news. Omar and Derek have been dating for the better part of two decades, but what's a long-term relationship when you can live forever? Or as close to forever as Skylar can guess.

It's Omar's turn to shrug. "We always end up in each other's bed at the end of the night. This just makes it easier."

"You here with Derek this evening?" Skylar's eyes scan the crowd for the taller demon with a beak-like nose and white feathers instead of hair.

Omar shakes his head. "He's at home tonight customizing his skateboard. Said he isn't in the mood for big crowds. I guess that means you're stuck with me tonight." The last word is said with a bit of a leer.

The wolfy demon may end up with Derek by the end of the night, but Skylar knows from first-hand experience that isn't always where he starts.

Sometimes they start somewhere else together, but Skylar knows their relationship is pretty open. Omar can be just the distraction she is looking for.

Skylar finishes the last of her drink. "Dance with me and let's see how stuck to me you stay," she says with her own suggestive grin.

Omar's tail picks up speed as it wags behind him. He jumps off the stool and holds out a hand to Skylar, but she just waves it off. The glass disappears from her hand, and she stands from the stool on her own before strutting towards the dance floor without a backward glance. It's really up to Omar if he chooses to follow or not.

When Skylar works her way into the crowd and turns, she finds that Omar has indeed followed. The other demon's golden eyes rise from where they must have been staring at Skylar's ass, the skirt leaving little to imagination. The beat flows over them and Skylar starts gyrating her hips to the music. She eases her way into the music with her whole body and Omar steps in to close the distance. His hands latch onto her hips and pull her closer. Skylar chooses to run her hands up over Omar's firm torso and hook them behind his neck. They find a rhythm together just shy of dry humping one another. Skylar keeps her wings as close to her back as possible to avoid taking up someone else's dance space.

Gradually Omar's hands migrate from Skylar's hips to the full swell of her ass. She feels his fingers spread wide to encompass as much space as possible before giving a firm squeeze. The result has Skylar jerking forward and grinding against Omar's evident excitement, stoking a fire of interest in her belly. Perhaps this is the exact distraction she is looking for.

"You look like an absolutely sinful angel," Omar growls in Skylar's ear, his hot breath ghosting over the sweat beading on her neck.

"Isn't that a bit of an oxymoron?" Skylar laughs, her fingers sliding up Omar's neck to bury themselves in the thick hair at the back of his head.

Omar then does something Skylar wasn't expecting, but probably should have. He drags his tongue across her throat from just above her collar bone to below her ear. The wet warmth sends a shiver through Skylar's body that causes even her wings to tremble. Skylar feels her tummy tighten in response to Omar's mouth on her and the grinding of his hips.

"You taste so good," Omar whimpers as he nuzzles her throat. "I want to swallow you down."

Skylar gives a throaty laugh. "Just admit you have a kink for demons with feathers and go."

"Only if you let me eat you out first," Omar whines. His hands slide up over her hips to press against her lower back, hot skin against the bare flesh just above her skirt.

"You want me to fuck your muzzle so you can go back home to Derek and kiss him with your filthy mouth?" Skylar teases.

"Yes," Omar pulls back to meet Skylar's gaze. "Say you will."

Skylar nods. "Lead the way."

Omar, like an excited puppy, takes Skylar's hand and all but drags her from the dance floor toward one of the side rooms. Skylar trails after him, trying to temper her own excitement. The idea of forgetting about her worries on the wet warmth of Omar's mouth is highly appealing. She watches the demon's strong back as he shoulders his way through the crowd.

The side room has a smaller crowd of people compared to the dance floor. There are two women and a man having their own carnal fun in one corner, but Skylar is kind of thankful Omar turns away from them to find their own spot. The far wall has X-crosses built in and one is in use by demons that Skylar doesn't get a good look at. Whatever they are doing involves blood and that is not of particular interest to her.

Skylar is relieved when Omar leads her to a booth that can be used for drinks, eating, drugs, or gaming. The booth seats, however, are not accommodating to Skylar's wings, so Omar pulls out a chair so she can sit with her back to the rest of the room.

She comes around the chair and settles on the padded seat, her wings flaring out behind her as she gazes up at Omar, her legs falling open. The man sinks to his knees between two tables and runs his hands up Skylar's thighs, pushing the leather skirt up the short distance to reveal her black satin panties, already damp from their provocative dancing. The demon wolf's tail wags so fast it thuds into the booth seats behind him, but he doesn't seem to notice or mind.

Skylar scoots her ass forward to the edge of the chair and leans back. She watches Omar's eyes drink her in and she nudges his leg with the toe of her boot.

Omar doesn't need any further prompting. He ducks down and noses the apex between her thighs, breathing her in deeply. Skylar uses this opportunity to card her fingers through the demon's hair, scratching around his ears to encourage him. Like a good boy, Omar's hands slide up her thighs so his thumb can hook into the fabric of her panties and pull them aside. Then a hot, firm tongue licks over her opening, bringing a heavy sigh from Skylar's lips. Omar begins licking at her in earnest, lapping her up like the most delicious treat and making her pulse race.

Skylar hooks a leg over Omar's shoulder, digging the heel of her boot into his back. He groans into her mound before pursing his lips around her clit and sucking. Her breathy moans join the wanton and depraved sounds coming from the other side of the room. It's been too long since she's sought out this kind of release and she feels her thighs trembling as one long finger slips past her folds, Omar's mouth still sucking her sensitive button.

The hand in his hair grips tight, holding him just where she wants him. Her other hand slides up over her chest to cup at her breast. She gives herself a firm squeeze as a second finger slips inside, opening her up and pressing against her quivering walls.

Skylar digs her heel sharply into his back, spurring the demon on. His fingers speed up, thrusting into her and tilting upwards to the find the most perfect angle until pleasure makes her groin clench. Her hips begin to move in little circles as she holds him in place, grinding against his face and he lets her. The wet sound of his fingers fucking into her mix with her own growing moans. Even her wings shiver as pleasure tightens through her core.

Just as her release feels imminent, she feels that familiar tug sneak in. She squeezes her eyes shut and tries to focus on Omar's mouth and the way his tongue flicks across her clit. She chases *that* feeling as the tug comes again, this time mixing with her arousal.

"Fuck," she groans as Omar seals his lips around her once more to suck, pounding the tips of his fingers against her sensitive walls when a third powerful tug comes and she's falling over the edge. Waves of pleasure course through her as her thighs tighten around Omar's head, his fingers coaxing her through and extending the orgasm pulsing around them. Behind Skylar's eyelids are the wide eyes of a warlock staring up at her from the edge of his shitty-looking summoning circle.

Her eyes fly open, worried she has lost control of her ability to ignore the summons, but she's still sitting in *Dante's.* Omar's hair is in her tight grip and only then does she think to let him go, petting him for his job well done.

The demon sits back on his heels letting her leg fall from his shoulder, his mouth and chin shiny with spit and her arousal. He takes his two fingers from inside of her and runs his tongue over the slick mess.

"Tastes so good," Omar murmurs before he pops them in his mouth to suck them clean.

Any other time, Skylar would be recovering from the quick and meaningless pleasure, but now her heart is pounding from anxiety that she was nearly summoned. She waits, her breath heaving, for the final tug, but it never comes. Her brow furrows as she runs her fingers through her own hair, feeling the sweat clinging to the strands stuck to her forehead.

Had she imagined the summons?

"You okay?" Omar asks, pulling her back from her thoughts. He pushes himself off the floor to collapse into the booth behind him. There's a dark wet spot spreading in the crotch of his slacks, evidence that he enjoyed their time together, too.

Skylar does her best to give him a reassuring smile, tugging her skirt down to cover herself once more. "Yeah, that was great. Thanks for the distraction."

Omar gives her a wolfish grin. "Anytime."

7

Summoning Problems

RYAN SLAMS THE BOOK shut. His heart races and he closes his eyes to block out the sight of the summoning circle in front of him. This has been a bad idea, but it takes setting everything up and chanting a few times before Ryan realizes that.

Nothing Ethan had told them last week gave Ryan any kind of reassurance that Skylar is a being to be trusted. If anything, maybe Ethan is wrong about some things. He said the association between demons and devils exists because of religious beliefs, but maybe there is a kernel of truth to it? Skylar looks like a fallen angel, not that Ryan has ever imagined one before: beautiful dark wings, unbelievably alluring, dark shining eyes. And when she isn't calling Ryan an asshole, her words have been very tempting.

Ryan takes a few more deep breaths and then chances to open his eyes once more. The circle stays as it was: messily drawn and empty. For a moment he is worried that Skylar will appear even though he has stopped chanting. A cold wind blows sharp enough to cut through his hoodie and make him shiver. He sits on the rooftop terrace, unsure how long to wait before he is sure the demon isn't going to make an appearance.

A drop of water hits Ryan's cheek and he cringes, glancing up. Another drop falls and he barely has a moment's notice to tuck the tome under his hoodie before it starts raining in earnest. He feels the cold binding of the book through his t-shirt as he contemplates the circle. He shouldn't leave a summoning circle on the rooftop for anyone to find, but with how quickly the rain is picking up he doubts there will be much left of the circle soon.

Deciding it is probably safe enough to leave the chalk circle to the elements, Ryan awkwardly gets off the ground while trying to keep the book safely tucked away. He rushes down the stairs and back to his apartment. Despite his hustle he is still very wet by the time he makes it to the safety of his living room.

The basement apartment never gets very warm and being wet is just going to make it worse. He kicks off his shoes and makes his way into the bedroom. The book gets tucked into a cheap fire safety box he had delivered earlier that day before he starts stripping off his wet clothes to take a hot shower.

The rain continues into the next day, which leaves Ryan grumpier than usual as he huddles underneath a clear umbrella while making his way to *Much Loved Books*. His mind is at ease that the book is locked away in his closet, but he hasn't replaced his broken bag yet. He's left carrying his work laptop and supplies around in a reusable shopping tote.

Ryan scurries under the cover of the bookshop's overhang to shake as much of the rain off as possible before closing up the umbrella and heading inside. The shop bell tinkles as he enters and already he feels relief from the damp cold outside as he's enveloped in the shop's cozy warmth.

"Hey," he says to Ethan as the man steps out of the stock room.

Ethan, his arms full of books, gives him a nod. "Hey, man. How goes it?"

"Wet," Ryan remarks and gestures to the weather. "I'm going to go get to work, don't let me stop you." Then he shuffles off towards his spot.

Work is just what he needs to take his mind off of magic and demons and shining black feathers. Ryan sets up his little corner and dives straight in. The work isn't hard, but it's detailed enough to not leave his thoughts a chance to meander.

He senses Ethan passing by from time to time, but he must look as prickly as he feels because the shop owner doesn't stop to visit. Several hours pass and Ryan has torn his gaze away from the computer only long enough to take a sip from his water bottle before getting back to work. There's a complaint of neglect coming from his stomach, but he really just wants to finish this data set.

Suddenly, there's a pounding on the table strong enough that Ryan's laptop vibrates. He blinks, his neck stiff as he looks up for the first time in a long while. Justin is standing next to his seat, smiling. "Hey, Ryan! Sorry if I'm interrupting."

"You are," Ryan scowls at him.

Not taking the hint, Justin pulls out the seat next to Ryan and settles down. He puts his camera bag on the table in front of him. "So, is now a bad time to talk?"

Ryan huffs at him. "Give me a minute to save what I'm working on." Justin nods and folds his hands on the table.

Sighing, Ryan saves the project. A quick glance at the time tells him he should have stopped for lunch an hour ago, so really he should be thanking Justin for dropping by unannounced. That doesn't prevent him from glaring at the younger man and then nodding. "So, to what do I owe this interruption?"

Justin's smile lights up. "I've got some more information," he announces proudly.

Ryan just blinks at him. "About?"

"You know." Justin leans in to whisper. "*Demons.*"

Ryan's eyes go wide and he immediately glances around their corner of the bookstore. There aren't any customers that he can see, but the shelves are tall and he can't be sure there isn't someone lurking.

He narrows his eyes and glances back to Justin. "How?" he whispers back.

"Oh, right." Justin chuckles. "I asked Kris last night."

Ryan waits for him to elaborate, but he doesn't. "Who?"

"You know . . . the demon I summoned when I did the thing? First, I might add." Justin's smile turns cocky, but Ryan's heart drops.

"What?" he gasps. "How! I've got the book locked up at my place."

"Well, you see," Justin says, shifting uncomfortably in his seat. "I may have made a copy of the summoning circle at my work studio. And it's not like the chant is all that hard to remember."

Fear spikes in Ryan's chest, but so does embarrassment. How is it that Justin did what Ryan got too scared to carry through? He tries to push away the shame and reach for something more useful, like concern. "That's so dangerous, Justin! What if someone finds your circle? And on top of that, what if the demon hurt you?"

Justin huffs. "I think you're overreacting. The demon is in the summoning circle and can't hurt me. Not that he wants to."

Ryan rubs his temple and squeezes his eyes shut. He swears he can feel a tension headache coming on. "And how do you know that?"

"Because I asked him!" Justin exclaims a little too loudlay, and Ryan hushes him. "I asked him if demons were evil, if they wanted to drag us to Hell, or take over the world. And he said no." Justin finishes so casually like he just told Ryan the rain outside has finally stopped.

"He could be lying," Ryan groans. He runs his fingers through his hair not caring that it tends to make it stick up in funny directions. "What made you think it's a good idea to summon a demon again? After Ethan warned us that it's not for beginners!" Because, honestly, Ryan would like to know why he had thought of doing it, too.

"Why not? Ethan has been a big help, but there's still a lot we don't know." Ryan pauses and takes a deep breath. He pushes his camera a little further to the center of the table so he can rest his elbows on the edge. "Now, I'm not saying there are no bad demons, just like there are bad people, but I trust Kris. We hung out for a while afterwards. Other than having horns on his head and living in another dimension, he seems like a pretty normal guy."

Ryan frowns. He really can't be upset with Justin since he very nearly did the same thing just the night before. "How is this our life?" he laments. "If you'd asked me last month I wouldn't have even believed demons existed and now we're arguing over whether they are trustworthy or not."

Justin nods in agreement. "It's wild, but I may have an idea."

"I'm open to it." Ryan slumps in his chair, resigning himself to this wild ride he has found himself on. "It's not like anything else we've done has been entirely logical or sane."

Excited, Justin scoots his chair closer until their knees are bumping under the table. "What if we summon *my* demon together? Then you can ask him questions, too. Decide for yourself if he's trustworthy or not."

Ryan frowns. "I don't know, Justin. It doesn't seem safe."

"What if we made rules! Like, you don't have to tell him your name. Or you don't even have to be in the room." The excitement radiates off Justin in waves and Ryan just isn't sure he's going to be able to dissuade him.

"That doesn't make any sense," Ryan points out. "Tell you what. Let's invite Ethan, too. I trust his judgment. If he agrees to do it, then we'll do this the three of us. But if he says no we don't summon anymore demons. Together or alone. Deal?"

"Deal," Justin says with a confident grin.

Ryan just smiles back and nods. *No way will Ethan agree to this scheme,* he thinks to himself.

"Sounds like a great idea," Ethan exclaims moments later and Ryan's jaw drops. The two of them had approached the bookshop owner while he was re-stocking books on botany. Justin practically vibrates with excitement as Ryan stands next to him.

"Seriously?" Ryan gasps.

"Yeah," Ethan nods. "Give me some time to see if I can do some more research on the topic, but this can be a great opportunity."

"You think this demon is going to be okay with continually being summoned and pumped for information?" Ryan asks in an attempt to scare Ethan out of this foolish path. "What if he gets angry?"

"Kris wouldn't get angry," Justin protests. "He's nice, you'll see."

"Besides, he'll be inside the protective summoning circle and won't be able to get us," Ethan reasons.

"Exactly," Justin nods. He crosses his arms and puffs out his chest in victory.

Ryan groans and rubs his face. "Fine, fine. Let us know when you're ready, Ethan, and we'll figure it out." He drops his hands and points to Justin. "And you! No summoning by yourself until then."

Justin holds his hands up in surrender, but that doesn't remove his shit-eating grin.

Apparently Ethan doesn't need that much time to research the practice of summoning, because they are meeting again the following Monday. For privacy, they agree to perform the ritual at Justin's studio.

Ryan brings the book even though Justin has managed to do a summoning without it at this point. He uses it as an excuse to test the limits of his new messenger bag that is weight-rated for 25 pounds and should be able to easily handle the hefty book and his work gear. Taking both a bus and the train to get to Justin's place is a great test run, in his opinion. His bag holds up fine, but Ryan is less certain about his shoulder by the time he arrives at the studio.

"I really can't keep lugging this thing around," Ryan complains as Justin opens the door for him. He rushes inside and dumps the weight onto a computer chair.

Justin rents his workspace from a local community of artists. It has its own darkroom for developing film. There are tables for matting photographs and a desk with a full computer set up to handle his digital editing, emails, and website. For a guy in his mid-twenties, Ryan's seriously impressed with Justin's setup. Even more so that the guy also has a television with a gaming system in one corner.

Justin comes up behind him and starts rubbing his neck. Instantly, the warm hands ease Ryan's sore muscles. "It's okay. You really didn't need to bring it this time," he points out. "I'll give you a ride home after. How does that sound?"

"Fine," Ryan grumbles, but it does make him feel better. Justin gives him a quick hug and then goes off to a corner of the studio. He pulls out a large, rolled up piece of paper, the roll standing almost as tall as him. "What the fuck is that?" Ryan asks as he starts rubbing his own shoulder.

"My summoning circle," Ryan chirps as he begins to unroll the paper out in the open space at the center of his studio.

The circle is drawn in black sharpie and is an exact replica of the one out of the book, but on a larger scale. The lines are thick and dark, the symbols clear and precise. No wonder Skylar had shat all over Ryan's own crudely drawn circle. Justin uses double-sided tape to tack down the corners to the hardwood floor in order to keep it from curling up.

Ryan watches in amazement and Justin steps back to make sure the circle is in place. "That works?" he asks in disbelief.

Justin shrugs. "It is how I summoned Kris the first two times. Why? How did you do it?"

"I drew the circle in chalk on the roof of my building," Ryan admits. "The demon told me it was kind of shitty."

"Aw, I'm sure it was fine." Justin comes over and claps Ryan on the shoulder, making him hiss in discomfort. "Oooh, sorry. The circle worked, though, didn't it? Maybe your demon is just an asshole."

Ryan is about to argue that his circle was really bad, but there comes a knock at the door.

Ethan joins them and Ryan pulls out the tome. He opens to the page for summoning and gives the newcomer a chance to go over the details. The scholar of their trio takes his time looking over the pages and comparing the drawing in the book to Justin's larger version. It's nearly perfect as far as Ryan can tell.

"Did you learn anything new this past weekend?" Ryan asks when Ethan finally sets the opened tome on one of the work tables.

"I did a lot of reading," Ethan nods. "I don't know how much of it will be useful, though. There's a lot of mythology and stories around demons. Realistically, it'll be hard to separate the truth from the fiction. A lot of the most popular and prolific stories have a religious basis, but I really can't tell if the demons referenced in magic texts are older than that, or if they were named demons based off of the religious connotations."

Ryan and Justin just nod along before Ryan clears his throat. "Do you think summoning one will help clarify anything?"

"I think it will be a fantastic way to gather first-hand data," Ethan says, excited.

"Do you think the demon can be trusted?" Ryan presses further.

Ethan shakes his head with a laugh. "Oh, not at all. But I think we can learn a lot from what it'll tell us, what it won't, and what we can observe about it."

"He's not an *it*," Justin cuts in.

"My apologies." Ethan does look contrite.

"Alright," Ryan says. "Ground rules. I don't want to give him our names. Other than Justin's since they already exchanged names." Once both Justin and Ethan agree, he goes on. "We don't give him any personal information about ourselves, either." Again, they both agree, but Ryan doubts there isn't much Justin hasn't told the demon about himself already. It's too late to do anything about that.

"Great," Justin smiles and pulls some sheets of paper out of his pocket. "Here, take these."

"What are they?" Ethan asks, accepting his.

"It's a modified version of the chant so we can summon my demon contact specifically," Justin explains. Ryan glances down at the piece of paper and, honestly, it's better than what he'd done to summon Skylar. Maybe that's why it didn't work?

Trying not to crumble under the weight of his own inadequacies, Ryan gets the ball rolling. "Alright, I think we should each take a point around the circle. Justin, were do you usually stand?"

"Here," Justin says as he takes a spot between the edge of the circle and the entrance to the studio with his back to the door.

"I'll stand here," Ethan suggests, moving so his back is to the darkroom door.

"Fine, I'll stand over there." Ryan moves to put his back towards a bookcase filled with books on photography and digital art. It feels pretty safe compared to having his back to a door. "I think we should all chant. Maybe he won't be able to tell that Ethan isn't magically inclined."

Ethan smiles wide. "Okay."

Justin beams back at him and Ryan is unnerved with how excited the other two are by the whole thing. An uneasiness sits in the pit of his stomach that he can't really identify, but there's no turning back now.

"On the count of three?" Ethan asks, holding his paper at the ready.

"One, two, and three," Justin counts them in. Together, they all begin to chant.

"From this realm to the next,
I seek the demon Kris's aid for trade.
For this night I bring you forth,
Until a bargain is made
You're mine for the stay."

Justin and Ethan are speaking the loudest, enunciating their words most clearly. Ryan mumbles along, but he still gets that strange tingling sensation. It grows with each repetition of the phrase.

Suddenly, without any preamble, a ball of flame erupts in the center of the summoning circle. Ryan gasps and Ethan makes a very audible yelp. Only Justin doesn't seem to react, his grin growing wider. The smell of sulfur, perhaps a little sharper than Skylar had left when she was summoned, fills the room. Ryan isn't sure if it is simply because they are in an enclosed space, or if it is actually different.

In the center of the fireball stands a tall demon with sharp, shiny horns peeking out of thick, curly brown hair. As the flames dissipate, he stands facing Ryan with his head thrown back and his eyes peering down at Ryan's own surprised look. The demon is dressed in tight black slacks and a blood red dress shirt. The top three buttons are left open to show a smooth expanse of collar bone and chest. When the flames dissipate, the center of the circle is unburned.

"What mortal summons me?" The demon's voice booms in such an enclosed space. The feeling of spiders crawling over Ryan's skin returns and he has to fight back a shiver. His heart is beating against his ribs in an attempt to escape, knocking the breath out of him as he meets the demon's cold glare.

"Kris!" Justin calls for the demon.

The cool look shifts to one of surprise as the demon turns his head. The disinterest melts away as his eyes seem to take in his surroundings before finally landing on Justin. "Bunny!" A giant smile appears on the demon's face as he turns to take a few steps towards Justin, still bound within the circle. "What's with the circle jerk?" He gestures to Ethan and Ryan.

"Aw, these are just my friends. They didn't believe me when I told them about you, so I thought I could get you here so they could see for themselves." Justin laughs, but suddenly he stops. Concern brings a frown to the corner of his lips. "I hope that's okay."

The demon waves away his worry. "Any friend of Justin is a friend of mine," he insists. He then looks back towards Ryan, then Ethan. "Hi."

"It's nice to meet you, Mr. Demon, sir," Ethan says with a warm smile. Ryan simply nods towards the demon. The difference between the demon's demeanor upon arrival and his countenance now is like night and day.

"Well, since you already know my name, you can call me Kris," the demon says kindly. He turns his attention back to Justin. "Sorry for not coming straight to you. The magic has a different feel to it and I didn't realize where we are at first."

"Really?" Ethan interrupts. "Magic has a feeling?"

Kris looks over his shoulder towards Ethan and shrugs. "Well, yeah. I mean, it feels a lot stronger, but that's bound to happen when there's three of you doing the ritual."

"So, it was just by chance you appeared in front of Ry—ahem, my friend instead of me?" Justin asks.

"Hmm." The demon strokes his chin as his gaze shifts to Ryan. Then, as if he becomes smoke, Kris's form distorts and shifts until he solidifies in front of Ryan once more. He is much closer to the edge of the circle and Ryan feels as if he's being seen through by the demon's regard. "Not really by chance," Kris murmurs. "This warlock is the strongest of you three."

Ryan frowns. "What makes you say that?"

As if the demon's persona just melts away, Kris is relaxed and is friendly once more. "It's kind of hard to explain. If magic has a flavor, this summoning tastes more like you than it does Bunny or the other one. Which is how demons usually decide who to address when being summoned by a group. Nine out of ten times the most powerful warlock is the one leading the group."

"Fascinating," Ethan comments. Ryan shoots him a glare, but at some point the bookstore owner has pulled out a small notepad and is scribbling inside of it. He doesn't even look up as he continues. "Do you mind if we ask you some more questions?"

Ryan watches as Kris glances toward Justin, receiving a small smile and a nod. The demon then takes a step back so he can address all three of them at once. "Fire away," he says with a smirk as a flame licks along his fingers. He points towards Ethan.

"Where do you come from?" Ethan asks without hesitation.

"The demon realm," Kris answers with confidence.

Ethan is just picking up speed. "Okay, but the demon realm was created by warlocks. Where did demons originate from? How are demons made?"

Kris blinks at Ethan then shoots an uneasy glance towards Justin. He swallows. "Well, there are two ways to become a demon. I was born one, which means that at least one of my parents was a demon."

Ethan doesn't even wait a moment before continuing his questions. "Do you know which one?"

Kris shakes his head. "Nope. I knew I was adopted from a young age, so I never knew my birth parents."

"I'm sorry," Ryan finds himself saying, because it feels like the right thing to say. It may also keep Ethan from just plowing through with his questions.

"It's okay," Kris says as he looks at Ryan, but the look is more of surprise than reassurance. "I had a good childhood, and they were kind to me. I had it better than many other demons."

Ryan can just nod. He catches Justin's warm smile out of the corner of his eye, the man's attention never leaving the demon.

Ethan, however, seems oblivious to the moment. "What's the other way demons are made?"

"Don't know." Kris shoves his hands into his pockets. "My mentor was a born a demon. I only know there's another way because other demons mention it."

Ethan hums at that response and scribbles faster.

When there isn't another follow-up question, Justin clears his throat. "How have you been, Kris?"

Kris smiles warmly back at Justin. "I've been doing okay. Just hanging out with my friend."

"You have friends?" Ryan asks more sharply than he intends. He only realizes how skeptical the question comes across by the look of surprise he gets from Kris and the other two humans present.

"Of course," the demon responds. "I don't stop existing when I leave this place. I have to do something with my time."

Ethan hums some more. "How many other demons are there?"

"Hmm." Kris crosses his arms and gazes up towards the ceiling as if lost in thought. "I'd say probably in the hundreds. While there are a fair number of born demons in the demon realm, it doesn't happen all the time. The fact that I have a friend who is my age is kind of remarkable. And I don't even know the last time a demon was made that wasn't born. Does kind of keep the population down."

"So demons don't procreate with other demons?" Ethan asks.

"Well, they try," Kris says with an eyebrow wiggle. "But no. Demons are only born when a mortal and a demon *procreate*." The demon leers towards Ethan, purposefully drawing out the word in a crude suggestion, which is totally wasted on the man since he doesn't look up as he writes.

When Kris doesn't seem to get the reaction he is looking for, he turns his leer on Ryan. He just rolls his eyes at the demon and shoves his hands in his hoodie pocket. "Charming," he smirks.

"I can be very charming," Kris gasps in mock offense. He then looks to Justin. "Right, Bunny?"

Ryan's eyes go wide as he looks towards Justin. The other man's ears have turned red as he glances towards the floor.

Ethan interrupts with his questions once more. "Are demons compelled to answer the warlocks that summon them truthfully?"

Kris's face screws up in confusion. "What?"

"Can demons lie to warlocks?" Ethan rewords the question.

"That's kind of an interesting question," Kris hums. "Most warlocks just ask for things, which demons are compelled to supply in order to complete the pact. I guess they could say no, but then there's no benefit in doing so. Most warlocks don't try to play twenty questions with us. I suppose a demon could lie, or at least not tell the full truth."

"Then how do we know we can believe anything you're telling us?" Ryan challenges.

This time Kris's look of hurt feels a bit more genuine. He glances towards Justin. "Because we're friends, Bunny and me. I don't have any reason to lie."

"I'm sorry," Justin whispers. "I told these guys they were being ridiculous to not trust me about you, but I thought if they saw you themselves they'd be less of a dick." That last bit is hissed and obviously directed towards Ryan.

"Sorry," Ryan repeats after Justin. "I guess I'm finding this all really hard to believe. Especially since you're being so helpful."

Kris smiles at Ryan, but it doesn't reach his eyes like his previous smiles. "It's okay. You guys are definitely different than the usual warlocks that summon us. I guess that's part of the reason I'm happy to answer your questions. Most warlocks assume they know more than me, or at least better than me."

"That sucks," Ryan admits. He feels bad for being so harsh, but the tingling feeling hasn't really dissipated. It makes him feel on edge. This is the longest he's been part of a summoning circle, and he wonders if that has anything to do with it.

The demon turns his full attention on Ryan. Under his gaze the feeling of spiders crawling across Ryan's skin returns as those warm brown eyes feel like they are seeing through him.

"What is it that you desire?" the demon asks when his eyes meet Ryan's own.

"Honestly?" Ryan frowns. "For the world to make sense again. When did magic and demons become a part of my reality?"

"If I had to guess," the demon says, his voice impossibly deep as he closes the distance between them in a few strides, "the possibility of magic has been with you all your life. It radiates off of you."

The sense of something crawling over Ryan's skin intensifies. "Bullshit," he huffs. Not because he doesn't believe the demon, but he doesn't want to.

"Oh, honey," the demon purrs. "That one is a magical dud," he points a thumb over his shoulder towards Ethan. He looks up from taking his notes with a murmured: *I told you so.* "Even Bunny doesn't have much innate magic, but he is naturally talented enough to use the tools of the trade." Kris finally breaks his gaze to glance towards Justin. "No offense."

Justin shrugs. "None taken, but what about him?" He tilts his chin towards Ryan.

"There's like an aura of power around him," the demon says, gaze settling on Ryan again. "I can feel it even from here. And the entire circle is laced with his magic. Bunny made an amazing circle, but this one's magic took it over and infused it with the power to bring me here."

Ryan squirms under the demon's gaze, but not just from that. If what he is feeling is his magic, then it is beginning to build around him like static. The hairs on his arms are standing on edge. "I didn't ask for this," he says plainly. "I didn't even know about this stuff until we found that stupid book."

Kris's look sours and Ryan feels a punch of guilt in his stomach. "You're not the only one who didn't ask for the power to bend reality, but we play with the hand we are dealt."

"I don't even know the game we're playing," Ryan says, more gently than before.

The demon shrugs, the look of hurt vanishing into a flippant smirk. Ryan is certain it is a facade. Now that he knows that, he can see the whole act the demon has been putting on since he arrived. "Then learn, warlock," he sneers.

The energy Ryan identifies as magic stings along his skin so sharply he gasps. "I release you back to the demon realm from which you came," Ryan grinds out through clenched teeth.

The demon disappears in an instant. Like a bubble bursting, the energy around Ryan dissipates quickly and leaves him feeling drained as he sinks to his knees.

No, he thought after a moment. It didn't just dissipate. He directed it. He didn't just release Kris like he did Skylar. Ryan had used the building energy to thrust Kris back out of their realm.

"Are you okay?" Ethan rushes around the outside of the circle to get to Ryan, even though the spell has ended and there is nothing more than paper covered in sharpie on the floor.

"What was that?" Justin cries. He strides across the circle more directly to kneel at Ryan's side. "Kris was talking to us, and you just sent him away?"

"It's not that simple." Ryan is shaking his head, trying to clear his thoughts.

Ethan, approaching his other side, presses the palm of his hand to Ryan's forehead. Ryan flinches at the cool touch. When had he begun sweating? "You're burning up," Ethan says.

Justin's frustration turns to concern. "Wait, are you actually not okay?"

"I don't know what it is," Ryan admits. "It was like this energy was building up and if I didn't use it for something it felt like it was going to start poking me like needles."

"Magic," Ethan says in awe. "I think the demon is right: you have a lot of magical energy. Maybe you just don't know how to control it?"

"Control it?" Ryan groans. "Last month I didn't even know it existed! I think the answer is simple."

Justin reaches out and rubs a hand along Ryan's back to soothe him. Even there Ryan can feel how his shirt sticks to his skin under the hoodie. He shrugs Ethan and Justin off so he can slide out of the sweatshirt. The other two stand back and let him, but their worried gazes linger on him.

"What's the answer?" Justin asks softly.

The cool air against his skin is a relief. He looks from Ethan to Justin. "I went for thirty years without knowing I could do magic, so I think the best option is to just stop."

As soon as Justin processes Ryan's words, the look of disappointment is evident in his eyes.

8

Cuddles & Espionage

SKYLAR'S PHONE BEEPS IN the middle of the night. It's not like she has a service plan or anything, but it is a device through which demons can easily send messages to one another that mimics the technology in the mortal realm. There are only two demons who would be texting her this late at night, and she hasn't heard from Warren for months.

Groaning, she reaches out and feels around in the darkness for the phone she left on her bedside table. Another message comes through, lighting up the screen and making it easier to find. She brings the device close to her face so she can squint at the messages.

Kris

Hey Sky, I know it's late . . . but are you awake?

If you're not at a summoning, can I please come over?

Or even if you are?

Skylar frowns as she blinks at the messages.

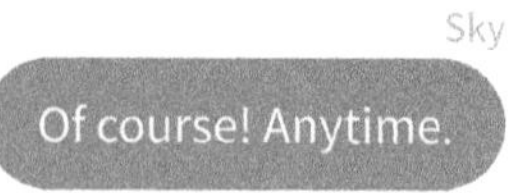

Within moments she hears Kris's voice coming from her living room. "Are you home, Sky?"

"In bed," Skylar croaks, her voice thick with sleep.

She can hear him shuffling through her apartment as she pushes herself up to at least turn on the bedside light. As she rubs the sleep from her eyes, Kris creeps into her room.

"Sorry for waking you," he says in a low voice.

Skylar just shakes her head. "Don't be silly." She peers at her friend in the dimly lit room. Kris is dressed in comfy-looking sleep pants and a soft baggy shirt. His hair is a wavy mess as if he's been running his fingers through it. "Everything okay, Kris? Did you have a bad dream?" Skylar immediately slides over and pulls back the sheets for him to join her.

Without hesitation, Kris crawls into the bed and curls up against Skylar. Even though she is a good deal shorter than her friend, she knows Kris likes being the little spoon when he's upset. She happily drapes an arm over him to encase her friend in the warm bed.

"Want to talk about it?" Skylar asks gently, pulling Kris close. She nuzzles the hair that curls behind the demon's ear with her nose.

"I don't want to hear an 'I told you so,' so no," Kris complains.

Skylar runs her hand up and down Kris's arm in a slow path. "If I promise not to say that, will you tell me?"

There's a pause and Skylar begins to wonder if Kris has already fallen asleep. Then there's a quiet, "Maybe."

"I promise I won't say 'I told you so' and I'll be the best, most supportive BFF," Skylar swears solemnly.

She feels Kris's chest expand when he takes a deep breath and lets out a heavy sigh. "I had a bad summoning," he admits softly.

Instantly Skylar's heart seizes in her chest. She begins to imagine what could have happened, but she knows "who" right away. If Kris's Bunny did anything to upset him . . . Skylar's temper is already rising. She has to bite the inside of her cheek to keep from saying something harsh.

After a few slow breaths, Skylar reins in her anger and tries to focus on Kris. "Do you want to tell me what happened?" The question is less soft than the first, with just an edge of the worry and anger that she's trying to control.

"I want you to remember what you promised before I continue," Kris warns.

Skylar realizes she has stopped stroking Kris's arm and is gripping it firmly. She forces her hand to relax and snakes it around Kris's waist to hug him. "I promise. If it'll help you to talk about it, I will listen."

"Bunny summoned me tonight," Kris explains. "He wasn't alone, though. He had two other mortals with him."

That is not what Skylar is expecting. She feels her brows pinch together in confusion. Once she's processed that bit of information, she nods and presses a gentle kiss to Kris's hair.

He takes it as a signal to go on. "Bunny was fine," he says and Skylar doesn't doubt it's in an effort to reassure her. "He is nice and sweet and even defended me against the other warlock."

"So, one of the other two warlocks were mean to you?" Skylar attempts to ask the question as even-tempered as possible.

Kris sighs. "There was only one other warlock. It took me a minute to realize the third guy was a dud. That one seemed more interested in just asking me questions."

"Weird," Skylar comments.

"Right?" Kris rolls over to face Skylar. "Like, I was fine with everything up to a point. The human was asking me questions about the basic stuff you learn when you first come to the demon realm. It was kind of nice knowing something that the warlocks didn't."

Skylar reaches up and cards her fingers through Kris's hair. "So, what went wrong?"

A frown immediately appears on Kris's lips. "The other warlock started to get mean. His words were harsh and he asked why they should even trust me."

Skylar takes a moment because this is the exact thing she's expected from the beginning. She tries to find a supportive thing to say instead. "What happened next?"

"Bunny defended me, but the other warlock seemed too . . ." Kris trails off. "I don't know how to put it. He had so much power, but he seemed too uncertain. He seemed to think that standing around talking to a demon was an impossible thing, but it is *his* magic that pulled me through this time. It was that powerful it eclipsed what little power Bunny has."

Skylar nods. "I wonder if warlocks are different than what Warren remembers," she muses aloud. "He seems to always talk about warlocks recruiting one another, teaching each other, and forming groups. Your warlocks don't seem to know jack-shit about being a warlock."

Kris nods. His eyes are looking glassy, like he might actually cry, and it hurts Skylar's heart. "Exactly! And I was trying to help, but the warlock didn't seem to want my help. He said he never asked to be a warlock, as if I ever asked to be a demon."

"Oh, sweetie," Skylar coos and pulls Kris closer to tuck his head under her chin. It is a bit of a feat with his horns atop his head, but it is a practiced maneuver at this point. "Of course you didn't. I don't think any demon, born or not, asked for this."

"You don't know that," Kris cries and Skylar feels the dampness of tears against the collar of her sleep shirt. "I think that's the other reason I'm frustrated. There's stuff we don't know, either, Sky. And I was fine with that until these warlocks started questioning me. Is there a way to become a demon without being born? Maybe our mentors are lying to us? But why?"

Skylar hushes him gently, rubbing his back to comfort him. "It's okay, Kris. We don't have to have all the answers tonight. Why don't we visit Warren tomorrow?"

"As if he'd tell us," Kris mumbles. "You've been asking him for years and he refuses to say."

Skylar frowns over Kris's head. "Maybe he won't refuse the both of us? You never know."

"And what could we possibly say that would make him tell us anything?" Kris argues, even as his arms wrap around Skylar to hold her closer.

"We could tell him about these clueless warlocks," Skylar suggests. "He may not have run into them before. Or maybe we can ask if he has advice on how to deal with untrained magic users?"

There's a moment of silence and then Kris's shoulder shrugs. "Maybe that could work."

Skylar pats Kris on the back. "Now, get some rest. I promise, everything will feel better in the morning. You just need some sleep."

Kris pulls his head back and looks up at Skylar. "And what if Bunny summons me again? What if that other warlock is there?"

Skylar thumbs away the tears wetting Kris's cheeks. "Well, I doubt that's going to happen tonight. Or even before we talk to Warren. So, we have some time to think about it. Let's hope, if your Bunny is as you say he is, that he would have better sense than to do that to you again."

"Yeah, I think so," Kris nods, but his tone feels less sure.

Skylar presses a kiss to Kris's forehead. "Sleep," she murmurs against the demon's skin.

"Thanks, Sky," Kris says, followed by a big yawn. He turns away again to let Skylar spoon him once more.

She turns off the light with a snap of her fingers so she doesn't have to unwrap herself from around her poor friend. She holds him close as they both drift off to sleep.

The next day Skylar treats Kris to a big stack of strawberry pancakes for breakfast. The demon is smiling and cheerful as if he hadn't crawled into bed with her in the middle of the night with tears in his eyes. Kris also sends a message to Warren that morning.

She knows flattering Warren makes him more likely to invite them over: either his good looks or his experience. The demon holds both in high regard, so Skylar has no shame in appealing to either one of those to get the answers she wants. She wants to butter him up, since she knows that the demon isn't going to want to answer their questions.

Warren replies before Kris has even finished his absurdly huge stack of pancakes.

Warren

For my favorite protégé? I have a meeting on realm-planning this morning, but come by this afternoon. We can have a late lunch and discuss your concerns.

Skylar is sure the older demon left off the phrase "due to your lack of experience." Sure, she and Kris are among the youngest of the demons in the demon realm, but she overheard once that Warren himself has been a demon for less than a century. So, how much older could the other demons be?

"What's up, Skylar?" Kris licks the last of the strawberry syrup from his plate, interrupting her thoughts.

She had frozen, her phone in her hand. "Nothing," she shrugs. "Warren says we can come over for a late lunch this afternoon."

"Great!" Kris beams at her. "What do you want to do until then?"

Skylar and Kris do what they usually do when they're together. They go for a walk, Kris summoning his camera so he can take pictures as they stroll through the park. The sun is warm on Skylar's skin as she tilts her face towards the sky, but now she wonders: is she experiencing the sun like someone in the mortal realm is, or is this a pale reflection? It's been over fifteen years since she was first called to the demon realm and she isn't sure she can remember anymore.

That afternoon they arrive at Warren's front door in their best visiting clothes in an effort to ingratiate themselves with the older demon. Kris makes sure his hair is styled with his curls under control, wearing his black slacks and a white button up under a patterned sweater vest. Skylar does her best to match the mood with a black blouse and matching A-line skirt. She knows Warren cares about appearances, so whenever she does visit she makes sure to put in the effort. They couldn't just teleport to the door because Warren's building has anti-teleportation wards since some of the most senior demons reside here.

Warren answers the door dressed in (as Skylar would have guessed) a pair of tan slacks with a pale pink silk blouse. "Skylar. Kris. Please come in," he says as he steps aside.

They both smile and walk into the apartment. It's just as Skylar remembers it from the first time she arrived in the demon realm as a frightened thirteen-year-old. Even the last decade has not brought much change to Warren's décor.

The furniture very much reminds Skylar of visiting her grandparents when she was young, but much more lavish and expensive. There's no television in sight as they enter the sitting area where soft, plush velvet couches are arranged so that company can look at one another rather than at a wall. A large, low coffee table takes up the center of the space and Warren has already laid out refreshments: a tea pot with cups, plates of fruit, cheese, and meats alongside small cakes and pastries.

"Thank you for taking time out of your busy schedule to talk to us," Skylar says as they all settle around the table. She and Kris sit on a couch while Warren reclines in an armchair.

Warren simply shakes his head. "It's nothing. In fact, it's been far too long since we last visited one another. How have you been?"

Kris sets to pouring tea for everyone, and, as he does, Skylar carries on the pleasantries. Once enough small talked has passed, she does her best to maneuver the conversation in the direction she wants.

"You know how the day-to-day summonings go," Skylar is saying. "Just recently Kris and I both have gotten a couple of unusual warlocks requesting our services. Perhaps you've encountered something similar?"

Warren hums and nods as he sips his tea. He takes a delicate bite of a petit four. "Unusual in what way?"

Skylar gives Kris a little nudge of encouragement. So far, he's been letting her carry the conversation. "Well," he says, glancing at Skylar, a little uncertain. "How would you deal with warlocks who don't seem to know much about the magic they are performing?"

"As if warlocks ever really know what they are dealing with," Warren laughs. "Most are just greedy children."

"But more than the normal ignorance," Skylar presses. "So untrained that they are surprised a demon even showed up in the first place."

A frown crosses Warren's face as Skylar watches him, waiting for a response. "Really? How could they complete a summoning without formal training? That's not something just anyone should be able to do."

"That's what we'd like to know," Kris insists. "Have you never, in your years of experience, come across such a warlock?"

"I can't say that I have." Warren puts his teacup down and dabs at the corner of his mouth with a cloth napkin before draping it over his knee. "Which of you experienced such a summons?"

"Both of us," Skylar explains. "Warlocks in normal street clothes without wants or desires summoning demons. Just testing to see if they can do it."

Warren narrows his eyes at the two of them. His forked tongue slips out between his lips, something Skylar learned under his mentorship happens when he's getting irritated. "Are you pulling my leg? Is this some sort of trick or prank that you're trying to get over on me out of boredom?"

Both Skylar and Kris immediately shake their heads. "No, sir," Kris rushes to say. "We were hoping you could help us get out from under their pact with some tried and true tactic of demoning."

Demoning? Skylar tries not to laugh.

"I don't have any experience with such a circumstance," Warren says, relaxing back into his seat. "There have been warlocks reluctant to give up a pact with a demon if they thought it gave them an edge. Perhaps we can apply similar tactics to your situation. Give me more details."

"Kris, you go first," Skylar urges her friend.

So Kris tells Warren about the first time he was summoned by Bunny, but leaves out a lot of the personal details such as the warlock's name, and his fondness for the man. Just that he was summoned by a man in gym clothes who sprayed him with a fire extinguisher.

Skylar follows up with her own story, again leaving out Ryan's name. "The warlock tried to abandon me in the circle and walk away. The only thing he had with him was a large book."

Warren holds up his hand to interrupt her. "Large book? Did you get a good look at it?"

"No," Skylar admits. "Just that it is quite large and he seemed to be using it as a source for the summoning circle. When I talked to him about how the deal would work, he started flipping through the pages of the book as if trying to verify my statements."

"Hmm," Warren hums. "It's possible that at least this warlock came across a tome written by one of the established warlock orders. Though how he got his hands on it without being inducted to such a group is strange."

Skylar puts her own teacup and saucer down on the table and neatly folds her napkin once more. "Then, what should we do when we're summoned by these warlocks again?"

"Do your best to get out of the deal," Warren says simply. "If they are truly this inexperienced, it should be relatively easy. Get them to make a wish, even if it's something silly. Use that as a way to get out of the pact. Even if it's something as simple as 'I wish I had a sandwich.' Get them a damn PB&J and be done with it."

Skylar nods. "That makes sense," she says, even as she feels Kris stiffen in the seat beside her. "It may take some creative word twisting, but I think I can do it."

Warren smiles confidently. "I have faith in the both of you. You may be the youngest demons here, but you've got the training to do this. It just may be more elementary than you're used to."

"May I ask another question?" Kris cuts in before Warren has a chance to change the subject.

"I'm feeling magnanimous," Warren nods, picking up a piece of cut pear and popping it into his mouth. "Go ahead."

"The warlocks asked me a question I didn't know the answer to. Perhaps this knowledge would help me get free of their influence?"

Skylar arches an eyebrow. She knows Kris isn't really looking to get out of his bond with Bunny, but it seems that he has figured out that this will be their best strategy to get the answers they both want. It is difficult not to beam with pride at her best friend.

"And why wouldn't you ask *your* mentor?" Warren seems smug like he knows the answer to that question. He really does think too highly of himself.

"You see, sir, it's due to the nature of the question." Kris leans forward as if he's trying to draw Warren in.

It seems to pique the older demon's interest because he leans in close as well. "And what would that be?"

Kris replies in a low voice as if concerned with being overheard. "You see, it's about the origin of demons."

A dark shadow seems to fall over Warren's face. "What *specifically*?" Already Skylar can see Warren pulling away from them.

"Well," Kris forges ahead, either not caring about or unaware of the shift in Warren's demeanor. "I know that demons can be born, obviously, from experience. However, given that a demon can be born only between a human and another demon, it leaves me wondering where the first demon came from."

Warren sits up straight and levels an even gaze at both of them. "And why would that be of importance?"

Skylar gulps. She has tried time and time again to get Warren to give up this bit of information and it seems they've lost their edge in this conversation.

"It's just that these new warlocks don't seem to have a clue either. Perhaps this is something I can use to get out of my pact." Kris is trying to appeal to Warren's manipulative nature, which Skylar has never tried to do before.

"Interesting," Warren says. "These warlocks are either very new or have no formal education from other warlocks. That's a very basic threat warlocks use against one another." The last sentence is spit out bitterly, even though it doesn't make any sense.

Skylar's familiar frustration starts bubbling up with Warren's cryptic answers, but she remains absolutely still holding her breath. She hopes that Warren will keep going this time. His thoughts seem to pass over his face before his gaze settles on them one more time.

"Perhaps the practice has gone out of vogue. And if that's the case, I expect we won't see any non-born demons ever again," Warren addresses them. "And if that's the case, you need not worry your little heads over it."

As if the air were being let out of a balloon, Skylar feels the breath she's been holding escape her in a long sigh. As expected, there are no new answers.

Just more questions. What threat? What practice? Warren continues to speak in riddles.

Kris nods. "Thank you for your wisdom and your insight," he says. "Skylar and I will try to figure out how best to rid ourselves of these warlock pacts. I'm sure your words will be of use to us."

"Very well," Warren says. "Now, if that's done, shall we have more treats?"

Skylar does her best to hide her disappointment. The rest of the afternoon is forced chitchat about a new expansion opening up in the demon realm: an art museum. Kris is thrilled, but Skylar can't be bothered to care at the moment. She and Kris finish their visit and go on their way.

As the pair are riding down the elevator in Warren's building, Kris turns to her with a giant grin on his face. "That was brilliant!"

"What?" Skylar pouts now that she doesn't have to pretend anymore. "I'm really happy for you and your art museum, but really—"

Kris gently smacks her shoulder. "Not that, silly! Though, yes. That's cool, too. I'm talking about what we learned today."

"Nothing," Skylar continues to sulk. "We learned absolutely nothing."

Kris rolls his eyes. "Yes, we did. You just weren't paying attention."

"What did I miss?" Skylar blinks up at him.

The elevator doors open to reveal they've reached the lobby. Two demons in burgundy robes step into the elevator without giving either of them a chance to get off. They have to scramble to get through the doors before they get trapped inside.

Once the doors are closed behind them, Kris leans in to whisper in Skylar's ear. "I'll tell you once we get back to my place."

With a shrug, Skylar follows him out of the building. The residences are all in close proximity to one another, but because they are the youngest, their homes are in the newest buildings and farthest away. The walk is good for Skylar's mood, though. The sun is still shining, and the stretch of her muscles feels refreshing after sitting on the too-soft couch cushion.

They get back to Kris's and change into their comfy lounge wear. As is their practice, they settle onto the couch together: Skylar draping her wings over the back and Kris curling up against her side.

"So, what did I miss?" Skylar asks again.

Kris sighs and shakes his head, a grin on his face. "What were we trying to learn today?"

Skylar frowns at him but goes along with his antics. "Ultimately: if demons aren't born, where do they come from?"

"Right," Kris gives her a playfully condescending pat on the head and she smacks his hand away. He just laughs. "And what did Warren say about demons and warlocks?"

It is obvious Kris is leading her somewhere, but she can't quite figure it out. "That we should try to get out of the pacts with these clueless warlocks?"

Kris shakes his head. "No, that's us specifically. What did he say in general about warlocks and demons?"

Skylar frowns and pokes Kris in the side to make him squirm. "What? Kris! He didn't say anything!"

"But he did!" Kris wriggles away to settle on the other side of the couch, out of her reach. "He said: that's a very basic threat warlocks use against one another."

"The threat of what?" Skylar exclaims, frustration boiling over.

It's Kris's turn to frown. "I don't know," he admits. "Something about demons. We were asking where demons came from and said that our warlocks don't know. Which means: warlocks usually *do* know where demons come from."

Skylar nods as she starts to catch on. "Yeah. Warren once told me that the creation of the demon realm and the first demon happened at the same time. And we both know that warlocks created the demon realm."

"So," Kris says drawing out the "o" sound. He crosses his arms over his chest. "If warlocks created the demon realm and demons were created at the same time, then warlocks created the first demon!"

Skylar's eyes go wide. "And that is a threat they used against other warlocks!" All of a sudden, a lot of pieces feel like they are finally fitting together. "Do you think the first demons used to be warlocks?"

Kris reaches over and smacks Skylar's thigh in excitement. "That makes sense, doesn't it? Old demons wear those stupid ceremonial robes that most warlocks wear."

"Maybe," Skylar concedes, but it feels like that's not the whole picture. "The robes look a little different, but I guess they could be connected. No two robes have ever been exactly the same between warlock groups."

Silence falls between them as they both fall into their thoughts.

"Okay," Skylar finally says after a long pause. "What does this mean for us now?"

Kris deflates and flops down across the couch, his head landing in Skylar's lap. "I don't know," he sighs. "It may mean the answer to the origins of demons is in the mortal realm."

Skylar threads her fingers through his curls. "Therefore, out of our reach."

Kris tilts his head up to catch Skylar's eye. A mischievous grin spread across his lips. "Or is it?"

9

Avoidance Tactics

THE RAIN FINALLY LETS up and the sun returns a week later. During that time, Ryan doesn't want to leave the dark and damp apartment, so he puts off working at *Much Loved Books*. Instead, he makes do with his spotty internet at home so he doesn't have to face the outside world or either of his friends. He also doesn't hear from Justin during his self-isolation other than some passing comments on work and a picture of a cat curled up on his building's doorstep during a particularly bad storm. They used to talk about non-magic stuff all the time and he's worried that his friend is upset with him for calling it quits on the warlock stuff. He's going to have to figure out the best way to reach out to Justin.

Now that the sun is back, Ryan waits until the afternoon to make sure it stays that way. Since he no longer has the weather as an excuse anymore, he packs up his bag and makes his way out into the world. There's still a chill in the air, but the sun's rays do a lot to warm him as he makes his way to *Much Loved Books*. His work bag is a lot lighter now that he doesn't have to carry the massive book everywhere he goes.

His first surprise when he walks through the doors of the bookshop is that Ethan isn't the first person there to greet him. The bell rings and a woman pops up from behind the counter and gives him a blinding smile. "Hey, Ryan," she chirps, her dark wavy hair pulled back into a high ponytail.

Ryan blinks. "Oh, hey, Nadia," he greets Ethan's part-time employee. "It's been a while. What are you doing here so early?"

The petite woman shrugs and picks up a stack of magazines from the countertop. "The dance studio cut down on my class load, but Ethan's been nice enough to let me pick up some extra shifts."

Ryan remembers Nadia mentioning she teaches dance somewhere in the city, but he can't remember what kind. He can appreciate the art form, but he honestly couldn't tell you the difference between much other than ballet and tap dance. "Cool," is all he can think to say. "I'm going to set up and get some work done. Let me know if you need a hand with anything." He starts to shuffle towards the back of the store.

"Sure thing," she calls after him before making her way to the magazine rack.

Despite only being gone for a week, Ryan feels an odd sense of comfort as he settles back into his usual chair. Once he's plugged in, he sets to moving information around and creating new data sets. The work is actually mind-numbing and not enough to keep his thoughts from circling back to Justin.

Upon reflection, the week apart has been very good for him. He's feeling more or less back to normal without magic complicating his life. All he really wants to do is reassure Justin that he's still here for him, magic or not.

A bottle of water appears next to his elbow and Ryan blinks, glancing up. Nadia is smiling down at him. "Hey," she says. "Boss man says I need to force you to hydrate when he's not around."

"I'm not one of his plants," Ryan says, amazed that Ethan is able to pester him even when he's not in the store.

She shrugs and shoves the water into his chest. "I take my store duties very seriously."

"I guess so. Thanks." Ryan accepts the water.

She lingers until he uncaps the lid and takes a sip. "So, um," she says, her hands shoved deep in her jean pockets as she sways in one spot like her body can't help but move. "Can I pick your brain for a minute?"

Ryan glances at his computer with the windows opened side by side and various tabs waiting for his attention. "Yeah, sure," he says.

With a little bounce, she settles into the chair next to him. "So, I was so wondering how was it that you got into doing this kind of work." She gestures towards his laptop.

"Remote work?" he asks, unsure what she means.

"Yeah," she nods. "I'm always looking for stuff that I can pick up in a pinch. I love teaching classes at the dance studio, but my extra gigs doing choreography or dancing are kind of few and far between. Sometimes I need to make some extra cash."

Ah, the hustle life. Ryan is familiar with it, and he hates it. "Wouldn't it be better to focus on getting other dance jobs?" he asks instead.

She nods. "Yeah, it would," she admits. "It's just hard sometimes. It'd be nice to have something to fall back on."

Ryan's already shaking his head. "Trust me: you don't want to be doing what I'm doing. It's far too stationary and soul-sucking."

She tilts her head, confused. "Then why do you do it?"

"Because I have no soul," he answers flippantly, and she laughs. "Rather than trying to find something else, maybe you should focus on expanding your reach for dance work. Do you have an online presence? A way for people to find and connect with you other than networking at your performances?"

"Kind of," she says and pulls out her phone. She shows him a really simple splash page with her phone number and links to her social media.

He considers it for a second before handing it back. "You should have some videos of yourself dancing front and center," he comments. "And if you're worried about money, I'm sure Ethan will always let you work extra here. He's definitely got a soft spot for you."

Color rises to the apples of her cheeks and Ryan does his best not to smirk. He may not be the most emotionally intelligent person around, but it's obvious the way Nadia and Ethan dance around one another. "Ethan has been really understanding with my chaotic availability," she says, but shakes her head. "I don't want to make things hard for him by asking for more hours."

Ryan just shrugs. "I doubt he'd find it a hardship, but that's cool. I just recommend focusing on updating your contact site. You don't want to do the kind of work I do."

She smiles. "Thanks, Ryan. For a Grumpy Gus, you're actually a pretty nice guy."

Ryan rolls his eyes. "Don't go telling anyone," he deadpans. "It'll ruin my reputation." Nadia just laughs and lets him get back to his soul-sucking work so she can tend the shop. He drinks the water as suggested.

By the time he is ready to call it quits for the day, it's already dinner time. Ryan did himself a disservice by not stopping to eat so he knows he has to do something about that on his way home. He packs up his gear and heads out of the store, giving Nadia a friendly wave as she's helping a customer in the children's section.

As he steps out onto the sidewalk, Ryan pulls his phone from his pocket. He's getting ready to shoot Justin a text message when the sound of Ethan's laughter greets him.

Blinking, Ryan shoots a glance over his shoulder to find Ethan coming out of the little stairwell that leads up to the bookstore owner's apartment over the shop.

"Oh, Ryan!" Ethan stops short so as to not physically plow into the surprised Ryan. Trailing behind him is Justin.

"Justin," Ryan gasps in surprise.

The smile on Justin's face shrinks. "Oh, hey. Fancy meeting you here," is all he says.

"You mean here, outside of Ethan's home? Or did you mean here, outside of Ethan's bookshop where I work most of the time?" Ryan looks from Justin and back to Ethan. The bookshop owner is looking a little uncomfortable.

"Yeah, I know. I was just kidding," Justin says with a shrug. "How's it going?"

Ryan feels his insides twist. Why does it feel like he caught his friends avoiding him? That's ridiculous. They can hang out without him. It's silly to think otherwise. Besides, he's the one that's been avoiding them. "Not bad. I was just about to text you." He holds out the phone to show the chat conversation already on the screen. "I was going to see if you had some time to hang out. Maybe we could grab a bite."

"Why don't you join us?" Ethan quickly interjects. "If you're done for the day, we were about to go back to Justin's for some take-out and a movie with Ashe."

"I don't want to intrude." Ryan presses his lips into a thin line as he glances between the two men. He can't squash the distinct feeling he's been purposefully left out for a reason, no matter how much he wants to ignore it.

"It's not intruding," Justin insists. "We're all friends, and we should all be able to hang out together." He throws an arm around Ryan's shoulder and gives him the patented "Justin-pout" that never fails to sway any conversation his way.

And it works once again, despite Ryan's misgivings. "True," he says. "I didn't have any other plans tonight, so lets go."

"Awesome! My car is just around the corner," Justin smiles brightly as if there was never any awkwardness there to begin with. Even Ethan smiles as the three of them turn to head down the street.

They walk to the corner parking lot, exchanging pleasantries about their day. When they get to Justin's car, he clicks the fob to unlock the doors as he walks around to the driver's side.

It is at this moment Ryan finds himself standing shoulder to shoulder with Ethan at the passenger side door. Ethan had obviously been reaching to open the door, only stopping when Ryan does the same. To be fair, Ryan is accustomed to driving around with Justin, just the two of them, so it didn't occur to him not to go for the front seat. Simultaneously they both take a step back as the realization dawns on them, each muttering apologies.

"I'm sorry, you should sit in front. You were obviously going there first," Ryan mutters.

"No," Ethan insists. "You and Justin should catch up on the ride over. Of course you should sit in front."

"We can do that while I'm in the backseat," Ryan counters. "You've got longer legs. You should sit in front."

"Guys!" Justin interrupts them. He is standing with the driver's side door open as he leans against the roof of the car watching them. "It's not a big deal. Can someone please just get in the car?"

Since he is closer to the rear, Ryan quickly takes a sidestep over and reaches for the rear passenger door. "There. It's no problem."

"Thanks," Ethan says as he gets into the front seat. Then everyone is on their way.

The drive to Justin's apartment is usually a pretty quick one, but they get caught in early evening commuter traffic. Ryan tells them about his day working in the bookshop for the first time after the rains. He mentions seeing

Nadia in the bookstore and Ethan seems inclined to moon over how helpful she's been, but it's sad she has fewer classes to teach.

Ashe is already at the apartment by the time the other three arrive. "Ryan! It's been a while. Happy to see you." He wraps his long arms around Ryan in a familiar embrace before Ryan can escape it.

"Thanks," Ryan murmurs. He's not much of a hugging person, but Ashe hasn't caught on. "How was your trip?"

The model steps back and lets everyone come in. They're dressed in casual clothes but manages to still look photo-ready. "It was good, thanks. I got to make some really good connections with brands I haven't worked with before. And Farah and I got to spend the day together before she had to fly out to New York."

Ryan takes off his shoulder bag and drops it on the floor next to the door. "That's nice," he says. "Did you two do any sight-seeing?"

"Not exactly," Ashe says with a smirk and turns to stride towards the living room.

"What does that mean?" Ethan asks, just above a whisper.

"It means they spent their day indoors," Justin tries to gently intone.

Ethan blinks. "So?"

Ryan huffs a laugh. "It means they didn't leave their hotel room, Ethan. Come on."

The ice is broken and the rest of the evening passes in good cheer. With the inclusion of Ashe, Ryan doesn't even worry that the topic of magic might come up during the course of the night. He's able to relax a bit and agrees to some beer to go with the fried chicken they've ordered. He also manages to cover the tab before any of the others can beat him to it. It is amazingly chill for a Monday evening, but then again three out of the four of them have non-traditional jobs and the fourth set his own hours.

One movie turned into two. More beers come out as the four of them sit around talking over the film more than watching it. Ryan feels comfortably floaty and weightless as the night goes on. At some point he dozes off curled up in the armchair he has claimed as Ethan asks Ashe about his experiences abroad. He wakes up to Justin gently shaking his shoulder.

"Hey, you doing okay?" Justin asks softly.

Ryan realizes the television is off and there are no other voices. "Mm, yeah. What time is it?"

"Just about two," Justin replies. "Did you want me to give you a ride home?"

He groans, rubbing his eyes. "I can just crash on the couch," Ryan yawns.

"Sorry, that's already been staked out by Ethan." Justin steps aside and Ryan sees the tall, lanky man spread out and down for the count.

"Oh," Ryan frowns. "You good to drive?"

Justin gives him a small nod. "Yeah. I stopped drinking hours ago."

With no excuse not to take the offer, Ryan agrees. "Fine. Thanks, Justin."

Justin helps Ryan out of the chair, and they head out. He still feels buzzed, but mostly sleepy, as they get in the car. Justin turns on the heat and lets Ryan sit back in the passenger seat to doze. Time moves the way it does only for drunks and exhausted people: too slow and all at once. Doubly so since Ryan is a bit of both.

Before he knows it, Justin is shaking him awake once more. "Do you need help getting inside?" he asks softly.

Ryan shakes his head as he unbuckles himself. "I think I can make it." He grabs his bag from between his feet.

"Hey, Ryan." Justin stops him from opening the door. "Are we okay?"

Ryan blinks to focus on Justin. His mind is still fuzzy, but he knows this is important. "I wanted to know the same thing. I hope you're not avoiding me."

Justin shakes his head "Not really. I just wanted to give you some space, but I didn't know when to reach out again."

"This is just fine." Ryan reaches over and pats Justin on the shoulder. "We're good. Get home safe."

"Thanks. Sleep well." Justin is smiling at him and the last little bit of unease that was still sitting like a lump in his chest disappears.

Ryan gets out of the car and waves Justin off before ducking down the alley that leads to his basement apartment. Once inside, he sheds his outer layers and collapses into bed in hopes that he is still drunk enough to slip back into sleep. The sheets are cool against his alcohol-flushed skin and darkness pulls him under.

The room is still dark when Ryan becomes conscious once more, but that's nothing new. Even in the middle of the day, very little light makes its way into his home. He kicks back the sheets in discomfort, as if needles are pricking him everywhere the soft fabric touches. Sweat makes his shirt and underwear cling to him as he thrashes about.

Confused and gasping, Ryan sits up and peers around the dark room. It still feels like the middle of the night, but he can't tell how long he's actually been asleep. He tries to figure out what woke him, and he feels uncomfortable in his own skin. After pressing a hand to his forehead he can feel that his skin is flushed. His groggy brain tries to process if this is just the effects of a hangover, but his skin is too hot and his stomach doesn't feel upset. His head isn't throbbing, but the sensation of spiders crawling over his skin makes him squirm.

He doesn't know how it's possible, but the sensation is the one he associates with doing magic. It dances along his skin and drives him from his bed. He stumbles over to the switch and turns on the bedroom light. Glancing around the room, he tries to find the source of the magic affecting him. Everything is as he left it yesterday with the inclusion of the trail of clothes going from the door to the bed from when he got home.

Never has the feeling of magic happened unless he was actively doing something, but he's been asleep. His focus is on how to *stop* the sensation instead of why it's happening in the first place. The summoning circle with Kris showed Ryan that he can get rid of the feeling by channeling it into magic. The problem is he only knows how to do one kind of magic and it's the last thing he wants to do. He groans as he glances towards the closet where the tome sits in its fire safety box, ignored since the last summoning circle.

"Fuck," he curses as he stumbles over to the closet and pulls the door open.

Maybe there is something quick he can do to get rid of the energy building around him. He drops to his knees and pulls the black fireproof box out of the corner and into his lap. It's the size of a chunky laptop case and outrageously heavy, even before he'd placed the hefty book inside. He tries to pop the lid open and realizes the damn thing is locked.

"Damn it!" he curses, struggling with the latch. "Open says me!" The magic crawls down his arm and dissipates the slightest bit across his fingertips pressed to the lock before the box pops open.

Ryan is left blinking at the tome sitting inside the box. Everything he thinks he knows about magic tells him that shouldn't have been possible. Don't warlocks need tools to do magic? Maybe he is remembering wrong, but that isn't his biggest concern. Despite focusing the magic into something, it still crawls along his skin.

Quickly, Ryan pulls out the tome and lets the box drop to the floor with a heavy thud. He flips open the book and tries to skim the first couple of pages. Despite everything he's learned with Ethan's help, the pages still don't make any sense. Nothing in this book is beginner level or three-ingredients-or-less spells-type magic.

"Shit," Ryan slams the book against the top of his thighs. He knows how to do only one thing.

10

Let's Make A Deal

SKYLAR IS PULLED OUT of a deep sleep by a sharp tug inside her belly. At first she thinks it's just nature calling, but a second stronger pull follows quickly after and she realizes she's being summoned. She grabs her phone to check the time to find it's half past four in the morning. The timing is unusual for a summoning, but she supposes time zones are a thing. She rubs her eyes and tries to wake up before she can let the metaphysical cord rip her through dimensions. The pull comes back, strong enough to make it feel like her insides are twisting themselves into knots.

"I'm coming," she groans and stretches.

With the next tug she lets the magic pull her from her bed and to the mortal realm. She envisions herself in a deep scarlet suit with matching slacks, shirt, and blazer. She slicks back her bedhead and adds a pair of black pumps to complete the ensemble. She keeps her wings tight to her back as she feels her feet hit the floor with a click. The magic hums over her skin with a familiar feel to it. Something she's felt once before and has been waiting for ever since. She forgoes the usual cloud of smoke and brimstone as to not frighten the warlock this time. "Ryan?"

Skylar blinks against the brightness of the light as she looks for the warlock. They're not on the rooftop, that's a given. Tiled counters line the wall to the left and past her. A fluorescent light shines off the silver fridge in the corner beside a white stove top. The stained and scuffed concrete floor at her feet has a crude summoning circle drawn across it in chalk. And there, on the floor, sits a crumpled and sweating Ryan with a piece of paper clutched in his fist.

Skylar glances around the kitchen, but they are alone. She kneels inside the circle, which is barely large enough for her to take a step or two, and tries to get the warlock's attention. "It is Ryan, right? What's going on?"

The warlock finally looks up to meet Skylar's gaze. His eyes are a clear blue, their color made almost translucent against the flush of his skin. His hair sticks to the sweat on his forehead. The man is wearing only a pair of boxers and a t-shirt, but he is too sweaty for the cool air of the kitchen. "Something's wrong," he says, his voice hoarse.

"Are you sick?" Skylar asks. That seems like the most obvious answer to her, and she feels silly even asking. What does she know about mortal illness anymore? "Why aren't you in a hospital?"

Of all the times she imagined being summoned again by Ryan over the last month, this is not even close to being one of the possible scenarios. In most of her scenarios she's brought back to the rooftop by the hapless warlock wishing for fame. Or fortune. Maybe even wishing for more power, since the man doesn't seem to know his own strength. And maybe there was one night she dreamt of being summoned back for more carnal desires.

To be fair, that was after her encounter with Omar at *Dante's*. She can't be blamed for where her mind was that night. She was already worked up from getting off once, and it is a little too easy to imagine Ryan's large hands roaming over her skin in place of Omar's.

"Not sick," Ryan shakes his head. His breathing is a bit more regular, but he still looks completely exhausted. "It's my magic."

"What about your magic?" Skylar prompts him to explain.

"It woke me up. Biting along my skin. It felt like it was going to swallow me whole if I didn't do something with it." Ryan's face is screwed up in pain and he drops his gaze once more.

"So you decided to summon me at this ungodly hour?" Skylar scoffs, but she feels her own heart rate pick up. Maybe it's the rush of the warlock's power, or the uncertainty of what is happening.

Ryan's jaw clenches in a grimace. "I don't know any other magic and it has to go somewhere!"

Skylar blinks at the warlock in disbelief. "It's been how long since we last saw each other and you haven't bothered to learn anything else in that time?"

She ridicules him, but only to mask her own mounting concern. Her knees are beginning to complain so she sits down in the middle of the circle to stay on an even level with the warlock. She crosses her legs and rests her elbows on her knees.

"Was kind of the point," Ryan shrugs. "If I didn't do any more magic, I wouldn't have to learn about magic."

"I see that really worked out for you." Skylar rolls her eyes at the warlock's stubbornness. "That's like someone who can breathe underwater swearing off swimming." Ryan glares at her, then winces. Skylar's flippant attitude shrinks. "So, how are we feeling now?"

"Casting the summoning circle took the edge off," Ryan admits. "But I can still feel it across my skin. Like it's building up again. I don't know how to channel it into anything."

"Hmm," Skylar hums as she studies Ryan. "I don't remember ever hearing anything like this before."

Ryan moans and squeezes his eyes shut. He stops breathing for just a moment, but then sighs as if a wave of pain has just passed. "So, you're saying you can't help me."

Skylar's lips pull together in a pout. "I didn't say that. Let me think. Your magic builds up around you and using it releases some of the, um, tension, shall we say?" Ryan nods. "You sound like you're clogged."

Ryan rubs his face, pushing the sweaty hair back from his forehead. He throws the crumpled piece of paper to the side. "Are you calling me a pimple?"

"Not exactly," Skylar smirks, glad he's got some of his attitude still. If the warlock can joke, maybe it isn't that bad. "Imagine magic is like an element in the atmosphere. It's something you can't see, but it's all around you. Some people can sense it and others can't. And those who can sense it are able to sense it to varying degrees. Warlocks are people who can not only sense it but make use of it."

"Okay," Ryan nods along. "So, I'm just hypersensitive to it?"

Skylar runs her fingers through her hair and tries to rethink how to explain this. "Do you feel it all the time?" The warlock shakes his head. "But you do seem very sensitive to it when you use it," she guesses.

"Yeah, sure," Ryan says. "The only time I've ever felt it was when I was summoning. And then tonight it came out of nowhere."

"Okay, new metaphor!" Skylar claps her hands together. "Let's pretend magic is like water. And when you use magic, it flows through you like water flowing through a stream."

"Really?" Ryan groans.

"Not really, that's why it's a metaphor," Skylar sighs. "Anyway! You, Ryan, have the capacity to move a lot of magic through yourself. Less like a stream and more like a giant river. However, there seems to be a dam somewhere along the river's path and it's causing it to back up. At least, that's my guess."

"So, how do I fix it?" Ryan says through gritted teeth.

Skylar frowns caught up in her own metaphors. "Get rid of the dam?"

Ryan growls and covers his face with his hands. "If I knew how to do that, I wouldn't be in this mess."

"Well, Mr. Smart-Ass Warlock. You've told me that you feel this building power of magic that hurts unless you use it. Right?"

"Yes," Ryan huffs and drops his hands into his own lap.

"Then I think the quickest way to expel the excess energy is to do some magic." Skylar feels unsure of her conjecture. She badly wishes she could ask Warren for advice, but Ryan doesn't look like he has the time to wait.

"I did! I summoned you!" Ryan gestures towards Skylar. "And I think I did something else . . ."

Skylar leans forward, intrigued. "What?

Ryan rubs his legs and glances away. "I think I unlocked something using my magic."

"Really?" Skylar gasps. "Did you use a spell? Or a wand or something?"

Ryan looks back at her with a skeptical smirk. "A wand?"

She shrugs. "I've seen it. Lots of warlocks who have only the most minimal access to magic need tools in order to accomplish anything. If most warlocks are like double-A batteries, you're like a nuclear power plant."

"Then what are demons?" Ryan asks, slack jawed.

"Demons are part-human, part-magic itself. None of us needs tools to do magic," she explains.

The color drains from Ryan's face. "Am I a demon?" he whispers.

Skylar can't help but laugh, both at the ridiculous question and as an attempt to calm the warlock. "No! If you were a demon, you'd have been recalled to the demon realm years ago. You're just a very powerful magic user."

Ryan swallows and nods. "Okay, so what do I do now? I can still feel it. I think the only reason it hasn't gotten overwhelming is because I'm channeling it into the circle right now."

"Do something else," Skylar suggests.

"Like what?" Ryan moans. "This, what we are doing right now, is the only thing I know how to do."

Skylar looks Ryan over. He's tired and desperate. Maybe this is the best opportunity for her. "Tell you what. Let's make a deal." She smiles at him.

Ryan frowns at her. "What kind of deal?"

"I offered before to help you learn how to use your powers. I'll help you with your magic, but in return I have something you need to find for me here. In the mortal realm."

"What is it?" Ryan asks, ever cautious, it seems.

Skylar just waves her hand. "Just some information, which you'll be needing more of anyway."

Ryan's blue eyes seem to roam over Skylar, judging her. She feels a heat rise to her cheeks and ears as those almost icy eyes take her in. She swallows and tries to keep a neutral face.

"Deal," Ryan finally says. "Now, what can we do right this instant? I'd like to be able to sleep without feeling like a ticking time bomb."

Skylar stands up and gestures for Ryan to do the same. The warlock pushes himself to his feet with only minimal effort and stands facing her. The shoes make enough of a difference that she's nearly eye-to-eye with him.

After taking a deep breath, Skylar lets the air out slowly and begins. "I think the easiest thing we can do right now is a glamour. It doesn't involve actually changing anything in the universe, just people's perception of it."

"Huh?" Ryan comments.

"Like this," Skylar says.

She closes her eyes and pictures the illusion she wants to create. Slowly, Skylar lifts both hands to her forehead and then smoothly runs them back over her hair. She hears Ryan's sharp gasp, which means the illusion must be working. When her hands have made it over the top of her head and down the back of her neck, she drops them to her sides and opens her eyes to find Ryan gawking at her.

"How does it look?" She smiles at him.

"Wow," Ryan says. "Your hair looks like strands of silver. It's catching in the light . . ." His sentence trails off.

"That's just how you're perceiving it," Skylar explains. "I pictured what I'd look like with silver hair, and then I made it so that anyone looking at me would see what I imagined. However, it's not real." Skylar shakes her head to dispel the glamour and Ryan gasps again. Strands of deep blue hair fall into her face and she blows them away. "Back to normal, right?"

Ryan frowns. "That's your normal hair color?"

Skylar chuckles. "As far as you or anyone else who can remember knows, it is. Now you try. Imagine what you want your hair to look like, then channel that excess energy into making it visible."

"Gee, you make it sound so easy," he grouses, but he shuts his eyes.

Skylar crosses her arms and waits, watching the warlock. His skin is less flushed than before and Skylar takes that as a good sign. The shirt he wears is just a baggy white shirt that hangs off his shoulders down to mid-thigh where she can only get a peek of his green plaid boxers. Ryan's legs are thin and pale beneath that, but they look soft to the touch.

Skylar is so distracted at thoughts of warm skin and long legs that she almost misses when Ryan reaches up to copy her own motion. He runs his hands over the sweaty mess of straw-colored hair. What is left in the wake is untangled, bright fire engine red hair that falls neatly over his forehead. Not only has he managed to make the hair a different color, but he styled it as he went. It isn't any shorter or longer, just combed through. Skylar is impressed by the warlock's natural intuition.

"Very nice," she honestly compliments the warlock.

Ryan blinks at her. "Did it work?"

Skylar nods. "Yeah, just a sec. She reaches into her pocket and pulls out her phone. She aims the camera at Ryan and snaps a quick picture.

"Demons have phones?" Ryan eyes the device skeptically.

"Not strictly speaking," Skylar shrugs. "It's not like I have an actual phone number or data plan. It's more like a magical photocopy of the technology that humans have here in the mortal realm, but it makes it easier to send messages and stuff to one another." As she explains, she turns the screen towards Ryan so he can see.

The warlock stares at the picture and nods. "So, it worked. I changed my hair?"

Skylar tsks and drops her phone. "It's just the *perception* of your hair."

"How long does it last?" Ryan asks.

"Depends," Skylar considers. "I've made glamours that last a lifetime. Any demon can do that. For warlocks, I'd say it depends on the power of the warlock. Anywhere from hours to days or weeks. You, though? I'm not sure. But how do you feel?"

Ryan blinks at her as if he just realized something himself. He looks down at his hands and arms as if checking for something, then back to Skylar. "It's gone. I can still feel the hum of it, but it doesn't hurt anymore."

"I bet the hum will disappear when you end the summoning," Skylar guesses and smiles as if she'd planned this all along. Secretly, she is just glad it worked. She wasn't sure how much magic training she could cover in a single night with a clueless warlock who doesn't know the extent of his own power.

"So," Ryan says. "Should I keep it?" He gestures towards the hair.

Skylar tilts her head and inspects the look. "I like it," she declares. "And now that you know how to, you can change it whenever and however you want."

Ryan nods and as he does, the strands of hair gradually turn back to their natural color. It's also a bird's nest again. Skylar lifts her phone once more and snaps another quick picture. She captures a surprised Ryan looking at her with messy hair and wide blue eyes.

"Hey," he protests. "Why did you do that?"

"It was too good not to," Skylar chuckles and shows Ryan the picture.

"Delete that," he frowns.

Skylar shakes her head. "I don't think I will." She slips her phone back into her pocket and gives Ryan a shit-eating grin.

Ryan crosses his arms. "So I guess you not having a phone number means I can't call you while you're in the demon realm if I have any more questions."

Skylar is stumped. "I don't know. I've never tried something like that before," she admits. Skylar crosses her arms, unconsciously mirroring Ryan's stance. "Other than summoning, I've never heard of anyone trying to communicate across dimensions. That may be something worth looking into."

Skylar is considering what would need to happen for that to work, forgetting that the two are still just standing in the middle of Ryan's kitchen just before sunrise. She is pulled out of her thoughts when Ryan clears his throat.

"Thanks," the warlock says.

Skylar is caught completely off guard. No warlock has ever thanked her before. "You're welcome?"

"So, what is it that you wanted me to find out? For our deal?"

"Oh, that." Skylar tries to figure out how to form the question. "I don't know how much your book told you about demons, but their origins are supposedly here in the mortal realm. Do you think you can find out more about that?"

"I don't know," Ryan hedges. "If you don't know, how am I supposed to find out?"

Skylar throws her arms up in frustration. "All I know is that warlocks created both the demon realm and the first demon. Maybe there's a record of how that happened somewhere here."

"Do you know how long ago that was?" Ryan asks.

It's a reasonable question, Skylar has to admit. "I don't know. I think the oldest demons are centuries old."

"Hold on," Ryan says and darts out of the kitchen. He comes back a few moments later with a spiral notebook in hand and a pen. "Centuries ago is a pretty big time span. I don't know if there would still be any documentation of it," he says as he writes.

Then the metaphorical light bulb goes off above Skylar's head. She claps her hands and hops in place. "What if I know a demon who wasn't born, but was created within the last hundred years? Do you think there may be proof of that?"

"Maybe," Ryan says slowly as he jots that down. "If I find something, I guess the only way I have of letting you know is if I summon you back."

"Yeah," Skylar agrees. "But can we try to keep it to a reasonable hour? Even this demon needs her beauty sleep."

Ryan actually smiles. Skylar's heart does an unexpected somersault at the sight, and she almost misses what Ryan is saying. "Sure thing. But what if I have another episode like tonight?"

"Then glamour yourself. Or anything around you. But you should probably also try to learn some other magic spells. I'll try to think of some more things we can do while I'm gone. Deal?" She goes to hold her hand out to him to shake on it, and realizes that's not going to happen. She can't cross the circle and no warlock with half his sense would willing reach inside. She lets her hand drop awkwardly.

"Deal," Ryan says as he finishes scribbling, not even noticing her faux pas. He sets the notebook down on a table that is halfway blocking the door out of the kitchen.

"Can we also not do this here again?" Skylar asks gently. "This is kind of cramped." She shifts her wings to relay her discomfort.

"I think I know a better place we can meet that's not outside," Ryan suggests.

Skylar gives a short nod. "Then I guess that concludes our business for tonight."

"Thanks, Skylar," Ryan says with a small smile, a bit softer this time. "I'm sorry for waking you."

"It's fine," she reassures him. She surprises herself to find she actually means it. "I hope you feel better."

"Good night," Ryan says, maintaining eye contact with her.

Skylar fights the urge to squirm under the warlock's gaze and settles for just shifting her wings instead. She is getting uncomfortable with this level of familiarity. "Goodnight, Warlock," she teases to break the discomfort.

Ryan cringes, but it doesn't look painful. "I hate that," he says. Before Skylar can apologize, he continues. "I release you, Skylar, back to the demon realm."

And with that, the cord keeping her in the mortal realm snaps and Skylar is sent flying back to land with a gentle bounce on her own bed. She changes back into her pajamas, but she really isn't sure she'll be able to fall asleep again that night.

Skylar shifts over on top of her cool sheets and stares out the bedroom window where the dawn is beginning to break. She feels as if she's just woken from a strange dream and that the world around her has changed. Ryan really isn't anything like the warlocks she's interacted with on a regular basis. And, for better or worse, it looks like they aren't done with one another yet.

No, that's better. Definitely better.

It isn't until midday that Skylar finally sends Kris a message. She's been thinking about how to broach the subject all morning, but finally can't wait any longer. Her interaction with Ryan in the early hours has left her feeling wound up with a curious excitement. From the couch of her living room, she sends Kris a text.

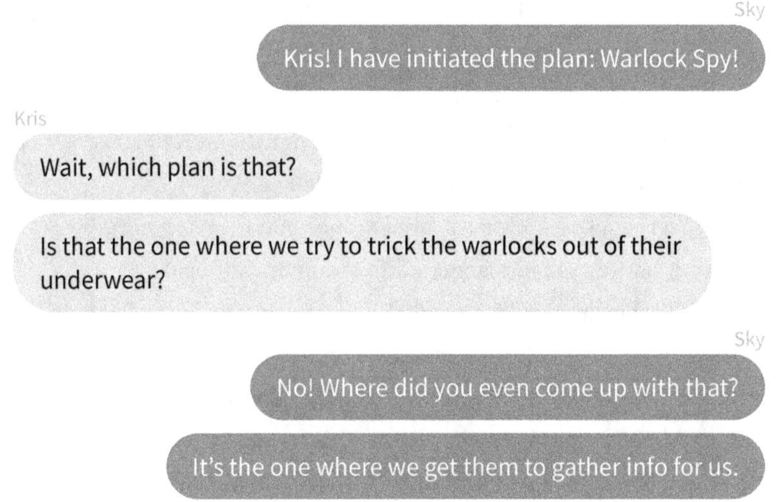

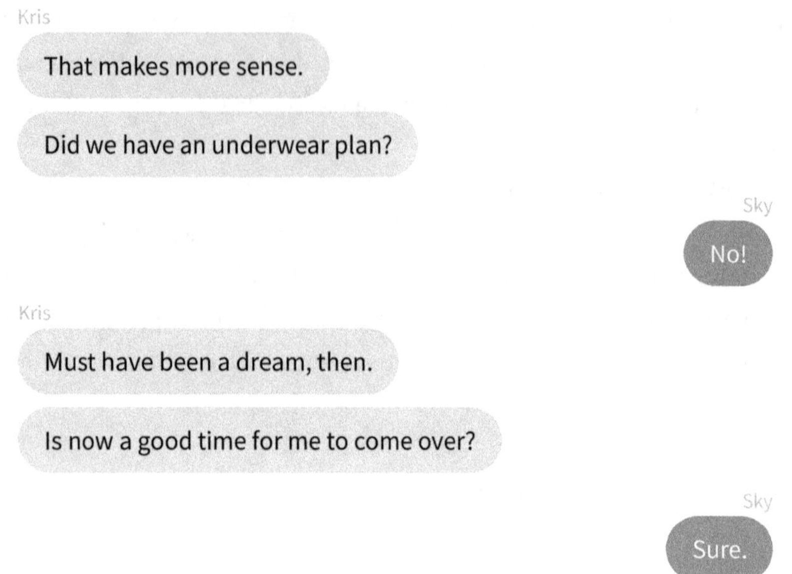

Kris walks in through Skylar's front door a few moments later. He scurries over to the couch and plops down to face her. The other demon is wearing wide pants and a baggy button-up shirt. His hair is a casually tousled mess of curls as he beams at Skylar.

"So, what happened? What warlock did you get to do it?" he prompts.

Skylar smiles and turns in her own seat, folding her legs underneath herself to face Kris. She's in a pair of casual sweats and a rose-colored sweater. "Ryan summoned me early this morning."

"And which is Ryan?" Kris asks her, no recognition on his face.

"The one who tried to walk away," she rolls her eyes.

"Really?" Kris gasps. "It's been weeks since you first saw him. I was beginning to think he was too embarrassed to summon you back."

"Right?" Skylar laughs. "He needed help. So, in exchange for helping him I asked him to look into the origin of demons."

Kris raises an eyebrow. "Really? Did the guy finally pick a wish?"

"Not exactly," Skylar shakes her head. "It's more like I'm giving him magic lessons in exchange for information."

Kris breaks out into such a hysterical fit of laughter that he flops backwards on the couch and holds his stomach. "A demon! Teaching a warlock!" He pants between guffaws. "That's hilarious!"

Skylar reaches out and smacks Kris on the thigh. "Hey! This guy is a complete novice. I know stuff!" She pouts and kicks out at Kris, threatening to shove him off the couch.

After Kris finally calms down enough to collect himself and sit up, he playfully pouts at Skylar. "You're right, Sky. I'm sorry."

Skylar tries to act outraged a little longer. She crosses her arms and turns her head, chin up in the air, but her friend is just too endearing. "I forgive you," she says and throws her arms open wide.

Instantly, Kris is ducking in to give her a hug. He then sits back and looks at her. "So, what great mysteries of the universe did you teach this baby warlock?"

Skylar waves her hand at the implication. "Nothing major. Just a simple glamour. I had him practice changing his hair color. Kid stuff." As she speaks, she plucks her phone up from the cushion where she dropped it. She opens it to the picture of Ryan with red hair and passes it over to Kris for him to see, like she is a proud teacher showing off a student's progress.

Kris takes the phone to look at the picture, a wide grin on his face as he looks down. Slowly, the grin shrinks. "Skylar, is this Ryan?"

"Yeah," Skylar replies, suspicious. "All he did was turn his hair red. Why?"

"This is the warlock who is friends with my Bunny," Kris says, his voice low and serious. "The one I told you about."

Skylar scoffs. "Yeah, right. Seriously, look." She leans forward to swipe her finger across the screen and show Kris the goofy picture of Ryan with his normal hair. "It can't be the same guy."

"No, really! It is," Kris insists. "He has the same hair and blue eyes. He was wearing jeans and a baggy hoodie. Bad attitude."

"What the hell," Skylar gasps, taking her phone back to look at the picture. Confused-blonde-Ryan is staring up at her. She looks to Kris. "What are the odds that we got summoned by two warlocks who are friends with one another like that?"

Kris shrugs. "I've no idea, but I haven't heard from Bunny since that night. I was hoping he'd summon me so I could ask *him* to do plan Warlock Spy."

Skylar frowns, swiping back to the picture of Ryan with the red hair. She liked this one better only for the facial expression. "Weird," she mutters.

"Well, if they are warlocks who summon together, maybe he'll ask Bunny for help."

"Maybe," Kris says, but he's pouting. "The atmosphere was not good when I got sent away. And I don't know what has happened since then."

Skylar puts her phone down on the coffee table and grabs her friend's hands. "I'm sorry, Kris. If I get summoned by Ryan before you hear from Bunny, I'll ask. Okay?"

Kris squeezes Skylar's hands. "But when will that be? It's been over a month between summonings for you and him."

"I don't know," she has to admit. "But I think it will happen again. I have information he wants, and he's supposed to be getting the information we asked for. There's a reason to summon me back now."

"I guess," Kris frowns. "I just miss him, Sky."

Skylar feels her heart sink for her friend. As much as she has teased him that summons are not dates, she knows Kris has formed a bond with the other warlock that isn't the usual warlock-demon pact. "I know, Kris. There's something adorable about these clueless warlocks." Without waiting for permission she slides across the couch and wraps her arms around him. Kris's arms circle Skylar's waist to hold her close, clasping below the junction of her wings. They sit for a long while, just holding one another.

"Thanks," Kris finally says, easing his hold on her so they can both sit back.

"Well, I have something new I need to find out that may be able to help both of us," Skylar adds, cautiously optimistic.

"And what's that?" A small smile returns to Kris's lips.

"Ryan wanted to know if there was a way he could contact me from the mortal realm without summoning me. If we can figure that out, maybe you can connect with Bunny the same way?"

Kris's smile grew ten-fold. "Do you think it's possible?"

"Maybe," Skylar smiles back being swept up in the excitement. "But you know who we're going to need to visit to find out."

Kris lets out a very put upon sigh. "You best make the call," he suggests.

So Skylar picks up her phone once more to send another message.

Sky

Hello, Warren. Do you think you have time for another brain-
storming session with me and Kris?

11

New Tricks

RYAN COLLAPSES INTO BED after summoning Skylar and falls right asleep. He sleeps through the sunrise and (thanks to how dark his apartment always is) late into the afternoon. He probably could keep on sleeping if he isn't roused by the sound of pounding at his front door.

"What the fuck?" he mumbles, sitting up in bed to rub his eyes. Ryan's mouth tastes terrible and his mind is still fuzzy. The pounding continues as he tries to untangle himself from the bed sheets. His stomach gives a loud growl as he finally stumbles out of bed.

In an effort to keep his door from being caved in by the incessant pounding, Ryan slips on a pair of sweatpants over his boxers and staggers to the living room. He throws open the door to find a frazzled Justin on the other side.

"Oh, thank god," Justin cries. "I was worried you'd choked on your own vomit in your sleep and died."

Ryan frowns at him. "That's a bit over-dramatic, wouldn't you say?" He then turns on his heel and shuffles back towards his bedroom. "I just woke up. Need a bio break."

Justin follows him as far as the living room, shutting the door behind himself. "Are you sure you're okay? You look like death warmed over. It's four in the afternoon and you're just waking up?"

"I had the wildest dreams last night," Ryan calls from the bathroom with a toothbrush in his mouth. "I didn't think I drank *that* much!"

He uses the toilet to relieve his bladder, brushes his teeth, and slowly comes back to the land of the waking. When he finishes washing both his teeth and his hands, he re-emerges into the living room.

Justin has collapsed onto his couch. "You look better already," he comments. "I tried to call you this morning to check on you, but you didn't answer.

Then Ethan said you never came into the bookstore today, so I kept trying to ring you."

Ryan frowns and picks his bag up off the floor from where it was abandoned the night before. He pulls out the phone which, is about as useful as a brick. "I forgot to charge it last night," he admits.

He quickly takes the phone back to his bedroom to put it on the charger beside his bed. While he's there, he changes into a fresh set of clothes since he has company and runs a comb through his hair. "Have you eaten yet?" he calls out to Justin. "I'm starving."

"Let me see what you've got in the kitchen," Justin replies. Ryan hears him get up and move through the apartment.

"Don't bother," Ryan sighs loudly. "I need to do some shopping. I was thinking we should just go out and eat. Maybe Ethan is free, too?"

"Um, Ryan?" Justin's voice calls from the other room.

Ryan comes out of the bedroom feeling a little more like a human being now that he's freshened up a bit. "Did you not hear me?" he asks as he enters the living room.

Justin's back is to him where he's staring into the kitchen. "What happened in here?" he asks.

"Did the fridge die again?" Ryan groans. "I swear to whoever is listening, if I have to mop melted ice up off the floor again -"

"No," Justin shakes his head.

Ryan finally comes up behind Justin and has to bodily shove him out of the way so he can see into his own kitchen. The small table that's usually in the center of the room is blocking their way. And there, on the floor scrawled in messy chalk, is his summoning circle.

"Shit," Ryan gasps. "Fuck, no!"

He moves into the kitchen stepping over the circle to look around. The crumpled piece of paper with the re-worked summoning chant is still on the floor. The tome he copied the circle from sits open on the kitchen table next to a notepad and pen.

In a panic, Ryan drops to the floor and starts rubbing at the chalk lines with a dish towel. All he manages to do is blur the line, but it looks like it'll come up if he properly washes his floor. He really isn't that worried about getting his security deposit back. The place is a sty and his landlord is more like a slumlord. His issue is just that everywhere is evidence that the events of last night are not some strange fever dream.

Justin comes in and grabs Ryan by the shoulders, pulling him up off the floor. "Ryan, seriously. Calm down. Take a deep breath." He forces Ryan to look at him.

With Justin's guidance, Ryan takes a few deep breaths, and his heart rate begins to slow down. He didn't even realize it was racing, or that Justin had been calling his name.

"What happened?" Justin asks once Ryan seems more collected. "Are you okay?"

"I didn't think it was real," Ryan explains, gesturing to the floor. "I thought it was a weird, alcohol-induced dream."

"What wasn't real?" Justin's voice is soothing, but firm.

Ryan's eyes slide to the floor again. His heart starts to pound and he worries that standing in the circle now could bring on another fit of magic sweats like last night.

Justin must sense his distress rising again. "No, don't look at that. Look at me. We can clean the circle up later. Come on."

He forces Ryan to look at him again, then slowly leads him out of the kitchen. Justin guides him to the couch where he forces Ryan to sit. The springs creak under him as he eases down onto the worn-out cushion. Justin kneels on the floor in front of him. His hands gently stroke up and down Ryan's arms in a soothing motion.

"Now, from the beginning," Justin says very calmly. "Can you tell me what happened last night?"

Ryan swallows, despite his mouth being dry, and nods. "I think there's something wrong with me," he says softly. Justin doesn't urge him to go on. He just nods and waits for Ryan to continue at his own pace. "I woke up at some point last night and I had that feeling again. You know that one I told the demon about at your place? The way it feels when I'm using magic?" Ryan waits for Justin to nod before he continues. "It was like that, but ten times worse. It felt like I was going to explode if I didn't do something. So I did the only thing I know how to do: I summoned a demon."

"Kris?" Justin asks gently and Ryan shakes his head. "You mean the one from the first time you did it?"

Ryan nods. "We made a deal."

Justin sits back on his heels, his hands resting on Ryan's knees. "What kind of deal?"

"She said she would help me control my magic if I could find something for her here. In the mortal realm," Ryan explains, the memory becoming clearer as he recalls it.

"Wow." Justin lets out a low whistle. "That's really heavy. But she helped you?"

"Yeah," Ryan nods. He looks Justin in the eye, finally feeling more like himself again. "I think we need to call Ethan. I can't do this by myself."

Justin pats his knee even as he reaches for his phone. "Of course, Ryan. You're not alone. Okay?"

Together they call Ethan and invite him over. Ryan warns the man that he should bring his books with him. While they wait for their scholar to get someone to cover the shop, Justin helps Ryan mop up the summoning circle from his kitchen floor and rearrange the furniture once more.

They then bring both Ryan's notebook and the tome back into the living room. Justin even calls for some Chinese delivery since Ryan is still absolutely ravenous. Meanwhile, Ryan puts the coffee on. He has a feeling tonight is going to be a long night.

When Ethan and dinner finally arrive, the three of them sit down in the living room to go over the series of events one more time. Ryan's place definitely isn't as spacious as Justin's apartment, but Ashe is home and they can't risk him overhearing their conversation. Over take out boxes of noodles and stir-fried vegetables, Ryan tells the story one more time to an extremely intrigued Ethan.

"Wow," Ethan says, garlic noodle sauce smeared across his bottom lip. "That's intense. But you're doing okay now?"

Ryan nods, putting his empty bowl aside and leaning back on the couch. He was so hungry, but after the meal he feels comfortably full. "Yeah. The magic the demon showed me really helped dispel the built-up energy."

"What did you learn?" Ethan leans forward in interest.

"Nothing big," Ryan insists, but he can't help the thrill of knowing something the other two do not.

"C'mon," Justin insists. "You have to show us."

A slight smile tugs at the corner of Ryan's lips as he tries to wave away their pleas before giving in. He sits back up and closes his eyes. Suddenly he's not so sure he can do it since he doesn't feel the static of magic pulsing along his skin. He tries to push away the uncertainty and instead focuses on the glamour he wants to create.

Slowly Ryan reaches up like he'd done the previous night, focusing on changing the perception of his hair. There is a slight tingle of power across the palms of his hands as he slides them over his hair and imagines turning the blonde strands a vibrant blue reminiscent of a certain angelic-looking demon. When he's done, he slowly peeks through one eye to gauge Ethan's and Justin's reactions.

They both sit with their mouths slightly ajar. Ryan confidently lets his hands drop back to his lap as he grins at his friends. "Did it work?" he asks, already knowing the answer.

"Your hair is blue," Ethan exclaims.

"Wow," Justin murmurs with wide eyes. "Imagine never having to bleach your hair to get a dye job again."

Ryan huffs. He's only dyed his hair once, just out of high school to impress a girl. He wasn't fond of it, but this new trick does hold a lot of possibilities. "It's just a glamour," he explains. "My hair isn't actually blue. The demon says that I just change people's perception of it."

"Still, that's pretty amazing," Ethan confirms. "And you did it without any incantation or ritual components."

"I think I did something else without that stuff either," Ryan admits. "The tome had been locked up when I woke up last night, but I was in too much pain to find the key. So, I think I forced the lock open with magic."

Justin bounces in his seat and beams at him with pride. "That's great! Kris was right: you're super powerful."

Ryan frowns and looks down at his hands. "Yeah, so powerful I nearly got consumed by my own lack of control."

"That's okay," Ethan says, and Ryan feels a warm hand on his shoulder. "We're here to help you, too. I've got my magic primers. Maybe we can find something in those that you can do if you ever need to channel magic like that again."

"Actually," Ryan peers up at the other two through his blue bangs. "I kind of need your help with something else."

"What is it?" Justin asks, always eager to help.

Ryan twists his hands together. "In exchange for their help training me with magic, the demon wants me to find some information here in our world."

"Ooh," Ethan says, clearly excited by the prospect. "What kind of information?"

"That's the thing," Ryan sinks back into the couch. "She wants me to find the origin of demons, but we already tried to ask Kris that. How are we supposed to figure that out on our own?"

Ethan hums and settles back onto the couch beside him.

Justin leans his elbows on the coffee table from his seat on the floor and also looks lost in thought. "If the demon needs us to find the information, it *must* be here. It's the one place they can't look for it, right?"

Ethan nods. "Yeah, but why would that information be here and not in the demon realm?

"Well, the demon said that warlocks created both the demon realm and the first demon. So, maybe there's a spell or something on this side?" Ryan feels like he's grasping at straws.

"Maybe, but the most advanced book we have is the one you found," Ethan argues. "If the answer is in there, we'd have found it by now."

The three sit in silence, stumped as the leftover noodles and soup across the coffee table go cold.

"Wait!" Ryan cries suddenly, causing the other two to startle. "I think I wrote this down."

Ryan shuffles through the pile of books to find his notebook from the night before. He flips to the back of the book where his notes from last night are scribbled. "The demon told me that the last demon who wasn't born was probably made within the last hundred years."

"Well," Ethan says slowly, "we know of at least one active warlock group in the last century."

"Oh!" Justin reaches for the pile of books that Ethan brought over. "It's that book Ryan was looking at the first time, right?" He pulls out the booklet and reads the cover. "The Order of the Knowing Well. Do you think it's in this?" He begins flipping through the flimsy pages.

"No," Ethan disagrees. "That's just a guide for membership. And we know that Ryan's relative was one of the co-authors of his book with other members of the Order."

Ryan frowns. "Do you think Thomas Andrew Smith has other books about magic? This was the only one we found in my mother's attic."

Ethan shakes his head and pulls out his phone. "I don't know, but we know of a more modern site for the Order." He taps on the screen and hands it over to Ryan.

"What am I looking at?" he asks Ethan.

The web page is dark and looks like it was made back when the internet first became a thing. There is a string of mysterious symbols and then just a field to enter your own contact information.

"Remember when I said some guy told me I was a dud?" Ethan asks. "This is the website where I found him. And I think he's the current gatekeeper of the Order."

"And how are *we* supposed to get into the Order?" Justin slumps in defeat.

Ethan doesn't look pessimistic at all as he turns his eyes to Ryan. "Well, you're a descendant of a member. And you have the tome as further proof. I bet you can get a meeting with the Order."

Ryan blinks as he slowly connects the dots Ethan has just laid out for him. "And maybe *they* have the information we're looking for."

Justin's energy returns as he jumps up from the floor. "It's worth a shot," he declares and moves around to the couch to force himself between Ryan and Ethan. "You should send them your email."

Trusting Ethan that this is a legit website, Ryan goes ahead and puts in his junk email. "Okay," he says as he presses send and hands Ethan his phone again. "Now what?"

Before anyone can offer a suggestion, Ryan's phone dings in the bedroom.

"Wow," Justin says. "That was fast!"

Ryan extracts himself from the couch and goes to get his phone. He pulls up his email as he comes back into the living room. Settling back on the couch, he reads it over.

The email is a simple form letter thanking him for his interest without actually naming what his interest is in. Then there's a link to a calendar site so he can pick the best time to meet with a "recruiter."

"I swear, Ethan, if you're getting me into a cult, I expect you to be getting me back out," Ryan warns as he goes ahead and picks a time.

There aren't actually a lot of slots to choose from, and they seem a little random. The soonest one he can pick is Friday morning. He takes it, just wanting to get the whole ordeal over with. Within moments of selecting his time slot, Ryan gets a confirmation email. The meeting is set at a coffee shop in town.

"That's the same place I went," Ethan confirms. "I think this is part of their screening process. Obviously, I didn't get past this part."

Ryan gives the man a sympathetic look. It's obvious that if Ethan could, he'd be all over this magic stuff. "Don't let that get to you," he says. "Justin and I wouldn't have been able to do any of this without you. Who cares if you can't do magic yourself?"

Ethan smiles. It isn't the brightest of smiles. "Thanks." He takes a deep breath. "So, are you going to go alone?"

"I wasn't counting on it," Ryan says and watches the hopeful look in Ethan's eyes grow. "I would feel more comfortable if you were both there. Ethan for his knowledge, and Justin for his muscles. Just in case the guy tries to mug me."

"I don't think that'll be the case," Ethan laughs. "I'll see if I can get Nadia to cover opening the bookstore. You should probably bring the book. I don't know how much they can sense your magic ability like the demons can, but the book itself is pretty solid evidence. If that doesn't get you in the door, I don't know what will."

Ryan pouts. "I don't know," he complains. "That thing is pretty heavy, but maybe you're right. Especially if Justin is coming and can give us a ride?" He playfully bats his eyelashes at the youngest.

"I can definitely move some stuff around," Justin agrees with an excited thumbs up.

Friday is a bright, sunny day and it's obvious that summer is just around the corner, making a gathering of warlocks even more inappropriate in Ryan's mind. He wears a pair of skinny jeans with his baggy black hoodie despite the weather warming up. He also makes sure his hair is back to it's natural color, making it far less noticeable than the shocking blue he's had most of the week. He leaves his work computer at home, loading up only the heavy tome in his messenger bag that he slings across his body.

Justin picks up both Ethan and Ryan at the bookstore before taking them downtown. They get to the café at a quarter to eleven, fifteen minutes before Ryan's scheduled meeting. After they each collect orders, they gather at a booth where they can watch the door. This late in the morning, there aren't a lot of people around. They've managed to hit just after the morning rush, but before the lunchtime crowd, it seems.

Finally, a guy in black slacks and a white button-up neatly tucked in under a black blazer comes through the door and Ethan swivels in his seat to tap at the table top between them. "That's the guy," he whispers. "The one I met with."

Ryan glances over at the man again. He looks more like an actor who has stepped out of a television drama than a warlock, in his opinion. The man's clothes look expensive, and his dark brown hair is styled back. "Are you sure?"

"I remember," Ethan nods solemnly. "It's not every day someone tells you that you'll never be able to do magic. Ever."

Justin reaches over and pats Ethan's hand where it rests on the table-top. "But you did," he insists. "You were as much a part of that summoning circle as any of us."

Ryan continues to watch the man in question. He goes up to order his coffee, then sits at a table by the window. "Now what?" Ryan hisses.

"You should go over there," Ethan encourages him.

"By myself?" Ryan feels his heart sink now that it's actually happening. There's a reason he chose a line of work that involves no direct human interaction.

Justin nudges him with an elbow. "You won't be alone. We'll be right here."

Ryan frowns but slides out of the booth anyway. He grabs his iced americano and shifts the bag over his shoulder before crossing the café. Awkwardly he steps up beside the table and waits for the other man to acknowledge him.

When the slick-looking man finally does look up, he gives Ryan a bit of the side-eye. Maybe Ryan isn't what the guy was expecting. "You're rs spamkiller at mail dot com?" he asks.

"Yeah," Ryan nods. "Ryan, for short."

"Hello, Ryan," he says, already looking disinterested, but he gestures to the seat across from him. As Ryan settles into the chair and puts his drink on the table, the man introduces himself. "I'm Alexander Kim. How did you happen to come across our web portal?"

Ryan blinks at him. "Um, my friend had come across your organization before. He suggested you to me."

Alexander casts a glance towards the table Ethan and Justin are sitting at. They aren't very subtle about the fact that they are watching them from across the café. "Is he one of them?" the man asks.

"Yeah." Ryan can't think of a reason to deny it.

"Hmm," Alexander hums and looks back to Ryan. "So, what's your interest in our organization?"

Ryan has spent the last couple of days thinking about how to answer this kind of question. "I came across an old book at my mother's house recently. I didn't realize what I'd found right away, but I believe it's a book that my great-great-grandfather had. The inside cover attributed it to The Order of the Knowing Well."

Alexander's eyes widen briefly before the stoic man could school himself, but it was just enough for Ryan to catch that he is on the right track.

Ryan forges ahead. "Everything in the book is way beyond me, but my friend helped me understand what it was that I had gotten my hands on. I'd really like to learn more."

"Do you have the book with you?" Alexander takes a sip from his coffee mug, but Ryan catches the way his eyes never leave him.

"I do," Ryan nods.

"May I see it?" Alexander leans back in his seat to cross his legs under the table, but his eyes drift down to the bag in Ryan's lap.

Ryan holds onto the strap across his chest tightly as if an at any moment Alexander may try to snatch it away from him. "Only if you understand that *if* this book is in fact legitimate, it is mine and will not be leaving my possession."

Alexander bites his bottom lip for a moment before he nods. "Understood. This is just to confirm your statement."

Ryan reaches into his bag and clumsily pulls out the book. "It's kind of hefty," he mentions as he does his best not to drop it on the table. Even with his best effort, their cups rattle as the book settles on the surface.

Alexander pushes his coffee mug aside as he reaches forward and slides the book closer to himself. Ryan keeps his hands on the table surface, ready to snatch it back if he feels any doubt. Slowly, Alexander opens the cover of the book and looks over the title page. He gently turns the page to the list of contributors where it plainly says *The Order of the Knowing Well.*

"May I take a picture of this page for proof?" he asks, his eyes not leaving the printed words.

"Um, sure?" Ryan can't think of a good reason to deny him.

A moment later, Alexander has his phone in his hand and is snapping a picture. Ryan can't help but notice it's one of those fancy models with the folding screen that opens up to be almost as big as a small tablet. The man then starts tapping away like he's sending a message.

While he's busy, Ryan slowly reaches out and slides the book back to his side of the table. They sit in silence for a few minutes as Alexander carries on a back-and-forth text exchange. Ryan casts a nervous glance back towards his friends, reassured that they are still nearby.

Without looking up at him again, Alexander asks: "What did you say your surname was?"

"I didn't," Ryan replies. "It's Smith. Ryan Smith."

Some quiet tapping later and then the phone in Alexander's hand begins to buzz. His eyes open wide as he closes the phone over and brings it to his ear. "Yes?" His gaze shoots across to Ryan. "It's for you." He holds the phone, which is probably more expensive than Ryan's second-hand laptop, out to him.

"Me?" Ryan blinks. Hesitantly, he takes the phone and brings it to his ear, not close enough to touch his face out of fear of smudging the damn thing. "Hello?"

A woman's voice comes across the line. "Yes, good morning. To whom am I speaking?"

"Ryan Smith," he repeats himself, feeling kind of silly. "Who might this be?"

The woman gives a warm chuckle. "Yes, of course. I'm sorry. This is Dahlia Jones. Alexander is my direct report. May I ask you one more question?"

Ryan glances to Alexander who seems interested in him for the first time since he sat down. "Sure."

The woman's tone of voice stays friendly, but it feels kind of forced. "Who is the relative you got the book from?"

Ryan feels his heart rate pick up. "I think it was my great-great-grandfather's," he tries to answer without saying too much.

"And what was his name, Ryan?" the woman urges.

He hadn't wanted to show all his cards right away, but if this is the only way to get access to potential answers, Ryan doesn't see another way around it. "Thomas Andrew Smith," he says. Even as he speaks, he sees Alexander's eyes drop to the book.

"That's amazing!" Dahlia's delighted laugh comes across the line once more. "We haven't had a Smith descendant in the fold for about half a century. I'd be very interested in meeting you, Ryan Smith."

Ryan shoots a glance across the café towards his friends. "Can I bring my friends with me? One of them can do magic and the other one is a scholar."

"This is a very exclusive offer," Dahlia says. "The Order of the Knowing Well is one of the oldest orders still in operation. We don't just invite anyone into the fold."

Ryan nods before he realizes she can't see that. "I see," he says. He reaches out with his spare hand and begins to pull the tome into his lap. "I guess I'll just have to take my ancestor's book elsewhere."

"However," Dahlia adds sharply. "It's just a meeting to get to know one another. Consider it like an entrance interview. We'd be happy to meet potential new members."

"That's great," Ryan says, still holding the book in his lap.

"I'll have Alexander contact you with a date and location. I look forward to meeting you, Ryan." Dahlia's voice is back to all sugar.

Feeling like he managed to keep the upper hand, Ryan smiles. "Likewise, Dahlia." The line goes silent and Ryan hands the phone back to Alexander.

The man lifts the phone to his ear only to realize that the woman is no longer there. Instead, he clears his throat and tucks the phone back into the inside pocket of his blazer. "That seems to be a promising conversation," he says.

Ryan nods. "It seems like I'll be hearing from you again in the future, Mr. Kim."

"Does it?" Alexander raises an eyebrow. "Very well. Have a good afternoon, Mr. Smith." He grabs his coffee and takes one last drink from the mug. Then he stands and leaves, depositing the mug at the pick-up counter on his way out.

Right away, Ethan and Justin rush over to where Ryan is now sitting alone. He takes a moment to tuck the book back into the bag as the duo sit across from him.

"What happened?" Ethan asks. He looks anxious, where as Justin seems to be bouncing in his seat with excitement.

Ryan smiles smugly at the other two as he picks up his americano to take a sip. "I just scored us a meeting with The Order of the Knowing Well."

12

Making Connections

"I DON'T WANT TO talk to him again," Kris whines on Saturday morning as they take the elevator back up to Warren's apartment.

Skylar gives her friend a curious glance. "Why not? You did such a good job last time."

"That was last time," Kris pouts. "I can't guarantee that'll happen again."

"Fair," Skylar concedes. "But this time we aren't trying to extract information he's hiding from us like before. Maybe it'll go much smoother today?"

"Maybe." Kris stands up and straightens the lapels of the vest he's wearing.

Skylar watches their reflection in the mirrored elevator doors. Once again, they are dressed in what she now thinks of as their "visit Warren" attire. Kris is wearing maroon slacks with a black button-up under a matching maroon vest. His hair is slicked back, and his horns are freshly shined. Skylar is dressed in cream this time: cream slacks with an off-white blouse that has a loose bow around the neck. The neutral colors really set off her dark features and wings.

Their reflections disappear as the elevator doors slide open and they step onto Warren's floor. Side by side, they approach Warren's door. After one final thumbs up of encouragement, Skylar knocks.

"You're early," comes Warren's voice from the other side along with the sound of rushed footsteps.

They're not early. In fact, they are right on time.

The door is flung open to find an impeccably dressed Warren in black slacks with a white dress shirt undone at the collar. He is shucking off the burgundy robe, tossing it to the side where it disappears from view before it can hit the floor. "I just got back, please come in."

Skylar nods to him before stepping inside. "Thank you for taking the time out of your schedule to see us again so soon."

Kris follows after. "We really hope we aren't interrupting your day."

"Not at all," Warren reassures them. "You two have been bringing me the most interesting quandaries lately. Why don't we take the meeting in the library?" He leads them past the living room which is not set up for visitors this time and to Skylar's familiar classroom: the library.

Warren brings them through the double doors. It's late morning, so the sun shines brightly over the city landscape through the large windows. Their host gestures to the table where Skylar took all her demon lessons. This gives her confidence a boost feeling like she's on home turf.

Skylar motions for Kris to sit in the chair next to her usual spot facing the windows. Warren moves around to his customary seat across from them. "Can I offer you any refreshments?"

"It's still early," Skylar remarks. "Water is fine for me."

"I do enjoy some orange juice in the morning," Kris says.

Warren gives a wave of his hand, and their requested beverages appear. A saucer and a teacup filled with dark liquid appears in front of himself. Sure, they could have conjured their own drinks, but these niceties of hospitality are still observed. Skylar and Kris thank him before taking sips from their glasses.

"So," Warren begins after his own sip of tea. "Have there been any developments with your little pact issue from last time?"

Kris nods. "Kind of? I think I've successfully settled my bond with the warlock. I haven't heard from him in weeks." He does a good job of keeping a straight face, but Skylar knows that Bunny's lack of contact makes the horned demon sad.

Warren takes another sip and shifts his gaze to Skylar. "And you?"

"My warlock is being a bit more difficult," she says, glad the conversation is naturally going where she is hoping it would. "It's actually one of the reasons we came to see you."

A smile slides across Warren's lips and he leans forward, those snake-like eyes focused on Skylar. It's been years since she's found it unnerving. There are far more creepy demons than Warren in the demon realm. "Oh? Do tell. Do you need a more nefarious way to rid yourself of the pact bond?"

Skylar's eyes widen at the suggestion, and she feels her heart skip a beat at the offer. She doesn't know what Warren is insinuating, but it doesn't sound friendly. "He's just so inexperienced, you know? But he's still asking questions that I have never even considered."

"I suppose the lack of training can do that. It leads you to think outside of the box when you don't know even know what shape the box is," Warren comments. "What questions do you have this time?"

Skylar glances towards Kris, who just gives her a nod of encouragement. She turns back to Warren. "I'd never considered it before, but is there a way to create a line of communication between realms? From mortal to demon without using a summoning circle?"

Warren laughs and sits back in his seat. "That's it?" He chuckles and shakes his head as he reaches forward to pick up the teacup and saucer. "That's something that was done ages ago."

"Really?" Kris asks, his own surprise mirroring Skylar's. "I've never heard of it before."

"Are you sure?" Warren asks, amused. It feels like he's playing with them, teasing the information over their heads. "I'm sure you have."

Skylar and Warren both shake their heads.

"No warlock has ever asked to communicate with me outside of a summoning before," Skylar says. "And I don't recall us ever talking about something like that."

"It's not a common practice anymore," Warren admits. "But the tools for doing so are well known."

"What do you mean?" Kris implores.

Warren gives a self-satisfied grin before sipping his tea again. "Have either of you ever used a spirit board before?"

Skylar feels her brow furrow. "No," she says slowly. "Isn't that a board game kids use to scare one another at sleepovers?"

"I did!" Kris smiles and shifts in his seat. "My siblings and I would take it out and pretend to talk to ghosts, but what does that have to do with anything?"

Warrens looks at them over the rim of his teacup as he takes another long drink. He then settles the cup and saucer back on the table and folds his hands in his lap. He is going into teacher mode, and Skylar feels herself leaning forward with anticipation.

"Warlocks created spirit boards," Warren explains. "Non-magic users just copied the design. It was a means with which to contact demons without having to summon them physically to the mortal realm. It was a common practice for warlocks who only wanted information. Or to converse with a well-known demon before summoning them over."

"That actually makes a lot of sense," Kris is nodding. "So, all spirit boards can do this?"

Warren laughs and shakes his head. "No! No, not at all. Only those imbued with warlock magic. Once a connection is made, though, that board can act as a communication device until disenchanted or destroyed."

"How does someone make that connection?" Skylar asks, honestly curious now.

"Due to the restrictions placed on demons, only a warlock can forge a connection," Warren explains. "From inside the demon realm, nothing we do can influence the mortal realm. The lesser-known bit of knowledge is that nothing we do in the mortal realm can influence the demon realm. So a warlock has to forge the connection."

"And how does a demon communicate with a warlock on this side?"

"A corresponding board appears on the demon's end here, of course. It's kind of tedious for extended communication, but it works for short interactions." Warren waves his hand as if this is obvious.

Skylar frowns. So, this is something Ryan is going to have to figure out. He may be powerful, but he is severely lacking in training.

"Are spirit boards the only devices that can be used to forge a connection?" Kris asks the question and Skylar glances at him in surprise.

Warren seems pleased by the query. "I suppose not," he says. "Do you have something in mind?"

"What about a phone?" Kris asks, and Skylar could have kissed him. Why didn't she think of that?

Warren nods thoughtfully. "Perhaps? The board was created before things like telephones existed. It's not something I have personal experience with."

"Do you think a human with a cellphone could create a connection to our version of cellphones?" Skylar pulls out her phone as an example. "These are simply magical recreations of mortal technology that we use in a similar fashion anyway."

Warren raises an eyebrow. "I suppose," he grants. "These are extremely specific questions. Are you trying to give a warlock your phone number?"

Skylar huffs and places her phone on the table as if trying to physically distance herself from it. "As if," she shakes her head. "I just found the entire thought exercise extremely fascinating."

"I'm sure," Warren says with a sly smile. Then with a flick of his wrist, Skylar's phone is sliding across the table and into Warren's hand. He picks it up to inspect it.

"Hey!" Skylar cries and jumps to her feet. Kris, however, erupts into a fit of giggles. Skylar shoots him a look of betrayal before marching around the table to get her phone back.

Meanwhile Warren is poking at the device, laughing to himself. "What is it, little Sky? Do you have something naughty on your phone?"

"Warren!" Skylar huffs as she comes around the table towards him. "I'm not a child anymore, c'mon."

As she comes up to Warren's side, she glimpses that the elder demon has in fact opened her camera roll. Warren stops laughing immediately as he looks at the picture of a confused Ryan with his sandy hair. Skylar takes the opportunity to try to reach out and snatch the phone away, but Warren is too quick. He darts out of the chair, turning his back on Skylar.

"Where did you get this?" he demands, all mirth gone from his voice.

Skylar frowns. "What do you mean? I got it from the same place all demons get their phones." Which is basically out of thin air.

Warren takes two long strides away from Skylar to the head of the long table before he turns to look at her. "Not the phone, Skylar. This picture," he demands, holding the phone up so that both Skylar and Kris can see the picture of Ryan.

"I took it," she replies, genuinely confused. "That's the warlock who's asking. He's so completely incompetent." Skylar tries to force a laugh to make the situation sound ridiculous.

Warren turns the screen back towards himself. "What's his name?" the demon asks as he glares at the picture.

Skylar moves around Warren's abandoned chair to try to get her phone back once more. "What does it matter?" She forces a chuckle. Kris, however, has stopped laughing. He sits, watching Skylar and Warren very carefully like one of them may attack the other at any moment.

Warren raises his eyes, stopping Skylar in her tracks with a death glare. "His name, Skylar."

Warren looks so intimidating that it shocks her into answering. "Ryan."

"What's his surname?" Warren hisses.

Skylar swallows her heart back down as it tries to escape through her throat. "I don't know."

A grimace crosses Warren's face. "I'd bet all of my scales he's a Smith." He tosses the phone onto the table as if it bit him. The phone slides past both Skylar and Kris to the opposite end. Then Warren's eyes train on Skylar. "I'd recommend you do your best to avoid this warlock."

"Why?" Skylar gasps.

"A Smith cannot be trusted," Warren all but declares.

"But this guy is completely clueless," Skylar balks. "He's practically harmless."

Warren shakes his head. "Then either the Smith line has completely fallen, or he is tricking you, Skylar. I'd bet everything I have on the latter."

"What happened?" Kris asks softly as if trying not to spook an angry animal.

All he did was successfully get Warren's attenuation off of Skylar as he looks at Kris like he'd forgotten he was there. "It is not a matter that is up for discussion. I'm afraid I'm going to have to ask you to leave."

"Warren -" Skylar tries to interject softly.

"Do not trust the warlock," Warren cuts her off. "Best leave that warlock alone."

There is no arguing with Warren once he's put his foot down. The man is stubborn and, in this moment, extremely frightening. "Yes, sir," Skylar says. She slowly makes her way to the other end of the table to retrieve her phone. "Thank you for your time."

Kris stands up and gave a short nod of his head. "Thank you, sir."

Warren's jaw clenches and un-clenches before he lets out a long slow breath. "I trust you can see yourselves out?"

They nod and leave the library. Kris and Skylar don't speak. Skylar doesn't even breathe until they are safely back in the elevator. She is still clutching her phone to her chest as she tries to puzzle out Warren's words. It's shocking to be thrown out *again.*

As if they had some sort of unspoken agreement, Kris and Skylar both teleport to Kris's place as soon as they're on the street. Skylar is just too shocked. How could Warren possibly know Ryan? What was with that warning about Smiths not being trustworthy? She's never seen Warren look so angry. Not even that time Skylar accidentally set the apartment on fire while practicing her magic.

Kris leads the way into his apartment and Skylar plops down onto the couch. Only then does she put her phone down on the table in front of her.

Kris sits next to her and makes two beers appear. "These seem appropriate for the mood," he says before he picks one up and takes a long swig.

"I think I agree," Skylar nods and grabs a can despite the early hour. She pops it open and lets the cold, bitter drink wash away the taste of fear from her mouth. "What the fuck was that?"

Kris shakes his head in disbelief. "I really don't know. Maybe Warren had a bad run-in with these Smith warlocks?"

Skylar cocks her head to the side. "Maybe?" She looks over at Kris. "But we don't even know if Ryan's surname is Smith."

"I guess we'll have to just wait and see," Kris says before taking a long drink. "What are you going to do?"

"I don't know," Skylar shrugs. "Unless Ryan summons me back, I don't have a way to contact him."

Kris puts down his beer. He scoots to the end of the couch and leans his back against the arm before holding his arms out to her. They rarely sit this way since Skylar's wings are so prohibitive, but in that moment, she wants nothing more than to be comforted. She puts her beer on the coffee table and lays down on her stomach between Kris's legs. Wrapping her arms around Kris's waist, she rests her head on her best friend's shoulder. A hand reaches up and starts carding through her hair while the other gently strokes a wing. Skylar sighs and feels herself relaxing. No one ever touches her wings. Even Kris rarely does so.

"Are you going to tell the warlock how to make the connection?" Kris's voice is gentle.

Skylar chews her bottom lip as she considers the question. "Should I?"

"It's up to you," Kris says. "I mean, he could always just summon you. Wouldn't another way be easier?

"Maybe," Skylar says slowly. "But what if Warren is right and the warlock can't be trusted?"

Kris takes a deep breath, his chest expanding beneath Skylar. "Want my honest opinion?"

Skylar just nods her head and waits for Kris to speak again.

"The one time I met him, he was kind of an asshole," Kris says bluntly, and Skylar huffs a laugh. That's kind of true for her, too. "But," Kris continues, "it feels more like he was doing it out of fear. He seems scared of his power."

Skylar frowns. She's noticed that, too. Especially the last time Ryan summoned her. If he is faking, it's an elaborate ruse.

"Maybe we're borrowing trouble," she finally says. "We don't even know if he's a Smith. Warren can still be wrong."

"Since when has Warren ever been wrong?" Kris chuckles. "He can be an insufferable prick because of it, but he knows what he's talking about."

With a heavy sigh, all Skylar can do is agree. "I guess our only choice now now is to hope it's not true."

Kris continues to stroke Skylar's wing for a while longer as they lay in silence. Eventually he switches hands so he can stroke the other wing. It feels like an incredibly intimate gesture to Skylar, but probably because so few people ever take the time to do so. In this case, it's extremely calming and Skylar feels herself beginning to drift off to sleep, despite it being just about lunch time.

"Do you want him to summon you back?" Kris's question is quiet and comes just as Skylar feels her consciousness beginning to slip away.

"Hmm?" She hums, trying to keep her eyes open. She squeezes Kris in a hug. "Ryan?"

"Yeah."

"I mean, I guess so. Hopefully he'll have answers about the origins of demons," she mumbles into Kris's shirt. They hadn't even bothered to change, she realizes.

Kris hums in response and places a soft kiss to the crown of Skylar's head. "Is that the only reason?"

Skylar blinks. "What other reason would there be?"

"The same reason you still have his picture on your phone?"

Skylar pushes herself up, despite how much she doesn't want Kris to stop petting her, so she can look the other demon in the face. Kris's eyebrows go up as he waits for a response. "There's no reason for that," Skylar denies. "I just haven't gotten around to erasing them."

Kris chuckles at her and reaches out to tuck a strand of hair behind her ear. "Okay, let's say that's the reason. There's not any other reason you'd want to keep your bond open with Ryan?"

Skylar frowns at him, but before she can come up with a rebuttal the familiar tug of a summons yanks at her belly. "What the fuck," she sighs, dropping her forehead to Kris's shoulder. "I'm getting summoned in the middle of the day."

"Time zones suck," Kris laughs and pats her on the back. "Come back here right after, okay?"

Skylar smiles. "Deal."

And just like that she let the warlock's magic pull her out of the demon realm. By the time she is making her arrival to the mortal realm she can sense that the magic is unfamiliar. She doesn't even bother to change her appearance as she conjures up the cloud of smoke with the smell of brimstone. Her shoes hit a soft carpet. She stands tall and waits for the smoke to clear.

If she'd been shocked when Ryan summoned her in his tiny kitchen, it is nothing compared to the sight before her. She is in a circle that is barely large enough to contain her and her wings in a room that feels overcrowded with four other warlocks. The only illumination comes from dozens of candles around the room, but a second glance reveals that they aren't even live flame candles. They are LED lights. Two sets of bunk beds line either wall, and the summoning circle is made out of masking tape.

Surrounding her are the "warlocks." She would be surprised if the youngest of them has even reached the age of majority. The one who apparently leads the circle stands before Skylar. He is tall and scrawny with an unfortunate case of acne. He has curly red hair and glasses so thick Skylar would hazard a guess that he is nearly legally blind. At least this collection of warlocks are wearing a set of stupid ceremonial robes like she's accustomed to. If they were in letterman jackets and sneakers, Skylar may very well have lost it.

"Warlocks, how may I serve you this . . . evening?" She tries to guess the time by glancing towards the window on the far wall. If it is night, it's only just past sunset. "Am I in a dorm room?" she blurts aloud.

"Shh, yes!" One of the four hisses at her. The hisser is a short girl. Pretty, but not in a way that young men are likely to appreciate until they're older. "Your smoke isn't going to set off the smoke alarm, is it?"

"It's an illusion," Skylar reassures her with a smile. She tries to turn on the charm, but all the girl does is roll her eyes at Skylar.

"Demon," the one who she'd first pinned as the leader addresses her. Skylar wishes she had a better grasp of accents. There's definitely some sort of European accent going on. "We seek your unholy blessing."

Internally Skylar cringes. For a bunch of kids who look very modern, they are taking this summoning in the direction of old school religion. Or maybe it's Skylar's fault. More than one warlock has commented that she looks like a fallen angel.

"And what blessings do you seek?" Skylar decides to just play along out of amusement. "As one of Satan's favored minions, my blessings can curry a lot of favor."

"Ahem," says the warlock standing behind her. When Skylar turns around, she finds a guy maybe a few inches taller than her with an unruly mop of shockingly blond (almost white) hair and sharp eyes. "There are four of us, so we'll require four blessings."

Skylar wants to laugh at the kid. "As my warlocks desire." Skylar would have bowed, but there's literally no room.

"I told you," the first one says drawing Skylar's attention once more. "Demon, I desire a blessing of comeliness."

Skylar arches an eyebrow. If all this kid wants is a glamour, this is going to be a quick trip. Maybe it will be worth her time having to "bless" all four of them. "As you wish," she nods.

Skylar raises a hand and snaps her fingers. The glamour, which is a really easy one, settles into place. The kid doesn't look so bad. If he just waits a few years, his acne will clear up, so that's what Skylar does. She basically pushes the kid through his rough patch of puberty. His acne disappears and he grows into his features. The glamour itself will fade away, probably before the guy finishes university, but sometimes a little bit of confidence can do wonders.

The group gasps at the results and Skylar smiles smugly. The warlock pulls out his phone and uses the front facing camera to check the results. He nods. "You've done well, Satan's spawn."

"Who's next?" Skylar asks, opening her hands out towards the group.

The girl wants to assure her scholarship status for the next three years. It kind of sucks that Skylar is basically guaranteeing that someone who may deserve it more doesn't get the scholarship, but it is a simple enough request to fill.

The guy at her back wants to ensure his place on the varsity golf team. Again, selfish but simple.

Skylar turns to the fourth warlock who hasn't spoken yet. He's a cute guy with smooth tawny skin, but he seems shy and a little too small for the robe he's wearing. "And what it is you desire?" Skylar all but purrs at him.

The warlock smiles bashfully and his pale green eyes glance away from Skylar's direct gaze. "You're so beautiful," the warlock mutters.

Skylar smiles warmly at him. "Thank you, Warlock. But what is it that you want?"

"Can I . . ." The warlock looks back at her, then drops his gaze lower over Skylar's body until he's staring openly at her. For someone who seems so shy, he is acting pretty bold.

Skylar leans forward, trying to catch his gaze once more. "Are you sure that's what you want?" she teases. "You'll either have to come into the circle with me or let me out."

And with that Skylar causes all the lights to flicker in the room. She uses the momentary darkness to shine a red light from below her feet up to cast stark shadows across herself. In the brief flash she creates the illusion of blood dripping from her lips, the whites of her eyes completely black, and her skin blotchy with a death-like pallor. The only thing she can't change is her wings. Some quirk of whatever it is that makes them demons prevents them from hiding their bestial attributes. When the lights flicker back on, she is back to looking like herself with a wicked grin on her lips.

The human gulps, his eyes wide with fear. "I'm good," he squeaks.

Skylar turns back to the head warlock of this motley coven. "If that is all, Warlock . . ."

"You're released back to the demon realm," the warlock says, and Skylar is sent hurtling back.

She reappears in Kris's living room. Skylar plops down on the couch and calls out into the apartment. "Honey, I'm home!"

Kris pops his head in from the kitchen. "You're back! How was it?"

Skylar shrugs and picks at her nails. "It was a bunch of college kids. I swear, where are these kids getting the idea that summoning demons is how to get a college degree?"

Kris disappears into the kitchen only to reappear a moment later with a plate of nachos. "Aw, poor Sky. Need a treat?"

Skylar pouts, batting her eyes at him playfully. "Yes, please."

Kris has changed out of his visiting clothes into a pair of sweatpants and a baggy designer shirt. Skylar uses the opportunity to change into a pair of gym shorts and a tank top.

"At least you came back really quickly," Kris points out, settling onto the couch next to her.

"I wouldn't have if this one kid had gotten his wish," Skylar grumbles. She reaches over to pick out a large chip covered in melted cheese, sour cream, and a healthy dose of hot sauce. The salty, cheesy spice is perfect!

Kris picks out his own chip. "What did he want?"

"Me!" Skylar laughs. "We were with three of his classmates in a tiny-ass dorm room in a standing-room only summoning circle, and he made a pass at me."

"You *are* pretty hot," Kris nods crunching into the chip.

Skylar smiles and pokes Kris in the cheek. "That means a lot coming from my hottest friend who is not interested in the female form."

"So, what did you do?" Kris reaches for another chip, trying to scoop up some of the taco meat in the middle of the mess.

"I scared the living daylights out of them, and he gave up his wish," Skylar says smugly.

"Oh!" Kris cries and shifts so he's sitting with his legs folded under himself on the couch. He turns to face Skylar. "This leads me back to what we were talking about before you left."

She blinks at him, honestly confused. "What was it again?" At least at this angle she can get good leverage to get her own meaty nacho chip.

"About why you don't want to break your bond with Ryan," Kris rolls his eyes. "So, my new question is: if Ryan summons you to his bedroom, would you scare him away like you did that kid?"

Skylar feels a heat rise to her cheeks. "That's ridiculous," she scoffs and fumbles as her chip breaks when she tries to scoop up the taco meat. She brings the broken chip to her lips anyway. "You're just projecting because if you had the chance, you'd jump Bunny in a second."

"Yeah," Kris sighs heavily. "I would."

"Kris!" Skylar gasps. She didn't think the demon would actually admit to that. "If you want to get laid, there's plenty of demons here to choose from."

"Not the point," Kris shrugs. "I just want to talk about what happened last time. And ask why I haven't heard from Bunny since."

"I'm sorry, Kris." Skylar pats Kris's knee. "I guess we're both waiting on those stupid warlocks to get their act together."

Kris laughs. "Tell you what: if you get summoned by Ryan, tell him I'm waiting for Bunny. And if I get summoned by Bunny, I'll tell him you're waiting on Ryan. Deal?"

"Sounds like a plan," Skylar nods, reaching for another chip.

13

The Order of the Knowing Well

SUNDAY AFTERNOON, RYAN GETS a ride out to a large, rolling estate across the bay with Justin and Ethan. He doesn't like how far he is having to roam from his familiar little part of the city. Yet here he is rolling up to an address he got from Alexander Kim.

Ethan had insisted they all dress appropriately for the occasion and treat it like a job interview. Apparently, for the bookstore owner, that means dressing like a high school chemistry teacher: corduroy pants, white button-up, navy vest, and a matching corduroy jacket. He's wearing his thickest rimmed glasses and looks every bit the part of a scholar. Justin, on the other hand, is in a primary blue suit with a white button-up, but no tie. Ryan didn't even consider wearing the suit his mother had pulled out of storage and goes with black slacks and a creme polo shirt. He wore it to his last in-person interview and that was easily five years ago.

"Why do I feel like we're about to go to the Mad Hatter's tea party?" Ryan grumbles.

Ethan is practically vibrating with excitement. "This will be fine," he tries to reassure Ryan.

"Don't leave me alone while we're in there," Ryan pleads before he knocks on the large double doors that look like they were stolen from the set of a horror movie about hauntings.

Alexander Kim opens the door, and at first look, Ryan is glad they all chose to dress up. Their point of contact is also in a suit that is black on black. "Ryan Smith," he greets.

Ryan nods. "Mr. Kim. This is Justin Perez and Ethan Forrest."

Alexander looks at both of them and gives a nod. "Nice to meet you," he says flatly. It doesn't sound very earnest.

"We've actually met before," Ethan says with a warm smile. Either he didn't notice the neutral welcome, or he doesn't care.

Alexander looks Ethan up and down before blinking at him slowly. "If you say so." Ethan frowns, but Alexander is already looking back to Ryan. "Please, come this way." He turns and leads the three of them into the large entryway.

The doors shut behind them without anyone closing them, which does nothing to calm Ryan's nerves. There is the distinct tingle of magic on the skin at the back of his neck, but not like when he is using it himself. It's more like he brushed too close to a live power line. A crystal chandelier hangs from the ceiling over an ornate wooden table in the center of the room. There are two curved staircases that go up to a second floor and doors that lead out of the entryway to the left, the right, and between the two staircases.

"The estate has been the main headquarters of the Order of the Knowing Well since 1927," Alexander explains as he leads them around the table and between the two staircases. "You'll forgive me for not giving you the full tour. Only members are permitted outside the entry and the ballroom."

"Of course," Justin says with wide eyes, his head swiveling to take in everything.

The walls are decorated with large portraits of people Ryan doesn't recognize and he doubts they are in any history books. Nothing screams "satanic cult," but Ryan isn't really sure what he was expecting when they arrived. The place looks more like a museum than the headquarters of a secret organization.

Alexander brings them to what must be the ballroom and Ryan continues to find himself caught off guard by how normal everything looks. It's a large space with a stage on the far side. A string quartet is playing chamber music as people mingle. Large round tables are spaced throughout the dance floor and a posh buffet is laid out along the right wall. Fruits, little cakes, sandwiches, cookies, and warmer trays with closed lids line the banquet tables. A punch bowl filled with a rich, red liquid sits at one end alongside as carafes for either coffee or tea.

A woman wearing a pale pink pencil skirt and matching blazer approaches them as they enter. "Is this the man of the hour?" she beams at Ryan. She looks like she's maybe only a few years older than him with perfectly coiffed hair and immaculate makeup.

Alexander gives a thin-lipped smile. "Indeed, it is," he says and motions to Ryan. "Ryan Smith, this is Dahlia Jones. Now, if you'll excuse me." Without waiting for acknowledgment, he turns and walks away, immediately joining another group of people nearby.

Ah, Ryan thinks to himself, *the woman from the phone*. "It's nice to meet you in person," he says as he holds his hand out.

She immediately takes his hand and gives it a firm shake. "Likewise, Mr. Smith."

"These are my friends," Ryan says, introducing Justin and Ethan once more.

"Charmed," she says as she briefly glances at the other two before her full attention swings back to Ryan. "Did you happen to bring your ancestor's book as well?"

Ryan isn't surprised she is asking for the book, but he frowns at the fact that she's making the request upon meeting him. "No, I'm afraid I didn't," he says, watching Dahlia. He didn't want to lose his only bargaining chip right away, so he left the book at home.

Her smile looks stilted for just a moment before she can recover. "That's fine," she says with a laugh. "I'm just curious about it. Today's just a 'getting to know one another' kind of day. Please feel free to mingle. Everyone here is a member of the Order and will be happy to answer any questions you have about membership."

"Thank you," Ethan smiles. He looks genuinely excited, even though Ryan doubts her words were intended for the bookshop owner.

"Are *you* available to answer questions?" Ryan asks Dahlia. She seems to be pulling the strings to get them invited, maybe she'll have the info they are looking for.

"Of course," she says. "But please, take a moment to get some refreshments. We have all afternoon."

Ryan, Ethan, and Justin thank her and make their way over to the buffet. There are actual plates and silverware as opposed to paper and plastic like Ryan expects at such a huge gathering. Even the napkins are cloth rather than paper. He quickly finds that the covered trays hold slices of ham, turkey, chicken, and prime rib. As tempting as all of this is, he chooses to stick with finger foods.

Justin apparently has no such qualms and is loading up his plate with piles of meat. "I skipped breakfast this morning," he says sheepishly as he piles on more than seems structurally sound.

Ethan seems to be striking a happy medium between a variety of food and not too much but looks torn as Justin takes his plate and wanders off to sit and eat. "I thought the plan was to stay together," he whispers to Ryan.

"He may need more watching after than I do at this moment," Ryan reassures Ethan. With a nod, the taller man trails off after Justin.

That leaves Ryan alone, which he isn't exactly thrilled about. However, the chilly welcome his friends received makes him think he'll have an easier time getting answers on his own. He isn't the most comfortable in social situations, but that doesn't seem to be a problem here. With his plate of sandwich wedges and fruit, Ryan finds himself swept into conversations with nearby people.

Everyone is extremely friendly when Ryan is on his own. There are men and women of all ages, from college students to elderly retirees. When he introduces himself as Ryan Smith, there are more than a few that seem to know the name.

"You're a descendant, then," says an older gentleman who introduces himself as Henry Archibald. "Have you grown up with magic training?"

"Not at all," Ryan admits. "I only recently discovered my connection to the Order by chance when I was going through a relative's belongings."

"Shame," Henry shakes his head. "At least you found your way to us now."

Ryan nods. "Thank you, sir." He isn't sure how he feels about the exchange, but he doesn't want to do anything to alienate his hosts. This is the only place he can think of that may have any information about the demon realm.

After Ryan finishes his plate and a cup of coffee, Dahlia finally makes her way back around to him. "Are you having a good time?" she asks. She approaches him from behind as he's leaving his cup on a tray for used flatware.

He turns to face her and smiles politely. "Everyone has been very friendly."

"I'm happy to hear that," she smiles. "Have you had a chance to make any judgments about the Order? Or have your questions answered?"

"I actually do have some questions." Ryan glances around and starts walking away from the buffet table, Dahlia following at his side. "It seems that some people here know my family name. Was my great-great-grandfather a person of importance?"

"Thomas Andrew Smith was a member of the Council of Elders during his tenure," Dahlia explains. "He was also lead a number of important projects the Order was running during the late 40's. His passing was a devastating event for the organization."

That certainly wasn't what Ryan was expecting. He blinks, amazed. "Really? Do you know what happened to him?"

Dahlia frowns. "I'm sorry, but I can't say. Certain details are privileged information for Order members only."

Ryan's heart races. It feels like he's so close to finding out something real. "Not even to me? He was my relative," he tries to insist.

"Only if you were to join the Order would I be allowed to share that information with you," Dahlia shakes her head. She sounds reticent, but Ryan's gut twists with uncertainty. "I understand that it's not kind, but we adhere to our rules very strictly. When you can do magic and change the fabric of reality, strict structure is a must. I hope you understand." She reaches out and places a gentle hand on his shoulder. It takes everything in Ryan's control to not shrug her off.

Ryan nods. "When you put it that way, it makes sense. I want to know more about the Order before I make a commitment, though. I want to know that this is the right place for me, you know?"

"Of course," Dahlia smiles warmly. "Is there something specific you'd like to know?"

This is it, this is the moment, Ryan realizes. He feels like he's trying to figure out the right combination of words to get to the right answers. Ryan bites his bottom lip as he considers how to phrase the question without giving away how much he already knows. "I've had Thomas Andrew Smith's book for a little over a month now. While I've had a chance to look through it, it's all way over my head. I want to make sure that your organization has the resources and ability to help me understand some of what I've read. When I first opened the book I thought it was fantasy."

Dahlia gives a chuckle. "We have the most extensive library of magic books in this hemisphere," she says if she is pitching a college program. "As a member, you'd have access to all those books as well as connections to more experienced warlocks."

Ryan hums and guides them to the edge of the room, away from the others. "Mind if I ask you some questions about what I read to make sure you can actually help me?"

"I can try," Dahlia replies. "I may not be able to answer fully, but maybe I can help clarify some things."

He stops in a corner and turns to face her, his eyes roaming over the room to make sure they have some semblance of privacy. "The most unbelievable chapter I read was one on how to summon demons. That can't be correct, can it? Demons and angels aren't real."

"Demons, huh?" One of Dahlia's eyebrows arches. "Demons are real, but they aren't like biblical devils. Demons are a very powerful and dangerous tool used by only the most experienced of warlocks."

"So, they are *tools*? Like a hammer?" Ryan does his best to sound completely clueless. It isn't too hard recalling his conversation with Skylar when she gave him a pitiful look.

"Yes, and no," Dahlia replies, gesticulating with her hands. "They are creatures made of magic that can be used to perform powerful spells beyond a single warlock's capabilities."

"So they boost a warlock's power?"

"In a way." Dahlia's responses seem guarded, but Ryan feels like he's chasing down his first solid lead.

"But where do they come from? How are they made?"

"It's best not to go into details," she says firmly. "At least, for now."

The feeling of being stonewalled makes Ryan's fists clench. "My friend, Ethan, has a glossary of magic terms. Can you confirm how accurate they are? For example, it says that demons come from a demon realm created by warlocks."

"That's fairly accurate." Dahlia looks surprised. "It's rare for actual magic tomes to fall into hands of non-practitioners like your friend."

Ryan wants to scoff given how easily he got his hands on his tome. Instead, he presses on. "But if warlocks created the demon realm, where did the demons originate from?"

Dahlia's lips press into a thin line as she studies him. His breath stops as he waits for her to decide if she is going to share or not. "I can't go into too many details, but being banished to the demon realm was used as a punishment for dangerous warlocks."

Ryan's jaw drops. "Is that why summoning demons is dangerous?"

"Partially," she nods.

"But—" Ryan begins, but she holds up her hand and shakes her head.

"If you want to learn more, you'll have to join." Dahlia crosses her arms as if that is the final word on the subject.

"That's fair," Ryan regretfully admits. "Thank you for taking time from your day, and for letting us join this gathering to answer my questions. My friends and I appreciate your hospitality."

"Our doors are open to you, Ryan. Please consider our offer." Dahlia smiles at him in an overly sweet fashion before she turns and makes her way towards another group of party attendees. Ryan watches her like she could turn into a snake at any moment before he sets out to find Justin and Ethan.

His friends are parked at one of the round tables having a lively discussion with some of the Order's members. Or, more accurately, Ethan is having a lively discussion as Justin continues to eat his way through the buffet.

"That's been the accepted theory," an older woman who sits next to Ethan is saying as Ryan approaches. "Those who have the ability to do magic inherit it from at least one parent, if not both."

"So, it's genetic?" Ethan asks.

"This chicken is amazing," Justin announces to no one in particular.

Ryan hovers for a moment before clearing his throat. "Hey, guys."

"Ryan! You're back," Ethan smiles. He then gestures to his conversation partners. "This is Dolores and Sunmi. They are both research heads here with the Order."

"It's nice to meet you," Ryan smiles at them. "I'm Ryan Smith."

"What do you think of the Order, Mr. Smith?" the woman referred to as Sunmi asks with a kind smile. She has straight black hair with streaks of white cropped short at the shoulders.

Ryan looks around as if trying to find something positive to comment on. "It's very impressive," he finally says. "Unfortunately, my friends and I have another engagement to get to."

Ethan's frown is immediate. "Really? Must we?"

Ryan tries to shoot him a serious look. "I think it's best if we don't overstay our welcome." Justin belches and at least has the sense to look embarrassed as he apologizes. "Or the limits of Justin's digestive system."

They say their goodbyes and are escorted out by a different Order member, who leads them back to the front door. Once they are outside, Ethan turns on Ryan. "I thought we were—"

Ryan shushes him and shakes his head. "Not until we're back in the car," he hisses.

Ethan's eyes go wide and he glances over his shoulder at the large, imposing building. Justin grumbles all the way back the long driveway about the items of food he hadn't tried yet. Even as he complains, he pulls a cookie from his pocket that Ryan hadn't even seen him snatch off the table.

Once they are safely inside Justin's car and driving away from the estate, Ryan feels like he can finally breathe again. "That place is intense," he sighs.

"Really, Ryan?" Ethan sounds surprised. "I thought it was amazing and the people were absolutely fascinating."

From the backseat of the car Ryan huffs. "Maybe to you two, but didn't you notice how Alexander and Dahlia didn't seem to pay the two of you *any* attention?"

Ethan shifts and faces forward in the passenger seat. "They did seem a little snooty."

Justin laughs. "They really only wanted to talk to Ryan and didn't give a shit if we were there or not."

Ryan feels reassured by Justin's assessment. "I picked up on that, too," he says. As the car rumbles along the two-lane road through the forested hills, Ryan crosses his arms and gazes out the window. "They have a lot of secrets and aren't willing to share much if you're not a member."

"Shit, was this a waste of time?" Justin asks.

"Maybe," Ryan sighs. "Dahlia did tell me one thing."

Ethan twists in his seat to glance back at him. "And was what that?"

Ryan glances at him. The man's endless curiosity about magic is kind of catching. "That being sent to the demon realm was a punishment of sorts for warlocks."

"Really?" Ethan frowns. "But what about Kris? Didn't he say he was born that way?"

"I don't like the sound of that." Justin shoots a worried glance through the rearview mirror. "Maybe we should talk to Kris again. Or you can summon your demon. There has to be something more to this that we don't know."

Ryan hums and nods. "Maybe, but one thing's for sure. I'm not getting any more information from the Order unless I join."

Ethan looks at him expectantly. "Well, are you going to?"

"I'm not inclined to join their club." Ryan rolls his eyes. "They creep me out."

"Any large crowd of people creeps you out," Justin unhelpfully points out.

"True." Ryan turns his head and goes back to looking out the window. He can't wait for the trees to give way to tall buildings once more so he can feel more at home.

Rather than go home, they all end up back at Justin's studio space. The long drive has given them plenty of time to talk and the best conclusion they can find is to bring Kris back over.

Ryan can't really explain it, but he is hesitant to summon Skylar in front of the others. He knows that sharing a demon's name may give them power over that demon. He hasn't asked, either. And he isn't as close to Skylar as Justin seems to be with Kris.

They shuffle into the studio, shedding suit jackets and loosening the buttons at their collars. "Water?" Justin offers them as he crouches down in front of a mini fridge that's plugged in under his desk.

Both Ryan and Ethan accept the offer and the three of them relax, stretching for a bit after the long drive. It isn't quite dark yet, so they have to wait to summon the demon. Justin tries to show Ethan how to play a video game as Ryan watches on in amusement.

Finally, once the sun begins to disappear past the horizon enough that they have to turn on the interior lights, Justin pulls out his summoning circle. Ryan just shakes his head as he watches the younger man unroll it and secure the corners to the floor with heavy books.

"I don't know why having a portable summoning circle seems wrong to me, but it's super convenient. Maybe if it were used for something other than summoning demons, it'd be something you could sell to warlocks," Ryan muses.

Justin laughs. "I bet I'd make bank off of warlocks who can't draw well. Like you." He pokes Ryan in the shoulder and then darts out of the way before Ryan can retaliate. Ethan just chuckles and shakes his head.

Once everything is ready, Justin hands out the pages with the chant written out for each of them. They take their former places around the circle—even Ethan—and begin the spell. The words begin to feel a little too familiar on Ryan's tongue and he isn't sure how he feels about that. As they chant, the feeling of power begins to tickle and shift over his skin. He does his best to focus that power into the circle rather than letting it build up around him.

Let it flow, he thinks to himself. *Don't be a pimple.*

It takes a little longer than it did before, but finally the demon appears within the circle. There is no fire this time. No smell of brimstone. One second the circle is empty, then it feels as if the air in the room shifts and the next there is a tall, horned demon. He stands facing Ryan once more with his chin up and his eyes cast down towards him. Kris is dressed in black leather pants and a matching jacket. Under the coat is a black shirt with the word FREEDOM printed in white block letters.

"Well, if it isn't Mr. Scaredy Warlock," Kris sneers.

Ryan frowns. He supposes he deserves that after the last time they'd seen one another. "I'm sorry," Ryan says. "I was freaking out and I didn't handle it very well."

Kris blinks in what looks like stunned surprise.

"Hey, Kris," Justin says gently from his spot along the circle.

Kris's gaze snaps to him, but it doesn't look much friendlier this time. "Oh, hello, stranger. I'm sorry, what's your name again?"

Justin pouts. "Don't be like that, Kris."

The demon turns to take a few steps towards Justin. "Like what? *You're* the one who hasn't summoned *me*. It's not like I can drop by on my own."

"I'm sorry," Justin says. "I'd promised Ry-ahem, *him* that I wouldn't summon again."

Kris's eyebrows shoot up. "Two apologies from two warlocks in one night? Even just one seems unprecedented." He looks over to Ethan. "Are you going to apologize, too?"

Ethan glances at Ryan, then at Justin with a mild look of panic on his face. "I'm sorry I'm friends with these two?"

Finally the demon smiles as he spins to look at all of them. "This night is off to a weird start." He steps to one side of the circle so he can face all of them at once. Then he gestures towards them, taking in their attire. "What's the occasion?"

"We were on a fact-finding mission," Ethan says eagerly.

Kris's eyes light up with delight and looks over at Ryan. "Oh, for Skylar?"

Ryan gasps. "Wait, how did you know that?"

"As it so happens," Kris smirks, "she's my best friend. Which reminds me: you're supposed to talk to her. She's been waiting to hear from you."

"I didn't have any information to share until tonight," Ryan says defensively.

The demon shrugs. "Fair enough, I suppose. So, why are you summoning me?"

"I hadn't told the others who my point of contact was," Ryan explains, nodding his head towards his friends.

"Oh!" Kris covers his mouth. "Did I say something I shouldn't have? My bad." He smirks like he isn't really all that sorry. "Like how I'm not supposed to know that you look adorable with bright red hair."

It's Ryan's turn to gasp. "I asked Skylar to delete those photos!"

"And yet she didn't." Kris crosses his arms and brings one hand up to tap at his chin. "I wonder why that is."

Ryan feels a blush rise to his cheeks. It is hotter than the magic flowing over his skin, but so far that's all the magic does: flow. He drops his eyes to find a point of the circle to focus on instead. "I can't fathom why."

"Well, you're friends with Ryan's demon, maybe we can bring them here, too?" Justin (oh so helpfully) shifts the conversation.

Kris looks back at Ryan. "I suppose you could," he nods. "It's not like I can bring her here myself."

"Can two summonings be done in one circle?" Ethan asks in awe.

"With enough power, yes. And I'm willing to bet that between Bunny and Warlock Ryan, you could probably pull it off."

The power crawls over Ryan's skin and he grimaces. "She told you my name?"

Kris leans towards Ryan, putting his hand up to his mouth like he's going to share a secret even as he stage whispers. "She's my best friend." He then gives an exaggerated wink and a lewd lick of his lips.

Another weird wave of emotions sweeps through Ryan that leaves him uncomfortably warm at the insinuation. He clears his throat. "Okay, then. Let's give it a try."

Ryan closes his eyes and focuses that nervous, anxious, frenetic energy into pushing the magic back into the circle. He begins the chant again, but instead of calling for Kris, he uses Skylar's name. The energy spikes through him but keeps moving, unlike that one morning he woke up in a sweaty panic. After he repeats the chant a few more times, Justin joins him. Ethan, however, just sits back and watches.

"You're not going to chant too?" Ryan hears Kris ask Ethan.

"Like you said before: I'm a dud. I'm mostly here for research purposes." Ethan sounds defeated, but accepting. If Ryan weren't currently trying to summon a second demon into the mortal realm, he'd go over and hug the gentle giant of a man.

"I'm sure that's not the only reason you're here," Kris says kindly.

"Thanks," comes a bashful reply.

"Aren't you the cutest," Kris coos.

"Hey," Justin interrupts the chant.

Ryan has to shut his eyes to block out the distraction, but he hears Kris laughing. He tries instead to think of the subject of his summoning. Skylar's large, black wings that look like they would be unbelievably soft to touch. The demon's dark hair that shines blue when it catches the light. Her sharp jawline and piercing brown eyes. How her pants hug her thighs and her ass and—

Something in Ryan's nether region starts to stir. He clenches his jaw and tries to focus on the flow of magic rather than the blood flowing south. Just as he thinks he's losing the battle between his brain and his hormones, he hears that silky smooth voice.

"Why, hello, Ryan."

14

Plan: Warlock Spy

SKYLAR IS AT HOME, blasting music and dancing around her apartment as the lazy Sunday afternoon comes to an end. Dance classes were something her parents supported for her as a kid and she missed them the longest after becoming a demon. It's a great way to work off some of the stress she's built up trying to puzzle out Warren's comments about Ryan. Is Ryan tricking Skylar into thinking he is some hapless warlock in need of a demon's help? If so, to what end? If only Warren wouldn't keep his cards so close to his chest.

The classical music swells over the sound system in her living room as Skylar throws herself through the air with her wings held up and back to prevent a loss of momentum. As she lands, she feels the tell-tale tug of a summoning in her belly. She stops, panting as the music continues to sweep over her. She stands up and wipes the light sheen of sweat from her forehead as she considers how to appear for her summoner.

The second tug comes on faster and stronger than normal. Skylar doesn't want to feel what a third tug will be like, so she lets the metaphysical cord rip her out of the demon realm. The familiar taste of Ryan's magic quickly puts her in a better mood as she materializes in the mortal realm. Skylar chooses to appear in her chunky black boots and ripped skinny jeans topped with a fitted black v-neck.

Ryan stands in front of her with a bookcase and game system behind him. Quickly Skylar concludes they aren't on the roof or in the warlock's kitchen. The warlock's eyes are squeezed shut and his skin is flushed. Skylar crosses her arms and smirks at the man. "Why, hello, Ryan."

The warlock's eyes pop open in surprise, but before Skylar can enjoy the moment, she has the wind knocked out of her. A pair of arms wrap around her from the side as a weight nearly knocks her over. "Sky!" cries a familiar, cheerful voice.

Skylar feels her own eyes go wide. "Kris?" she gasps as she turns her head to find her best friend looking like a whole snack and attached to her side.

"I knew it would work," Kirs squeals. "Look at us: two best buds in the mortal realm."

Skylar grips Kris's arm across her chest and hugs it. "What's happening?" She looks to Ryan who is watching them with a smile which surprises her almost as much. He should definitely smile more.

"Summoning party!" Another voice cries and draws Skylar's attention to the fact that there are two other people—one on her left and the other almost directly behind her.

Kris finally releases her. "Oh, right!" He grabs Skylar's hand and pulls her towards the edge of the summoning circle, closer to the warlock who just spoke. "Skylar, this is my Bunny," he announces with a giant grin.

"Oh?" Skylar smirks as she looks the warlock up and down. For some reason the three warlocks seem to be wearing dressed-down suits, and this warlock's muscle definition is clearly visible beneath the dress shirt. "Bunny is way too cute a name for this much of a man," she mutters to Kris. She watches as a blush rises to the warlock's cheeks.

"Bunny" sputters and before he can recover, Skylar shoots a look over to the final warlock. "And who is this tall drink of water?" She slips out of Kris's grasp and goes to stand before the professorial human with warm brown skin and a bright smile appearing on his full lips.

"Hi," the warlock replies with a small wave. "I'm Ethan."

Skylar smiles at the tall man. She is flustered at being confronted by so many people, so she goes to her comfort zone: flirty and overconfident. She finds it usually throws other people off, and that puts Skylar more at ease. "Pleasure to meet you, Warlock Ethan."

"Oh," the man shakes his head and brings his hands up to wave off her assumption. "I'm not a warlock. I'm a magical dud."

Skylar playfully pouts at him. "Well, I'm sure you're not a dud in *all* aspects." She lets her eyes drop to the man's belt buckle and back to his face. She then winks at him as his eyes go wide in surprise.

"Wicked, Sky," Kris laughs from where he still stands by his Bunny.

"*Ahem*," Ryan clears his throat rather forcefully.

Skylar spins on her heel to eye *her* warlock. Ryan stands with his arms crossed over his chest and a very sour pout on his face. "Oh, you're very handsome, too. Don't worry." Skylar gives him a wink.

"That's not why we brought you here," Ryan grumbles.

Kris claps. "Oh, right! Sky! They have information on our plan: Warlock Spy."

Skylar smiles and strides across the circle so she can turn and see everyone at once. Perhaps she's a little closer to Ryan than the others. "Oh, is that so?"

"Wait, you called it 'Warlock Spy'?" Bunny asks.

Kris shrugs. "It was for fun."

Skylar levels her gaze at Ryan. "So, you found the origin of demons?"

The corner of Ryan's mouth pulls tight as he practically glares at Skylar. "Not exactly."

"Then why are Kris and I both here?" Skylar challenges him.

Ryan throws his hands up in exasperation. "Look: I found out that warlocks used to send people to the demon realm as punishment. That's all I was able to get so far."

Skylar shoots a look at Kris, who meets her gaze right on. She hears Warren's voice in her head: *a prison is still a prison, no matter how nice it may seem.* Maybe he hadn't been exaggerating.

"That doesn't make any sense," Kris says slowly. "There aren't any mortals in the demon realm."

Skylar frowns at him. "Maybe because they aren't mortals anymore."

Kris shakes his head. "No, that can't be right." He looks at Ryan. "You said it was something warlocks 'used' to do. Maybe there aren't any mortals there *now*, because they haven't been sent there in a long time."

"Kris," Skylar sighs. She feels sorry for her friend trying to rationalize away the obvious answer: demons were once humans.

However, if that is true, what does that say about the demons that weren't born? Are they evil, wicked people? Warren likes to pretend he is, but that doesn't feel right. Skylar has known the demon for so long. Wouldn't she know if Warren were an evil man?

"Is that all you were able to find out?" Kris ignores Skylar and turns his eyes back to Bunny. "That can't be everything."

"They won't tell us anymore unless we—or more specifically, Ryan—join their organization," Bunny frowns at Kris. The warlock lifts his hand like he's going to reach out to the demon but stops himself.

Skylar looks back to Ryan, who is frowning at the floor. "Why don't you just join?" she asks him point blank.

His eyes come up to stare at her in shock. "I don't know if that's a good idea," the warlock says. "They don't seem to take kindly to people leaving their order."

"Oh," Skylar sighs. "I don't know how else to get the information then."

Ryan nods. "I don't know either, but we can think about it. I was hoping the information I did get could help you figure out more."

Kris laughs, the sudden mirth surprising Skylar. "We *do* know something else," he teases.

Skylar blinks at him, then recalls the conversation with Warren before he went all scary-demon. "Right!"

Ethan straightens up from where he's been slouching. "About the origin of demons?"

"No," Skylar shakes her head and turns back to Ryan. "There is a way to communicate from the mortal realm to the demon realm."

Ryan's eyes widen. "Really?"

"Yup!" Kris grins and looks at Bunny. "Have you ever heard of a spirit board?"

Bunny blinks at the demon. "The party game?"

"Yeah," Kris nods. "It wasn't always for that, though. Warlocks could create a spirit board to communicate with the demon realm."

"That makes sense," Ethan pipes up. "Does that mean we just have to go get one from the store? I can order one online."

Skylar shakes her head. "Maybe, but it wouldn't work on its own. Either Ryan or Bunny would have to enchant one for it to work."

"But," Kris chimes in, "Skylar's mentor said that a warlock *might* be able to forge a connection from your phones to ours."

"Right," Skylar nods. "I'm not sure how or if it'll work. The basics are the same as the spirit board: creating a connection between a real object and a magical replica from the demon realm."

Ryan's brow furrows. "I wouldn't even know where to begin. Why can't you just do it for me?"

"Just like demons can't affect the mortal realm from the demon realm, apparently we can't affect the demon realm from the mortal realm either. Only warlocks have the ability to bridge the two," Skylar rattles off to the group. Doubt darkens Ryan's face, and she turns towards him to catch his eye. "If my opinion matters: I think you can do it."

"But how?" Ryan whines.

Bunny and Ethan both stifle a snicker, which leaves Kris blinking at them, but Skylar keeps her attention on Ryan. She steps closer to his edge of the summoning circle, so they are face to face. "I can't do it for you, but I can tell you how I'd approach it."

"Okay," Ryan nods.

"Take your phone out," she directs. Ryan pulls his phone out of his pocket and holds it up as if to show Skylar. She takes out her own phone and holds it up, level with Ryan's. "Now imagine as clearly as you can being able to connect your phone with mine. Either with a wire, or a rope, or a tunnel. Some way to get your phone to reach mine."

Ryan's eyes drop to the two phones, and he stares at them for a few moments. He blinks and looks back up at her. "This isn't going to break my phone, is it?" he asks Skylar. Then his gaze shifts over her shoulder towards Ethan. "Right?"

"Honestly? I don't know," Skylar admits. She glances towards Ethan. "What do you think non-warlock?"

Ethan clears his throat. "I mean, it's not a physical connection. You're not doing anything physically to the phone. I don't see why it'd break the device," he logically lays out. "But I've never read about someone doing it before. So there's really no telling."

Ryan exhales a long breath. "Fine, but if it breaks, you owe me a new phone," he mumbles.

Skylar rolls her eyes. "That's something I can easily do."

"Really?" comes Bunny's voice.

Kris snickers. "Of course, silly. Honestly, it's kind of a waste to summon a demon to ask for a phone, but it's possible."

"I've had a lot dumber requests over the years." Skylar chuckles.

"Really? Like what?" Bunny smiles and, honestly, Skylar can see why he got the nickname. He's just so energetic and cute.

"Shh," Kris hushes him. "I can tell you more about it later. Especially if they can figure this out."

Bunny's eyes go impossibly wide. "Oh, right!" He looks back to Ryan and Skylar. "You can do it, Ryan!"

"Thanks, no pressure," Ryan grumbles.

Skylar finds herself smiling at Ryan as he concentrates on their phones. The warlock is so endearing when he's grumpy.

The warlock continues to stare at the phones as if blinking will make them disappear. The room goes silent as Ryan continues to just stare, but Skylar can feel something is happening. Magical energy is swirling in an aura around the warlock, Ryan seems to shiver as the magic moves around him and expands until Skylar can feel it brushing over the palm of her hand holding the phone. Sweat begins to bead at Ryan's temples, but still the warlock stays focused on the phones. His pale skin flushes down his neck and Skylar starts to worry that he is going to hurt himself when the magical aura finally bursts.

Ryan is panting like he just ran a mile. With bright eyes he looks up and meets Skylar's. "Did it work?"

Skylar feels a heat rise to her own cheeks as Ryan holds her gaze. She swallows. "I don't know."

Ryan breaks eye contact to look at his own phone. He takes it in both hands and begins tapping his fingers along the surface of the display. When he's finished, he looks back at Skylar.

A moment later, Skylar's own phone vibrates in the palm of her hand, and she nearly drops the thing in surprise as a text alert rings out. Everyone gasps as Skylar grips the phone more firmly and looks at the screen.

"Shit," Skylar curses. She opens the message, but that's all there is to it. She frowns and looks at Ryan. "You create a metaphysical connection between cross-dimensional devices and all you say is *testing*?"

He shrugs. "It seemed appropriate."

"Holy shit, it worked?" Bunny gasps. He runs around the edge of the summoning circle (rather consciously or unconsciously not stepping over the barrier) to look over Ryan's shoulder.

Ethan, who seems to realize he doesn't need to stand where he's standing, comes around after him to look as well. Kris takes the opportunity to sidle up next to Skylar and look over her shoulder.

"Send a reply," he urges her.

Skylar taps out a quick response.

Ryan's phone buzzes in his hand and the humans gather together to see.

"Really?" Bunny rolls his eyes. "You two are the lamest."

"So, it worked!" Ethan beams. "That's amazing."

Skylar nods in agreement. "It is impressive. The test will be whether or not the connection works while I'm in the demon realm."

"Do you want me to send you back there now?" Ryan asks, looking up from his phone.

Skylar and Kris both shake their heads. "You don't have to do it right this second," Skylar insists.

"If it does, can you do it to mine and Kris's phones?" Bunny tugs on Ryan's sleeve. "Please?" The grown man is actually pouting at the shorter warlock, but it seems effective.

"This wasn't exactly easy," Ryan points out. "I feel exhausted."

Bunny looks a little deflated. "Of course. You need to rest." He pats Ryan on the back. "Good job!"

Ryan shrugs him off, but there's a small smile on his lips. "Get off of me," he moans halfheartedly. "If Skylar takes the phone back to the demon realm and it works, then maybe I'll consider connecting your phones, too."

Bunny and Kris both cheer and bounce in place. "Thank you, Ryan," Kris sing songs.

"Hey, don't thank me yet," Ryan says. "We don't know how well this is going to work."

"I believe in you," Bunny encourages him.

"Me, too," Ethan chimes in and pats the warlock on the shoulder.

"Me, three!" Kris cheers.

Skylar smiles at all of them. "I think you've done it, Ryan. Good job," she says, gaining the warlock's attention once more.

Ryan cringes and shrugs his friends off of himself. "Stop being so sappy! And give me some room to breathe," he complains, but despite his protests a grin is spreading across his lips.

Both Ethan and Bunny back off to give Ryan some space, but they are smiling as they do so. They must be accustomed to the warlock's quirks.

"So, what do we do now?" Ethan asks looking around at everyone. They're all still gathered on one side of the summoning circle.

Kris shrugs. "I mean, do you guys have any other leads to hunt down information?"

The three humans shake their heads. "The Order of the Knowing Well seems like the best resource for information," Bunny explains. "And I agree with Ryan that joining without really wanting to be a member seems like a bad idea."

"Most of the people I talked to were nice," Ethan protests. "I can't imagine them hurting anyone for wanting to quit being a member."

"Or sending them to the demon realm," Bunny nods in agreement. "But most of the people we talked to seemed pretty low level. None of them were – what's it called? Elder Council level?"

"Fair. I spoke to the heads of research, but they surely won't tell us every-thing." Ethan sighs and puts his hands in the pockets of his slacks.

Kris and Skylar exchange a look. "I don't know what else to say," Kris admits.

"Right. I mean, Ryan is a pretty powerful warlock. I doubt it'd be easy for them to keep him if he chooses not to stay, but I don't know." Skylar's lips twist into a pout. "Maybe Kris and I can offer some extra protection?"

"Maybe." But Kris doesn't seem entirely convinced.

Ryan heaves a put-upon sigh. "I'll think about it, but only if we can't figure out anything else."

"Well, if that's all there is to cover tonight, you should probably send us back." Kris is frowning as he says it, his eyes drifting back towards his Bunny.

"Kris," Bunny whines softly.

The horned demon smirks. "What? It's not like you don't know how to bring me back later. Maybe after all your friends are gone." He wiggles his eyebrows suggestively and Skylar gasps in mock surprise.

"That is, if I'm allowed to." Bunny shoots Ryan a glare.

Ryan holds up his hands in defense, or maybe surrender. "I'm not going to stop you."

"Yay!" Kris claps.

"Thanks for your help," Ryan says as an aside to Skylar.

"And good job on your information gathering. Good luck," Skylar smiles.

"I'll text you," Ryan promises.

It is such an innocent thing. A phrase easily exchanged between friends, but those three words make Skylar's heart flutter in her chest. Maybe it is just the implication that he'd be able to reach her from the mortal realm. The thrill of finding out if the experiment works. "I'll talk to you soon, then," she gives him a wink.

"Kris and Skylar, I release you back to the demon realm," Ryan intones.

And just like that, the floor drops out from under Skylar's feet and she is back in her own living room once more wearing her gym shorts and tank top that she'd been dancing in. She doesn't wait even one second before teleporting over to Kris's building.

She walks into this apartment to find Kris in his own living room wearing a pair of black and white checkered pajamas. "Sky!" He squeals. "You got to meet my Bunny!"

"Ryan wasn't too mean again, was he?" Skylar asks sternly.

"Nope!" Kris shakes his head. "He actually apologized! They all apologized, in fact."

Skylar blinks in amazement. "Really?" Before she can ask anything else, her phone goes off from inside her pocket.

"Is it him?" Kris bounces over and starts slapping his palms against her arm. "Check! Check!"

She has to nudge Kris away to pull her phone out of her pocket. Skylar opens her chat without checking the notification first.

Omar

Hey, you and Kris free for a party tonight? Derek wants to celebrate our co-habitation. Show up whenever. Clothing optional. ;)

Skylar frowns and even Kris sighs over her shoulder. "Maybe he hasn't tried yet?" Kris offers.

"Maybe. Do you want to go to this thing?" Skylar tilts the screen towards Kris as if he hasn't already been reading the text over her shoulder.

"It could be fun," Kris says slowly, but he doesn't sound as enthusiastic as he normally does at the prospect of a party.

"You just hope Bunny summons you back." Skylar pokes at Kris as she teases him.

Kris grins. "That might be part of it."

Skylar's phone goes off again.

Warlock Ryan

Hey, did you and Kris make it home safe?

Skylar gasps. "Kris, this one's from Ryan!" She shows him the message.

Kris laughs. "That's the stupidest question, but it's sweet."

"He's trying," she sniffs as she taps out a reply.

Skylar is deciding if she should send another message, but then the phone starts to ring in her hand. She was getting a phone call? From the mortal realm? The contact name *Warlock Ryan* lights up the screen. She shoots a confused look at Kris.

"Answer it," he hisses.

Skylar accepts the call and puts it on speaker. "Hello?"

"Hey," comes Ryan's voice through the phone. It sounds tinny, and like he's speaking from the end of a long tunnel. "Can you hear me?"

"Barely." Skylar finds herself unconsciously raising her voice as if that would help with the connection. "Maybe texting is better."

"I can't really hear you," comes the broken reply. "I think we should stick to texting." And then the line goes dead before she can reply.

Skylar chuckles and shakes her head. "Well, phone calls aren't great, but texting seems pretty solid," she concludes.

"Try sending a pic!" Kris grabs her phone out of her hand and pulls up the camera. He takes a quick selfie of the two of them before handing the phone back. The pic isn't the greatest with Skylar staring ahead in surprise. "Send that!"

"Really?" She scoffs but opens the chat to try anyway. The phone says it's sent, but she isn't sure how clear it'll be on the other end.

Before Ryan can reply, she goes into her contacts. None of the contacts in her phone have actual phone numbers, since that's not how phones work in the demon realm. She pulls up the contact for Ryan and attaches the picture she took of blond Ryan to the name. Then her phone dings a text notification.

Warlock Ryan

I didn't even think about picture messages.

You both look pretty comfy.

Demon Skylar

Kris wanted to test it. Good to know.

Warlock Ryan

It was a good idea.

Well, have a good night.

"I guess that's it for tonight," Skylar says and slips her phone into her pocket. "Want to make an appearance at Omar and Derek's party? Celebrate our friends' milestone?"

Kris smiles and nods. "Sounds good."

Skylar and Kris roll up to Omar and Derek's new place an hour later. They took their time picking their outfits and actually walking over to the party. The effort not to be the first ones there pays off.

The party is in full swing as Kris and Skylar stroll in through the front door. Music is playing and demons are seated in the living room and around the kitchen table or standing in small groups. Food and alcohol are out on the kitchen counter for the taking. Everyone is dressed to the nines, making Kris and Skylar no different. Skylar opted for a leather mini skirt and sheer button up top with just a simple black bra underneath. Kris is sporting black slacks with white pinstripes and a black t-shirt under a leather jacket.

They are arm in arm when Derek approaches them, dressed in his own white slacks and a sheer white tank top that matches his white feathers. "You made it," he greets them. He wraps an arm around Kris for a hug first, then Skylar. "Make yourselves at home."

"Thanks for inviting us," Skylar says. "And congrats."

Derek cups Skylar's cheek as he smiles at her. "I'm sure Omar can think of a way you can congratulate us." He winks and Skylar huffs a laugh.

"I think we'll need libations first," Kris says and politely begins pulling Skylar towards the refreshments. Once they are out of Derek's earshot, Kris starts snickering. "Those two really have a thing for you."

Skylar shrugs. "They have a thing for each other, but sometimes I'm there to facilitate it."

"So I've noticed," Kris chuckles. "Speaking of things for people: what about you and Ryan?"

"That is you projecting." Skylar rolls her eyes as she reaches for a bottle of beer in a bucket of ice on the floor.

"Uh huh, okay." Kris gives her some serious side eye. "So you're saying I didn't see him turn green with jealousy when you flirted with Ethan and Bunny?" He reaches for a pitcher full of a fruity cocktail that's on the counter-top and fills a glass.

"Didn't happen." Skylar pops the cap on her beer with a flick of her fingers and takes a swig.

"And you don't still have his pictures on your phone."

Skylar shoots him a glare. "And it's convenient I did. Now there's a profile pic for his contact."

"Yes, how lucky," Kris smirks.

Skylar is saved from rebuffing his accusations further as another demon Skylar knows only in passing approaches them.

"Kris," the demon says and throws his arms around him in a big hug.

"Giles!" Kris easily hugs the demon back.

Giles is a tall, handsome demon with horns as well. His horns, however, are large and curved and complement his goat-like eyes. Skylar smiles at the other demon as he pulls back and gets a polite smile in return. His attention turns right back to Kris.

"It's been a long time," he says. "How have you been?"

"Same old, same old," Kris says, and Skylar chooses to tune them out.

Instead, she sips her beer and looks around for anyone else she may want to head towards. Derek has gone to speak with another friend of his. Omar is busy entertaining a small crowd with goofy dance moves and jokes. He is so personable and animated that Skylar finds herself just watching from the kitchen, even if she can't hear what's being said.

"Oops," Kris announces and draws Skylar's attention once more. Her friend is downing the last of his drink. "Looks like I've got to run. Summons."

Skylar blinks at him. Is Bunny summoning him back already? Or is it someone else? "I hope it doesn't take too long," she says in condolence.

Giles nods in agreement. "Yeah, come find me if it isn't too late." The other demon gives Kris a flirty wink, and Skylar has to school her face to keep from rolling her eyes. If only Giles knew that Kris is completely obsessed with a certain mortal warlock.

"I'll try," Kris says before glancing back to Skylar. "Have fun for the both of us." And with a wink he disappears.

Skylar looks to Giles, but the other demon is already wandering away. She laughs and takes a drink from her beer, which she nearly chokes on when she is startled by a sudden cry of excitement.

"Oh, did I just miss Kris?" Omar is on the other side of the kitchen island, just behind her enough that she didn't notice him approaching.

She coughs and wipes her mouth with the back of her hand. "Looks like. He offers his congrats to you and Derek, though."

Omar smiles and shrugs. "It's no big deal. Just an excuse to throw a party."

"Fair," Skylar nods and takes another sip of her beer. The alcohol is bitter and doesn't seem to really be having its desired effect yet. "You look like you're having a good time."

"It's been fun." Omar runs his fingers through his hair before scratching behind one of his ears. "I wouldn't mind having some fun with you, though." The demon's wolf ears swivel forward as he steps around the kitchen counter to Skylar's side. He slides a hand around Skylar's waist to pull her into a side hug. She shifts her beer to her other hand as Omar leans in to nuzzle her neck just below her ear.

"Derek said something along those lines," Skylar laughs. It wouldn't be the first time, but for some reason she's just not feeling it tonight. Something about Kris's comments earlier keeps bouncing around in her head. "But I'd hate to take you away from your party guests."

"I wouldn't hate it," Omar whispers, his breath hot against Skylar's ear. Strong fingers dig into her hip, holding her in place as Omar grinds against her side to show his *appreciation*.

"I knew he'd find you," Derek laughs as he makes his way over to them. He sets his empty cup down and picks up another, this one filled with a neon green liquid.

Skylar shoots Derek a smirk. "It's a relief that you're here," she teases. "Your boyfriend is about to rut himself silly against me. Don't you take proper care of him?"

Derek reaches over and threads his fingers through Omar's hair. He grips the thick strands and yanks, pulling the demon's head back from where it's buried against Skylar's neck. "You know I do," Derek says, speaking to Skylar though his eyes are on Omar. "You know how badly he misbehaves. Especially around you, Sky. You seem to bring out the worst in him." He sounds scolding, but it's playful.

"Then maybe he should get disciplined," Skylar suggests.

Omar's eyes light up with excitement and Derek smirks. "Look how much he likes that idea," he points out. "I don't think our past disciplinary sessions have done much good."

"A change of tactic is needed then," Skylar hums. She takes her free hand and slides it along the outside of Omar's thigh towards his ass. "Instead of giving the naughty pup what he wants, we should deny him." Before her fingers can caress his firm glutes, she steps away, going as far as to twist out of his grip.

Omar whines as his eyes follow her. "No," he pouts.

"I think she might be right, pup. I indulge you too much." Derek also backs away from Omar. "If you can behave for the rest of the party, I'll give you a treat."

"Really?" Omar's eyes go wide as he looks at Derek. Then his gaze slides back to Skylar with a wicked grin.

She holds up her hands. "Do not include me," she shakes her head. "I came to congratulate you both, but I don't know if I'm staying all night."

"Will you consider it if you're still here as things die down?" Derek's question is so polite and unassuming.

Skylar looks between the two of them. "No promises," she points at both of them. "Go be good party hosts." She waves them off as she takes her beer and goes around to the far side of the kitchen counter, away from them.

Instead of catering to Derek and Omar's inclusive sexual proclivities, Skylar socializes with some of the other demons she doesn't know very well. She finds herself in a discussion about new music with two other demons. They are talking about their favorite vocalists and Skylar contributes from time to time. As her beer empties, she just summons more to fill it again, so she doesn't have to bother wading through the party again.

Sometime around her third refill, Skylar's phone buzzes in her back pocket. She just assumes it's Kris back from the mortal realm, so she lazily sips her beer before pulling the phone out to check. However, it's not Kris's name on the notification. She didn't expect to hear from the warlock so soon, but that doesn't stop a silly grin from coming to her lips.

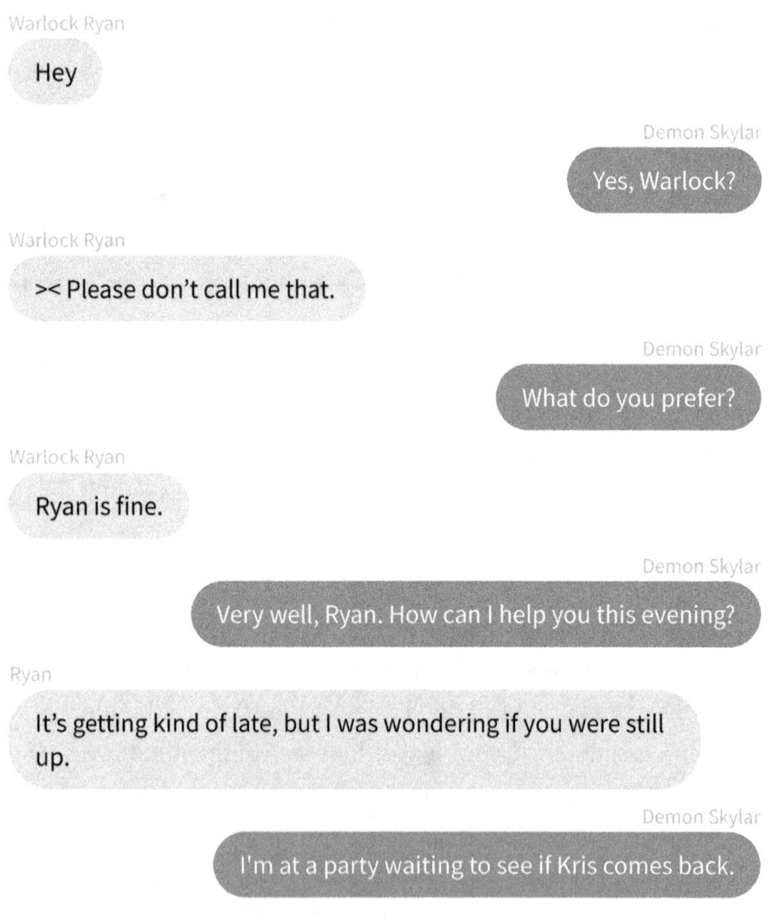

Skylar slips her phone back into her pocket and does a scan of the party for Derek and Omar. She spots Omar sitting in Derek's lap on the couch and sucking open mouthed kisses into his neck as Derek speaks to other party guests. His hand is lazily stroking up and down Omar's back as the wolf-like demon's tail wags. *So much for behaving*, Skylar thinks to herself.

She extracts herself from the conversation she'd mentally checked out of already. After making eye contact with Derek over the shoulder of his conversation partner, Skylar waves and points to the door to indicate she's leaving. He just smiles back and nods before going back to his conversation.

Skylar takes the short walk home, letting her troubled mind continue to tumble over Kris's words. She still firmly believes her friend is reading into her connection to the hapless warlock. Before she knows it, she's wandering back into her apartment. Without turning the lights on, she shuffles into her bedroom. She pulls her phone back out of her pocket before changing into an oversized sleep shirt and crawling into bed. As she settles into her pillows, she checks her messages again.

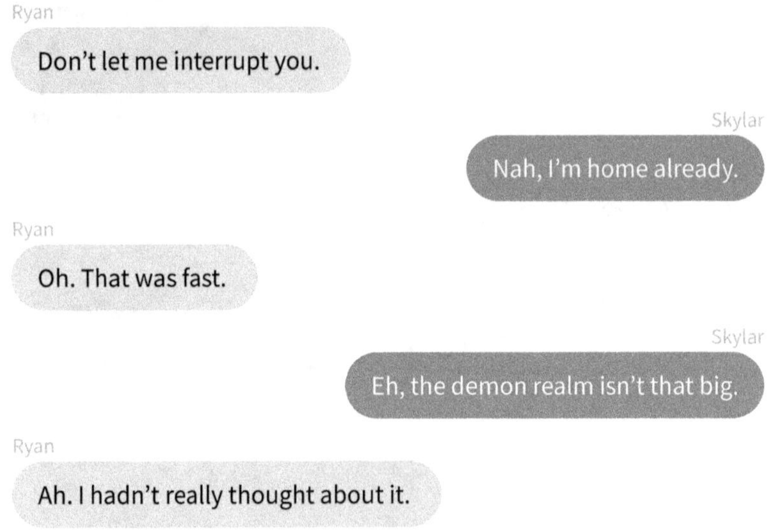

Skylar chuckles as she reads over the exchange, the only light in her room coming from the screen of her phone. She feels like a teenager in one of those dramas she'd watched growing up in the demon realm.

Ryan

Do I have to?

Skylar

I'm waiting . . .

Skylar snickers as she kicks the sheets down the bed so she can slip her feet under the covers. It takes a few extra moments before her phone goes off again. An image comes up of Ryan with green hair in a black t-shirt as he sits propped up against some pillows. He is smiling and Skylar feels herself smiling back at the picture.

Skylar drops her hand holding the phone to the bed as she stares at the ceiling in the dark. What can she teach him? Will there be something she can come up with that would take longer to teach? Or maybe something that would involve convincing him to break the summoning circle so she can touch that soft hair? Or hold those long fingers?

A heat rises to her cheeks, and she shakes her head to clear the wandering thoughts. Where had that line of thinking been leading her? She blames Derek and Omar for coming on to her so strongly. That has to be why she's so worked up.

Her phone goes off again and she brings it up to her face once more.

I don't know where else you can find better information.

But you're not going in there completely blind. You are aware enough to be nervous, so I think that gives you an edge.

And you've got Justin and Ethan. Maybe they can be your safety net?

Plus Kris and me.

Ryan

I think having demons on my side is both something I never thought I'd say and more reassuring than just having my human friends.

I'll think about it.

Thanks, Skylar. Goodnight.

Skylar

Goodnight, Ryan.

Skylar smiles fondly at her phone as she curls onto her side and closes her eyes. She tucks her phone under her pillow and lets her mind drift to images of a gently smiling warlock.

15

Membership Has Its Benefits

RYAN SITS WITH ETHAN, Justin, and Ashe in Justin's living room. They're having another movie night, but his mind is anywhere other than the comedy that is playing on the television.

It's been almost two weeks since his meeting with the Order of the Knowing Well. He's gotten a few polite messages asking if he is interested in pursuing membership, which he does his best to stall with vague excuses of considering it. Meanwhile, he's been working with Justin and Ethan to find other sources of magic history and information. They've run down a lot of dead ends and it's getting frustrating.

Hence the movie night break.

However, he's been texting Skylar at least once a day under the guise of checking in on their progress for plan: Warlock Spy. He's scrolling through their most recent exchange as his friends laugh along with the film. It started as just something to do with his hands, but he's long since stopped paying attention to the film.

Skylar

Learned anything new?

Ryan

Not since the last time you asked.

I thought we set up this connection so I could contact you. Not have you constantly harass me.

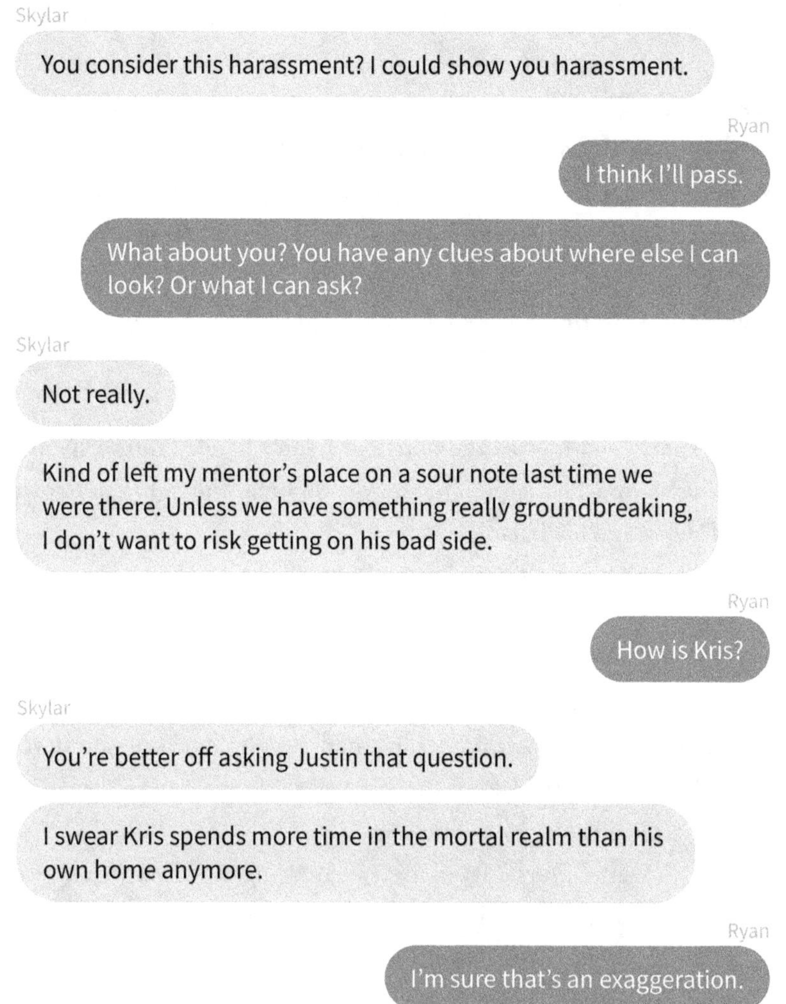

Ryan bites at the skin around his thumbnail as he scrolls through the messages. As much as Ethan has tried to help find avenues for other information, Ryan hates to admit that the Order is still their best and surest bet. Besides, whatever happened to his ancestor was nearly seventy years ago. A lot could have changed in the Order since then.

Absently, he continues to scroll through the messages until he comes across some of the pictures Skylar sent him. Somehow, they'd gone from talking about where demons come from to where bad photo filters come from to whether or not demons are capable of taking a bad picture. Unfortunately,

Skylar took it as a personal challenge to prove that she can't possibly take a bad picture. Ryan has been sent an onslaught of photos of her looking increasingly cute from every possible angle. A smile unconsciously tugs at the corners of his lips as he scrolls through the collection of images.

"Boyfriend or girlfriend?" Ashe's voice interrupts Ryan's thoughts.

Ryan glances up to find that the movie has ended. Justin is gathering the trash from their snacks as Ethan tries to help. Ashe is sitting on the spot of the couch closest to the armchair Ryan occupies and is leaning towards him with a conspirator's smile.

"What?" Ryan asks dumbly.

Ashe dips his head toward the phone in Ryan's hand. "You've spent more time looking at your phone than the movie. So I'm asking: do you have a new girlfriend? Or is it a boyfriend?"

Ryan frowns at him. "Neither."

"No way," Ashe scoffs. "No one looks at their phone that fondly if there isn't a sweetheart of some sort." He tries to lean forward as if he could glimpse Ryan's screen, so Ryan pockets the device.

"Seriously," he reiterates. "I haven't had a girlfriend since first year of college and my last boyfriend was . . ." He trails off trying to remember when he and Jake stopped seeing one another.

"Six years," Justin offers. "Ryan hasn't dated anyone in six years."

The number shocks Ryan himself. "How is it that *you've* kept track of that better than I have?"

"It's one of my many talents." Justin smirks before turning to leave the living room, his hands full of partially devoured bags of snacks.

Ethan follows after him with arms full of empty cans and bottles. "That's impressive, Justin," he mentions as they disappear into the kitchen.

"I can introduce you to someone," Ashe offers as he settles comfortably back into the couch.

Ryan laughs, a bit uncomfortable with the direction the conversation is going. "That's really not necessary."

"Why not?" Ashe's head tilts to the side. "I work with tons of beautiful men and women. I'm sure we can find someone who is willing to lower their standards for a hermit gig worker."

"Fuck off." Ryan smiles sweetly and then flips Ashe the bird, which causes both of them to erupt into laughter.

Ashe just shakes his head and gets up from the couch, stretching his arms over his head. "Speaking of beautiful women," he says around a yawn, "I'm going to go call my girlfriend."

"Good night," Ryan calls after Ashe when he heads down the hall towards his room.

Ethan and Justin come back just in time to bid him a good evening as well. Then the two settle back on the couch, closer to Ryan.

"So, were you talking to Skylar?" Ethan asks, his eyes bright with curiosity.

Ryan lets out a heavy sigh. "No, I wasn't! I may have been looking through our past messages for new ideas of where to look for info about magic next, but it was kind of useless."

"So, now what?" Justin is kind enough to shift the topic and not push any further.

Ryan rubs his eyes before combing his fingers through his hair. It isn't that late yet, but he is suddenly very tired. "I think this means we have only one choice."

"No!" Justin shakes his head. "There must be other warlock orders that have information about demons."

Ethan crosses a leg and rests his elbow on his knee. "True, but I don't know if Ryan's name is going to carry as much weight with any of them."

"That," Ryan groans. "And the fact that no other organization is going to have information on what happened to Thomas Andrew Smith."

"So that's important now, is it?" Justin's eyebrows are climbing towards his fringe. The question doesn't come off as rude or a challenge, but genuinely surprised.

Ryan leans towards them, keeping his voice down. They should have been more careful talking about this with Ashe in the house. "It is to me. I keep finding myself getting more immersed in this magic stuff. His name was like a free pass to join this Order and they are the only ones with answers about what happened to him. It feels like it's connected somehow." Ryan watches as his friends exchange a somber look. "What?" he demands.

Justin looks back at him. "We're just worried. We want to help you, but if you join the Order of the Knowing Well, you're going to go somewhere we can't follow. You'll be on your own."

"But I'll agree to whatever you decide," Ethan quickly adds. "Maybe we can come up with some way that you can signal us if you're in trouble. I'm sure, between the three of us, we can come up with something."

Ryan feels a fondness swell up in his chest as he smiles at his friends. "I think we can do this."

The next day Ryan sends an email to the Order. Instead of another email back, he gets a personal phone call from Dahlia Jones to arrange a return visit to the estate. Despite his misgivings, Ryan agrees to return later that week on his own.

He is sitting on a park bench with Ethan the day after the phone call. He's not sure how, but Ethan has managed to lure Ryan out of the bookstore for some natural light over lunch. Ethan also just *happens* to have an extra lunch box for Ryan so that he'll eat something other than convenience store food. That's how he finds himself crunching on some carrot sticks as he tells Ethan about the upcoming meeting.

"Are you really sure this is what you want to do?" Ethan asks as he sips his water. "Justin and I can be nearby if you need to make a quick escape."

Ryan nods slowly as he considers the logistics. "I'd appreciate that. It'd also save me the money on a really expensive ride share to get all the way over there. I also think I'll be less nervous if I know you guys are nearby."

Ethan caps his water bottle and takes another bite of his sandwich. "I'm sure Justin will agree."

"It's going to be a Thursday afternoon," Ryan points out. "He may be busy."

"As if he won't rearrange his schedule for this," Ethan chuckles. "And I'm sure I can get Nadia to cover the store."

"You're going to be in big trouble if she ever gets her big break in dance," Ryan shakes his finger at Ethan.

"I know," he admits with a laugh. "I'm going to be severely lacking if she goes, but I hope she makes it."

Ethan is right about Justin. When Ryan calls to talk to him about his plans, the younger says he'll make sure he is free. Which leaves a few days, once plans are made, for Ryan to obsess over everything that could possibly go wrong.

———

Ryan finds himself lying in bed the night before his meeting, staring at the ceiling in the dark. What will taking an oath with the Order of the Knowing Well entail? Will he have to swear a blood oath? Sacrifice an animal? What if he has to promise his first-born? Not that he has ever planned on having kids. Maybe he could adopt? Would being a member of the Order get in the way of a family? First, he'd have to find a partner. He isn't really keen on being a single dad. Fuck, he hasn't gotten laid in two years.

Seeking a distraction from his mind weasels, Ryan grabs his phone to look at the latest dance videos Nadia has shared. She has started filming her group's practice sessions and sharing whenever they nail a particularly hard piece of choreography. He is happy to be a hype man when needed.

The camera is set up in a dance studio space with a group of men and women in a starting formation. A beat starts and everyone makes identical isolated movements. It is impressive how synchronized they are. When the performance ends, he watches it twice more to make sure he caught all the details Nadia put in the dance. Then he sends her a comment praising Nadia for the performance. He suggests getting permission from the students to add it to her portfolio.

This is a nice distraction, but it went by too quickly and he's still wide awake with a phone in his hand. Without really thinking about it, he opens his chat app. His text chat with Skylar is right there at the top. The last several messages are images Skylar has sent him of her apartment and a nearby park. The demon realm looks disappointingly normal, but Ryan isn't sure what else he expected. Pits of fire and torture devices were definitely what classic art and literature brought to mind, but Skylar's home actually looks like its in a nice part of town. Nicer than his apartment, at least. He decides to text Skylar on a whim.

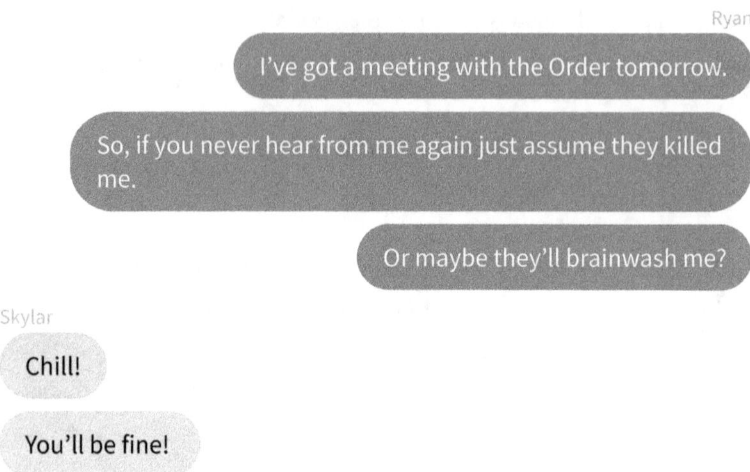

For some reason, those last three words do more to make him feel better than anything else possibly could.

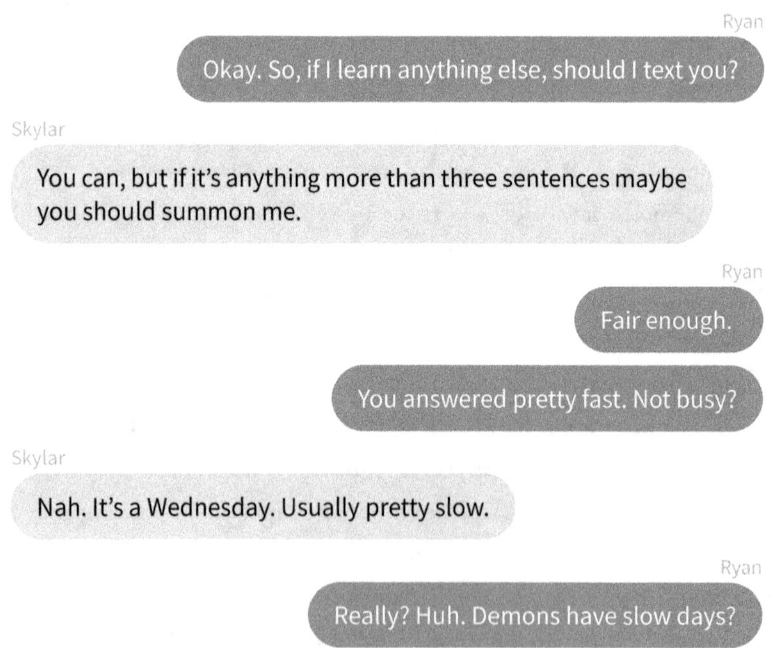

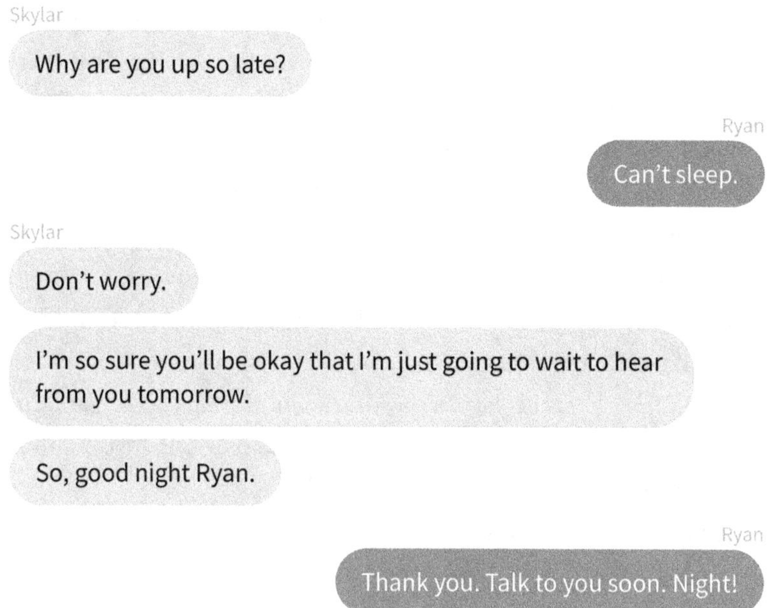

Ryan smiles at the glowing phone screen. He really can't explain it, but he feels much better than when he first picked up his phone. Skylar's confidence in him feels like a comforting weighted blanket over him.

He turns his phone off and sets it on his bedside table. Ryan rolls over, feeling more at peace than he has in weeks and falls fast asleep only minutes later.

Justin picks up Ryan from his apartment just after lunch on Thursday. Ethan is already in the car, so Ryan hops into the back seat. They spend the long drive out to the estate talking about contingency plans.

Justin is going to drop Ryan off at the driveway and then park off the road less than half a mile away. There he'll wait with Ethan for either a pick-up call or an emergency message. Ryan keeps a typed text in their group chat that says "get me out now." If things go bad fast, he can send it quick. If Ryan doesn't come back before sundown and there's no message that everything is okay, they are going to summon the demons and come get him.

Ryan feels better (if not a little silly) with all these plans in place, but not as comforted as he was after talking to Skylar last night. Too bad that calm didn't last past breakfast.

It is just ten minutes before his scheduled meeting with Dahlia Jones when Justin lets Ryan out at the driveway to the estate. He crawls out of the car and pulls at the collar of his white dress shirt.

Early this morning Ryan had pulled out the old suit from his mother's attic and ironed it. The grey suit fits better than his graduation one and he looks even more like his ancestor when he glances in the mirror. The only problem is the rising summer heat this late in the afternoon. He runs his fingers through his hair as he looks up at the large building once more. If Justin and Ethan had to bust in the door, would they even be able to?

"Good luck," Ethan calls from the passenger seat.

Justin nods. "You can do it! We'll be waiting for you."

Ryan does his best to give his friends a reassuring smile. "Thanks. See you soon." He gives them a short wave before shutting the car door and beginning his march up to the doors of the estate. It feels incongruent to be joining an occult organization on such a bright, sunny day.

Instead of Alexander Kim greeting him this time, Dahlia is there herself. She is dressed in a smart beige pantsuit and already Ryan is glad he opted for the suit over his usual clothes. "Ryan! I'm glad you decided to come back."

"Thank you," he says with a small bow of his head.

Dahlia gives him a once-over and he has to fight not to squirm under her gaze. Her smile seems to grow as she gives him a nod of approval, but she doesn't say anything. She turns and leads Ryan through the entryway, but this time they go up the left set of stairs.

The landing at the top of the stairs splits into a hallway where a large group portrait hangs. It gives Ryan the impression of a class picture. Everyone in the photo is wearing a crimson robe, about fifty of them, and stares stoically ahead at the camera. The man front and center holds a sign: *Order of the Knowing Well, 1947*. Dahlia stops beside the photograph and smiles widely at him.

"Have you noticed already?" she asks.

Ryan leans in to peer at the photo. In fact, the first thing he notices about the portrait is that it includes only one woman who sits in the front left corner. Everyone else is male. "That this photo is in color even though it's pre-1950?" he asks.

Dahlia laughs and shakes her head. "No, silly. We're warlocks. Color photography was easy for us."

Ryan blinks at her. "I'm sorry, then what am I looking for?"

"Your great-great-grandfather is in the portrait," she says proudly. She then gestures to the center, in the second row. "You look a lot like him."

"I guess we look alike," Ryan admits as he eyes the photograph more closely. His relative, wearing the same crimson robes as the other warlocks, stands between two taller men. His ancestor is about half a head shorter than either man. The one on his left is the more portly of the two. The man on his right is taller with broad shoulders and a classically handsome face.

"Why don't you follow me," Dahlia gently interjects. "Everyone is waiting for us."

Ryan swallows as he looks back at her. "Everyone?"

She chuckles. "It's not a big deal. The elder council likes to be present when a new member is sworn in. Especially if the person is a legacy—which you are, of course."

He can only nod along as he follows her down the hall. "Oh, yeah. Of course."

Ryan is led down the hallway to a large room. There are comfortable high-back chairs around short tables that look like they are meant for small groups of people to gather. A huge fireplace is at the center of the longest wall opposite the door, but the day is far too warm for a fire to be burning. Portraits of people Ryan doesn't recognize hang on the walls between tall bookcases filled with hardcover books.

People are milling about, but far fewer than at the gathering he'd attended with Justin and Ethan. He feels like he's the youngest person in the crowd today, with Dahlia being the next youngest. Most of the attendees have hair that ranges from silvering to pure white strands. He is struck by the fact that today they are all wearing crimson robes, just like the people in the photograph they'd stopped to look at. In fact, when Dahlia enters the room, she pulls a matching robe from a coat rack at the door and pulls it on.

"Let me introduce you around," she offers after the robe is in place.

Once again, Ryan is introduced to a whirlwind of people whose names he has no hopes of remembering in this instant. A few people he vaguely remembers from the first visit to the estate. There are also more mentions of his family name: Smith.

An older man by the name of Jang, white haired and hunched over a crane, cries out in delight when they meet. "It's about time we had a Smith back in our ranks! Come, my boy." He hobbles away leaving Ryan no choice but to follow him. Dahlia trails behind, her smile never fading.

The man brings him to a corner of the room that Ryan had not previously noticed because there were enough other people around to block his view. There, on the wall, is a large portrait with a name plaque: Thomas Andrew Smith. His great-great-grandfather stares out of the portrait over his head with a stoic expression.

The more he stares back at the image of his ancestor, the more Ryan feels like he is looking at himself. His own eyes stare at him from this man's face. He recognizes his own sour expression whenever someone catches a candid of him on the man's turned-down lips. What is different is the air of authority his great-great-grandfather projects, even from an old photo. Maybe he had a confidence that Ryan doesn't share.

"You're the spitting image of him," the old man says. "I met him once when I was still a young man. He was giving a lecture on how to build on existing magic systems in order to create something new." Ryan nods like anything the man says makes sense, which seems to urge him to continue. "It's a damn shame what happened to such a great man. He had so much more potential to give."

Ryan's heart leaps. Here's the opening he's been hoping for. "Can you tell me what happened?"

Of course, that's when Dahlia cuts in. "Maybe after the ceremony. Speaking of which, we should get started." She turns and claps loudly to get the room's attention. "Let's begin."

The crowd begins to organize into a circle in the center of the room where a space has been cleared on a gray rug designed with intersecting black circles. Dahlia leads Ryan to the circle and directs him to stand between two others: a man in his late forties whose name Ryan has already forgotten and an older woman in spectacles who he'd never met. Dahlia steps into the center of the circle and commands everyone's attention with sheer charisma.

"Welcome, everyone, to the swearing-in of our latest legacy: Ryan Smith. Great-great-grandson of the esteemed member Andrew Thomas Smith. The Council of Elders has granted me the honor of leading this prestigious ceremony. Thank you." She turns and bows to a section of the circle before continuing to address everyone. "Let's keep this short and sweet." The crowd chuckles as she turns back to Ryan. "Ryan Smith, step forward to be seen and judged by your peers."

All eyes are on him and Ryan squirms under the weight of their gaze. With Dahlia's gentle urging, Ryan steps into the circle. Rather than focusing on everyone around him, he keeps his eyes on her. She leads him to the very center where they stand face to face.

"We invite you to join the Order of the Knowing Well. We seek to learn the secrets of magic and we invite you into our fold. To share our knowledge and add yours to our own. Share with us something you have learned. Show us that you have the drive to learn more."

Ryan gulps. "What?"

She smiles and leans forward to quietly whisper, "This is just part of the ceremony. You can show us a piece of magic you know or recite something from your tome."

Ryan frowns. Only two things come to mind, but like fuck he's going to summon a demon in front of everyone here. That really only leaves the glamour trick Skylar taught him. The magic is probably something very easy compared to the spells the others in the circle can accomplish.

After he makes up his mind, he sets his jaw and closes his eyes to imagine the change he wants to enact. Ryan holds his hands up, first placing them over his eyes until can feel the tingle of magic along the palms of his hands. He imagines that the next time he opens his eyes, instead of their usual blue, they'll be a rich brown color. Then he slides his hands over his forehead, pushing his hair back slowly as he goes imagining that each strand turns from straw-colored to pure white. Just as Skylar had shown him, he focuses on the illusion as he runs his fingers over his hair.

Before he even opens his eyes, he hears a gasp from the others in the room. When he does open his eyes, Dahlia is staring at him, her own eyes wide in surprise. She lets out a startled cry when their eyes finally meet. "How?" she gasps.

Murmurs from the crowd fill the room. Ryan glances around at them, which draws even more sounds of surprise. He looks back to Dahlia, his heart thudding in his chest. "Did I do something wrong?" he whispers. In an effort to put everyone at ease again, Ryan shakes his head and imagines the glamour falling away so he's back to his blue-eyed, blonde-haired self.

"No." Her answer is stilted, but she blinks as if breaking free from her own shock. "Not at all! I just don't think anyone expected you to be able to do magic without any tools. No chants or words of magic."

Internally, Ryan cringes. He should have known better. Even Skylar pointed out to him that what he did was unusual. "I didn't know—"

"It's amazing!" she interrupts him. "You're obviously *very* talented."

"Yes," comes a cry from elsewhere in the circle.

"Just like his ancestor," cries old man Jang.

The sounds of surprise turn to noises of appreciation and cheer.

"Warlock Jones," someone says, their voice ringing out over the crowd. Everyone stops and looks towards the tall man with salt and pepper hair. "You did well in bringing Warlock Smith into our fold. I think he's proven himself more than enough. Let's complete the ceremony."

"Yes, Warlock Houghlin." Dahlia nods to him and turns back to Ryan. "With your gifts of magic, we welcome you to our circle."

"Welcome!" The crowd echoes the sentiment.

Someone from behind Ryan steps forward with a brass bowl. They hand it to Dahlia and then rejoin the circle. "This represents our Knowing Well, the well of knowledge," Dahlia explains. "We each have sworn an oath of loyalty both to the well and to each other. If you take this solemn oath, know that the Order will be here for you in all things. Never will you be left seeking knowledge alone. Our knowledge is your knowledge. Do you swear to uphold this solemn oath?" She holds the bowl out to Ryan.

He reaches out and takes the bowl. It is cold to the touch, but it also thrums with an energy Ryan is growing to recognize as magic. It isn't Dahlia's magic, but magic endowed into the bowl itself. A clear liquid, looking very much like water, sloshes slightly in the bowl as Dahlia lets go and Ryan holds it alone.

"I swear it," Ryan says with a lot more confidence than he actually feels.

Dahlia smiles at him proudly. "Then drink, Ryan Smith, and become a member of the Order of the Knowing Well."

Ryan lifts the bowl to his lips. The rim is cool to the touch, but the water is even colder. It is fresh and clean but carries with it the sensation of magic. For the first time it feels like he is taking magic *into* himself instead of just feeling it on the outside, dancing along his skin. It scares him but also feels exhilarating. Like the magic isn't just surrounding him but becoming part of him.

The crowd applauds as Ryan lowers the bowl and hands it back to Dahlia. "Welcome, Warlock Smith," she says. Then the circle folds inwards so everyone can shake Ryan's hand and congratulate him. He is helped into a matching crimson robe that feels a little heavy for the season.

The first to approach him is the man called Warlock Houghlin. "Welcome, Warlock Smith. I have a feeling you're going to do great things during your time with us."

"Thank you," Ryan says as he shakes the man's hand.

Once everyone has had their chance to shake his hand, Dahlia takes Ryan on an official tour of the grounds. There is a giant library, meeting rooms, a research facility, a decent kitchen, temporary dorms for visiting warlocks, and an archive of the history of the Order. Ryan feels overwhelmed by the sheer size of the place.

They stop in the archive, which is a basement room of the estate that is large, cold, and smells of old books. Ethan would love it. "This place is amazing," Ryan says honestly, looking at the shelves of books and various trinkets. "Is this where information on Thomas Andrew Smith would be?"

Dahlia smiles. "Yes, but I may be able to answer some of your questions. My grandfather was an apprentice under your great-great-grandfather, so I grew up hearing stories about his greatness." She gestures for him to sit at a long wood table probably used for looking at any of the books and artifacts stored in the archive.

"Did he do a lot for the Order?" Ryan asks as he sits next to her, genuinely curious.

She nods. "Yes. He was a great leader. I can only imagine what he could have accomplished if he hadn't been killed so early."

Ryan frowns, turning away from the shelves to turn towards her. "So, he *was* murdered."

"Sadly." Dahlia clasps her hands in front of her and drops her head. "By one of his closest confidants, too. The only man closer to him than my grandfather."

"What happened though? His obituary is extremely lacking, and you said I could only find out when I joined." Ryan might be pushing a little hard, but all this dancing around the subject is making him frustrated.

She sighs and moves to sit at a long table. "I did, didn't I? I'm sorry, it's not something any of us really like to talk about."

Ryan nods in sympathy, but he's come so far to get this information. He isn't going to give up now, so he goes over to sit beside her. "I understand, but since he's a member of my family, my ancestor, I'm sure you can understand why I would still really like to know."

"Like I said, he was betrayed by his closest friend in the Order. He had been planning to take the Order to new heights, and the warlock struck him down out of jealousy. He was worried he'd lose his place in a new power structure, but all he did was destroy everything Thomas Andrew Smith had been building for years." She pauses and takes a deep breath. "If I'm totally honest, it's part of the reason I was hoping you'd bring his tome. He was one of the contributors, but when he passed, all existing copies went with him. I was surprised his personal copy alone survived, but perhaps it had been warded against such an event."

Ryan blinks in surprise. "What do you mean that the copies went with him?"

"They simply went up in a flash, leaving nothing but ashes in their wake," Dahlia replies.

"So, he knew it was going to happen?" Ryan is shocked.

"Knew it?" Dahlia ponders the question, one immaculate nail tapping the tip of her chin. "I don't think he *knew* it would happen, but I suppose he suspected that someone may not want to move forward with the future he had in mind."

Ryan frowns. "And the Order knows who it was? They punished him?"

Dahlia reaches out and puts a hand over where Ryan's is clenched against his knee. He hadn't even realized he was that tense until she touched him. He tries to relax. "Yes," she says. "He was delivered the harshest punishment given to anyone who betrays the Order."

Ryan feels his heart racing. He's no closer to learning exactly what he's been looking for, but some details remain stubbornly hidden. The very thing he'd taken the oath to discover. "And what's that?"

She looks him dead in the eye. "He was banished to become a demon in the demon realm," Dahlia says. "Forever bound there and made only to serve warlocks."

Ryan gasps. So that *was* how demons were made if they weren't born. They were once warlocks. Evil ones at that. "This punishment is something the Order came up with?" he asks, mind reeling to process this revelation.

"Oh, no," Dahlia gives a sad smile. "It's a centuries-old practice, but the Order has used it in the past."

"In the past?" Ryan gulps. "Does it happen a lot?"

"No," she reassures him, giving his hand a squeeze. "We haven't had a murder in the Order since Thomas Andrew Smith's death. It really is saved for only the worst crimes. The man who killed your great-great-grandfather was the last to be banished in that fashion. By us, at least."

"Who was he?" Ryan asks. Maybe Skylar would know of him? *Or what if she's been lying? Maybe there are no born demons.* He tries to ignore the cynical voice in the back of his head.

Dahlia gives him a pitying look. "His name was Warren Hayes."

16

Trust Issues

KRIS IS HOME FOR once. It seems to Skylar that he is gone most evenings lately. Either her friend is on a random summoning trip or spending any free time with his Bunny. Skylar doesn't begrudge him the happiness that evenings with Justin brings him, even if it seems extremely limiting. What could the two of them do together that either of them can't do from the comfort of their own homes? Justin can't cuddle Kris through a summoning circle. Rationally Skylar knows that's beside the point, but with Kris gone so often, it really leaves her with too much time alone in her own head.

Which is why she's especially glad to see Kris today, a day when she hasn't heard from Ryan at all, an unusual occurrence in and of itself. Normally they check in with one another, but today in particular is worrisome. She knows Ryan is going to meet with the Order to get answers. As much as she reassured the warlock that he would be fine, the fact that she can't be there herself to make sure he stays fine is agitating. So, instead, Skylar finds herself pacing around Kris's apartment to work off her anxious energy. Her wings constantly twitch, and she comes very close to sweeping a few knickknacks off tables as she paces.

To Kris's credit, he does his best not to be annoyed at his best friend's nervous demeanor. He sits on his couch and tries to coax Skylar to join him. "You're making me tired just watching you," he complains gently. "Cuddles are the fix for everything! I'm sure you're worried over nothing, and you'll feel silly later. Now, sit your cute ass down and let me pet you."

Skylar has been gnawing on her bottom lip, which she releases to stop and look at Kris. "We have to be ready at a moment's notice. If Justin summons you to go rescue him, you have to make them summon me too."

Kris pats the empty spot on the couch next to himself. "Come sit down and we can talk about our daring rescue plan."

Lower lip jutted out in a pout, Skylar begrudgingly plops down next to Kris. She is immediately pulled into a hug as Kris falls back on the couch and brings Skylar with him. With Skylar on her stomach across his chest, Kris can pet her wings as he tries to calm her down. "I'm sure if there was a problem, we would have heard from either Bunny or Ryan by now."

"Why haven't either of them texted us even if there isn't a problem?" Skylar whines as she buries her face in the crook of Kris's neck. Kris's fingers stroke gently over her wings and it does have a calming effect on her nerves.

"Maybe they're busy." She hates how reasonable Kris sounds. "Besides, didn't you tell your warlock to summon you if it was a long explanation?"

"Yes," comes Skylar's muffled reply.

"Then he's probably has to wait until he's somewhere he can do that," Kris points out. "And hopefully this means he has a lot to report."

Skylar sighs and slowly melts into Kris's embrace. "I guess you're right."

Together they lay on the couch for a long while. Kris puts soft jazz music on in the background and, despite how wound up she has been, Skylar feels her eyelids grow heavier as Kris continues to caress her wings. Her best friend has long fingers, a lot like Ryan's.

Lazily her mind drifts to wondering what Ryan's fingers would feel like against her feathers. Would they be so soothing? Or would they spark something else in her? Ryan always has an aura of power around him because the magic he commands is so powerful but untamed. It feels like getting too close to a large Van de Graaff generator. Skylar suspects if they ever touch, she'll get shocked. It is kind of exhilarating.

"Are you doing better?" Kris's soft voice interrupts her thoughts.

Skylar hums an affirmative reply. She braces herself against his chest so she can look down at him. "I'm sorry for being such a nuisance."

"It's okay." Kris smiles up at her and gently tucks a lock of her hair behind her ear. "You're worried. If it were my Bunny, I'd be worried too."

Skylar pushes herself into a sitting position so Kris isn't crushed beneath her anymore. "It's different," she protests, adjusting her wings over the back of the couch.

Kris sits up, curling his legs underneath himself. "I really don't see how it's different."

"Because," Skylar says as if it is obvious, "you and Bunny are cute and flirty and becoming unreasonably close for a warlock and a demon."

"You're flirty with Ryan."

Skylar levels him with a skeptical side-eye. "I'm flirty with everyone."

"It's different with him," Kris argues. "You also try to help him without him having to make a wish or request."

"Now, that's different. He's giving us something in return."

Kris raises an eyebrow. "Is that really it? You're helping him learn to control his magic just because he *might* be able to tell us where demons come from? Since when do we care that much to begin with?"

Skylar crosses her arms over her chest. "Just because you didn't care doesn't mean that I didn't. Don't you want to know why, as kids, we were pulled from our homes?"

"Will knowing change anything?" Kris frowns.

Skylar's heart sinks. He's been trying to cheer her up and all she does is bring Kris down with her. She's about to open her mouth to apologize when she feels the urgent tug deep in her belly. "Oh, I'm getting summoned!"

"I hope it's Ryan," Kris offers, but it doesn't feel very hopeful.

Skylar reaches out and clasps Kris's hand, giving it a gentle squeeze. "I'm sorry for what I said, but we'll talk when I get back. Okay?"

Kris nods. "Yeah. Now go. I'll try to be here when you get back."

With a last exchange of somber smiles, Skylar lets the metaphysical cord rip her from the demon realm and drag her to the mortal one. As soon as she's making her way through whatever the in-between space is made of, she knows it's Ryan summoning her. Relief floods through her before she even sets foot in the mortal realm. She is so anxious to see the warlock, she doesn't even really focus on what she's wearing. She finds herself in Ryan's kitchen once more, dressed in her comfy gray lounge pants and an oversized t-shirt that hangs precariously off one shoulder. Her bare feet touch down on the tile and her eyes immediately take Ryan in.

The warlock is dressed in nice grey slacks with a white dress shirt. The sleeves are rolled up to the elbow and the top couple of buttons are undone so his pale collarbone peeks out from the opening. The shaggy blond hair is a bit of a mess as if he's been running his fingers through it. Skylar looks him over to make sure he's still in one piece.

"Ryan," Skylar says as the warlock seems to take her in as well. "I see you made it back okay."

"Uh, yeah," Ryan mutters and gestures towards her. "Did I catch you at a bad time?"

Skylar shrugs. "I was just hanging out with Kris. It's fine. So! I'm assuming you summoned me here rather than texting because you have some news."

Ryan blinks and meets her gaze right on. There's something cold and a bit distant there. "Yeah. I met with the Order today."

"I remember," Skylar says. Silence draws out between them, and she wonders why this feels so awkward. Why does her heart do a little flip when they make eye contact? Skylar ruffles her wings to let loose the energy singing around inside her. "Have you decided what else you might want in exchange for the information you gathered?"

Ryan's brow furrows. "I told you when we first met there wasn't anything I wanted."

Skylar sighs and rolls her eyes. "Yes, yes. I remember. How I could I forget?"

"But," Ryan says quickly, "what if there's something I want now that you can't give me?"

"Impossible," she scoffs, even as her heart sinks a little.

Ryan rubs the back of his neck with one hand and drops his gaze to the floor between them. "I want to believe you," he says quietly.

It feels as if the air has been sucked out of Skylar's lungs. "What?" she asks, equally as soft.

"I want to believe everything you've told me," Ryan explains further. He then looks up at her, his eyes seeming to pierce her chest with their intensity. "I want to believe that you're just an unwitting victim in all of this. That you were dealt a bad hand when you were born."

A lump begins to form in Skylar's throat. "What do you mean?"

"Skylar, I learned something today that . . ." He trails off and his eyes dart around the room as if the right words to say would be hidden somewhere on top of the fridge or on a countertop. "Something that made me wonder if I should doubt everything you've told me."

"Ryan," Skylar urges the warlock to look back at her once more. She shifts in the circle, but she has little space to move around in within the lines that lock her in place. Instead, she spreads her wings to block the view of the kitchen behind her as best she can in hopes that those sweet, blue eyes would look back at her. When they do, there is so much emotion swirling in them Skylar can't pick just one out. "I have *never* lied to you," she says, trying to put all her sincerity into the words. "Never."

"I want to believe you," Ryan repeats. "I want . . ." The words trail off again.

"What do you want?" Skylar asks, her heart racing. Something in the way Ryan won't look away now makes her skin prickle under the weight of his gaze.

"I want to trust you."

Then he does the last thing Skylar could have ever expected. Something no warlock has ever done in front of her. Ryan, in his black socks, steps across the chalk lines of the summoning circle towards her. Skylar's eyes go wide as she looks down to see that he has purposefully crossed the lines.

"Ryan, what are you doing?" She gasps and tries to take a step back, but the size of the circle won't allow her. "You should never cross the protective barrier of a summoning circle. It's the only thing that keeps you safe from a demon's magic working against you."

Ryan reaches out across the small distance between them. He presses his fingers to Skylar's chin and gently lifts her face to look up at him. Skylar wraps her fingers around his wrist and forearm as if to keep herself grounded.

"I'm choosing what I want," he says firmly. Ryan's voice is so deep it sends shivers down Skylar's spine despite how hot her skin feels at the warlock's touch. "And I want to trust you. I want—" Skylar sees Ryan's gaze drop her to lips. "No," he corrects himself. "May I, Skylar? Without me being a warlock and you being a demon, may I kiss you without it being a wish you have to fulfill?"

Time freezes as Skylar's heart skips a beat. And in that moment she can see only the sadness and the longing in Ryan's eyes. It feels like Ryan really does want nothing more than to trust her, nothing more than to seal that trust in a kiss. Only then does Skylar realize that she wants that, too. Never was a summoning with a warlock about what Skylar wants, but here she finds herself. "Yes," she breathes.

Ryan's hand comes up to cup the back of Skylar's neck and pull her closer. His other hand, still trapped in Skylar's grasp, drops from her chin, which leads Skylar to clutch his arm to her chest as her eyes flutter shut. The warlock's soft lips are warm as they press with so much certainty against Skylar's. The kiss is relatively chaste for all of the heat that it carries with it, just lips and the mingling of their breath. Skylar's blood pounds in her ears as her hands slip from Ryan's arm to grab at his waist, her fingers digging into the unbelievably soft fabric of his slacks. Ryan uses his free hand to ghost his fingertips along Skylar's exposed nape before gently gripping her shoulder, goosebumps rising along on her skin.

When the kiss finally breaks, Skylar is left searching to find her breath again. Her eyes flutter open to find Ryan already looking back at her. "I am choosing to trust you," he reiterates.

Those words dampen the thrill of the kiss. Skylar's initial smile turns into a frown. "You learned something horrible today, didn't you?" Her words come out a whisper.

Ryan swallows and his hands drop from her, leaving her bereft of his touch. In return, Skylar releases her hold on Ryan's hips. Freed from the embrace, Ryan takes a couple of steps back until he is on the outside of the circle once more. Skylar's heart drops. Despite the man's claims to trust her, he's left the circle before sharing his knowledge.

"I learned how demons are made," Ryan says, his voice filled with something heavy. Sorrow? Regret?

Fear shoots through Skylar. This is the information she's always sought, but the look on Ryan's face makes her second guess how badly she wants to know. Still, they've come too far now. Ryan can't carry this knowledge alone, even if in this exact moment Skylar wishes he would. It takes an eternity for her to force her mouth to form the word. "How?"

Ryan licks his lips as his hands become fists at his sides. "When a warlock kills another warlock, the murderer is sentenced to become a demon in the demon realm."

Skylar gasps, her hands flying to cover her mouth. That is so much worse than she'd ever imagined. Over the years she has wondered if it was some sort of punishment, but she'd never fathomed murder.

A prison is still a prison, no matter how nice it may seem.

"That can't be." Skylar shakes her head as she tries to make sense of this new information. "Why would they send *children* to a prison for murderers? I was only thirteen when I was taken from my home and sent to the demon realm against my will!"

"I don't know." Ryan's voice is quiet and sounds far away through the blood rushing in Skylar's ears. "I just know that for centuries it has been common warlock practice. The ultimate punishment for warlocks. They did it to the man who killed my great-great-grandfather."

The last statement is cold and Skylar's eyes open wide, both in surprise and to stop the tears that threaten to spill from them. Ryan is watching her as if weighing her reaction. This is all too much. She wishes that she could undo this. That she could give back this unwanted information. If Ryan's relative was killed by a warlock, and that warlock was sent to the demon realm, that means Skylar is trapped in the demon realm with that murderer.

"Who?" The question comes out unbidden, but it's too late now. Skylar has to know.

Ryan, for what it's worth, looks torn. She doesn't know what Ryan expects from her, but he seems swayed by Skylar's shock. He frowns and glances away. "He was my great-great-grandfather's closest friend. The name the Order gave me is Warren Hayes.

All the confusion, all the anger, all the fear – all of it just stops. "No," Skylar says firmly. Warren is a lot of things, but Skylar refuses to believe he's a killer. "That can't be right."

Ryan blinks. "Skylar, do you know him?"

"Better than I know you," Skylar huffs. As soon as the words come out of her mouth, she regrets them. "Warren took me in when I was sent to the demon realm. He's a lot of things: pompous, arrogant, stuck in his ways. The one thing he isn't is a murderer."

A grimace forms on Ryan's face. "Are you sure about that?"

Is she?

Skylar feels like she is sure, but then she remembers her last visit to the demon with Kris. Warren had been scary. He also reacted very badly to Ryan's picture on her phone. Suddenly, Warren's words come back to her.

"Are you a Smith?" Dread bubbles up in Skylar's chest as Ryan's gaze snaps up with surprise. "Is that it? Ryan Smith?"

"How did you know?" Ryan seems frozen in place, but the air is static with tension. Or is it magic?

"I didn't," Skylar admits. "I think you need to send me back, *Warlock Smith.*"

A visible shudder ripples through the warlock, like it does anytime she invokes his title. "What?"

"I don't know what's going on here," she tries to explain. "Either the Order lied to you, or I've been lied to. I need to find out which it is, but I can't do that from here."

Even as she says it, she knows that isn't the whole truth. Warren has never lied to her. He's withheld certain truths, but never flat out lied. And despite the memory of Ryan's lips on her own, she needs to put some distance between herself and the warlock so she can think clearly.

"Skylar," Ryan says, confusion and hurt in his eyes. "I don't understand what you're saying."

"I was warned to avoid warlocks named Smith," Skylar replies. "And I think it's time I found out why."

Ryan nods as if that makes sense, but he still looks a bit like a kicked kitten. "Will you text me when you find out?"

Skylar wants to say yes, but she knows that depends on what she learns. "I don't know," she offers instead, honestly.

"Skylar—" Ryan's voice sounds defeated.

Only then does Skylar realize the kind of day Ryan must have had before he had to deal with her own freak-out, but it's too late to try to fix it. Before she can try to reassure either Ryan or herself, the warlock is muttering the words.

"I release you back to the demon realm."

The last thing Skylar sees is Ryan's trembling bottom lip. She very much wants to reach out and stop it, despite whether or not he is a Smith. However, that's never an option even if she could reach through the barrier as the floor drops out beneath her feet and she is sent back to her prison. A prison for murderers and children.

Well, more specifically, she's sent back to Kris's apartment.

Skylar looks around, wide-eyed, for any sign of the horned demon. Fear shoots through her at the thought of telling Kris what Ryan just shared with her. She knows her best friend won't believe her. Skylar doesn't want to believe it, but she has to know for sure.

Luck is with her in that case. A purple piece of paper sits on Kris's coffee table with one word written in her friend's neat handwriting: *summoned*.

So Kris is out for the time being. For once, Skylar hopes it isn't with Justin. Ryan may have told his friends what he learned, and Skylar doubts Bunny would think twice about sharing that information with Kris. She secretly hopes that Kris has been summoned by a crotchety old warlock who wants something petty and vain to cover how awful they are as a person. That would save Skylar from having to explain to her best friend that things are so much worse than she catastrophized.

Skylar pulls out her phone and taps out a quick message.

Skylar

I'm coming over, now. You better be there.

She puts her phone back in her pocket and looks down at her outfit. It doesn't scream "power suit," so she quickly changes. Instead of lounge clothes, she opts for black slacks with a matching double breasted coat. The white shirt underneath is made of sheer lace.

Then, without waiting for a reply, she makes her way toward Warren's as fast as she can: leaving Kris's apartment and teleporting directly to the older demon's building. She then storms through the lobby and takes the elevator up to Warren's floor. She all but flies down the hall, her wings held high behind herself, to pound on Warren's door.

"Let me in!" she cries. "I swear, Warren, if you're in there and ignoring me . . ." Skylar trails off. She doesn't know what she *can* do, but it feels like the appropriate thing to say as she continues to slam her fist against the door.

After a few minutes it becomes increasingly obvious that Warren is not coming to the door. Perhaps he isn't even home.

Skylar pulls out her phone and checks the message. It hasn't even been read. She grunts and slams her forehead against the door impeding her as the anger and fear deflate within her chest. She is no longer welcome past the wards since she hasn't lived with Warren in years.

Perhaps this is for the best, she tries to reason with herself. Warren will not respond positively to a yelling Skylar. She tries to rein in her fear and doubt so she can talk to the demon rationally. Warren never responds well to emotional outbursts. She needs to find the right words to throw the guarded man off kilter enough to get the truth from him.

Either time goes faster than Skylar notices or Warren is home more quickly than she expects. Suddenly the door is thrown open and Skylar has to throw her hands out to catch the door frame to keep from toppling over. Warren stands in the open doorway, wearing a dark green suit with a black button-up underneath which only further brings out the green of his scales. He stands tall, towering over Skylar as she rights herself.

"Skylar, I didn't expect to see you this evening. Is everything all right?" His eyes glance over Skylar's shoulder. "Alone this time?"

"Yes," Skylar replies curtly and straightens the lapels of her jacket. "May I come in?"

"Of course." Warren steps aside and lets Skylar brush past him into the sitting room. "To what do I owe the pleasure of your company?" He shuts the door before trailing in behind her and conjuring a tea tray onto the coffee table.

Ignoring the tea, Skylar strides past the seating area to the far side of the room before turning to face Warren. The other demon, ever a gracious host, remains standing as he watches Skylar. She has no idea how to start the conversation, so she goes for blunt and straightforward.

"Warren, I believe you've never flat-out lied to me, but I need you to be very honest with me right now," Skylar begins. "I know you haven't told me certain things out of some strange sense of superiority or misguided protection, but I've been told something I can't believe unless you confirm it."

Warren's eyes widen in surprise, the only sign of his state of mind before his cool exterior slides back into place. "Skylar, if I haven't told you something, has it ever occurred to you that I was doing it for your own good?"

Skylar bites her bottom lip as she watches this man, her mentor, the first demon to take care of her after she was brought to the demon realm. "Yes," she replies honestly. "But I'm not a thirteen-year-old kid anymore. I think I deserve more than that."

A frown forms on Warren's full lips as he glances down. "Yes, I suppose you do," he says. He then goes ahead and sits in the large Chesterfield chair. His long, thin fingers run through his dark hair, pushing it back from his forehead so the scales along his hairline are visible for a brief moment. "Have you ever considered that maybe I couldn't tell you everything for my own protection?"

Skylar's jaw clenches. "Not until this evening," she says through clenched teeth. She moves to the armchair across from where Warren sits. Skylar doesn't feel comfortable closing the distance between them just yet. The man's quiet stillness feels like a coiled snake, able to strike at any moment. "Would you like a chance to tell me the truth yourself, or are you going to make me ask?"

Warren glances across at her and, for the first time ever, he looks tired. "I don't know what you think you know," he says, "so I don't know what truth you seek. But I doubt it's anything that will improve your life."

A growl crawls it way up Skylar's throat. "I don't care about if something will make me happy or not, only if it's the truth," she declares. "So tell me the truth: where did the first demon come from?"

The snake-like demon's yellow-slitted eyes lock onto hers. He folds his hands in his lap, but his knuckles turn white with tension. "From the mortal realm."

"Tell me," Skylar demands. "Tell me why we are forced to live *here*." She gestures to the room, but the intention is clear.

Warren's eyes narrow at her. "I don't know what you want me to tell you."

"The truth!" Skylar throws her hands up in exasperation.

"Legend was that the first demon sent to the demon realm was sent here as a punishment," Warren states as a matter of fact, as if reciting from a book.

"For murder," Skylar prompts him.

Warren's face hardens. "That's supposedly why," he grants her. "I've never spoken to the first demon. And so many of the old ones claim to be him, so who knows? Documentation is lacking."

"And that's why *you're* here." Skylar states it as if it's fact, trying to get something from the other demon. Anything.

This time heat flashes in Warren's eyes. "No," he seethes.

"I told you not to lie to me!" Skylar springs up from her seat. "Why are you lying to me, Warren *Hayes*?"

As soon as those words leave her lips, Warren looks as if he's been physically struck. There's no doubt in Skylar's mind that Hayes is his surname as his jaw drops and his eyes go wide. "How do you know that name?"

"Surprised?" Skylar practically laughs with the amount of anxious energy shooting through her. "You murdered a warlock named Smith and that's why you were sent here to the demon realm!"

"Lies!" Warren slams his palms against the arms of his chair before he shoots up from where he sat. "I warned you, Skylar. All Smiths do is lie and manipulate people. Thomas Andrew Smith was a madman! He was going to put everyone in danger!"

"So you murdered him?" The question slips through her lips before she can second guess herself, not sure if she is goading Warren anymore or if the energy has wound so tightly it's out of her control.

"I *stopped* him," Warren hisses. "I did what no one around him would do. He had his cult of fanatics, but I saw though his bullshit and was able to understand the consequences of what he was trying to do."

Skylar cries out in frustration. "What does that even mean? What was he trying to do?"

"Thomas Andrew Smith wanted to create an army and take over the world." Warren strode around the coffee table to close the distance. "Did I kill him? Is that what you really want to know, Skylar?"

She looks up at Warren, whose breath was ragged and eyes hard. "Yes," she replies firmly.

"Then yes, I did. I killed him or he would have killed me," Warren says quietly, and it sucks the wind right out of Skylar's sails. Tears, real actual tears, threaten to spill from Warren's eyes as he meets Skylar's gaze. Only then does she realize tears are already streaming down her own face. "He was my best friend. I didn't want to kill him, but he left me no choice. Then his followers accused me of murdering him out of jealousy. *That* is how I wound up here, Skylar."

Skylar feels her heart swell with sympathy for this man before her. Warren always seemed so strong to her, but now she can see past the mask to the broken individual underneath. "How do I know you're telling me the truth?" she asks meekly. She doesn't want to believe this horrible story.

"I guess that's up to you to decide," Warren says, his voice thick with emotion. "For what it's worth, no one else has believed me either."

"Warren," she says softly.

The older demon sighs. "I think I've had enough baring my soul for one evening," Warren says quietly. He looks more than tired. He looks bone weary exhausted. "Think about what I said. About everything I've ever taught you. You're a smart woman, Skylar. You can figure it out."

"Why?" Skylar asks. This is the real answer she wants. "Why would they send children to a prison with murderers?"

Warren shrugs. "If I had to guess? The first warlocks that created a demon didn't expect there would ever be children of demons. We can't breed with one another so where would children even come from? They didn't take into account or just didn't know that we could still copulate with mortals."

Skylar's lip trembles. It's a horrible answer, but it makes so much sense. "Warren—"

The demon holds up his hand. "No more tonight, Skylar. Please."

How can Skylar refuse when Warren looks so dejected? "Okay, but we will talk about this again." She doesn't make it a request.

"If we must," he sighs. "Just be careful, Skylar. Don't trust what any warlock tells you. They only care about themselves."

"I guess you would know," Skylar replies before her brain can filter the words coming from her mouth.

"Better than most." Warren sighs deeply. "Now, kindly get the fuck out."

Skylar nods. Seeing Warren look so sad and hurt takes all the fight out of her. She doesn't want to believe any of it, but Skylar feels completely overwhelmed. So she strides out of Warren's apartment and makes her way out of the building. Without even thinking of where she is going next, she keeps walking.

Thoughts swirl around in her head as she tries to untangle everything she thought she knew from what she's been told this evening. Her tears dry on her face.

Unfortunately, what Warren has already taught her lines up with Ryan's assertion. The demon realm is a prison, a prison made for murderous warlocks. The offspring of demons and humans are just an unfortunate side effect of the spell the warlocks built to create demons. However, that doesn't align with what she knows of Warren. Could being a demon for half a century have changed him so much from the warlock he was? Or was he falsely accused?

It isn't until she's walking through the door that Skylar realizes she auto-piloted home. She finds herself standing in her living room.

It is late.

She is tired.

After checking her phone, she realizes she doesn't have any new messages from Kris. She quickly shoots him a text.

Without really wanting to, she checks to see if there are any messages from Ryan. There aren't. The last messages are them wishing each other good night before he went to join the Order.

Her bed is calling her. To avoid obsessively checking her phone, Skylar turns it off. Really, she doesn't need to. It never needs to be charged. This is the metaphysical equivalent of putting it on silent. She won't get any messages until she turns it back on. As further deterrence from wanting to check it, she leaves the phone in her living room before slumping off to her bedroom. A quick change into a pair of sleep shorts and a large, soft sweater occurs as she crawls onto the bed and settles between the cool sheets.

As she closes her eyes, the memory of Ryan crossing over the protection circle comes to her mind unbidden. How she wishes that was where the evening had ended. Her chest swells with sadness at the memory of how Ryan's lips felt against hers. What if that is the last kiss they will ever share? Skylar didn't even get a chance to properly embrace him before the warlock stepped back out of the circle. Could Skylar disregard everything Warren said about the Smiths in some ridiculous hope to taste Ryan's lips one more time?

Trust isn't something demons deal with very often. There doesn't need to be trust between them and the warlocks who summon them. In fact, the very existence of a protection circle reveals an inherent distrust on the part of the warlocks.

As a child Skylar had trusted easily and made many friends, but as a demon there are only two beings she really trusts. Warren (though she also trusts Warren to keep things from her) and Kris. She doesn't even fully trust Omar and Derek. They are fun, but she knows in the end they are devoted to one another. Skylar is just an occasional party favor. So, can she trust Ryan? Did Ryan's choice to believe in her make a difference?

At some point she falls into a fitful sleep. Only Kris arriving at some point to crawl into bed with her finally calms her turbulent mind. The demon's long arms wind around her and pull her into a hug, his fingers brushing over her wings as she lays on her side. Warm, friendly lips press to her forehead. Skylar takes a deep breath and smells only Kris's clean, reassuring scent.

"Shh," Kris whispers. Skylar isn't even sure she tried to speak, but that doesn't stop Kris from trying to soothe her. "Sleep. We'll talk in the morning."

And just like that, Skylar is out like a light. No swirling thoughts of murder, unfair punishments, or kisses disturb her for the rest of the night.

17

Going Digital

SKYLAR VANISHES FROM THE circle and Ryan collapses into the kitchen chair behind him, dropping his head to the tabletop. His skin feels like it is burning compared to the cool table surface. The magic he swallowed that afternoon still hums through his body and it came alight at the first touch of his fingers to Skylar's skin. Maybe that's why he got carried away? He squeezes his eyes shut and tries to get his thoughts in order. Nothing this evening went the way he had planned.

He's gotten the answer Skylar has been looking for, but apparently it isn't what the demon wanted to hear. Ryan has also learned what had happened to Thomas Andrew Smith, which he wishes he could unlearn. The thrill of getting into the Order is suddenly feeling like regret. And now he is stuck there. He has sworn an oath, was given a fancy robe, and his own membership book. When he finally got back to Justin's car after the meeting, able to prove he is okay, Ethan had been so excited. It was contagious. There is still a wealth of knowledge inside the Order that Ryan has access to. If he no longer has Skylar to teach him (which scares him as he sits alone in his kitchen) then he isn't completely without options.

Ryan sits up and pulls his phone from his pocket. The urge to text Skylar and make sure she's okay is strong, but he knows it's too soon. Instead, he turns the phone off and trudges to his bedroom. He peels himself out of his clothes before collapsing face first into the bed.

Fuck everything.

He just wants to go to sleep. To wake up tomorrow with a text from Skylar asking him what he's been up to. To pictures of the demon and her friend. To anything but this hollowed out feeling in his chest. He tries to push away the image of Skylar staring at him with a look of betrayal. Never has he seen

Skylar looking so soft and breathtakingly beautiful. She looked much like she did in the candid Kris had sent Ryan of the two of them in their comfy lounge clothes. There was a lack of artifice. If felt like the Skylar he's been texting for weeks and he drifts to sleep with hopes of seeing her again.

Ryan wakes up the next day to the sound of movement in his kitchen. He scrambles out of bed, not caring that he's in just his boxers and socks, and storms into the kitchen to confront the intruders. He finds Justin standing at his stove as the smell of bacon cooking wafts through the kitchen. Ethan sits at his tiny table facing Justin, but has turned his head to look at Ryan as he comes in.

"Good morning," Justin chirps as he flips the bacon in the sizzling pan.

"How did you get in here?" Ryan looks between them in utter disbelief.

Ethan grins. "That would be Justin's doing."

Smiling proudly, Justin puts the tongs down to reach into his back pocket. He pulls out a stick, no bigger than a pencil, that has been carved down and designed with an intricate swirling pattern.

Ryan blinks at him, then towards Ethan. "Really? A fucking wand?"

"Not everyone can do magic without tools like you," Ethan reminds him.

Justin pouts as he turns back to the pan. "I made it myself," he mumbles, slipping the wand back into his pocket before picking up the tongs once more to tend to his bacon.

Ryan feels guilty. As much as he's been scared of learning more about magic, Justin has been excited. And Ryan hasn't done anything to encourage his friend. "You did well, Justin," he says and goes over to pat the younger man on the shoulder. "But what does that have to do with you being in my kitchen?"

"He used the wand to cast a spell to unlock your door," Ethan explains. "It was really neat."

"And a little disconcerting," Ryan adds. "I'm glad it was you, Justin, but if anyone can do that—"

"Wards!" Ethan suddenly shouts, interrupting Ryan. "I've seen mentions of warding in the books I have. You can make a ward so that people can't enter your home without your permission. Or only certain people can cross the threshold."

"That would be handy against burglars," Ryan reasons, but he really just wants to make sure that none of his new "friends" at the Order can just come traipsing in. "Can you bring the book with you next time?"

Ethan nods. "I could, but if you want, I'll snap pictures of the relevant pages and send them to you as soon as I get home."

"Thanks." Ryan is relieved that Ethan guessed the urgency with which Ryan wants to prevent anyone else entering his home.

"Had another late-night summoning?" Justin asks as he finishes plating the last of the bacon. He brings the plate of meat over to the table where there are already three plates of toast with fried eggs on top.

Ryan looks down at the summoning circle still sketched across the floor. He didn't even bother to try to clean it up last night, which is careless. "Yeah. I had to tell Skylar what I learned."

Justin nods and piles some bacon onto one of the plates. "Did you tell Kris, too?"

"No, but I assume Skylar will tell him." Ryan picks up one of the plates and grabs a few pieces of bacon himself despite the way his stomach sinks at the thought. Will Kris be as untrusting towards him as Skylar? Ryan takes his plate and stands against the counter so his two guests can sit at the table.

"I guess I just assumed you'd tell them both." Justin slips into the empty seat without argument. He shrugs as he digs into his own food.

Ethan takes the last plate and starts to eat as well. "What did the demon say about your findings?"

"She didn't seem to like what I had to say," Ryan admits. He looks at the food on the plate before giving up and setting it on the counter beside him.

"Was she unhappy?" Ethan frowns around a mouthful of egg.

Ryan scoffs. "You could put it that way. You could also say she might have been angry. Shocked? Incredulous?"

"I wish I'd summoned Kris last night," Justin mumbles, mostly to himself. "Maybe I could have phrased it better."

"Hey!" Ryan gives a cry of indignation.

"No offense," Justin is quick to apologize. "You can just be really sullen."

Ethan nods in agreement. "You can be."

Ryan huffs. "Thanks guys. Good morning to you, too."

"Is she okay?" Ethan asks, his plate only half eaten in contrast to Justin's nearly empty one.

"I don't know," Ryan sighs. He glances back at his food, feeling even worse that Justin made food and he just doesn't have any appetite. "She demanded I send her back and I haven't heard from her since."

"Could it be because you left your phone in here?" Ryan points at the device still sitting on the kitchen table.

Ryan scoops up the phone and turns it on. The screen flashes as it powers to life and connects to both his world and the demon realm. He opens his messages, but there is nothing new from Skylar. Just texts in the group chat with Justin and Ethan that they were on their way over.

"Nothing new," Ryan confirms. He tries to put the phone back in his pocket to realize that he is still just in his boxers. "I'm going to go put clothes on."

Justin smirks. "I don't think anyone is complaining."

Ethan gives a shocked laugh as Ryan playfully flips Justin the bird before shuffling out of the kitchen and back to his room.

After a quick shower and a change of clothes, he comes back to find Justin has cleaned up from breakfast. His own plate has been cleared without a word. The three of them settle in the living room and Ryan runs his fingers through his damp hair. "So, now what?" He slumps into the couch.

"Are you going to text Skylar, or wait for her to text you first?" Justin asks. He is sitting on the floor facing Ethan and Ryan on the couch.

"I'll give it another day," Ryan decides. "Not what I was talking about, though. I was thinking more along the lines of: now that I'm in the Order, what's next?"

Ethan pulls his leg up underneath himself so he can twist in his seat and face Ryan. "Well, now you have access to all their books!" He smiles widely.

"Do you think they'll let me check them out? Like a library?" Ryan ponders aloud.

"That would be amazing." Ethan's eyes light up with excitement.

Justin has taken out his phone and is tapping away. "What do you think they're going to want from you?" He asks the question without looking up from his phone.

Ethan's eyebrows knit together in a frown. "What do you mean?"

Ryan crosses his arms over his chest. "It seems, to me, that this all went too smoothly." Justin nods, but lets Ryan continue. "There seems to be a lot of excitement about the fact that I am a Smith. And that is one of the things that Skylar seems most upset about."

That gets Justin to look up from his phone. "Wait, really?"

"Yeah," Ryan sighs and drops his head to the back of the couch. He shuts his eyes and can still see Skylar's look of betrayal. Or something akin to it. "I guess she was told not to trust any warlocks named Smith."

"Weird," Ethan comments before there's a long pause as if he's putting together the pieces. "Wait, if she knew your surname, then that means—"

"—that she has connections to the ex-warlock-turned-demon who killed Thomas Andrew Smith," Ryan finishes for him. He lifts his head to find both Justin and Ethan staring at him in awe.

"Fuck," Justin states succinctly. "That's some star-crossed-lovers shit right there."

"Hey," Ryan frowns, but feels a rush of heat to his cheeks. Ethan just nods in agreement and Ryan can't help but squirm in his seat. He hasn't even mentioned the kiss from last night, how the hell are they jumping to labeling him and Skylar as lovers? "Don't you think that's a bit hyperbolic?"

"Nope," both Ethan and Justin say in unison.

"You forget," Justin adds as he leans his elbows on the coffee table. "I've known you the longest. I know how infatuated-Ryan acts."

Ryan rolls his eyes. "And how does 'infatuated-Ryan' act?"

Justin starts ticking off the points on his fingers. "He texts the object of his infatuation every day. He makes up excuses to spend time with them, even if a simple text would do. He turns bright pink when you point it out to him."

Despite how much Ryan wants to dispute all of those, Ryan does feel the heat rushing to his cheeks and down his neck. "I feel like texting is a dumb indicator. It's the easiest way to contact the demon realm."

"You made a cross-dimensional connection in order to text her," Ethan points out. "That's kind of a big deal."

Ryan groans. "Okay, but what about the other stuff? It's not like I can just hang out with Skylar whenever."

"True," Just concedes. "But you did summon her here last night rather than just text her what you learned."

"I told her I'd summon her if it wasn't a simple response," Ryan huffs.

Justin holds up both hands and then drops each finger word-by-word. "Demons used to be warlocks who killed other warlocks." He only has one finger remaining. "Nine words. Done."

Ethan nods. "He has a point. You could have sent her that information over text."

"Okay, we are getting way off topic here," Ryan groans. "Enough about Skylar, what about the Order?"

Justin shrugs and picks up his phone.

"I guess try to learn more about being a warlock?" Ethan tries to help.

Justin sighs without looking up from his phone. "I'd be wary of them," he says ominously. "Remember the first time you met with Alexander Kim? The only reason you got a meeting with the Order was because of that tome you've got."

"Oh," Ethan exclaims and points a finger in the air. "Also, wasn't Dahlia kind of disappointed you didn't have the book with you when we all went to the estate together?"

"Yeah," Ryan admits. "But she didn't bring it up again when I went to join."

"Not at all?" Ethan asks.

"Well," Ryan sighs. "She may have mentioned it was the last remaining copy."

"I'd bet a hundred bucks the next time you show up without it, they ask you to bring it to them," Justin says. He finally puts his phone back down to look up at them. "If it's the only one of its kind left, they are going to want it."

Ethan shifts in his seat and stretches his long legs out under the coffee table. "Well, isn't preserving knowledge one of the Order's main tenets?"

"It is," Ryan confirms. "I'm just worried if I bring the book there, it won't be coming back home with me."

"That's a pretty legitimate concern," Ethan acknowledges.

Silence falls between them. Rather, Ryan and Ethan fall into contemplation whereas Justin goes back to typing on his phone. Ryan wants to figure out how to get the Order to trust him without bringing the book to them, but his thoughts eventually drift back to Skylar. Is she okay? Did she go to confront a murderer? Can demons kill one another? Is Skylar hurt? Or did this Warren guy convince her that Ryan isn't trustworthy?

"Know what would be helpful?" Ethan's voice breaks the silence. He shifts and sits up again to rest his elbows on his knees. "Finding out what your book has that the Order doesn't already know."

Ryan is thankful for the distraction. "Yeah, but I don't know how to do that without bringing the book there. I have one very thick book whereas they have a giant library and archives."

Ethan nods. "What if we make a copy of the book?"

"Do you have a skill set I'm unaware of that you can make books and not just sell them?" Ryan gives Ethan a deadpan look.

"No," Ethan rolls his eyes. "But I have a scanner. We can make a digital copy of the book, so that way if something happens to the physical one, we still have all the information."

As much as Ryan is reticent to hand over the copy of his book, the idea of having a digital back-up is highly appealing. Even if they don't lose the book to the Order, any number of other things could happen to it. "I like this idea."

"We can go back to my place and do it today," Ethan smiles. "It'll take a while since the book has so many pages, but if no one else is doing anything, we can all hang out."

Ryan smiles at his friend. He really appreciates Ethan's offer to let them all come over rather than just ask for the book. "I've got nothing pressing," he confesses. Work is the last thing he could focus on right now, even if he tries.

Justin groans. "I have a photo shoot this afternoon." He pockets his phone again. "I don't mind driving everyone over there now, but I've got a slew of consultations today." And so Justin drops Ryan and Ethan off at Ethan's apartment, only stopping in for a glass of water before taking off for his work appointment.

Ryan realizes he's never been inside Ethan's place before. The apartment is more like a studio space right above the bookshop and is much nicer than his own basement apartment. There's a set of stairs leading up to an open platform where the man's bedroom is arranged. The kitchen and living room are all one large open space separated only by a breakfast bar of sorts. There is a single door off the main room to the bathroom on the ground floor other than the door in and out, but there is a large wall of windows that allow a lot of natural light in. Which is great, because Ethan has a lot of plants. That doesn't really surprise Ryan about the man, but he does note that there is no television that he can see. Just a comfy seating area surrounded by plants and walls lined with bookshelves along with a home desk setup.

"Nice place," Ryan comments as Ethan settles at his desk and unburies the scanner from beneath a pile of books.

"Thanks," Ethan says. He boots up the computer. "Oh, while we're here, you can look for that warding spell we talked about."

"That's a good idea." Ryan pulls the large tome out of his bag, but he has to wait for Ethan to clear more papers out of the way. The desk is cluttered, but not a disorganized kind of clutter. Like a well-used mess of books and pages. Ryan then steps back and watches as Ethan opens the book to the first page and places it on the machine to start scanning. "Are you sure your scanner is weight-rated for that monstrosity of a book?"

"I'm sure it'll be fine," Ethan chuckles as he starts up the machine and it whirs to life. He then points to a bookcase closer to the couches. "The books I have on magic are over there. I forget which one has the wards though."

"That's fine. This is going to take a long time." As if emphasizing Ryan's point, Ethan lifts the heavy book to turn the page and places it on the scanner. "Tell you what, I'll order lunch and then start looking through the books."

"Thanks," Ethan smiles softly as he clicks the button to scan the next set of pages.

Ryan pulls out his phone and orders them lunch for delivery. Despite his lack of appetite, Ryan is aware he has to eat. He knows Ethan really likes ramen, so he gets them each a bowl.

Then he goes over to the bookcase and easily finds Ethan's small collection of books on magic. He bypasses the copy of The Order of Knowing Well's membership book. He has his own copy at home, and his own is a much more updated version. He goes ahead and picks up the glossary figuring it may be helpful and a handful of other beginner guides. The books on history of magic doesn't seem like the right place to look for actual spells. He then settles on the couch, placing the small stack on the wood coffee table, and begins looking through the first book.

Lots of the information in the small spellbook seems accessible to him. It is as if he's spent all his time trying to read an advanced calculus book and is just handed a primer on addition. The words are familiar and everything is explained at a beginner's level. In fact, the first spell he reads is how to create a tool for magic use. A warlock can enchant a small object such as an orb, a crystal, or a wand. Ryan figures this must have been what Justin did to create the wand he was carrying around that morning.

"Ethan," Ryan calls out over the thrum of the scanner. "Do you think I should create a wand or something?"

Ethan hums as he continues to scan pages. "To be honest, it doesn't seem like you need one," he finally concludes. "However, it could be useful. A way to focus the magic? Or make you seem more like a normal warlock?"

Ryan nods even though Ethan isn't looking towards him. "That's what I was thinking. Doesn't a wand seem a little, I don't know, silly?"

"I think it's cool." Ethan turns another page and re-positions the book. "But I think there's other things you can use."

"I'll think about it." Ryan pulls out his phone and takes a quick picture of the magic circle needed to enchant the item so that he can copy it at home. He then takes another quick picture of the incantation.

It is nearly twenty minutes later when the doorbell rings. Ryan has only gotten through about half of the book by just skimming the subtitles of each section and bypassing anything that doesn't interest him, but he does take a few minutes to look over a spell for repairing small broken items.

"Must be the food. I'll get it," Ryan says. He sets the book face down on the coffee table to keep his place as he stands up. After paying for the bowls of noodles, Ryan deposits one next to Ethan and takes the other back to the coffee table. He quickly eats the soup before picking up the books again. Ethan, he notices, will take a bite each time the pages are scanning and then carefully wipe his hands before touching the pages again.

Ryan gets through the first primer and is a quarter of the way through the second when the bell rings again. "I've got it," he reassures Ethan who is still eating as he scans. He half expects it to be Justin rushing back to join them after his photo shoot, but he's surprised to see a different face.

"Oh, hey!" Nadia smiles at Ryan. She has her lanyard from the bookstore around her neck and looks genuinely surprised to find Ryan at the door. "I didn't know you were going to be up here."

Ryan blinks. "Hey, Nadia."

"Is Ethan in?" Her eyes drift over Ryan's shoulder as if trying to find the bookstore owner.

"Ethan," Ryan calls, opening the door fully and stepping aside. "You have a guest."

The man swivels in the chair and his eyebrows climb high in surprise. "Nadia, hey," he says jumping up from the chair. He comes over to the door, so Ryan steps back out of the way. "Is there a problem?"

She tucks a stray curl from her ponytail behind her ear. "Yeah, sorry for bugging you on your day off." She shrugs. Ryan wanders back to the couch trying not to eavesdrop, but it's hard when they are all in the same open space.

"It's fine," Ethan shakes his head and Ryan eyes the man's back curiously. "What's the problem?"

"The P.O.S. system disconnected and while I can get it most of the way back up, they want the owner of the service to authorize new sales before they allow any more to go through," Nadia explains and half of the context goes over Ryan's head. "I have them on the phone downstairs, if you have a moment."

"Yeah, I'll go down and sort this out," Ethan agrees. "Hey, Ryan. I'll be back as soon as I can. Feel free to keep reading, or go ahead and take over the scanning if you're up for it."

Ryan blinks and glances towards the book laying open on the scanner. He doesn't know how long Ethan will take, but it feels kind of selfish to expect him to do all of it by himself. "Yeah, sure. I can take over."

Ethan shoots him an apologetic wave and follows Nadia back downstairs.

Ryan gets up and makes his way over the scanner. He's scanned stuff before, but he doesn't want to mess up the other man's set up. He tentatively pokes around and, realizing the pages face down in the scanner bed have already been scanned, he picks up the book and turns the page to keep the process going. He's a little disappointed to realize that it doesn't take very long before his arms start to get sore from the repetitive motion of having to pick the heavy book up off the scanner just to flip one page for each scan. Ethan's biceps are no joke if he's been doing it this long without complaining.

Ryan's mind begins to wander as he continues to work, not really paying attention to the information on the pages as he continues to input them into the computer. Unbidden, Skylar comes to the forefront of his thoughts. It hasn't been 24 hours yet, but he really wants to talk to the demon. Make sure that she's okay. That they are okay.

Maybe he should apologize for the kiss. He felt so drawn to the woman in that moment it felt unavoidable, but in the cold light of day he has second thoughts. Skylar hadn't rejected him or told him to stop. Maybe she thought Ryan had done it to butter her up for the news that was about to follow.

No, Ryan thinks to himself. That doesn't make any sense. In what world would kissing Skylar be any kind of service for her and not purely for Ryan? Shit, what if she couldn't say no? Fuck.

Ethan hasn't even been gone a quarter of an hour, but Ryan's arms are already dying. The sound of his text alert going off is a welcome distraction as he sets the book down to scan the next set of pages. He uses it as an excuse to take a break and see if the message is from Skylar.

Justin

Are you guys still working?

I'll probably be done here in another hour.

Do you guys think you'll still be working on scanning the book?

Ryan

> Don't rush.

> I'm scanning some pages while Ethan is downstairs helping Nadia in the bookstore.

Justin

> Oh, did he come up with an excuse to go down and talk to her?

Ryan

> No. What? Why? She came up and asked for his help.

Justin

> Shame. I was hoping he'd worked up the courage to finally ask her out.

Ethan

> Shut up! I'll be back up in a minute.

Justin

> Oops, back to work!

Ryan chuckles at the messages. By the time he's setting up the scanner to scan the next set of pages, Ethan is coming back through the front door.

"Did you manage to help Nadia with her P.S.O problem?" Ryan smirks.

Ethan gives an exaggerated sigh. "It's P.O.S. for point of sale, and yes—we did manage to get it fixed. So I could, you know, sell books and make a living. I thought you were up here scanning pages, but it turns out you were just gossiping with Justin in our group chat." He comes over and shoos Ryan away from the computer so he can take over, but he's very pointedly not making eye contact.

Ryan crosses his arms, grateful for the relief from scanning the heavy book. "Was he wrong, though?"

"She's an employee and a friend," Ethan grumbles as he waits for the pages to scan before picking up the book once more.

"But do you want there to be romance?" Ryan presses, curious.

"Maybe," Ethan groans and covers his face with both hands. "She's just so friendly. And personable. And always so busy—"

Ryan reaches over and pats Ethan's shoulder. "She definitely has the hustle thing going on. She once asked if I could talk to her about doing freelance work."

"She works too hard." Ethan shakes his head and continues scanning.

Ryan lets it drop. He isn't one to be giving out dating advice. Look where he's at.

They work in a comfortable silence for the next few hours until Justin shows up back at the apartment. He then takes his own turn scanning the book as Ethan and Ryan go through the other books some more.

"Found it," Ethan announces while holding a larger book Ryan had been saving for last out of sheer intimidation. It looks like it is the most complicated of Ethan's collection. Ryan slides across the open space of the couch to look at the pages over Ethan's shoulder.

It is a little more complicated than the simple spells Ryan has considered trying, but not nearly as intricate in design as the demon summoning circle. It involves getting four stones that are then enchanted in a magic circle. The stones are then placed in the four corners of the property or room. This keeps anyone the warlock doesn't grant permission to from entering. Permissions can be changed by re-enchanting the stones and temporary access can be given by invitation only.

"This looks like it could work," Ryan nods as he looks over the spell.

Even Justin has gotten up from the computer and is looking over both their heads from behind the couch. "So, are you going to grant any of us special permission?"

Ryan shoots him a glare over his shoulder. "Why? Do you want to be able to come in whenever you want like you did this morning?"

Justin throws his hands up in defense. "I'm just saying! What if something happens and you need our help, but we can't get through the door?"

"What am I? A senior citizen? Should I get a medical alert button for when I've fallen and can't get up?" Ryan scoffs, but he is only giving the younger a hard time. "Tell you what. I'll give you and Ethan access, but you better believe I will revoke it in a heartbeat if you abuse it."

"Of course!" Justin beams at him.

"Thank you for your trust," Ethan says solemnly.

Ryan feels flustered by their sincerity. "Whatever," he mumbles. "Let me get a quick picture of the pages so I can get the supplies together and do it at home."

Ethan shoves a clean napkin from lunch between the pages and closes the book, offering it to Ryan. "You can just borrow the book."

Ryan blinks at him, accepting the book. "Are you sure?"

Which is how Ryan ends up taking both his book and the spellbook home at the end of the night once the scanning is finished. He also fully intends to go through the loaned book for anything else that may be useful while he has it in his possession.

It does take the rest of the evening to finish going through the pages of the book from his mom's attic and compiling the scans into a digital copy. Since Ryan feels they are all in this together, he agrees to let both Ethan and Justin keep copies of their own. So, on top of the two heavy books he also has a thumb drive with the digital copy in his pocket.

It is late by the time Ryan is putting the original back in its fire safety box and collapsing on his bed, but his mind is still awake. Thoughts of the warding come back to mind. The stones for the spell are specifically hematite stones. Ryan isn't sure he even knows what hematite looks like, so he pulls out his phone and does some searching. Thanks to the wonders of the internet, he can order exactly the type of stones he needs and have them delivered.

He still feels a little antsy, so he gets up and does a little tidying around the apartment. He puts away the clean dishes from that morning and eyes the chalk markings on his kitchen floor. Magic hums along his skin, not intrusive like before but like static in the air. Should he wipe away the circle? What if Skylar texts him and wants to be summoned? He decides to give up on cleaning and wanders back to bed.

It's nearly one in the morning, but it feels like the wheels are still turning in his head. It's been over twenty-four hours since Skylar was last in his apartment. Ryan figures it can't hurt to reach out and try to text her. It is less intrusive than summoning the demon against her will.

Ryan grabs his phone from the bedside table and opens up the chat. He stares at the last exchange between them before he had gone to the Order.

Ryan takes a deep breath and starts typing out a message.

Hey, how's it going?

He immediately deletes it. Will it be better to be direct? Or should he try to pretend nothing is wrong and let Skylar bring it up first?

Hey, you would not believe how embarrassing Ethan is.

He deletes that message, too.

Groaning, Ryan collapses back onto his pillow and lets both of his hands flop to his sides as his phone rests on his sternum. Why is this so hard? He thinks about maybe starting by apologizing, but for what?

It feels insincere to apologize for the kiss because he honestly isn't sorry for doing it. The more he thinks about it, the more he really wants to do it again, actually. The likelihood of Skylar reciprocating those feelings, though, seems pretty low.

Maybe he should apologize for summoning Skylar to tell her the news? Justin is right, he could have done it over text. However, given Skylar's response, he is really glad he didn't do it remotely. He wouldn't have been able to see the demon's reaction.

Ultimately, he decides apologizing isn't the right thing to do either. There is really only one thing he needs to know from Skylar. Everything else is his own problem that he is working up in his head. He finally picks up the phone and types out a message. He hits send before he can second guess himself.

Ryan

Skylar, are you okay?

Ryan holds the phone and stares at the screen until the light dims. He isn't sure if Skylar is busy or just ignoring him. Then the thought that something could be wrong comes back. What if Skylar can't respond?

Quickly, Ryan switches his chat window to the one with Justin.

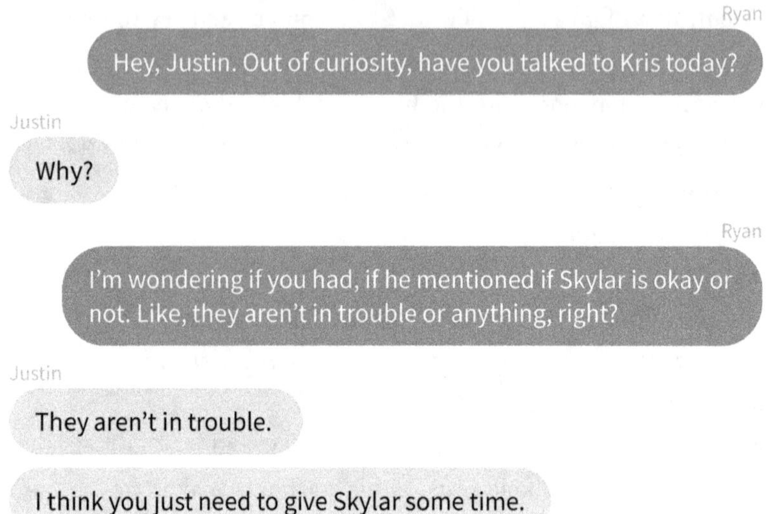

Ryan sighs. What has Skylar told Kris? What has Kris told Justin? Why does this suddenly feel like high school when his first girlfriend told his best friend he prematurely ejaculated in his pants while they were making out and that embarrassing story made its way around his class? He shakes his head.

They are all adults—demon or human—and he really does expect more from everyone involved than that. If Justin says that Skylar is physically safe, then he has to trust that they are.

Justin

Try to get some sleep.

Goodnight.

Before Ryan can even close his chat message with Justin, the phone's alert goes off once more. The notification banner that pops down says *Skylar*.

18

Finding Faith

SKYLAR WAKES UP ALONE after a long dreamless sleep, but Kris's warmth still lingers. She stretches and peers at the clock beside the bed. It is just after eight in the morning. No wonder her stomach feels like a bottomless pit. She went to bed without dinner last night.

She shimmies over and reaches for her phone. When it isn't on her bedside table, she summons it to her hand and turns it on. A brief glance shows she has two new messages, both from last night.

Warren

> I suggest you don't come back until I invite you over.

A thumb swipe and Skylar checks the next message.

Kris

> I was at a summoning. On my way now.

Nothing from Ryan.

She isn't really expecting anything from the warlock, so why is she disappointed? Skylar groans and forces herself out of bed. She follows the smell of baked goods out of her room and into the kitchen where Kris is pulling muffins out of the oven.

"You baked?" Her voice croaks, thick from disuse.

Kris shrugs. "You were out like a light, and I needed to do something with my hands." He sets the muffins out to cool and slaps Skylar's hand away when she reaches for one. "Give it a few minutes," he scolds before pouring each of them a glass of orange juice from a jug she definitely doesn't own and guiding Skylar to sit at the kitchen table. "Are you feeling better?"

Skylar thinks about the question, both hands settling around the cold glass handed to her. Did she feel better? No, she just feels kind of numb. She shrugs. "I'll be okay," she mutters before sipping her juice.

"Want to tell me what happened last night?" Kris gently asks.

Skylar eyes him curiously. "Didn't you talk to Justin last night?"

Kris shakes his head. "Bunny didn't summon me. I was off playing real estate mogul for a warlock. It was boring as fuck."

Not sure if that is better or worse, Skylar chews on her bottom lip. She wanted to be able to tell Kris the information she learned herself, but a secret part of her had hoped Justin would do it for her so she wouldn't have to watch her best friend's look of disappointment. Kris never bought into the notion that the demon realm is a prison like Skylar had been taught. Will he even believe her? Not telling him isn't even an option.

Skylar is pulled out of her thoughts by Kris reaching over and gently tugging her bottom lip free from her teeth with the pad of his thumb. "What's going on in that head of yours?" he prompts.

"I talked to Ryan last night," Skylar chooses to start from the beginning. "He came back from his meeting with the warlocks."

Kris nods. "I'm guessing he had something to report?"

Skylar feels her wings shift and flutter as she tries to think about what to say next.

"I have a feeling we're going to need some muffins for the next part," Kris announces. He jumps up and grabs a few of the muffins before sitting back down next to Skylar. He places one in front of her and then slowly picks at his own.

"Plan: Warlock Spy brought back some disturbing information," Skylar says after a deep breath. Phrasing it like a silly game makes it easier to tell her best friend. Kris reaches out and puts a hand on the back of Skylar's since she hasn't even bothered to touch her own muffin yet. With that bit of encouragement, she goes on. "Apparently demons used to be warlocks."

Kris's mouth drops open, a crumb from his muffin still clinging to his bottom lip. "That confirms our hypothesis! But *why* did they get changed into demons?"

She looks up to meet Kris's eyes. "They were sent here as punishment for killing other warlocks."

A sharp gasp comes from Kris. "No," he whispers.

"Warren all but confirmed it last night," Skylar says, but she feels the tears she's been trying to ignore welling back up. "Kris, he killed Ryan's ancestor. That's why he's here."

"Fuck, that's kind of insane." Kris scoots his chair closer to Skylar's so he can put an arm around her shoulders.

The tears finally win out and spill down her cheeks as a sob escapes Skylar. "Right? How could we end up in a prison for murderers when we were just children?"

"Shit, Sky, I hadn't even thought of that," Kris frowns. "My brain is still processing the implications of what you're saying."

Skylar's brow furrows as she looks at her best friend through the tears. "What are you thinking then?"

Kris hums as he lets go of Skylar's shoulder and rubs slow circles across her shoulders above her wings. "I just can't believe Warren is a killer."

Skylar groans. "That's just the tip of the iceberg," she exclaims. "I confronted Warren about it, and he says it was in self-defense. That Ryan's relative was dangerous."

"He really did seem distrustful when he thought Ryan was someone named Smith," Kris nods. "It must be how he recognized him if the two are related."

"That was why Warren said not to trust him," Skylar sighs, shoulders slumping forward. "And now I don't know who to believe."

"It sounds like a lot," Kris says gently, his voice deep and soothing. "Why don't you calm down, take a deep breath, and start from the beginning?"

Skylar takes more than a few deep breaths and finally feels calm enough to stop crying. She then starts with being summoned by Ryan and recounts the events of last night all the way to Kris crawling into bed with her. Once she is done, it feels like a knot has been undone inside her chest and Skylar is able to breathe a little easier. Kris continues to stroke her back and doesn't interrupt her until she is done.

"Wow, Sky," Kris utters. "That is a lot. And don't think we aren't going to be revisiting that kiss, because we will be. In great detail. But first: do you believe what Ryan told you?"

"It's kind of hard not to when Warren basically confirmed it." She starts to pick at the muffin. The baked good smells delicious and Kris has taken the time and effort to actually make it.

Kris nods. "Yeah, but Ryan is getting his information from another party. Warren was actually there," he points out. "So maybe the truth is somewhere in between?"

When Kris lays it out like that Skylar feels kind of silly for trying to decide which version to believe. "You're probably right," Skylar says, taking a bite of the muffin. It is warm and soft with just the right amount of sweetness from the blueberries baked in. "This is delicious, by the way."

"Let's do this," Kris decides while ignoring the compliment. "We finish our muffins, then you go take a long shower. Then we are going to talk about the kiss."

"*Kriiiis*," Skylar whines, but she can't stop the smile from coming to her lips.

Kris picks up the muffin and presses it to Skylar's lips to shut her up. "Shh, you big baby, and eat your breakfast."

After finishing their muffins Skylar opts to take the suggested shower. She doesn't really want to admit it, but Kris is right. She feels a lot better after a long shower. The tension in the muscles of her back and wings has melted away under the hot water.

When Skylar finally comes back out, Kris is sitting on the couch tapping away at his phone. He doesn't even look up as Skylar sits down next to him and curls into the other demon's side. "Feel better?" is all Kris asks as he continues to type on his phone.

"Maybe," Skylar sighs. She lays with her head on Kris's knee and waits for him to finish with the phone and play with her hair. Skylar has to lay facing his stomach so that her wings can have room off the front of the couch. "Who are you texting?"

Kris's hand finds its way to her head and starts to card through her hair, though his attention is still on his phone. "Bunny," he says. "He texted me while you were in the shower. He's asking if you're okay."

"Fuck," Skylar moans. She squeezes her eyes shut and feels a heat rush to her cheeks. Obviously, the warlock has been talking to Ryan, but how much did Ryan share?

"Don't worry," Kris coos. "I told him I'm taking care of you, but I didn't say anything else. So, of course now he's asking how I'm doing."

Skylar frowns. She was so worried about Kris's reaction all night, and this morning she completely blew past what he may be feeling to deal with her own breakdown. "How are you doing?" Her voice feels small.

Kris sets the phone aside on the arm of the couch so he can look down at Skylar. "Honestly? I think I've been preparing myself for this for a few weeks now. I know I always resisted Warren's views of this place being a prison, but now it all just makes too much sense."

"Yeah," Skylar sighs.

"So, we're trapped in a giant prison for misbehaving warlocks," Kris says. "Nothing has changed, except for how we view it, I guess. We're still stuck here. And those that are stuck here with us are the same ones who were here before we knew any of this."

"True." Skylar nuzzles her cheek against Kris's thigh.

The horned demon leans forward and presses a kiss to Skylar's crown. "I think I'm still trying to absorb the information, but there isn't really anything we can do with it now. So, let's talk about you and Ryan."

"What is there to talk about?" Skylar pushes herself to sit up, legs folding underneath herself as she faces Kris on the couch.

"Everything!" A wicked grin spread on Kris's face. "I knew he was hot for you, but the way you described how he approached you . . ." Kris's voice, already deep in it's own right, becomes gruff as he tries to mimic Ryan's voice. "I want to trust you."

Skylar covers her face with her hands in an effort to hide the ridiculous grin she's wearing at the memory. "That's your takeaway from this whole thing?"

"Seems to me that it's the part that you're trying to ignore." Kris folds his arms over his chest as he leans back against the couch cushions. "Let's pretend for a few minutes that your evening ended with this kiss and not any of the other stuff. How do you feel about the kiss?"

Skylar drops her hands to glare at Kris, but her friend doesn't let her shame him out of the question. Instead, she takes a moment to think about the kiss. "It was surprising," she admits after a long moment. "I knew I could get him flustered—"

"You can fluster anyone," Kris helpfully adds, earning him a small smile from Skylar.

"But it was more than that," Skylar continues. "I don't know the last time I was asked for something like that."

"Don't you make out with Omar and Derek whenever they corner you at *Dante's*?" Kris raises a skeptical eyebrow.

Skylar rolls her eyes. "That's different. Those two are obviously head over heels for one another. When I'm there, it's more like I'm helping facilitate whatever they are trying to do together. No, what Ryan was asking wasn't just physical. It was something more . . ." Her words trail off as she tries to describe the feeling from the night before. Even as she speaks, she feels the shadow of a thought forming in her mind. Ryan wasn't asking for just a kiss, but for something else.

"Well," Kris says aloud, tapping his chin with a finger, "if he was saying he wanted to trust you, then asked to kiss you, wouldn't that mean he was asking for your trust in return?"

"What?" Skylar blinks. It feels like the air has been sucked out of the room for a minute as Kris's words sink in.

Kris reaches over and takes both of Skylar's hands in his. "Skylar, think about it. I know we give Ryan and Bunny a lot of shit for being inexperienced warlocks, but really think about what Ryan did. They have been so careful about staying outside the protective circle, but you said he walked right into it on purpose. No negotiation to keep himself safe. Just blind trust." Skylar nods. "When was the last time a warlock did that to you?"

Skylar thinks about it, but the answer is obvious: never. She's had warlocks come onto her, like the dumb college kid, but they never willingly cross the barrier. "It doesn't happen."

"And once he was there, what did he demand of you?" Kris asks the question like he's guiding Skylar to an evident answer.

"Nothing," Skylar whispers.

Kris nods. "When was the last time a warlock didn't just take what they wanted? Since when do they ask demons for anything?"

Finally, with Kris's coaxing, the light bulb goes off in her head. "He asked to kiss me. I could have said no."

Kris's grin softens. "But you didn't." Skylar shakes her head. "Did you want to say no? Or did you just not think you could?"

Skylar's mouth drops open. There is a very important distinction between the two scenarios Kris is presenting, but she already knows the answer. "I wanted to kiss him," she confesses.

"About time!" Kris throws an arm around Skylar's shoulders. "I've been trying to tell you this for weeks."

He isn't wrong, Skylar realizes. There has always been something different about Ryan. With any other warlock Skylar would have taken the first utterance that seems like a wish and completed the warlock-demon pact. Instead, she keeps finding excuses to help the warlock without fulfilling the deal. And in return, Ryan never treats her like a tool for his own gain. He always gives Skylar an option to say no. He asks for help and never demands it. Skylar leans over to rest her head on Kris's shoulder. "I'm an idiot."

Kris rests his cheek against the top of Skylar's head. "Only a little bit." His hand then skirts around Skylar's wings to wrap around her lower back and grabs her waist in a side hug. "You're not the first one who has been enchanted by a warlock."

"I guess that's true," Skylar sighs. "I mean, we both had to come from somewhere. Do you think demon/warlock romances are common? I mean, there are more than a few of us born demons."

"Maybe," Kris muses. "I haven't been told anything from other demons about relationships with warlocks or humans. But I was talking more specifically about present company."

Skylar gasps and her head shoots right up which causes their heads to collide. Kris exhales in surprise as Skylar looks at him with wide eyes. "Have you and Bunny . . .?"

A slight blush rises to Kris's cheeks and a shy smile plays across his lips. He ducks his head. "Bunny may have set up a couple of chairs in the summoning circle so we can sit and watch movies or play video games."

"Why didn't you tell me?" Skylar emphasizes each word with a smack on the other demon's arm. "You just said that warlocks never willingly enter summoning circles!"

Kris turns his back to Skylar to avoid her playful strikes and laughs. "Because I knew you'd react like this," he calls out. Only when Skylar relents her assault does Kris turn back around. "You've made your thoughts on my behavior with Bunny *very* clear." The words are said with a pout and regret lances through Skylar. She suddenly feels like a giant hypocrite.

"I'm sorry if I made you feel like you couldn't talk to me about this." Now it is Skylar's turn to reach out and take Kris's hand in hers. "I was worried. I still am, but now for both of us. What could a relationship with a warlock ever turn into?"

"Maybe that's not the point," Kris offers. "Maybe we should just enjoy the moment and not worry about what comes next."

Skylar chuckles and bumps her shoulder against his. "That's real easy with Mr. Warlock-Supreme-Magic-Denier."

Kris shrugs and squeezes Skylar's hand. "You don't know until you talk to him."

"After how I reacted last night?" Skylar feels insecurity creep up in her. "This may be a moot point. I'm not sure he's going to be terribly interested in pursuing a demon anymore."

"I still think you should talk to him," Kris states, but pauses when he sees Skylar's look of dread. "Take some time to get yourself sorted, but nothing is going to get resolved if you don't talk to one another."

Skylar nods.

They sit in silence for a few moments, just holding hands. Skylar takes the time to ruminate on what Kris has said. Until she talks to Ryan again, everything is kind of up in the air. At the same time, she still feels too emotionally charged to have that conversation.

"So," Kris drawls and finally breaks the silence. "How was the kiss?"

A blush rises to Skylar's cheeks, and she remembers the feel of Ryan's lips against hers. "It was my first kiss with a warlock," she prefaces. "But it was really good. Warm and gentle. Not demanding at all."

"Aw," Kris gives an exaggerated sigh. "That's so sweet."

Skylar narrows her eyes and looks over at Kris. "So, are you going to tell me what you and Justin have been up to? It's been weeks and I know you've been infatuated with him since day one. So, spill."

Kris's grin grows and suddenly things feel back to normal. Like they were before Justin and Ryan had come into their lives. They rearrange themselves on the couch so that Kris can rest his head in Skylar's lap this time as he shares.

"Well, it started with just watching TV and playing games. Bunny would leave a chair for me in the circle, so I didn't have to sit on the floor or stand. Then he moved a second seat into the circle and joined me. That was the first night we kissed."

"That boy is too clever for his own good," Skylar laughs as she runs her fingers through Kris's curly hair. Occasionally, she runs the pads of her fingers over his horns. "So, only kissing?"

"I mean, that's where it started." Kris is lying on his back, his knee bent with one leg crossed over the other. He gestures with his hands as he talks. "He is just so sweet. And considerate. And unbelievably hot. You've seen him."

Skylar has to nod in agreement. "The boy does look like he takes care of himself."

Kris smirks up at her. "You have no idea. He has this itty-bitty waist, but such strong shoulders and arms. I'd let him pin me to the floor and have his way with me any time." He fans himself with his hand.

"Oh, you haven't?" Skylar guffaws.

"Not yet." Kris groans. "We've done plenty of other stuff, but I feel like a gentleman shouldn't say more than that."

"Hey!" Skylar smacks Kris's pectoral. "Since when are you a gentleman?"

"Since now?"

The conversation devolves into a tickle fight that neither of them really wins, but it is hard to say anyone actually loses either. A lot of the tension that has been building up disperses and Skylar feels like she is finally somewhere closer to normal.

They spend the afternoon watching TV and chatting, only pausing to get dinner. It is in the middle of their meal that Skylar has a revelation. "I should have talked to you before I went storming over to Warren's," Skylar abruptly says. "Maybe I could have handled the whole thing better. Warren looked really upset."

Kris puts his fork down and reaches across the kitchen table to pat Skylar's hand. "Warren has his own problems he hasn't dealt with, it seems. This whole thing does explain a lot about him."

"Really?" Skylar asks, feeling reassured.

"He was always haughty," Kris nods. "But his views on the existence of demons was always so much darker than anyone else's I know. Which seems at odds with his personality otherwise. He's peculiar, but he is also kind and funny when given half the chance."

"True." Skylar wipes a bit of adobo sauce from her lips. They'd agreed on some comfort food for dinner, and the chicken adobo reminds her of her childhood. "So, do you think what he said is true? That he only acted in self-defense and no one believed him?"

Kris takes a drink from a bottle of beer before continuing. "I think so, but it's hard to say until we can talk to him again. Which, I think, also deserves a grace period."

"I owe him an apology." Skylar shifts her rice around on her plate. "The way I stormed over there wasn't fair."

"He's been keeping a really big secret from you this entire time," Kris points out. "I think it's fair that you would be upset, but you're right that you could have handled it better. I think an apology would go a long way to mending that bridge."

Kris spends the rest of the night just hanging out with Skylar helping to distract her, and also letting her talk through her more complicated thoughts whenever they surface. Skylar isn't oblivious to the occasional text Kris is getting though the evening, but she doesn't pry.

Kris eventually mentions it himself. "Bunny is asking to summon me," he says after Skylar gives a big yawn. "I'll tell him not to if you still want me here."

Skylar gives an incredulous laugh. "What kind of luck do we have that we have warlocks asking us for permission to be summoned? But I'll be fine. You've given me a lot to contemplate. Hopefully I can manage to get away without any summonings myself this evening." She leans over and gives Kris a kiss on the forehead. "Go have fun with your warlock."

"Be kind to yourself," Kris says and gives her a soft smile. He then picks up his phone and taps out a reply. It takes a few minutes before Kris is tucking the phone back into his pocket. "I'll see you tomorrow, okay?"

"Be safe," Skylar teases and gets a playful smirk in return before he vanishes from the demon realm.

For the first time that day Skylar is left alone. She is happy for her friend, but too quickly her own uncertainties return to cloud her thoughts. In an effort to cut off her own mental spiral, Skylar turns on her sound system and plays music loud enough that she can't hear her own thoughts. Then she throws herself into dancing. She moves around her apartment letting the music move her body without having to think too hard. She lets her muscles stretch and flex and burn with effort as she continues to lose herself in the music.

It isn't until her shirt is drenched with sweat and her muscles feel like they can't move anymore that Skylar stops. She takes a quick shower just to wash the effort of her dancing away before collapsing in bed in a tank top and sleep pants. A last look at her phone shows there aren't any new messages. She lies on her side in bed and stares at the phone, contemplating messaging Ryan first.

"Hey."

She types out and then immediately erases it.

"Are you free to talk?"

Her next attempt meets the same fate and she deletes that message, too. Honestly, she can't figure out how to pick up from where they left off. Nothing feels good enough over text messages.

Instead, she tosses her phone to the side and rolls onto her stomach to bury her face in the pillows. Maybe if she just lies still long enough sleep will come.

Time passes, but with Skylar's stubborn refusal to move it is impossible to tell if it's been minutes or hours. Eventually sleep does pull her under, even if it is ever so lightly that her thoughts become more surreal and visual.

A sharp ting of a text alert pulls her back from the edge of slumber she's been teetering on. Skylar feels like she is moving in slow motion as her hand reaches out and sweeps along the bed looking for where she dropped her phone. Her fingers brush along the cool, hard surface of the phone and she grabs it to bring it close to her face. The alert on the home screen tells her all she needs to know.

Ryan

> Skylar, are you okay?

It takes an extra moment for Skylar's eyes to focus on the text, then another few moments for her groggy mind to process the words.

Of all the things Ryan could have opened with, Skylar is wondering why she is surprised by this message of concern. On every opportunity she gives the warlock to act like every other warlock she's ever met, Ryan chooses to do the opposite. Skylar's heart drops at the realization that she's been spinning herself up over Ryan being mad at her, but she should have known better. Her bottom lip trembles and she has to tuck it under her front teeth to keep from pouting outright as she considers a response.

Still, nothing seems sufficient over text. There is too much she wants to say to Ryan that her mind stalls out on how to respond. The light of the phone dims as she considers how to reply.

Skylar shuts her eyes and imagines Ryan at home in the mortal realm. It is well after midnight, but the warlock is still awake enough to message her. Does Ryan expect a message back right away? What if he sent the message and doesn't think Skylar will see it until morning? Well, fuck that.

Before she can doubt herself, Skylar shoves the phone under her pillow and buries her face in its surface once more. Her heart is pounding like she has just finished dancing again. It isn't until her pulse has become more regular and sleep begins to pull her under again that she feels the tugging sensation in her tummy. Skylar gasps aloud, her eyes fluttering open at the pull from the mortal realm. She lets the metaphysical cord haul her across the inter-dimensional divide.

It is Ryan's magic that pulls her through. Relief floods through her as her bare feet touch down on cold kitchen floor once more. The harsh kitchen lights blind her for a moment before she can focus on Ryan.

The warlock stands outside the crudely drawn circle in a black t-shirt and gray sweatpants. His shaggy hair is messy but his eyes are clear and focused when they meet Skylar's.

"Ryan," Skylar says, unable to break his gaze.

"You're really okay?" Ryan asks. His voice is low and gruff. It almost feels like a caress across Skylar's bare skin, and it makes her wings shudder in response.

Skylar shakes her head. "I'm sorry for how I reacted," she rushes to get out. "You showed me how much you were trusting me, and I didn't give you the same courtesy."

"Does that mean you confirmed what I told you?" Ryan swallows, his Adam's apple bobbing in his throat.

Skylar tilts her head back and forth. "Kind of. I think there's more to the story than you've been told, but that's not what I want to talk about."

Ryan blinks at her. "What do you want to talk about?"

"You," Skylar says firmly. She steps to the edge of the circle as close as she can get to Ryan with the thin chalk line the only barrier between them. "You said you wanted to trust me, and I did a poor job of giving you a reason to. Yet everything you've done has shown me that I can trust you. No, that I should trust you. And I'm sorry if I've done anything to make you doubt that."

"I dumped a lot on you." Ryan is shaking his head as he speaks. His hands come up and kind of hover in the air between them. "I think it's fair it took you time to process it. I'm just glad that you were willing to come back. And that you're okay."

"I'm okay. And I do, you know? I do trust you." Skylar nods, suddenly frustrated that she can't close the distance any further. Her wings flap in agitation as she lifts her own hands towards Ryan's, which flutter just out of reach.

The warlock looks down and, as if just realizing how much Skylar is trying to reach him, does the demon the courtesy of closing the distance. Ryan's hands pass over the invisible but ever present barrier to interlock their fingers together. He shuffles the one step closer, causing Skylar to take a step back, so that he can move into the protective circle and be just a hair's breadth away. Skylar takes the opportunity to crash their lips together. To return Ryan's precious gift to him.

19

Bonding

IT'S TAKING ALL OF Ryan's self-control to stay on his side of the summoning circle when Skylar appears in her sleep pants and tank top. Her hair is soft and fluffy. His fingers itch to touch the silky strands just as badly as he feels the urge to brush them over her feathery wings. How is this fucking fair? Her lithe form is framed by those large, black wings and Ryan can only make the comparison to a dark angel sent to tempt him.

Then Skylar moves closer, apologizing for absolutely nothing she needs to apologize for, and Ryan can't keep away. When their lips press together a thrill of electricity shoots through his body. Skylar may have initiated the kiss, but Ryan is dominating it.

He lets go of Skylar's hands so he can grab the demon's waist and pull her flush against his body. Feathers brush against the backs of his hands as the wings move, but Ryan is more focused on tilting his head and licking into Skylar's mouth. Those plush, soft lips easily allow him access to run his tongue alongside Skylar's and pull a soft moan from the demon's throat.

Ryan becomes lost in the myriad of sensations: the magic tickling over his skin, the feel of warm skin under his fingertips where Skylar's tank top rides up over the hem of her sleep pants, her warm mouth and wet tongue sliding against his own, the demon's fingers gripping his shoulders as they move together inside the circle despite having nowhere to go.

After aimlessly shuffling in a circle as they move against one another, Ryan reluctantly breaks the kiss. He pulls back and they are both panting softly. Skylar's lips are slick and red from the kiss as her eyes flutter open to look at Ryan, the eye contact like static in the air between them. Ryan moves one hand up to brush Skylar's hair back from her face and card his fingers through the unbelievably soft strands. The demon takes the moment of separation to run her hands down Ryan's chest before sliding around his waist and holding him close.

"If I open the circle, will you be sent back to the demon realm?" Ryan asks, his mind racing with thoughts of taking Skylar to his bed.

Skylar shakes her head. "No, I'll stay here until you release me. At least until sunrise. The circle is meant for your safety." Even as she speaks, Skylar brushes the tip of her nose across Ryan's and teases like she's going to kiss him again but doesn't make the connection.

Ryan swallows the desire rising up in him, the heat rushing south to his groin. "If I break the circle, would you like to join me in my bedroom?"

A tiny gasp escapes Skylar and her eyes open wide, searching Ryan's face. Ryan makes an attempt to relay all his want to her with just his eyes. "Really?" she asks softly.

"Only if you want to," Ryan emphasizes. "If you don't, we can stop right here."

Skylar's teeth bite into her bottom lip as she continues to gaze at Ryan as if considering him or the offer. Or both. Ryan's heart is pounding as he waits for the demon to decide, but he doesn't make any move to try to coax or lure her further. He just stands there with his hand on Skylar's hip and the other softly cupping her face.

When it feels like an eternity has passed and Skylar hasn't enthusiastically agreed, Ryan feels his heart drop. He gently removes his hands from her and tries to take a step back. "It's okay if you don't want to," he sincerely says. Perhaps he's rushing this.

Skylar's arms lock around his waist and keep him from moving away. "I want to," she says quickly with an emphatic nod. "I really, really want to. I was just surprised that you'd want to."

Ryan's brow furrows as his hands slide their way back up Skylar's arms to hook over her shoulders. "Why? You've been my lifesaver when it comes to this magic stuff. You're absolutely gorgeous. And you said you trust me."

"Because I'm a demon," Skylar replies. "I live in another dimension meant for evil warlocks. You have to use a circle of protection each time you summon one of us to make sure you're safe from our magic. There's lots of reasons for you to not want *this*—whatever this is."

"But you're not *just* a demon," Ryan argues. "You're *you*. You're Skylar. And I may be incredibly naïve, but I trust you. You could have harmed me as soon as I stepped over the circle, but you haven't. I don't believe you'll hurt me."

Skylar's eyes become watery as she continues to make eye contact with him. "I'd never hurt you," she breathes. She blinks and the first tear slips down Skylar's cheek.

"I know." Ryan brings a hand up to wipe the tear away with his thumb.

A gentle laugh breaks the tension and Skylar smiles and drops her gaze. "I'm kind of embarrassed."

Ryan hushes her. "Don't be." He tilts Skylar's head back to catch her gaze again. "You're still as beautiful as ever."

Skylar grips Ryan's wrist before she leans forward and kisses him once more. This kiss is gentler than the kisses they'd shared earlier, but just as heated. "Yes," Skylar says against his lips. "Take me to your room." She leans into him, her body all heat and soft curves, driving him to the edge of reason.

With one more firm kiss, Ryan steps back so he can break the circle. Using one socked foot, he rubs at the chalk outline until it smudges and disappears. He glances back up at Skylar. "Is this enough?"

Skylar takes one of Ryan's hands in her own before moving to the edge of the circle. She takes a deep breath and steps over the line before turning to smile at him. "Yes."

"Perfect." Ryan grins and with Skylar's hand in his leads her the short distance through his apartment to the bedroom.

"Your place is kind of small," Skylar comments as she trails behind him.

Ryan chuckles. "You live in a pocket dimension with far fewer demons than there are people here. I doubt real estate is at a premium like it is here," he huffs.

"True," Skylar admits and shrugs when Ryan turns to face her once more. They stand at the foot of Ryan's bed. "Now, where were we?" Without waiting for an answer, Skylar steps into Ryan's space and presses a kiss to his jaw. "What exactly did you have in mind?" she whispers. Ryan feels her hot breath against his ear and it sends a shiver down his spine.

"Not sure I thought this all the way through," he admits as his hand slides back around Skylar's waist to hold her close.

He plants a kiss on the column of Skylar's neck and the demon tilts her head to give him better access. With his face buried in her hair, Ryan finally catches this soft floral scent that makes his head swim as he continues to plant kisses up Skylar's neck until he's close enough to take the demon's earlobe between his teeth and give a gentle tug. He splays his hands against the demon's lower back and slides them up under her tank until his finger tips brush where the wings sprout from her back.

"Does it hurt if I touch them?" he murmurs before pressing a gentle kiss to Skylar's cheek.

"Only if you're rough with them," she sighs. Skylar's own hands have made their way to the hem of Ryan's shirt and are sliding up under the fabric to press against his waist before traveling up over his ribs.

Ryan drops his face to press a kiss to Skylar's shoulder and peer down her back. The sleep tank has a racer back that goes down between her wings and he can see where the they grow from her back. It looks more natural than he expected. Everything about Skylar is graceful and beautiful.

"Can I touch them?" he asks, eyeing the beautiful black feathers more closely than he ever has before.

"You have blanket permission to touch me anywhere you like," Skylar says and begins tugging at Ryan's shirt. "As long as you take this off first."

With a laugh, Ryan lets go of Skylar long enough to discard his shirt revealing skinny arms and pale skin. He feels a little self-conscious next to the gorgeously tanned and fit demon, but the way Skylar's eyes drink him in gives him a rush of confidence.

"You look like you're made of pure moonlight." Skylar sighs, her hands sliding up Ryan's soft tummy. The tips of her fingers graze Ryan's nipples which stiffen under the brief attention and pull a gasp from him.

"May I see your wings better?" he asks shyly.

Skylar nods and, with only a small pout, removes her hands from Ryan in order to turn around so she's facing the bed with Ryan at her back. The tank top vanishes and the sound of cloth hitting the floor somewhere in the room isn't enough to draw Ryan's gaze away from the vision before him. The wings spread out a little as if for Ryan's inspection. Her dark hair falls down her back long enough to brush the tops of the wings.

Carefully, Ryan brings his hands to brush his fingers over the feathers. He follows the way the feathers lay from the junction in her back up and over the highest arch of her wing before coming down towards the tips. The feathers are amazingly soft to the touch and shimmer in the dim bedroom light. Skylar shivers, her wings giving a gentle shake.

"Did I hurt you?" Ryan asks as he immediately pulls his hands back from the wings.

Skylar throws him a glance over her shoulder. "No, not at all," she reassures him. "It just feels very intimate. Not many people touch me there."

"Oh." Ryan smiles and feels a blush rise to his cheeks. He gently brings his hands back up to run along the feathers once more. Then he slips his hands from the wings to Skylar's lower back. He presses his long fingers into the warm, firm skin there before drifting further down to the waistline of her pants over the soft curve of her hips. "Can I remove these?"

"Yes," Skylar exhales.

Ryan dips his fingers under the waistband of the sleep pants and slides them down, crouching into a kneel as he goes. The plush curve of Skylar's ass comes into view as the fabric slips away. Once the waistband is over the swell of her hips, the pants easily fall the rest of the way.

Skylar leans forward and props herself up on the edge of the bed. The motion only leaves her on display for Ryan and he feels like drooling over the pure perfection that is Skylar's thighs. He leans forward and presses open mouth kisses over her enticing curves. Skylar's sweet huffs are going straight to Ryan's dick where it's tenting the front of his sweats at this point, but he can't even imagine letting go of Skylar for a moment to touch himself.

Feeling encouraged by Skylar's sighs of pleasure and her permission to touch her anywhere, Ryan brings both his hands up to gently hold her open. Then, without a moment's hesitation, Ryan leans forward to run the flat of his tongue across her honey pot, getting a mouthful of the most intoxicating slickness.

"Fuck, Ryan," Skylar cries, but she doesn't stop him. So Ryan continues to lap and lick at her center, using his tongue to tease her hardening pearl at the apex.

Only when his fingers dip down to join his mouth and press inside does she protest. "Wait, wait, wait," the demon chants.

Ryan stops instantly. "What's wrong?"

Skylar crawls onto the bed and Ryan lets her go, his hands falling to his lap as he watches the demon turn to face him. She has to lift her wings high to clear the surface of the mattress. "Nothing's wrong," she says. Her full breasts glisten with just the lightest sheen of sweat, her face a warmer color and eyes bright as she smirks down the bed at him. "It feels amazing, don't get me wrong. I just want to see you. This feels extremely one sided."

Ryan chuckles and glances down at the growing wet spot in the front of his pants. "Believe me, it's not," he smiles then looks back up at Skylar.

Skylar lifts her hand and beckons him closer. "Come here."

Quickly, Ryan pushes himself to his feet and hooks his thumbs into the waistlines of both his pants and boxers to push them to the ground. For the first time, he brings his hand to his dick and strokes it in a loose grip to give it *some* relief. He is pleased when he glances at Skylar to find the demon's eyes following the motion. "Like what you see?" Ryan asks, his voice deep and husky.

"Definitely," Skylar purrs back with a seductive smile. "It's just all the way over there, and I'm over here."

Ryan crawls onto the bed to join her, pausing on his knees when he's beside her. "Wait," Ryan frowns, eyeing Skylar's wings. "How are we going to—?"

Skylar laughs and even her laughter sounds musical. She shakes her head. "I've had these since puberty, I know how to move around them. It just means you won't be getting me on my back."

"Okay," Ryan licks his lips as he slides closer to her, his hand reaching out to trail his fingers over her shoulder and down her clavicle. "So, how do you want me?"

Skylar gives a wicked grin as she looks back up at Ryan. She shifts to her knees so they are kneeling in front of one another and brings her hands to Ryan's shoulders before leaning in for another kiss. It is slow and languid.

As their lips move together their bodies shift closer. Ryan feels the swell of Skylar's breast against his chest before he reaches down to grip the demon's hips once more, his fingers digging into warm skin.

Gently, Skylar presses Ryan back until he is reclining on the bed with Skylar over him. Ryan's hands roam from her hips, up her sides, and over her back. Meanwhile Skylar writhes on top of him, Ryan's cock caught between the press of her thigh and his hip.

Slowly Skylar's kisses migrate from Ryan's lips down over his neck and chest. She pauses briefly to lick and nip at each sensitive nipple as Ryan grips her shoulders and moans aloud.

"I love the sounds you make," Skylar whispers against the skin of Ryan's ribs as she shifts further south.

Ryan sighs when Skylar finally reaches her destination and wraps her fingers around the base of his cock. She brings the flushed and leaking member to her plush, spit-slicked lips to press a gentle kiss to the tip. A shudder runs through Ryan, and he grips the sheets at his sides in order to hold onto something, but he can't look away.

"Fuck," Ryan cries aloud as Skylar takes him into her mouth. Skylar swallows around him and Ryan can't stop his hips from bucking into the wet, warm heat of her mouth.

"Sky, fuck, fuck," Ryan chants. It's been a long time since someone other than himself has taken Ryan in hand, but he swears it has never felt this good this soon with anyone. Don't people usually have to take time to learn what the other likes in these situations? But already, as if it were the hundredth time, Skylar is bringing him such precise and exact pleasure he feels as if he could climax at any moment.

Just as he thinks he has the building pleasure held back, Skylar changes tactics to run the flat over her tongue over his length. "Sky!" Ryan gasps. Heat pools in his belly and he feels that any second he could tip over the edge. "Slow down or I'm not going to last."

Skylar pulls off, a string of spit between Ryan's cock and her bottom lip as she grins up at him.

Ryan groans and reaches down to grip her wrist, pulling her up his body to bring her closer. He presses a heated kiss to that wicked mouth, tasting himself there. "Give me a few to calm down," he pants as the kiss breaks.

"Sure thing," Skylar chuckles. She presses a gentle kiss to the corner of his lips as she settles against him.

He can't keep his hands off her as she ducks down to kiss him some more. Ryan's hands roam the expanse of her sides and down her hips. He lifts his thigh to press between her legs where she's settled and guides Skylar to grind lazily down on him.

When Ryan feels like he finally isn't about to burst at the slightest provocation, he breaks the kiss. He runs his fingers through Skylar's hair, pushing the dark strands back from her face so he can look the demon in the eyes. "Do you still want to . . .?"

Skylar grins. "Yes," she says, rolling her hips to grind down on his thigh more firmly. "Do you?"

Ryan smiles back and gives Skylar one more quick kiss. "Yes, give me a second." He has to shuffle out from under her so he can roll and stretch his arm out to his bedside table. He rummages around in the drawer, finding the half-empty bottle of lube and then pauses. "Shit," he mutters and collapses onto his back. "I don't have any condoms."

"No problem," Skylar laughs. She snaps her fingers and a box of condoms appears beside Ryan's hand.

"Did you just steal those?" Ryan deadpans.

Skylar shrugs. "Only technically. I mean, they have to come from *somewhere*. When I'm here I can't just summon them out of thin air." She smirks and leans forward to lick at the skin over Ryan's hip.

Fuck capitalism.

He takes the box of ill-gotten condoms and rips it open, pulling one from the container. "Are you ready for this?" he asks, holding it up. "I could eat you out some more."

She sits up and snatches the condom from his fingers. "Tempting, but I'm ready." Placing the corner between her teeth, Skylar tears open the condom and Ryan isn't sure he's ever seen anything sexier. Deftly she slides the condom over his cock, rolling it down to the root.

Throwing a leg over his hip, she positions herself over him. Ryan's heart is racing as he watches this beautiful woman settle over him. He bends his knees to plant his feet against the mattress and reaches for her waist as if to help her, but her wings spread out and seem to be helping her keep her balance.

Tight heat envelopes him and knocks the breath from him as she lowers herself over him. His body tenses as he fights the urge to thrust up, the taste of her still on his tongue. No, he's letting her take this at her pace.

Skylar's face twists in pleasure, relaxing only once she's fully settled over him. She sits and he lets her adjust to the stretch while his hands slide up her sides to cup her breasts, full enough to fill the palms of his hands. His thumbs come up to slide over her pert nipples making her gasp as her eyes flutter open and look down at him. She smiles and rolls her hips, making lightning flash behind his eyes at the sensation.

"Skylar," Ryan groans, his eyes never leaving the demon's face. She bites her bottom lip and swivels her hips again.

"You feel so good," Skylar sighs, her hair falling in tousled waves around her face. She reaches down and puts her hands on his chest to get better leverage to ride him. The eye contact is intense, and Ryan feels himself throbbing inside of her. "Do you feel good, *warlock*?"

Only then does the magic prickle his skin. With his senses so overwhelmed, Ryan had almost forgotten about the low current of magic still flowing over him. He jerks, unintentionally digging his fingers into the softness of her hips.

"Don't call me that," he says through gritted teeth. When the tingle of magic passes, Ryan realizes they've both frozen.

"Sorry," Skylar says, slowly rising off of him before settling back down more firmly as if testing the waters. "It really bothers you, doesn't it?"

Ryan can't keep the eye contact going anymore and his eyes flutter shut at the feeling of Skylar's wings brushing his knees. He throws one arm over his forehead and tosses his head to the side. "I don't like it," he pants. "It also hurts. The magic reacts to it in a stinging way."

Skylar pauses again and Ryan opens one eye to peer up at her. The woman is staring down at him. Her black wings twitch as she studies him. "I didn't know. I'm sorry."

Ryan's heart pounds as he finds himself smiling up at her. "If you're really sorry, kiss me."

Obeying the request, Skylar leans forward to press their lips together. The motion changes the angle of their meeting and makes Ryan's heart thud as he loses his control and thrusts up into her to follow the warmth sliding over him. The kiss itself is gentle and sweet, but the way Skylar grinds more powerfully over him is anything but gentle. He groans as they kiss and Skylar's rhythm increases.

When the kiss breaks, Ryan feels right on the edge of his orgasm once more. She must realize he's close because she starts panting into his ear. "That's it," she moans, her hot breath puffing against his neck. "Just like that."

As much as he loves her body blanketed over him, Ryan has a different focus. He gently grips her shoulders and helps sit her up right. He leaves one hand in the crook of her neck, his thumb brushing over her clavicle. His other hand slides down so he can thumb at her clit. She gasps, her thighs tensing as he continues to play with the sensitive bud, refusing to let up the pace they've built together.

"Come for me," Ryan coaxes as he continues to watch her grind and gasp atop him. "Please."

Skylar gasps and she's coming apart above him, her wings shooting out to their full impressive wingspan displaying her in her full wicked beauty. Her own pleasure squeezes him, sending him tumbling over after her, releasing into the condom, pleasure shooting through him like magic when it wells up inside of him.

"Fucking hell," Ryan sighs. "That was—"

"—something else," Skylar agrees.

Skylar pants above him, all sweat-glistened skin and heaving breaths. Ryan's fingers roam over her, feeling the way her heart flutters beneath his touch over her chest, or her leg twitches beneath his palm. Slowly, she climbs off of him with a lazy, blissful smile. Ryan reaches to grab the condom, but before he can Skylar snaps her fingers and the prophylactic is gone along with its load.

"That's nifty," Ryan points out as he languidly stretches. He's been so wound up and anxious since Skylar's visit the other night that now he feels utterly sated and exhausted.

Skylar smiles as she shuffles to lay down beside him. She cuddles up to his side on her stomach and rests her head on Ryan's chest where, beneath her cheek, his own heart continues to pound. Ryan puts an arm around the demon and strokes her wings. The feathers still feel incredibly soft to the touch and seem unreal. He is used to stroking sweat-slicked skin after sex and, while there is plenty of that, there is also these gorgeous wings. Skylar seems to like the attention, her wings stilling at the contact as she lets out a deep sigh.

"Can you fly?" Ryan finds himself asking before he can stop himself.

A dry chuckle comes from Skylar. "No, sadly. They're just for show. Great big wingspan, but it's not like I have hollow bones or anything." The demon's hands begin to trace nonsensical patterns over Ryan's stomach. "I mean, I can levitate and make it look like I'm flying, but it has nothing to do with the wings."

"Still pretty cool." He lifts his head to press a kiss to the crown of Skylar's head, his other hand pushing her hair back to tuck it behind her ear.

Quiet fills the darkness of Ryan's bedroom as the two continue to just lie together. Hands lazily pet over one another in exploration: skin, feathers, hair. Everywhere they can reach.

Ryan must doze off at some point. The next thing he remembers is Skylar pressing a gentle kiss to the corner of his mouth. "I have to go soon," she whispers.

A sleepy groan comes from the back of Ryan's throat as he tightens his grip around the demon. His hands press to Skylar's sides as if the force of his will can keep the woman from being ripped from this plane of existence. "I don't want you to go," he mumbles, his voice rough with disuse.

"I'd stay if I could." Skylar's voice is heavy and thick but tinged with sadness more than sleep.

Ryan reluctantly opens his eyes to peer down at Skylar where her head is resting on his shoulder. "What happens next?" he wonders aloud.

Skylar reaches up and brushes her fingers through Ryan's hair, pushing the shaggy strands from his eyes. "I don't know. What do you want?"

"I thought we settled that question already," Ryan says with a small chuckle. He presses his lips to Skylar's forehead in a chaste kiss. "But besides you?"

Skylar giggles and scoots up the bed to press a kiss to Ryan's lips instead. "Yes, besides me."

"I guess," Ryan considers, seriousness leaking into their quiet, calm space. "I guess I want to get to the bottom of this thing with Thomas Andrew Smith. What really happened." *Why the Order so eagerly accepted me into their fold*, Ryan doesn't say aloud.

Skylar sighs and gently presses her forehead to Ryan's as her eyes flutter shut. "Right? It happened so long ago, but it feels so relevant."

"Hey," Ryan murmurs and Skylar opens her eyes once more. Ryan makes sure he has her full attention. "Whatever we find, it doesn't change *this*." He presses a quick kiss to Skylar's lips. "I trust you. We're in this together."

A warm smile blooms on Skylar's face. "You, me, Kris, Justin, Ethan," she points out. "But thank you. I was afraid that you'd find something . . ." Her voice trails off.

"I'll text you, no matter what I find," Ryan reassures her. "And nothing I find will change the way I feel about you."

"Thank you, Ryan Smith." Skylar leans in and gives him another kiss. "I'll talk to you soon."

"Sleep well," Ryan says and dives in to plant another kiss to Skylar's plush lips. Time feels incredibly short all of a sudden, and there is no telling how quickly the coming dawn will steal Skylar away.

"Send me back," she pleads gently. "I'd hate to just disappear without a goodbye."

Ryan's heart twists, not wanting to let Skylar leave a moment sooner than he has to. "Goodbye, Sky."

"Bye, Ryan." Skylar sits up to lean over Ryan and give him another kiss. When the kiss breaks, Skylar sits back and runs her hands down his chest.

Their eyes are locked, but he knows it's time. "Skylar, I release you back to the demon realm."

Just like that Skylar vanishes. If it weren't for the warmth of her body on Ryan's sheets and the bone-deep satisfaction of last night's activities it would be easy to believe it had all been a dream. Ryan rolls over, burying his face into the pillows and imagines those soft feathers brushing against him as he falls back asleep.

After getting a few more hours of sleep, Ryan decides to get up and try doing normal things for a while. He's been so wrapped up in magic and demons and feelings that he's really let work fall behind. Instead of spending his weekend at home like he usually does, he chooses to go to the bookstore and try to get some more work done. Especially if he's going to continue to be busy with warlock intrigue.

It is kind of a shock when Ryan steps into the bookstore. He's used to coming in early during the week and staying through most of the afternoon. Now it's late Saturday morning and the bookstore is busy. Not only is Ethan there, but so is Nadia and another bookseller Ryan has never seen before.

Hugging his laptop bag to his chest, Ryan shuffles through the crowd of browsing people and nearly gets run down by playing children on his way to his usual table. As he turns the corner of the shelves, he finds that every space at his usual table is occupied. Students of college or high school age have laptops open and books piled high around them. Ryan sniffs and goes in search of another place to work. In the end, he finds an empty chair and pulls it into the corner of the gardening section, which seems to be the only section not inundated with people. He pulls out his laptop and gets to work, balancing the machine on his knees.

Once he's settled, Ryan finds it very easy to let all his concerns about murdering warlocks and secret societies fall away as he focuses on work. He and Skylar exchange messages at somewhat regular intervals, but Ryan really uses the time to get some distance from everything before trying to figure out what comes next.

"Oh, hey," Ethan says in surprise as he comes around the corner with a customer. "I didn't even see you come in."

Ryan, saving his progress, glances up to find the tall bookstore owner looking down at him in confusion. "Well, you're pretty busy."

"Speaking of," Ethan reaches over Ryan's seated form to pull a book from the shelf behind him. He turns to hand the book to an older woman dressed like she time traveled from about three decades ago. "Here's the book on succulents you were looking for." She wanders off happily and Ethan turns back to him.

"Don't worry," Ryan interrupts him, shoving his laptop back into his bag. "I'll be out of your way in a moment."

"Everything okay?" Ethan asks, putting his hands on his hips. "I never see you here on a Saturday."

Ryan shrugs, pushing himself out of the chair. "I'm fine. I was just behind on work. I didn't realize how busy you'd be today. Is it going to be like this tomorrow?"

Ethan shrugs. "It's less busy in the morning since it's Sunday," he offers.

"Cool, I'll get here earlier tomorrow then." Ryan picks up his chair to put it back where he found it.

Ethan's lips purse together. "I have a lot of questions for you, but I'm too busy to stand around and chat."

Ryan waves him off. "We'll talk later. Maybe after the weekend."

"Fine," Ethan says and points a finger at him. "I'm holding you to that."

***

After working through the weekend to catch up on all of his missed work, the stones he ordered arrives early Monday morning and he wards his apartment using the spell from Ethan's book. It doesn't take very long to sketch out the simple circle on a piece of notebook paper and chant over the stones a few times. He does just as he promised and gives Ethan and Justin blanket permission to come and go. Or at least he hopes he did. He isn't sure how to test the wards and can only go on blind faith that he did the spell correctly.

The tactic of giving himself distance from his problems all weekend seems to have worked, because Ryan wakes up Tuesday morning with an idea that hadn't occurred to him before.

He gets out of bed and dresses quickly, scheduling a rideshare before he can second-guess himself. Dressed in a pair of ripped blue jeans and an oversized black sweater, Ryan pulls a ball cap over his head to protect his eyes from the bright, sunny morning as he heads out.

As the car makes it's way out of the city and towards the outskirts, Ryan shoots off a couple of text messages. The first is to Skylar, telling her a good morning and that he'd talk to her that evening. The second message is to the group chat with Justin and Ethan to let them know where he is going since he still feels really paranoid.

Finally, the rideshare drops him off at the large gates of the Order's estate. Ryan marches his way up the drive to the main doors and lets himself in. It feels strange just walking in, but he has taken the oath. He's been promised access to the grounds and everything within. Then why does he feel like he's sneaking in?

The entryway is empty and there are no signs of anyone else around. The last two times he has come, they've been expecting him. This time he chose to just show up, so no one is waiting for him. That is the whole point.

As he tries to remember his way around, Ryan quietly moves through long empty halls. The quiet does nothing to calm his nerves as he creeps about, his heart pounding in his chest, afraid that he'll be caught even if he isn't doing anything wrong. He several blind turns before finding what he thinks is the correct door: the door to the basement archive.

He reaches for the doorknob, but suddenly the door swings open towards him. Ryan has to take a quick step back to avoid being smacked in the face as someone steps through.

"Ryan Smith?" comes a woman's surprised voice.

It takes Ryan a moment to recall the small, older woman standing before him with a large book in her arms. She is dressed in totally normal clothes: a pair of khaki pants and an embroidered sweater. She is one of the two women Ethan was speaking to at their first visit, but she wasn't at the oath-swearing ceremony.

"Oh, yes, hello," Ryan says with a small bow of his head. "I'm sorry, you surprised me."

The woman smiles at him kindly and steps into the hallway before shutting the door behind her. "It's okay. Are you lost?"

Ryan licks his lips and glances up and down the hall as if the answer is something he can find. He isn't sure he should admit his true intentions. "Maybe."

"Are you looking for the library? Most new members are eager to take a look at our collection of books about magic. I'm heading there myself." The older woman gestures down the hall.

A library may be just as good a place to start looking for answers as the archive. "Thanks, umm—"

"Sunmi Choi," she offers, her smile never faltering. "You can just call me Sunmi. Warlock Choi is so formal." She turns and leads him down the hall, back the way he came.

"Thank you, Sunmi," he says as he trails after her.

She nods as she slows down so he can walk beside her. "It was exciting to hear that you joined. I was hoping the offer would be extended to your friend, Ethan. He seems like a well-versed scholar for someone who is self-taught without any magic background. The Elders are more than ready to accept magic users before non-magic users." She tuts and shakes her head, then gasps. "Not saying that *you* shouldn't have been invited to join! Being a legacy on top of that, of course you should have been invited."

Ryan chuckles. She puts him at ease more so than any other person he's met at the Order so far. "Thanks, but I don't disagree. I feel like Ethan would be a better choice than me. I really don't know what I'm doing." He looks at her and the book she's carrying. It looks really heavy. "Did you want me to carry that for you?"

"You're a gentleman, but I've got it," she waves him off. "I'm not over the hill just yet."

"Of course," Ryan nods, not sure what else to do.

Sunmi leads Ryan into the largest of the libraries he was shown on his tour of the grounds. The other woman Ethan had met that day is sitting at a table with several other books spread out around her. She doesn't even look up as they enter. "Thank goodness you're back," she cries with the hint of a European accent Ryan can't quiet place. "I was about to send a search party after you."

"I wasn't gone that long, Dolores," Sunmi chides her. "Besides, I found young Mr. Smith wandering lost around the halls."

The woman looks up finally from her notebook she'd been scribbling in and smiles. "Oh, dear! Hello." She gets up and moves to tidy the space. "Sunmi and I were certain we'd have the library to ourselves this morning."

"Oh, don't let me interrupt." Ryan holds out a hand to motion for her to relax. "I had some free time and I thought I'd stop by and check out the resources here."

"Feel free to look around." Dolores gestures to the library. "We're just doing some research. Don't let us stop you."

Sunmi makes her way over to the table and sets the large book down on a clear spot on the surface. Ryan smiles at both the older women and makes his way over to one of the large walls filled with books. Even if he meant to come to the library to look for information, he doesn't know where to start. The two women huddle over the books and begin flipping through the pages.

After a few minutes of aimlessly looking at the titles of books along the shelves, he feels just as hopeless as when he started. The titles don't give him much of a clue to what he's looking at: *Alacastar's Guide to Ley Line Tapping*, *Pagan Practices Remastered*, *Herbs and Spices for More Than Just Spellwork*. Ryan pauses to turn towards them. "May I bother to ask a few questions?"

Both the women lift their heads to look in his direction. "Of course," Dolores says and gestures for him to join them at the table.

Ryan shuffles over and sits at the chair across from them. "Thank you," he ducks his head, bashful for a moment. He feels truly out of his depth and wishes Ethan were here to translate 'academic' for him. "I feel like I've been thrown into the deep end here."

They both chuckle kindly. "It's fine, dear," Sunmi says. "Do you need help navigating the library?"

"That's basically our job here," Dolores adds. "We're glorified librarians." They laugh like this is a common joke.

"Maybe some help with more than just books," he admits. "I was curious about my ancestor: Thomas Andrew Smith. Do either of you know much about him?"

"Oh." Sunmi's mouth forms a perfect little "o" of surprise. "I must admit, I don't know a lot."

Dolores nods along. "I'm sure I know even less. I was recruited from another warlock order when my late husband and I immigrated. I did notice your ancestor's portrait hanging in the sitting room upstairs."

Sunmi hums. "I've heard of him in passing. More so in the past week since you've joined. I was actually pretty curious about him myself, so I did some reading."

Ryan's eyebrows shoot up. "Really? The way some of the members talked about him, I thought he was more well known."

Dolores shakes her head. "The Order is just like any other social circle," she sighs. "There are certain cliques and crowds. I'd argue that the Smith enthusiasts are a small set of people in the Order who have family ties to the man, but that's all I've managed to discern."

"I agree." Sunmi folds her hands and rests them on the table in front of her. "From what I've read, he was rather influential during the late 1940s up until he passed. The most significant detail I learned was that he was the youngest member of the Council of Elders. He'd made a name for himself developing innovative magic practices."

Ryan feels lost. He understands the words she's using, but they don't make sense to him in the order they are presented. "What does that mean?"

Sunmi tilts her head as she considers his question. "It's like making advancements in technology, I suppose. He helped create new and improved spells or wards. He didn't create anything brand new as much as he expanded on previous warlock practices. Found ways to connect spells that seemed unrelated for new uses, but a lot of his work was lost after he passed. So I couldn't find much of the specifics."

Dolores gasps. "That sounds terrible. I can't imagine losing a lifetime's worth of discovery like that."

Ryan glances down at the books and pages spread out in front of the women. He can't make heads nor tails of it, but he imagines they'd feel much the same way if everything they are doing right now disappeared one day.

"Thank you," he says softly before taking a deep breath. "I'm sorry to bring up such a gloomy subject. Maybe you ladies can point me to a beginner's section here in the library?"

Both their faces light up and they point him towards the other end of the library while giving him suggestions on what to look for. He thanks them both before getting up to wander the shelves.

Ryan spends the rest of the morning looking through the books there. They are of a similar level to the books Ethan has in his collection, just many more of them. He can't help but feel guilty. The bookstore owner would love it here, but Ryan is the only one they allowed in.

He is on his way back out of the main entry once he finishes in the library, giving up on trying to sneak down to the archives for the day, when he hears a familiar voice.

"Yes, of course," Dahlia's voice comes down the hall. The sound of clicking heels against the hardwood floor between area rugs precedes her turning the corner. She is on her phone, dressed in a smart pants suit and carrying a briefcase. "Everything's coming together, I assure you." Her eyes widen when she looks up and meets Ryan's gaze. "I'll call you back," she says sweetly and hangs up the call. "Ryan! What a pleasant surprise."

He smiles at her, but it feels a bit stiff. "Dahlia, hello. I was just on my way out."

She pouts at him, but it seems more than a little fake. "That's a shame. Perhaps you can return again soon? There's still so much I want to discuss with you. And you really must bring Thomas Andrew Smith's book if you can! The information in there has been lost for half a century."

Ryan sucks air in through his teeth. This was bound to come up, especially after what Sunmi told him. "Sure, I'll bring it next time I come," he promises vaguely. "Today was kind of an impulsive visit."

Dahlia smiles at him. "Of course, you're welcome any time. Give me a call next time, though."

Ryan tries to return the smile, but he's worried it comes off as a grimace. "Thank you. I will. Have a good rest of your afternoon."

"You too," she says with a little wave. Then she is tapping on her phone as she strides past him like he wasn't there to begin with.

Ryan darts out of the large house like he can't leave fast enough. He's already called for a rideshare before he left the library and really hopes it'll be there by the time he gets down the long driveway. His next visit will have to be better planned.

20

Of Best Laid Plans

SKYLAR AND KRIS ARE seated side-by-side inside the summoning circle in Justin's studio. The addition of folding chairs is a pleasant reprieve for the meeting they are having with the warlocks, though Skylar's a little jealous that they weren't given the comfier computer chair the Ethan is occupying. It still feels a little chafing after being able to leave Ryan's circle in his apartment, but with Ethan and Justin there she doesn't want to object to the protection circle if it's for their comfort.

After summoning both the demons, the warlocks (and Ethan) sit down so they can all talk. Everyone is in casual clothes and it feels almost like a group of friends hanging out.

"I'm really not getting around this anymore," Ryan is saying. "I promised I'd bring the book with me the next time I go."

Kris has one leg folded under himself as he leans against Skylar's side. "Do you think there's something in the book that's bad?"

Ethan shakes his head. "Not that I can tell. We've read it, but we aren't the most well-versed in magic."

"You're doing pretty good," Skylar interjects with a small smile to the kind man.

"Thanks," Ethan says, bashfully dropping his head.

"Do you want *us* to take a look?" Kris offers. "We can tell you if something is particularly dangerous."

Justin and Ethan both glance at Ryan. He blinks at both of them. "I don't mind," he says, then looks back to the demons. "But I didn't bring it with me. The thing is fucking heavy."

"Oh!" Justin jumps up from his chair where he had been sitting next to Ryan. "I put my digital copy on my tablet." He darts off to his desk.

Skylar blinks at Ryan in surprise. "You digitized it?"

"Yeah," Justin answers for him as he returns with a tablet in his hand.

Kris hops up from his chair and holds out grabby hands as Justin passes the tablet over. With a small skip, Kris returns to his seat beside Skylar. The document is already pulled up on the screen. Glancing over from his shoulder, Skylar watches as Kris begins to flip through the scanned pages. He quickly bypasses the cover pages and pauses at the table of contents.

"We were worried if I brought the book with me to the Order, they would insist on keeping it there," Ryan explains as the duo looks over the scans.

"Smart," Kris comments, but his eyes never leave the screen.

After reading through the table of contents, both demons just shrug. "Nothing looks particularly dangerous or extraordinary," Skylar comments as Kris flips past the table of contents to begin going over the pages.

"As demons, we don't have to know spell components or magic circle configurations. Our magic is just a part of us, but that's what a lot of this is. Instructions on how to harness magic to do specific things," Kris is explaining as he continues to swipe through the pages.

Skylar eventually loses interest in looking at the scans and looks back to the warlocks. "So, what are you going to do?"

"Well," Ryan gestures toward the tablet in Kris's hand, "since we have the digital copy, we won't be actually losing anything if I take them the book and don't get it back. So, I guess I'm going to call Warlock Jones and arrange my next visit."

"And are you two going to go with him?" Skylar looks between Ethan and Justin.

"We'll take him," Justin reassures her. "But they won't let either of us on the premises again."

Ethan nods, shifting in the computer chair so he can lean forward to rest his elbows on his knees. He looks a bit tall and lanky in the squat seat. "We were allowed in for the first meeting, but they have it warded against non-members. Right, Ryan?"

"That's how it was explained to me," Ryan confirms.

"Hmm," Skylar hums and crosses her arms as she leans back in the chair. Her wings comfortably fit over the low back of the seat. "Wards can be a tricky thing. I'd almost guarantee a place meant for warlocks is going to be warded against more than just trespassers for their safety . No magic will probably be able to get in, either. Not unless allowed from within."

"You can't just bust down the doors with your demon magic?" Justin asks.

Skylar shrugs. "I mean, maybe? It depends on how the wards are set up, but I'd rather overestimate these warlocks than suppose they didn't prepare for that possibility."

"Maybe your, ahem, mentor can give you some insight?" Ryan gives Skylar a hopeful glance. She finds the man's hesitation to bring up Warren endearing and catches herself smiling fondly at the warlock.

"He might," she agrees. "I haven't spoken to him since—well, you know."

"Might be time to try and mend that bridge," Kris chimes in, looking up from the tablet. "I don't see anything in here that makes me think it would be bad to give the information to the Order. I mean, the way some of it is written out seems creative, but it's nothing any seasoned warlock shouldn't be able to do."

"Thanks for looking anyway, Kris," Justin smiles at him.

Kris smiles back and tucks the tablet under the folding chair for the time being.

"So, do we have a plan of action right now?" Ethan asks.

"Yes," Ryan nods. "I'm going to contact Dahlia and arrange my next visit. Regardless of anything else, you and Justin are going to drive me there."

"And," Kris cuts in, "Skylar and I are going to talk to her mentor. See if we can get more information about the Order that can be useful to you."

Skylar feels a weight drop in her gut. She really isn't looking forward to reaching out to Warren after how they left things, but she knows it has to happen. And this is as good a reason as any to try. "Yeah," she says with a heavy sigh, her eyes downcast towards her hands in her lap.

"Hey," Ryan's voice pulls Skylar's attention back up. His expression is so soft and kind, Skylar's heart skips a beat. "If that's not something you can do, I understand. We'll think of something else."

Skylar smiles at him. "I appreciate it, but it's something I have to do. We'll let you know if we learn anything new."

"Same," Ryan's smile grows wider. "Then shall we bid you a good evening?"

Kris and Skylar both stand up. "Maybe next time we can have a group summoning over something less dire," Kris playfully pouts.

"Are summonings used for social calls?" Ethan asks, standing to bid them farewell.

"Why not?" Kris shrugs with a large grin.

With that, they all bid one another goodnight from the respective sides of the circle. It is easier to not miss holding Ryan when everyone else is present, but secretly Skylar might have hoped the warlock would summon her into his home again.

Instead, Skylar and Kris are sent back to the demon realm where they reconvene in Skylar's apartment. Kris plops down on her couch beside her, throwing his arms around Skylar with a wide grin on his face.

"It was so much fun being all together," he squeals.

Skylar smiles, but it doesn't reach her eyes. "I guess."

Kris sits back to look at her. "What's wrong?"

"Didn't it feel kind of weird to still be stuck inside the circle?" Skylar picks at her fingernails, not wanting to look up at Kris.

"No," he says slowly.

Skylar shakes her head and drops her hands. "Never mind, I'm being silly."

"No, you're not," Kris protests and leans in to give her a peck on the cheek. Then he sits back once more, curling his legs up under himself on the couch. "Now come on. No time like the present. You should call Warren."

"Call?" Skylar gulps.

Kris nods, his expression serious. "This isn't the kind of conversation you can start over text. Call him."

"What if he doesn't answer?" Skylar asks meekly.

"Then leave a message," Kris shrugs. "And if he doesn't respond, we'll try again tomorrow. This is literally the only thing we can do from this dimension to help the warlocks."

Kris has a point and Skylar can't argue with that. She pulls her phone out of her jeans pocket and pulls up Warren's contact name. After a deep breath she presses the button and brings the phone to her ear.

The phone rings once.

Twice.

Three times, then goes to voicemail.

"Hello, Warren," she says gently after the tone to begin a message beeps. "I don't blame you for not answering my call, but I'm hoping you'll give me a chance to see you soon. I want to apologize in person for how I behaved. And I'd like to, despite not deserving it, hear about how *it* happened. Maybe ask some questions to keep something like that from happening again. Please? I'll be waiting for your call." Skylar hangs up the phone.

Instantly Kris's comforting arms are around her once more, pulling her into a hug. "You did a good job," he murmurs into her hair.

Skylar smiles as she wraps her arms around Kris. She suddenly feels emotionally drained.

It isn't until late afternoon a day and a half after that Skylar gets a call from Warren. She is at the park sitting on a bench watching the fluffy clouds drift by. Her phone rings and she answers it immediately when she sees who is calling.

"Warren, hi," she says, sitting up straight on the bench. She glances around at the other demons lazily enjoying the park. She gets off the bench and teleports back home, seeking some privacy for their conversation. "Thank you for calling me back."

"Skylar," Warren replies. He sounds tense, reserved. "I was surprised to hear from you."

"I understand," Skylar frowns, pacing her living room. "I was really out of line. Will you give me a chance to apologize?"

The line is silent except for soft breaths coming from Warren's end.

"You'll be more civil this time?" Warren finally asks.

"Yes, please," Skylar pleads, but she is feeling a little wronged. She can't just let Warren make her into his bumbling apprentice again. "I jumped to a lot of conclusions, but only because you've kept a lot of things from me. However, if you're willing to talk to me I want to know what really happened."

Warren hums. "As you might have guessed by now, it isn't exactly a topic I like to discuss."

"I understand that now." Skylar tries really hard to convey her sympathy. "However, the truth has come to light. Avoiding it now will only make things worse."

"Very well," Warren finally agrees. "Come to my apartment tomorrow. Let's do it after lunch. The topic doesn't really leave one with much of an appetite."

"Thank you." Skylar sighs in relief.

That evening, when Skylar is laying in bed, she texts Ryan to check in.

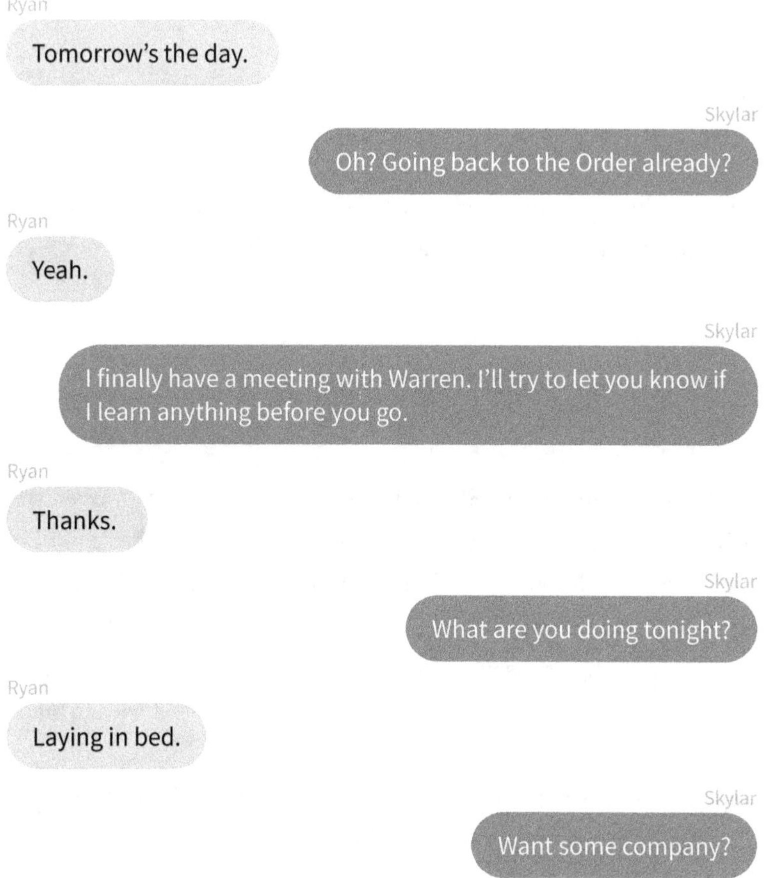

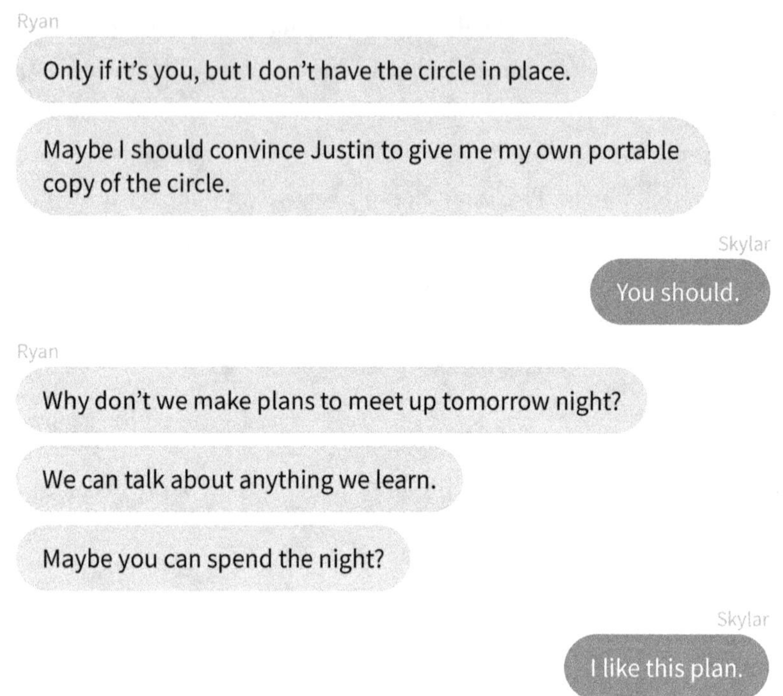

Plans in place, they wish each other a goodnight. Skylar drifts off to sleep with a pillow tucked under her arm as a poor replacement for a certain warlock.

Friday afternoon comes and Skylar makes her way back to Warren's apartment. Kris promises to stay at home and wait for her, so her plan is to go there after. Skylar doesn't get all dressed up this time. She doesn't feel like adding to the artifice that Warren always wraps himself in. Instead, Skylar is wearing a pair of blue jeans with a large gray sweater that hangs comfortably off her shoulders. She runs her fingers through her hair before she knocks on the door and waits for Warren to answer.

He opens the door dressed in a pair of slacks and a white button-up under a blue and gray argyle sweater vest. "Skylar," he greets her simply and steps side.

"Thank you for seeing me, Warren," she says primly. She then strides into Warren's apartment, head held up.

Warren leads her back to the library, which makes Skylar a little more comfortable. All their important conversations have taken place in the library. They take their usual seats, Warren with his back to the large windows, and look at one another for a long moment.

"Where shall we begin?" Warren crosses his legs under the table and folds his hands in his lap. "I haven't spoken about these events since I came to the demon realm. I can't fathom how to start."

"How did you know Thomas Andrew Smith?" Skylar asks. It feels like a natural starting place and more neutral than *Why did you kill him?*

Warren gazes down at his hands and takes a deep breath. "I met Thomas before I joined the Order of the Knowing Well," he begins, raising his gaze to meet Skylar's. "I did not come from a family of warlocks, but neither did he. We'd both started with just a scholarly interest in magic.

"I was studying world literature and mythology in university with a focus on the use of magic in fiction when he found me. I'd written a paper about magic realism as metaphor, but apparently it hit very close to describing the truth of real magic. It had been published in an academic journal and that's the sort of thing the Order looks for. Both as a source for knowledge but also for recruiting other like-minded members."

"So, you couldn't do magic yourself?" She asks when he pauses long enough for her to get a question in. It feels reminiscent of her lessons when she was a child.

"As it turned out, I could." Warren gives a short, harsh laugh. His eyes drop to the table, but they seem to lose their focus as if he isn't really seeing what's right in front of him. "I had never tried before because I didn't think it was real. I used to wonder: if Thomas hadn't been the one to find me, would things have ended up the way they did? Would I be here? Or would I have grown old in the mortal realm, blissfully ignorant of the magic that surrounded me?"

Skylar's heart squeezes at the regret in his voice. "Did you ever come to a conclusion?"

Warren blinks and looks up as if only just remembering that Skylar is still there. "In a way. If I hadn't ended up in the Order, no one would have stopped

Thomas. Then it wouldn't have mattered that I wasn't banished to the demon realm, because he would have brought the demon realm to us."

Skylar frowns, trying to parse what Warren is implying. "Wait, what?"

Warren holds up a single finger as if asking her to be patient. "Thomas Andrew Smith was a brilliant man and a very talented warlock," Warren nods as he speaks. "He took me under his wing. First, as an apprentice. Then, over the years, we became friends."

Skylar feels a weird envy worming its way into her chest. That was how Warren and she had begun, but they never became friends. Now, Skylar is beginning to perhaps understand why that was the case.

Oblivious to her inner feelings, Warren carries on with his story. "The only thing that was greater than Thomas's natural aptitude was his ambition," Warren sighs and leans back in his chair. "He was well respected and had a magnetic charisma. I don't know when it happened, but at some point, I looked around and realized there was a small coterie forming around him within the Order. Loyalties began to shift from the Order to Thomas.

"He once told me, almost as a jest: *'It's not about knowing well, Warren. It's about knowing better.'* He laughed and I had too at the time. However, I think that was when I started to realize the larger implications that split loyalties could have in the Order. Thomas had surrounded himself with yes-men and was willing to break codes of magical conduct to further his own objectives."

Skylar finds herself leaning closer, enthralled by Warren's story. "And what were those objectives?"

Warren gestures with his hands as he spoke next. "At first, I thought it was just about becoming the head of the Council of Elders. From there, Thomas could help shape the Order's codes and rules. Lessen restrictions on certain types of magic. A subsect had grown within the Order calling themselves the Coterie of Knowing Better, assuming progress was being inhibited by the rules. It was towards the end that I realized that he no longer had his sights on the council, but on something bigger.

"I kept trying to reel him in. Convince him that the regulations were there for our safety, but that was probably why it took me too long to figure out what was really going on. Since I wasn't blindly agreeing with him, he started sharing less and less with me. I'd foolishly assumed he'd taken my advice, but he'd simply stopped telling me what he was doing."

"And what was he up to?" Skylar's elbows are resting on the table in front of her as if trying to close the distance between herself and Warren.

"His goal wasn't just the council or the Order." Warren sits up and leans towards Skylar as well. "He'd done a lot of research on demons, the structures of the dimensional planes, and the bindings that keep us trapped here."

Skylar feels the blood in her veins run cold and her and her voice comes out a whisper. "Why?"

"Thomas Andrew Smith sought ultimate world domination," Warren frowns. "Not just within the Order, but everything. In order to achieve that, he needed the most powerful army in the world he could find. Stronger than any man and with limitless power."

"Demons," Skylar breathes.

Warren nods. "He believed he had found a way to summon the demons back to the mortal realm and keep them under *his* control."

Skylar shakes her head in disbelief. "That's madness."

"I wouldn't have believed it either," Warren agrees. "Except it was Thomas. He was going to try it, whether it worked or not.

"By this time I had been left out of his planning, but I managed to hear whispers of it from the other coterie members. I showed up as he was preparing to enact his plan. The circles had been drawn, the spell components gathered, and a dozen members of the coterie assembled for a mass summoning."

"How did you stop it?" Skylar is chewing on her bottom lip as she listens to Warren's tale.

"I tried to talk him out of it at first. Convince him that it was too dangerous to try. If he was wrong, he may summon something dangerous. Or he could end up getting rid of the pocket dimension without bringing any of the demons over. They'd be lost to all warlocks forever.

"But, really, I was afraid he'd bring the demons out of the demon realm, breaking their tie to that realm without having any control over them. Now, decades later, I think the only thing worse than that would be if Thomas Andrew Smith had actually succeeded. Imagine one power-hungry warlock in charge of every demon in existence here."

Skylar blinks at him. "But you weren't able to talk him out of it."

"No," Warren shakes his head and drops his chin. "I tried to convince him, then I tried to convince the others. When that didn't work, I tried to destroy the tools and components they'd gathered, but I was too outnumbered. I was restrained by the other coterie members as Thomas tried to start the ritual. Magic was filling the air and I felt desperate to stop him.

"I wrestled free from those that held me back and physically tackled Thomas. We struggled. The magic hung in the air like an omen of impending disaster. It was during our scuffle that it happened.

"He'd tried to stab me with the athame he was wielding, but I tore it from his hands and stabbed him instead. I must have hit something vital because he bled out then and there. The magic dissipated. I found myself covered in my mentor and best friend's blood while surrounded by his most loyal converts. You can guess what happened next."

Skylar's heart sinks. Warren sits before her not the arrogant demon and teacher she grew up with, but a broken man. "They brought you to the rest of the Order and accused you of murder," she finishes for him gently.

"You were always bright," Warren says with a sad smile. "Thankfully for me, the others waited for a proper hearing from the Order rather than just killing me themselves. The cowards." Warren gives a bitter scoff. "Naturally, no one believed my tale of the events. Thomas was too well known and respected by the Order. However, they delay gave me time to cast one last spell."

Skylar's mind races, trying to think what could possibly have helped him in that moment. "What was it?"

Warren runs his fingers through his short hair, pushing the fringe back from his face. He hasn't aged a day since he arrived in the demon realm so it's hard to imagine these events took place half a century ago. "I got rid of every last copy of the book Thomas had authored with the others in the coterie. Whatever secrets he'd been hiding to bring about his world domination could not be used again. Not without extensive reconstruction, which I doubt anyone but Thomas could manage."

"Thomas Andrew Smith's book?" Skylar feels dread bubble up inside her. "One that he wrote for the Order of the Knowing Well?"

"Yes," Warren says, his eyes narrowing at Skylar. "Why?"

"I think there may still be a copy left," Skylar says, hoping she is really, really wrong.

Warren leaps to his feet. "What? Why do you say that?"

Skylar swallows. "Because that's how I met my warlock, Ryan Smith. He found a book authored by his great-great-grandfather in an attic."

"Fuck!" Warren slams a fist down on the table with a resounding bang. "Shit. I was so sure I'd gotten every last one."

"I think you did, except for this one," Skylar says. "Ryan has been keeping it safe from the Order."

Warren's eyebrows rise in surprise. "Really? That's good. That's very good." The older demon crosses his arms over his chest as he begins to pace the length of the table. "As long as that book stays away from the Order, it should be fine. It's been so long, there's no way there's still anyone loyal to Thomas in the Order anymore."

"Actually, about that," Skylar chews on her bottom lip. "Ryan joined the Order to find out what happened to Thomas and some other things for me. They are kind of forcing him to bring the book back to the Order. Like, soon."

Warren's eyes go wide, the yellow of his irises on full display. "No, Skylar! That cannot happen! There's no way to know if there are any remnants of the coterie left in the Order's ranks."

"Fuck," Skylar mutters and pushes away from the table to dig her phone out of her pocket. She immediately texts Ryan as Warren looks on in panic.

"So, your warlock got that to work?" Warren says in surprise as he nods to the phone.

Skylar feels a blush rise to her cheeks. *Her warlock.* The messages sit, unread. "Uh, yeah, but he's not answering."

"It's absolutely vital that his copy of the book never makes it into the coterie's hands," Warren says with all seriousness. "Do you understand?"

"Of course," she snaps, feeling the weight of potential disaster preparing to crush her. Her mind races as she stares at the messages, praying for a response. Maybe Warren is being an alarmist? "But, I mean, Kris and I looked through it and nothing said *Demon Apocalypse 101.* Maybe there isn't anything about his plans in there?"

Warren shakes his head. "If it's Thomas's copy, I'm positive there will be."

"Fuck," Skylar curses again under her breath as she wills the phone to receive a response. Still nothing. Then she remembers Kris. "Wait! Kris has a connection to a different warlock. Maybe he can stop Ryan."

"Then what are you waiting for?" Warren throws his hands up as if ushering Skylar out.

"Right!" Skylar gets up and runs from Warren's apartment. She practically flies down the stairs and darts out to the street before teleporting to lessen the travel to Kris's apartment. She walks in through the front door, not bothering to announce her arrival.

Kris is sitting on his couch playing video games when Skylar storms in and comes between him and the television. "Skylar, I'm going to lose," Kris whines as he stretches out on the couch to look around her. An impossible task with wings like Skylar's.

"I need you to text Justin, now!" Skylar rips the controller from Kris's hands. "Tell him Ryan cannot bring the book to the Order under any circumstances."

Kris's face screws up in confusion, his hand reaching for the controller. "What? Why?"

"I'll tell you in a minute, but first we have to tell the warlocks to stop Ryan," Skylar growls in frustration.

Kris gives an annoyed huff and pulls his phone out to text Justin. Skylar moves around the back of the couch to look over his shoulder as he types.

Kris

Bunny, you have to stop Ryan.

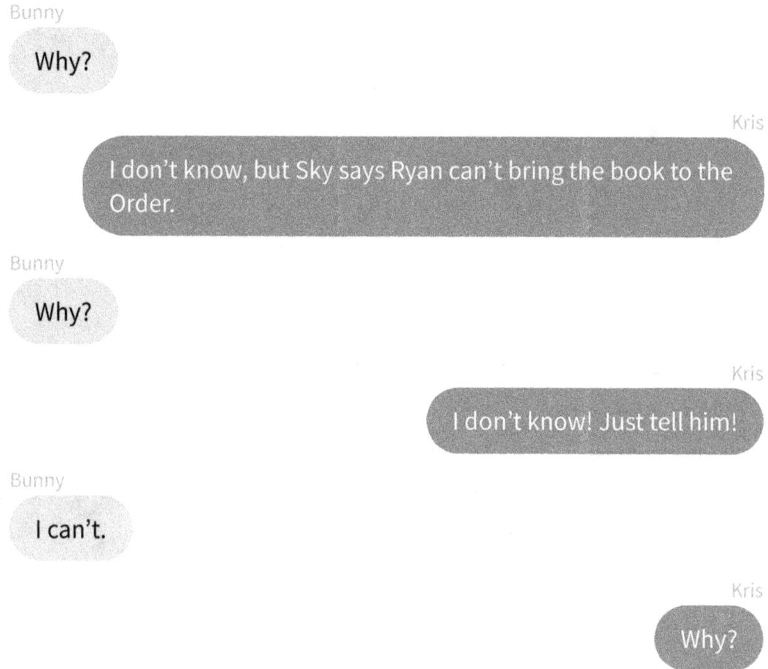

Skylar feels her heart pounding against her ribs as the words scrolling on Kris's phone. She hopes that she is wrong, but then Justin's next message appears.

21

Dungeons & Warlocks

AFTER THEIR TUESDAY EVENING summoning with Skylar and Kris, Ryan feels as confident as he can possibly feel that bringing the book to the Order isn't as bad as he thought. He hangs out with Ethan and Justin for a little while after the demons are sent home. The three just discuss scheduling and what their next few days looked like. Ethan could easily rearrange his schedule, but Justin has a few professional shoots lined up.

Wednesday morning, Ryan sends Dahlia a text message, because calling feels way too nerve-racking. Besides, what does one talk to another warlock about over the phone?

Ryan

Dahlia, this is Ryan. I'm contacting you about arranging my next visit. When might be best for you?

Then he goes about the rest of his day. He does his best to put everything to the back of his mind and treat today like any other day before he found the stupid book that has become the bane of his existence. He works at the bookstore, comes home, makes dinner for himself and texts Skylar. It's not until he's getting ready for bed that he gets a response from Dahlia.

Dahlia

Warlock Smith, thank you for contacting me.

Tomorrow isn't good because I have a client meeting. Friday is probably the best time. I have a meeting in the afternoon, but if you can get to the estate by four, I should be free. Does that work for you?

Ryan

Sure. I'll see you Friday.

With the new meeting set up, Ryan isn't as nervous as he thought he would be. He has the digital backup of the book, so even if Dahlia insists on keeping the original, he won't be without the book's contents. Besides, he's been to the Order's estate enough times fear around the unknown is fading.

He lets Skylar know the meeting is arranged, and he learns that she is also going to meet with her mentor the same day. Everything seems to be panning out. He manages to go to sleep rather easily after everything has been settled.

Friday comes and Ryan takes the hefty book with him to the bookstore early in order to get some work done before his meeting. There's time to get a few lingering projects completed before he has to ride out the estate that afternoon. It also gives him a chance to let Ethan know his plans for the evening. Sadly, Justin has a photo shoot he just can't cancel, but he's offers to pick up Ryan if he's still there after his shoot.

Ryan has the ride-share pick him up at the bookstore. The drive out to the estate is a little slower than their previous trips due to the fact that it's Friday afternoon. People are trying to get out of the city for the weekend, so traffic is backed up. It's a little after four thirty when the car drops him off at the driveway. He shoots Dahlia a text message that he's arrived as he makes his way up to the main doors.

Dahlia is standing inside the entry, smiling, as Ryan lets himself in.

"I'm sorry I'm late," he apologizes as the door swings shut behind him. "Traffic was a pain."

"No worries," she reassures him. "I've been working from my office here, so it wasn't an inconvenience to me."

Dahlia is wearing a pair of black slacks and a silky peach wrap-around blouse. Ryan always feels underdressed next to her, and today he has barely bothered with a pair of black jeans and a red-and-black-striped long-sleeved shirt.

Ryan nods awkwardly. "Okay." He doesn't know what else to say. He hasn't found an easy companionship with her like he has with Dolores and Sunmi.

Dahlia's eyes shoot to his bag. "Did you bring the book?"

He shifts the weight of the bag across his shoulder. "Yeah, I said I would."

Her smile widens. "Come, let's go down to the archives. We can safely inspect it there." Then, without waiting for an answer, she spins on her heel and starts down the hall.

Ryan trails after her through the halls with a little thrill of anticipation. Getting back into the archives is exactly where he wants to be. He feels reassured when she stops at the door he bumped into Sunmi last visit, reaffirming he had been going the right way. And maybe this will be his chance to look for that information about his ancestor he couldn't find last time.

She leads him down the staircase into the basement room. He is surprised to find there are others already gathered. Alexander Kim is there, as well as the member of the Elder Council from his swearing in called Warlock Houghlin. There are a few others whose faces he recognizes, but he can't recall them by name: another man in his late fifties and a woman in her early forties. They all turn and greet Ryan with a smile when he arrives.

"Come," Dahlia smiles at him and gestures for Ryan to join her at a large table in the center of the room. Everyone else gathers in a circle around the table. There is an air of excitement that makes Ryan nervous.

Ryan stands beside Dahlia as he puts the bag on the table and pulls out the large book. "Will Dolores and Sunmi be joining us?" he asks, trying to seem calm and casual. "I'd have thought something like this would be of interest to them."

"Oh, I'm sure they'll get their turn." Dahlia smiles, but her eyes carefully follow Ryan's hands as he extracts the book and puts it down on the table.

"Cool," Ryan murmurs.

As soon as his hands leave the book, Dahlia is pulling it closer to herself. She gently opens the cover and looks over the first few pages.

"Is it authentic?" Warlock Houghlin asks. He is standing directly across the table from Ryan and Dahlia.

"Only one way to tell," she replies.

Dahlia flips through the pages, her eyes skimming over the contents as she goes. Then, on the final pages of the book, she stops. There is nothing written between the final page and the back cover of the tome. Ryan watches on in confusion as she pulls a crystal rod from a pocket in her slacks. It's small enough to fit in the palm of her hand and no thicker than the wand Justin had made for himself. The crystal itself is a deep amethyst color. She holds it gently between her thumb and pointer finger.

"Reveal to me the things unseen," she murmurs as she waves the crystal over the pages of the book. Magic tingles along the back of Ryan's hand that's closest to the book just before a faint purple glow appears along the corner of the back cover.

Ryan's eyes go wide as Dahlia puts the rod down and picks her perfectly manicured nail at the paper covering of the back of the book. Carefully, she begins to pull back the paper revealing the cloth binding underneath. Ryan gasps as she gently tears open the back of the book. "What are you doing?"

There, behind the backing, is a folded sheet of paper that is different from the pages of the book. It looks like lined notebook paper to Ryan. Cautiously, Dahlia pulls the paper out of the binding and unfolds it. Her eyes light up as she reads the page. "This," she declares, "is your ancestor's true legacy."

"What?" Ryan asks, confused. He cranes his neck to look more closely.

"Let me see," Warlock Houghlin interrupts. His hands tremble as if he wants to snatch the page from Dahlia's hands, but it looks too delicate to do so.

Dahlia places the page face up on the table so that those close enough can see, which includes Ryan. The first thing he notices is the drawing that takes up the bottom third of the page: three circles, intersecting with intricate designs along the borders. Ryan has no idea what the design could be used for. His instinct tells him its purpose is to facilitate magic, like the circles to summon or create the warding stones. The top of the page contains tiny, scrawling print that looks like both an incantation and a list of materials.

"What is this?" Ryan tries again to get an answer as the other warlocks gathered gasp in amazement. He gets the distinct impression that everyone but him knows what they are looking at.

"This," Dahlia says with great reverence, "is Thomas Andrew Smith's crowning achievement. His final piece of brilliance that never got the chance to be made reality before he was struck down."

"Really?" Ryan feels his jaw drop as he looks back to the piece of paper. Whatever this magic is, was it what had gotten his ancestor killed? It feels like the blood in Ryan's veins has turned to ice. That all of his fears and paranoia about magic are coming true.

Unaware of Ryan's growing distress, Warlock Houghlin takes over speaking from Dahlia. "This is Thomas Andrew Smith's final vision for the Order. A way to secure our dominance and bring about a new era of magic. Not just for us, but for the world." He looks across the table to smile at Dahlia. "Warlock Jones, you've done a great service to the Coterie of Knowing Better. You'll have a place of leadership in the new world order."

"New world order?" Ryan is left looking between Warlock Houghlin and Dahlia, both of whom are grinning ear to ear.

"Yes," Dahlia beams at Ryan when she turns to face him. She reaches out to take his hands in hers and it takes all of his willpower not to shake her off. "And with you here, I'm sure it'll be a success this time. Thomas Andrew Smith was brilliant, but your raw talent is remarkable. There's no way the spell can fail a second time."

"Now, now," Warlock Houghlin interrupts. "It didn't fail the first time. It was interrupted, but I don't disagree." He looks to Ryan. "With you in our ranks I'm sure we'll reach new heights that, since the time of Thomas Andrew Smith, have never been imagined."

Ryan glances from Warlock Houghlin back to Dahlia. "What exactly is this grand plan? I don't know if I'm just slow to understand what the page says."

Dahlia laughs and shakes her head. "No, of course not. It's a very complex spell. We of the Coterie of Knowing Better have heard tales of the plan from our ancestors and previous Coterie members. The plan is to bring those who were cast into the demon realm back to the mortal realm, but under our complete control. That way no other order or individually practicing warlock will have access to the demon's magic. Then, with unlimited power at our command, we will bring magic to the whole world."

Ryan feels dizzy as his head spins with this new information. No wonder his ancestor died: that sounds like an unimaginable power grab. "Um," Ryan says, his mind racing for something to say. "This sounds dangerous. Maybe we should get some of the others to check the spell. Make sure it'll work. I bet you Sunmi and Dolores would be helpful."

For the first time since he stepped through the door that day, Dahlia's smile disappears from her face. "They are not a part of the Coterie," she simply says. "We are offering you a place of honor in our ranks. A chance to become more powerful than you already are. Don't you want that?"

Ryan is gobsmacked. "Fuck, no," he says, twisting his hands to pull them away from Dahlia. "This sounds really dangerous. And kind of power hungry. Do you guys even hear yourselves?"

Suddenly the excitement in the room drops and shifts to something distinctly hostile. Ryan looks around at the other faces watching him with suspicion.

"Are you not Thomas Andrew Smith's great-great-grandson? Do you not want to continue his life's work?" Warlock Houghlin demands.

"I am his great-great-whatever," Ryan shoots back. "I just think that this all sounds really out there. I don't think any person or group should have that much power."

"Says the one with the most raw power among us," Alexander scoffs, surprising Ryan. He'd forgotten the guy could even talk, what with how far his head was up Dahlia's ass. The small crowd begins to murmur. Concern about where Ryan's loyalty lies seems to be the main issue.

Warlock Houghlin silences everyone by clapping his hands with one sharp sound. "Warlock Smith, I do not think you have read the room correctly. You are either here to help us reach our goals, or you are in the way. Which is it?"

"I'm not going to be a part of this scheme," Ryan growls. His eyes dart to the page, but there are too many eyes on him. His intentions are probably too obvious, because before he can even think of reaching for the paper, Dahlia has her crystal rod back in her hand.

"Sleep!" She screams the word at him as she points the rod directly at his head.

The force of the magic feels like a physical blow against his skull. Ryan tries to push through the sinking sensation and grab the page, but everything seems to slow down and, rather than reaching for the paper, Ryan feels himself collapse to the floor. His vision slowly goes dark. The last thing he sees is everyone's feet in front of him as someone walks to the solid stone wall. It shimmers and an opening appears where none had been before, but then Ryan loses his fight against unconsciousness.

Darkness takes over.

The next thing Ryan is aware of is the feeling of cold stone against his back. Slowly, pulling himself out of a deep slumber, Ryan wakes back up. He blinks, trying to look around and figure out where he is. The dimly lit room is all stone floor and walls. He finds himself lying on the floor in the center of a metal cage. His body protests as he tries to push himself to a sitting position. He groans because his back hurts from lying on the hard floor for an unknown amount of time.

Once he is sitting, he takes a second to look around the room beyond the fucking cage. Actual real life torches are in sconces along the walls. Chains are also attached to the walls, both inside his cage and out. There is no door that he can find. The only furniture is a small wooden table and chair on the far wall where a familiar man sits: Alexander Kim. He is lounging on the chair reading a book and either hasn't noticed Ryan has woken up or doesn't care.

As Ryan slowly comes back to himself, he feels a flash of panic. These assholes locked him up in a dungeon! He has to let the others know what's going on. His heart drops to his stomach when he realizes his phone isn't in his pocket. He pats his other pockets: all of them are empty.

"We took your phone, idiot," Alexander says without looking up from the pages of his book. He turns the page with long, delicate fingers. "We aren't as stupid as you seem to think we are."

Ryan scowls at him. "You are if you're going to go through with that plan." He pushes himself to his feet and walks over to the door of the cage. The bars are cold beneath his fingers as he grabs the gate and rattles it.

"Sure, shaking the door," Alexander yawns. "That's going to work." He slowly turns the page of the book he is reading.

Annoyed at the other man, Ryan feels around the mechanism for a lock to the cage. Once he finds the opening for the key, he presses his palm to the lock. He shuts his eyes and tries to control his breathing to make his racing heart slow down.

When he finally feels calm enough to focus, Ryan tries to imagine the magic as he pulls it to himself. Ryan feels the energy tickle along his skin and focuses on the palm of his hand. He tries to remember what it felt like when he opened the lock on his fire safety box before. The feeling of magic stings as he imagines it flowing from his hand and into the lock.

"Open says me," he growls, imagining the magic moving through the lock and opening the door.

Instead, it feels like the magic hits the lock mechanism and then rebounds against his hand. A piercing pain shoots through his palm and Ryan yanks his hand away from the lock. Blood drips from a deep gouge in the middle of his palm and a wave of nausea passes through Ryan's stomach. He pulls his hand back in through the cage bars and grips the hem of his shirt in an effort to stop the bleeding.

Alexander sets the book down and finally glances at him with an unimpressed look. "The lock is warded against magic, dipshit," he sighs. "Though I will admit I've never seen anyone try to cast anything with their bare hands before. That must have hurt. You're better off just sitting there and waiting until they decide what to do with you."

Ryan scowls at him. "Why am I here? Why lock me up and not just get rid of me?"

"I was asking them that same question." Alexander stands up and stretches, still dressed as ever in an expensive looking suit of black and gray. "The higher-ups seem to think that you just need some convincing. You're too new to the Order of Knowing Well to understand what the Coterie of Knowing *Better* is offering you. And too powerful to just get rid of."

"Fuck that," Ryan spat. "I'm not a megalomaniac."

For the first time, Alexander looks at Ryan like he can actually see him. "You're short-sighted, but you're not a pushover either. I argued that keeping you alive is just asking for trouble, but I'm too new to the Coterie to have any real say."

"So that's why you're stuck babysitting me?" Ryan laughs harshly.

Alexander glares at him. "I would just put you out of your misery, but that would get me punished. So yes, I'm here to make sure you don't kill yourself trying to get out of your cage."

"You're doing a bang-up job so far." Ryan frowns as he looks down at his hand fisted in his shirt. Blood is spreading from where he holds the fabric.

"You're not going to die from that," Alexander sighs and settles back in his seat. "Just sit back and relax. It may be a while." He picks up his book and goes back to reading.

Sitting seems like a good idea to Ryan, even if he doesn't have a comfortable place to relax. He moves to the solid stone wall that makes up one side of his cage and sits with his back to the rock. It's better than nothing.

The only thing he has to occupy himself with for the moment is his wound. Slowly, he lets go of the shirt and finds blood still pooling in the cup of his palm, albeit a bit more slowly than before. He really wishes he'd read more of Ethan's books rather than just assuming he'd have time to do it later. There has to be a way to stop the bleeding at least. Healing is definitely a magic people study.

Skylar's voice comes to Ryan's mind. *Imagine what you want . . .*

Sure Skylar was talking about making illusions, but that level of imagining had seemed to work for Ryan in other aspects of magic so far. A pang of longing distracts him from the pain in his palm for just a moment. If Skylar had been there, Ryan is sure he wouldn't have found himself in this situation.

Ryan tries to push thoughts of Skylar away so he can focus on his hand instead. He tries to imagine the magic again, coming to his palm like it had before. Squeezing his eyes shut so he won't focus on just the blood but on the invisible magic that is already tingling along his skin he tries to imagine the magic knitting his skin back together like a 3D printer or something. That the magic could weave his flesh closed.

Once he has the image planted in his mind as firmly as possible, he gives a soft command. "Heal."

The magic prickles along the skin of his palm and causes the wound to sting even worse. Ryan holds his breath and tries to push through it. The pain makes it feel much longer than the actual seconds it probably takes, but finally the magic dissipates.

Ryan peels his eyes open and looks down at his hand. The small pool of blood still sits there. He reaches his hand out to his arm's full extension and dumps the blood from his hand onto the stone floor. Then he wipes the remaining blood on his already bloodied shirt. There is a rough looking lump of shiny, pink flesh in the center of his hand that looks like fresh scar tissue, but at least it has stopped bleeding.

A sigh of relief escapes his lips as his head falls back to rest against the hard stone behind him. He is no longer bleeding, but he is still trapped. And his friends have no way to find him. Even if they could get through the warded front doors.

Despair settles in his chest as he realizes he is now at the mercy of a band of warlocks seeking world domination. He should have known better. Why had he let his guard down?

Ryan peers through the bars of his cell at Alexander. The warlock has gone back to completely ignoring him.

There had been only five warlocks gathered in the archives, but was that the extent of the Coterie's membership? Ryan can't be sure. He only knows for sure that Dolores and Sunmi aren't members because Dahlia said so. But could even that be a ruse?

With nothing else to do but sit, Ryan isn't going to just wait for them to come to him. No matter what the Coterie offers him, there is no way he is going to willingly join their ranks. His only option is to try and find a way out.

The bars of the cage are too narrow for even his skinny body to make its way through. And they seem to be made of the same material as the door and lock. He is afraid to push his luck trying to break through with magic in case the bars are also warded and he hurts himself worse.

The only thing he has on him is his clothes. Nothing to draw with or make a circle other than his own blood. He looks at the drying puddle and determines that, even if he had the summoning circle memorized, that wouldn't be enough blood. Besides, that would be very obvious. Even Alexander would notice if Ryan tried to do something as elaborate as drawing a summoning circle with blood in his cage. Ryan already proved he could do magic within the cage when he healed himself. He just can't risk directing the magic at the bars.

So, with magic off the table Ryan is left with just himself. Just being on his own has served him well up until magic came into his life. Will he be able to talk his way out of this one? He isn't sure, but time is on his side. As long as they are willing to keep him alive, he has time to think his way out of this problem.

22

Bypassing the Wards

"THERE'S STILL HOURS UNTIL sundown," Skylar exaggerates. "What are we going to do?" She paces back and forth in Kris's living room.

"*We* aren't going to do anything until we hear back from Bunny," Kris says from the couch. His phone is still in his hand as he waves it at Skylar. "We are going to wait until we know there's actually a problem."

Skylar stops pacing to look at him. "But then what? We can't do anything to help from the demon realm."

Kris takes a deep breath and looks up at her with big, sympathetic eyes. "There may not even be a problem. Warren even said this group existed over fifty years ago—maybe they're all dead now. We could be worried over nothing."

"I feel it in my gut," Skylar says, wringing her hands. "Ryan shouldn't bring that book anywhere near that place."

"And if there is a problem, big emphasis on *if*, then Bunny will contact us and we can come up with a plan." Kris reaches to grab Skylar's wrist before she can start pacing again. "Don't waste your energy pacing a groove in my floor. Come. Sit down. Chill out."

Skylar is shaking her head even as she sits down next to him. "I should have told him to wait. I should have made him delay his plans until we could be there."

"Stop," Kris insists. "You're going to drive yourself up the wall with these 'should haves.' Let's focus on what we can do when we can do it."

It's been almost two hours since they first texted Justin. The warlock promised to get Ethan and head directly to the estate. Skylar has tried sending multiple texts to Ryan, but there is still no response. No one is able to get in touch with Ryan from either realm. The lack of contact is just adding to the sour pit growing in Skylar's stomach.

Kris must see the wheels spinning in her head, because he reaches over and begins running his fingers through Skylar's hair. "Hey, look at me." Skylar turns her focus to her best friend. "We've got this. I believe in Bunny. Hell, I even believe in Ryan. He may be clueless, but he's powerful. It's not going to be easy to make him do anything he doesn't want to do."

Skylar swallows. "Yeah, you're right. Of course you're right." The soothing petting and the calm words help her mellow out. At least until Kris's phone starts pinging again. Skylar's heart leaps into her throat as her eyes shoot to the phone in Kris's hand.

Bunny

Made it to the estate.

Cannot get in. No answer at door.

Still no response from Ryan.

Please advise?

And just like that, all Kris has done to calm Skylar is undone. "Fuck, I told you something was wrong!"

"Shh," Kris says, stroking Skylar's arm with his free hand as he texts Justin back.

Kris

Is there another way in?

Bunny

We'll look, but Ethan thinks it's not going to work.

They are definitely warded against anyone who is not a member of the Order.

Skylar groans and jumps back to her feet. The nervous energy shooting through her won't allow her to sit still any longer. "Shit," she curses.

"Skylar, please sit back down. We don't know if anything is wrong." Kris tries to coax her back to the couch. "Maybe his phone died? Or maybe there's no signal where he is?"

"I think we need to assume the worst here, Kris." Skylar begins pacing again, gesturing with her hands as she speaks. "The way Warren speaks about those in the Coterie that followed Thomas and how they set him up to be punished is bad news. What if they are still around?"

"I don't disagree," Kris finally admits. "So let's go at it like this: we can't do anything until the sun goes down and we get be summoned. If Bunny and Ethan haven't found a way in or heard from Ryan, then what can we do once we're there?"

"We storm the castle," Skylar exclaims. "We need to get in there and find out for sure."

"Okay," Kris placates her. "But the place is warded. Until we're there we have no way of knowing if the wards are resistant to demon magic or not. Since we are assuming the worst, how do we get in against wards meant to keep us out?"

Skylar's frantic mind finally feels like it clicks into place as an idea comes to her. She smiles as she looks to Kris. "We get a member of the Order to invite us in."

A skeptical eyebrow rises on Kris's face. "And how are we going to find one to do that?"

"We don't need to find one," Skylar says smugly as she pulls her phone from her pocket once more. "We already know one." She taps the screen and hits the dial button.

The line picks up. "Skylar," comes the familiar voice.

"Warren," she replies. "Do you feel like taking a trip to the mortal realm?"

It takes some coordination with Justin, but by the time the sun sets the summoning is taking place. Justin doesn't have the unbridled magic that Ryan has, but he is able to pull all the demons over to mortal realm one at a time. First Kris, then Skylar, and finally Warren.

"Am I standing on a piece of paper in a field?" Warren sneers as he looks around. They are, in fact, standing on Justin's paper circle which happens to be laid out over short cut grass in a field.

"It is the closest place we could find that's out of sight," Ethan explains.

Justin stands at the edge of the circle. His face is flushed and sweat drips from his temples. Summoning this many demons looks like it really took a lot out of him. "So," the warlock says once he seems to have found his breath. "What's the plan?"

"He doesn't look like a bunny," Warren comments, his gaze looking Justin up and down. Then his eyes shift over to Ethan. "Neither does he."

Skylar sighs. "This is Justin," she says as she gestures to the warlock. "And this is Ethan." She gestures to the scholar. "And be nice or they won't let us out of the circle."

"We most certainly will," Ethan says. "We can't do anything without your help."

Warren smiles at him. "Smart man."

"Yeah, yeah," Justin says. "We'll let you out, but first let's go over the plan."

"It's quite simple," Warren says as he crosses his arms over his chest. "The wards on the estate of the Order of the Knowing Well are strong, but there's one important failing. The stones that hold the warding are built into the foundation. So they can't recast the spell to change the specifics. The wards are set to let any members of the Order in and anyone else by express permission only."

"How does that help us?" Ethan gestures towards their small group.

Warren smiles at him then places a hand on his own chest. "I am a sworn member of the Order of the Knowing Well."

Justin frowns at the announcement. "They didn't take away your membership?"

"Eh," Warren shrugs. "It's unlikely anyone did that. Membership is supposed to last until death. And I, being sent to the demon realm, had no way to return to the estate of my own accord."

"So, you're saying there's a chance that you won't be able to get in," Ethan points out.

"A small one," Skylar pipes up, trying to keep the hope for their plan alive.

"As charming as it is to meet Sky's new friends," Warren drawls, "are we just going to stand here all night?"

"No." Justin drops to his knee and picks up a corner of the paper the circle is drawn on. He then rips it, destroying the border of the circle and effectively releasing the demons from within.

Kris frowns and rushes to Justin, draping his arm around the warlock's shoulder. "Aw, baby. Not your handy dandy roll-up summoning circle!"

Justin gives a short laugh. "I can make another one."

"Or two," Skylar suggests. "After we save Ryan like you summoned us here to do."

"Right!" Ethan raises a finger, then points off towards the tree line at the edge of the field. "That way." As the demons move off the circle, Ethan ducks down to grab the ruined paper up and shove it into the nearby bushes.

Warren chuckles and starts marching off through the grass. "Let's see if I still remember my way." He leads the eclectic team of warlock, mortal, and demons across the field and through the trees.

It doesn't escape Skylar's notice that Kris is walking with Justin hand-in-hand, their fingers interlocked. With Warren leading the way, Skylar falls into step beside Ethan. She looks up at the taller man. His cheery demeanor is gone and even his bashful grin doesn't make an appearance. His lips are set in a line as he keeps his eyes on Warren.

"Do you think I'm overreacting?" she asks, drawing Ethan's attention.

Ethan blinks, glancing over at Skylar is if just realizing she was there. "Overreacting?" Then he shakes his head. "No, I don't think you are. Ryan has never stayed in the estate past nightfall. And he always messages us if his plan changes. I think something went wrong."

Skylar sucks her bottom lip in between her teeth and chews on it nervously. She isn't sure if she had wanted Ethan to agree with her or reassure her.

Just as she is thinking of what to say next, the trees clear and they are walking across a well-manicured lawn. A large building sits ahead of them in the dim light of a full moon in a clear sky. It doesn't look like a castle, but any magic used to ward it could be stronger than stone walls.

"Welcome to the Order of the Knowing Well," Warren says he climbs the stairs to the main double doors. "Now is the moment of truth." Everyone crowds onto the front porch as Warren grabs the handles of the doors and throws them open. He steps into the entryway and turns to smile at them. "Please, come in."

Without hesitation, Justin crosses the threshold and enters the building. Hope rekindles in Skylar's chest as they all step inside, the door shutting behind them.

"Okay, where do we look?" Skylar asks out loud, looking at the various ways out of the first room. There are staircases going up and doors that lead out in every direction.

"That is the one room Justin and I have both been in." Ethan points at the large doors directly across from the entrance.

"The ballroom," Warren says with a nod.

"Where would they take the book? Maybe a library? That's could be where Ryan is," Kris guesses.

Warren tilts his head as if considering the suggestion. "That's as good a place to look as any," he admits. "This place has several libraries as well as an archives room. Those are the places books are most likely to be found."

"Lead the way," Justin says.

Warren's eyes narrow at the warlock. "Is that an order?"

Justin's brow knits together. "What? No! Please, help us."

Now it is Warren's turn to look surprised: his eyes going wide and his mouth dropping open just a bit. "Very well," he says once he's recovered.

The older, reptilian demon then strides off down the hall to the left. Justin and Ethan follow on his heels. Skylar lets Kris go before her since her wings will effectively fill the hallway and block the view of anyone behind her. So she walks at the tail end of the group constantly checking over her shoulder in case someone comes up behind them.

Skylar's heart is racing as they move down the halls. The five of them aren't exactly stealthy. And with the three of them being demons, it will be hard to excuse their presence. On top of everything, they are in unfamiliar territory.

They twist and turn down the halls and Skylar's mind is filled with so much static she can't be sure she'd find her way back out if they need to run.

Finally, they stop outside a set of doors. Warren turns to point at them. "This is the largest library on the grounds," he whispers so low Skylar has to strain to hear him.

"I'll go first," Justin says, equally as low. "No offense, but—" He gestures to his face as he looks at Warren.

"We'll be right behind you," Kris says as he pats Justin on the back.

With a glance at everyone crowding the hallway, Justin gives a nod and then quietly opens the door. He peers in, but Skylar is too far back to see what Justin is looking at. Slowly he opens the door the rest of the way and steps into the room. It feels as if everyone in the hall is collectively holding their breath. A moment later, Justin's face appears in the doorway.

"It's empty," he whispers.

Kris darts into the room before Warren strides in behind him. Skylar waits for Ethan to go in, but just as he is about to turn the corner into the library a woman's voice calls out.

"Ethan Forrest?" The older woman's voice is surprised and startles Skylar so much that she jumps, her wings fluttering. The stranger had just come around a far corner with a mug in her hand. She seems confused to find Ethan there.

Instead of going into the room, Ethan slams the door shut. It does hide the fact that there is anyone else with him, but it leaves Skylar out in the open. "Warlock Choi," Ethan says with a smile.

"What are you—" she begins to ask, but then her eyes shift past Ethan and fall to Skylar. She pulls her wings back as much as possible, but it is impossible to completely hide them. The moment the woman registers Skylar's presence, she drops her mug. "Demon," she hisses.

"Wait," Ethan cries, throwing his hands up to try and stop her.

Skylar grits her teeth and prepares to counter any spell the warlock throws at her. The woman is delayed trying to pull a wand out of her pocket.

"Please, Warlock Choi, hear us out," Ethan pleads as the wand comes up to point in their direction.

"Mr. Forrest," she says, the stress evident in her voice. "How is it that you find yourself in our estate with a demon outside of its summoning circle? I thought you couldn't cast magic."

"I can't, I swear! This is Ryan's, um, friend," Ethan stumbles over his words. "We're here looking for him. We think he's in trouble."

Skylar nods. She raises her hands to show she is harmless. To be fair, all she has to do is snap her fingers and magic would happen, but she wants to put the woman at ease. If the warlock yells for help things could go badly very quickly.

"I'm just here to make sure Warlock Smith is safe," Skylar reiterates Ethan's explanation while playing into what any warlock would expect of a bound demon.

Their ploy seems to be working, because Warlock Choi seems frozen in indecision. Her eyes dart to Ethan for a moment, but seem drawn to Skylar. She is the threat.

"May I?" Skylar asks and lifts her chin towards the mess in the hall. When the skittish warlock gives a small nod, Skylar lowers her hands and makes an elaborate gesture to remove the coffee stain in an offer of goodwill. She even goes as far as to refill the coffee cup and leave it sitting at the warlock's feet. "It's a little late for caffeine," she comments gently.

"It's decaf," the woman replies. Her wand dips ever so slightly and Skylar feels like she can breathe just a little again. "Why are you looking for Ryan with his demon? Why does Ryan *have* a demon?"

"It's a really long story," Ethan says, his own hands dropping from the "surrender" position they'd taken. "Dahlia Jones invited him to bring his great-great-grandfather's book this afternoon and we haven't heard from him since. We have reason to believe she wants something from him."

The wand dips further until it is at her side, but still held firmly in her grip. "There's been something about the accounts surrounding Thomas Andrew Smith," she acknowledges. "Then Warlock Smith's approval was rushed through and his swearing-in was done in secret. The whole thing is strange, but this is all above my pay grade." She blinks and then narrows her eyes. "How did you get in?"

Ethan's mouth opens, but nothing comes out. Skylar cuts in to save the floundering man. "Warlock Smith gave us permission to come in only if he could not come out." As she says it, she wishes they'd thought of that beforehand. She's not sure if such a stipulation would work with the wards. The good news is, this warlock seems to think it could, because she doesn't question it.

"Very well. I haven't seen Warlock Smith today, but if you believe he's here I think we need to take you to the Council of Elders. I suspect there's a lot of rule breaking going on, but they are the ones to decide such things." Warlock Choi sweeps her hand in front of herself, gesturing to them. "After you. Head back to the entryway."

Skylar purposefully lets Ethan go first so she can stand between the human and the warlock. Ethan is the most vulnerable of their party. And as long as the warlock doesn't know Skylar's name she can't be sent away from outside a summoning circle.

Once they are back in the main hall, the warlock orders them to stop. She goes to a side table and pulls a piece of chalk from the drawer. Quickly, the warlock pulls back a corner of the rug to reveal the hardwood floor underneath. With speed and precision, she draws a quick binding circle. Not like the protection circle meant for summoning, but one for simply containing. She then looks to Skylar. "You will wait here while I take Mr. Forrest to see the Elders."

Ethan takes a breath, perhaps to argue, but Skylar holds up a hand to stop him. "If it'll make the warlock feel more comfortable, I shall wait here for their judgment. But every moment we waste, my warlock may be in danger," Skylar warns. Wings held high and chin up, Skylar gracefully steps into the circle and faces Warlock Choi.

"Seal," the warlock says and points the wand to the circle. It flashes a brilliant blue color and Skylar feels the magic lock into place. With Skylar safely held, the warlock turns her attention back to Ethan. "This way, young man." She then leads him out of the room by going up the staircase and out of Skylar's line of sight.

Skylar sighs and looks down at the circle. She presses a hand against the invisible barrier and sees the ring light up blue against her attempt to cross it. "Fuck me," she says to herself, feeling useless.

"I'll pass," comes Kris's chipper voice.

"Kris," she gasps. Skylar looks up to find that Kris, Warren, and Justin have followed them in secret.

"Free her," Warren says to Justin and gestures to the circle.

Justin's eyes are wide in surprise. "Me? How?"

"Just rub your foot over the circle like you would a summoning circle," Warren sighs.

"Oh!" Justin smiles and speeds over to rub at the circle. "Why do I have to do it?" he asks even as he does the task.

"You didn't have to be the one," Warren admits with a smug smile. "I just wanted to try bossing a warlock around for once."

"Where's Ethan?" Justin asks, eyes wide with worry once more.

"The warlock took him to see the Elders," Skylar replies, unsure what that means. "They went upstairs."

"Is that good or bad?" Kris shoots his question in Warren's direction.

Warren frowns. "It depends. Back in my day, the council was not part of the Coterie. But who knows what may have changed since then?"

"That warlock doesn't seem to know what is going on," Skylar points out. "If she were part of the Coterie, wouldn't she have taken us directly to them?"

"True," Warren nods. "If the Coterie is still operating in secret, I think we best check the basement."

Warren turns to lead them back down the hallway they'd come from, but Justin calls out, "wait!" They all pause to look at him. "What about Ethan?"

"Either that warlock is taking him to the Coterie, which is where Ryan may be, or he's being taken to a legitimate head of the Order. In the second case, he may be able to solicit their aid," Warren explains. "So, for better or worse, the mortal is on his own and we will either be brought back to him, or he'll come looking for us."

Justin sucks a breath in through his teeth, glancing up the staircase as if he can see where Ethan has gone. He then looks back to Warren. "Okay, I trust you."

Warren blinks in shock. "Today is just full of surprises," he mutters as he turns and leads the way once more.

Once again, Skylar feels like they are being led through a maze that she has no hope of navigating on her own. They stop only when Warren once again points to a door. "This is the entrance to the archives. If I'm correct, this is likely a more dangerous place to check. Warlock," he looks to Justin. "Do you have a magic implement?" Justin nods and pulls out a small wand. "Very good, but I think we demons should go first this time."

Kris grasps Justin's free hand in both of his and looks nervously between Skylar and Warren. Skylar smiles and gives him a nod of encouragement, moving to stand beside Warren. Her wings could block Kris and Justin's view but could also protect them from being seen as well. She spreads them as wide as she is able to still pass through the narrow opening.

As silently as possible, Warren pulls the door open. Voices drift up the dimly lit stairwell. Skylar feels her jaw clench as nerves ping through her. She only hopes and prays that Ryan will be at the bottom of this staircase.

After Skylar exchanges a nod with Warren, the older demon begins to creep down the stairs first. Skylar follows close behind and can only assume Justin and Kris are following after. They make their way downward towards an opening at the bottom of the stairs. Light and voices are coming from the space beyond the opening. Skylar can pick out at least two voices, one a man's and the other a woman's.

Warren holds up a hand to stop Skylar. He then points to the stairs then back at Skylar. Does he want Skylar to stay in the stairwell? She isn't exactly sure, but before she can ask Warren is turning away and stepping from the darkness of the stairs and into the room at the bottom.

"Well, well, well," Warren says with bravado. "It seems the Coterie of Knowing Better is still lurking in the shadows."

"Demon," a man gasps. It is alarming not being able to see what is happening. Skylar takes one step down the stairs and tries to peer into the room from the cover of darkness.

She had been wrong about her warlock count. There are two men and two women in the room below. The walls of the stone room are mostly obscured by shelves. A large table mas been moved to one side and the floor of the room is covered in the strangest circle Skylar has ever seen: three intersecting circles with elaborate (if somewhat unfinished) symbols scrolling the edges. She doesn't have much of a chance to study the circle more, because her attention is drawn to the warlocks as Warren faces off against them alone. Her mentor is smart enough to not wander into the circle, but Skylar doesn't know if it is because he knows what it is or because everyone should be wary of unknown magic.

Warren sighs as he *tsks* at the warlocks. "Foolish warlocks meddling in things they shouldn't," he says, obviously antagonizing them.

"How did you get in here?" one of the men demands, the wide sleeve of his robe fluttering as he brings a hand up to point a wand at Warren. "Who is your master, demon?"

"Obviously not you," Warren says as he levels his gaze at the man. "I come for one warlock, and one warlock alone. Ryan Smith. Give him to me and you can carry on with your pathetic attempts at controlling that which should not be controlled." Warren continues to slowly pace around the circles.

Skylar has no idea where he is going, but the warlocks sidle around the circle to keep it between them and the unknown demon. If Warren keeps it up, eventually the warlocks will have their backs to Skylar. Maybe that is the plan?

Her heart is pounding against her ribcage as she watches the scene unfold. Skylar tries to think of what she can do to either help Warren or find Ryan. There is no way to get into the room unseen at the moment, so all she can do is wait. She feels Kris and Justin at her back, but she can't afford to look away in case she misses an opportunity.

"What do you want with Warlock Smith?" asks a woman. She's dressed in slacks and a peach blouse. The other two warlocks, though they moved as a group, have fallen back behind the man and woman who spoke. Obviously those two are the ones in charge.

"Me? What do I want with him?" Warren muses. "Nothing really, but I'm curious to see the pathetic excuse for a warlock."

The woman's eyes narrow. "Then you were sent here by someone else to get him. I didn't think his silly little friend had it in him to summon a demon, let alone let one loose. You accuse us of being foolish." She gives a harsh laugh.

"Why didn't you just strike your master down where he stood as soon as you could?"

Warren stops pacing. The warlocks haven't rotated nearly enough to be in front of Skylar. She is left with Warren to the far left in front of her and the warlocks only just coming around on her right side. "Maybe what the warlock offered was too good to refuse?" Warren muses. "Perhaps revenge is a better reward."

Skylar's heart drops. *No*, she wants to yell. Is that what Warren is really after?

But while those thoughts cross her mind, something else must have occurred with the female warlock Warren is addressing. Her gaze glances away from Warren for the first time and over his shoulder. Warren turns but all that Skylar can see directly behind him is a blank wall.

"Oh," Warren says with a laugh. "I see where you've hidden him. I guess the Coterie has managed to keep it secret all these years."

A quick expression crosses the warlock's face, but she recovers quickly. "And now I know who you are," she says with a smug smile. She shoots an arm out, pointing an amethyst rod at Warren. "Warren Hayes, I banish you back to the demon realm."

And just like that Warren vanishes. They'd lost whatever opportunity they had, but at least Skylar has a clue. She looks over her shoulder and hisses under her breath. "Justin, head to the far wall to the left where there's a blank spot. I think there's something hidden there. Kris and I will distract the warlocks. Now!"

She doesn't have time to wait for confirmation. She just has to hope that the warlock will understand what Skylar is asking him to do.

As soon as she finishes speaking, Skylar spins and rushes into the room. She opens her wings wide to help obscure Kris and Justin coming out of the stairwell behind her.

"Foolish mortals," Skylar cries with as much bluster as she can manage. At the same time, she creates a plume of smoke at her feet that reeks of brimstone. She knows the warlocks won't fall for the fallen angel persona she usually plays into, but anything to distract them will be helpful to Justin. "You think you've saved yourself by sending away the weakest of us?" Skylar manages to pull the lie off with a straight face only because Warren isn't here to protest.

"They are obviously slow-witted," Kris's deep voice echoes against the stone walls from behind the warlocks. Instead of walking into the room, he obviously took the opportunity to teleport the short distance. Flames erupt around him as he appears; they light his wicked smile in dancing shadows before they are dispelled. Skylar can't help the smile that comes to her lips as all the warlocks whip around to look at him. Their attention is definitely anywhere but the direction Skylar can only hope Justin is heading.

"And do you fancy yourselves the lords of the demon realm?" The woman who has been speaking rolls her eyes. "That must mean you've been there longer, trapped there by the warlocks who managed to best you."

For an instant Skylar is worried their ploy isn't going to work. The warlock who has sent Warren back doesn't seem at all intimidated by their display, but assumes they were once warlocks like her. The two that haven't spoken yet are cowering and the man in the robes seem at least a little bit cowed.

"It doesn't matter where we come from," Kris says, lowering his chin slightly so that his horns are more prominent. "What matters is that a warlock more powerful than you sent us here to take back what you've stolen."

"We haven't stolen anything." The robed man seems to have recovered from his stupor. "We took back what is rightfully ours!"

Kris has done a great job of keeping the warlocks' attention completely away from both Skylar and Justin. She risks a glance over her shoulder to find that Justin has managed to silently creep past all of them and is poking at the wall. He has his wand in hand he seems to be gesturing at the stone. If Skylar didn't know to look, she doubts she would hear the young warlock's low murmurs as he tries to find whatever it is Skylar hopes is over there. She turns her attention back to the warlocks. It won't do to have any of them happen to glance in her direction and accidentally catch Justin.

"Think you own whatever you can get your greedy little hands on, do you?" Kris is sneering, but the words sound eerily more like something Warren would say. He is doing an amazing job stalling for time and attention.

Skylar has to figure out how to help. She doesn't want to kill the warlocks they need to find Ryan. Thoughts of using magic to bind them comes to mind, but she knows once magic starts to get thrown about, the warlocks will respond in kind. It is best to let words be exchanged for as long as possible while Justin works to find whatever secret the wall holds.

"Perhaps we did make a mistake," the woman says, glancing to the man who has spoken. "Smith may have had the book, but his friend summoned three demons and got past our wards. Perhaps we don't need Ryan to finish our goal."

Skylar feels anger well up in her gut. Before she can react and let that outrage spill out, there is a cry of surprise from behind her.

Everyone turns to find a section of the wall has disappeared. Justin crouches there in the open doorway, looking surprised. Another warlock, younger than the rest, jumps up from a chair looking just as shocked to see Justin. And behind both of the warlocks is Ryan in a cage, pushing himself to his feet in a bloodstained shirt.

After that, all Skylar can see is red.

23

Consequences

RYAN IS SITTING IN his cell glaring at Alexander Kim. His ass is going numb from sitting on the stone floor. The dust jacket of the book Alexander holds is missing, so Ryan can't even guess what the other man is reading.

"Are we really just going to sit here and ignore each other?" Ryan asks.

Alexander hums and turns the page.

Ryan frowns. "Look, you don't want me here. I don't want to be here. Why don't you just let me out and I'll get out of your way."

"Sure," Alexander says without looking up. He sounds almost bored. "You're just going to walk away and not tell anyone what you've seen today."

"You don't know me. I might," Ryan bluffs. To be fair, he doesn't know who he would tell. He can't be sure who else is a part of the Coterie. Everyone at his swearing-in ceremony is suspect, but what about the others? What if he trusts the wrong person again?

No. The only people Ryan knows he can trust are outside of the Order. He needs to get to Justin and Ethan. Then they need to get Sky and Kris. Only after that will they have the magical firepower to stop these assholes.

Just as Ryan is opening his mouth to try a different tactic, the wall behind Alexander shimmers and disappears. Alexander jumps to his feet and there, in the new opening, is Justin with wide eyes. He is crouched awkwardly with his wand in hand as he raises his eyes up to Alexander, who is right in front of him.

"What the fuck?" Alexander cries out in surprise as Ryan pushes himself up off the floor. The muscles in his legs scream after sitting for so long.

Alexander drops the book and reaches into his pocket to pull out a wand. Before he can even bring the wand up to point, Justin lashes out with free hand and knocks the wand away. The thin piece of wood goes flying and skitters across the stone floor into Ryan's cage.

Even though his legs feel like rubber, Ryan does his best to scramble over and pick up the stick. When he looks back up Justin has rotated into the room, keeping his eyes on Alexander as he edges closer to the cage. Without his wand Alexander has his hands up in a fighting stance like he is going to physically attack Justin, but he seems hesitant to strike. To be fair, Justin looks more athletic than Alexander.

Ryan shoots his arm through the bars of the cage, pointing the wand at Alexander as he yells. "Sleep!" He doesn't feel the magic move over his skin like it usually does. Instead it feels like the power is drawn to the stick and doesn't touch Ryan at all as it then shoots out towards his target. Alexander drops like a marionette with its strings cut.

Without both of them between Ryan and the opening, he can finally see out into the next room only to realize it is the archives. He sees Dahlia and Warlock Houghlin with the other two warlocks, but this time they are flanked by Skylar and Kris. Hope bubbles up in his chest when he realizes that his friends have come to save him. His gaze locks with Skylar's and the demon looks back at him with wide, scared eyes. Then those eyes narrow as her attention turns back to the warlocks.

"Bind!" Skylar screams as she lashes her arms out at the warlocks. The two unknown warlocks closest to her go stiff as a board and collapse to the ground.

Justin takes Ryan's attention away from the fight that is breaking out in the next room when he rushes to the cage and immediately looks at the lock on the gate.

"Wait," Ryan warns him as Justin raises his wand towards the mechanism. "It's magic resistant. You can't open it with your wand."

"Oh," Justin says and drops his hand. He begins looking around the room.

Ryan points towards the collapsed warlock. "Check Alexander. He might have the key."

Justin spins on his heel and begins patting through the sleeping warlock's pockets.

Ryan looks up at the next room again. The two fallen warlocks are back on their feet. All the warlocks have a wand or other implement in their hands and are shouting commands back and forth with Kris and Skylar. Like the ozone in the air around a thunder strike, the sensation of magic begins to build from the other room.

Warlock Houghlin is breaking away from the group and heading towards the not-so-secret room Ryan is being held in. Skylar is distracted trying to keep two other warlocks from overpowering her as Warlock Jones faces off with Kris. Ryan watches as Houghlin raises his wand hand towards Justin.

With his new trick up his sleeve, Ryan points the wand at Houghlin. "Sleep!"

Houghlin quickly flicks his wrist, the tip of the wand cutting through the air from Ryan towards Justin. "Deflect," he says in a firm voice. Ryan watches in horror as Justin drops to the floor beside Alexander. He didn't know magic could be redirected that way and curses himself for accidentally putting Justin to sleep.

The warlock easily steps over the two sleeping men and approaches Ryan's cage. "Send the demons back to the demon realm now," he hisses.

Ryan glares at him through the bars. "Or you'll what," he challenges the man. "Kill me? If you were willing to do that, you'd have done it already."

"What makes you think I won't?" Houghlin sneers at him.

"Because then you'll end up like Warren Hayes," Ryan shoots back.

Houghlin narrows his eyes. "Maybe. Maybe not. I could always just kill your friend." The warlock steps back from the cage to point his wand at Justin's unconscious form. "There's no proof that he's a warlock, and he isn't even a sworn member of the Order."

"Then I'll tell everyone what you've done!" Ryan feels desperate. The wand is clutched tightly in his fist, but he's worried anything he tries will just get deflected again.

"You can try," Houghlin says with a shrug. "It'll be your word against mine. A new member of the Order versus a member of the Council of Elders. That didn't work out so well for Warren Hayes."

Ryan growls in frustration and uselessly rattles the door of his cage with his free hand. From the other room come the shouts of magic spells and zings of power, but Ryan's focus is on the warlock pointing a wand at his defenseless friend. "How do I know you won't just kill us once the demons are gone?" Ryan asks.

"I guess you don't, but your options are very limited right now, Smith. You really don't have anything to bargain with from where you are. Send the demons back, now." Houghlin doesn't have to yell, he has all the power.

Ryan is back to being completely helpless. So what if he has such a strong connection to magic when he doesn't know how to use it? "You have to swear not to hurt Justin," Ryan tries to stall, but he doesn't know what for. He has no other plan.

"I swear: no harm will come to this novice warlock," Houghlin says with a triumphant grin. He knows he's already won.

Ryan bites his lip as he glares at the warlock. He wants to wipe that smug look right off the older man's face. He looks past the bastard to find Skylar still in combat with the other warlocks. She and Kris are almost side by side facing Ryan's way with Dahlia and the other two warlocks between them. Skylar's wings are pulled tight against her body so she can move freely, ducking and weaving away from the magic bolts and physical blows coming her way. She looks like an avenging angel.

Ryan's heart stings at the thought that this may be the very last time he sees the beautiful demon. He takes a deep breath to shout out the command to return them to the demon realm.

"Halt!" A cry backed by power rings out. Ryan feels magic tingle over him and freezes him momentarily.

From the stairway come more warlocks dressed in crimson robes. Men and women with their magic implements drawn. Their focus immediately goes to the demons and Ryan feels like things are only about to get worse.

Then Ethan appears, pushing his way to the front of the group. "Wait," he calls out as the wands, crystals, and orbs are directed towards Kris and Skylar. "These are our friends!"

The distraction is enough that Ryan feels the order to halt pass. Instead of sending Skylar back, Ryan looks at Houghlin to see that the man has turned to look at the arriving warlocks. Ryan points the wand at the back of Houghlin's head. "Sleep," Ryan hisses. Houghlin crumples to the ground to join Justin and Alexander in their slumber.

Desperation shoots through Ryan as more warlocks file into the archives room. "Key, key, come to me," he chants, waving the borrowed wand towards the pile of sleeping men. A large metal key slides from Warlock Houghlin's robes and floats the short distance to Ryan's waiting hand. As do Justin's car keys. Ryan snatches all the keys out of the air, shoving Justin's into a pocket. He rolls his eyes as he inserts the key into the lock. "I'm the dumbass?" He grumbles to himself. "You're the idiots who made the lock resistant to magic, but not the key." The door opens with a clang, finally drawing everyone's attention in his direction.

Sunmi's voice rises about the others. "Why is Warlock Smith in a cage and covered with blood?" It's the first time Ryan realizes the warlock, dressed in ordinary clothes, is in the crowd.

Before Ryan can answer, Skylar appears in front of him. Her wings spread wide with her back to Ryan as she faces down the new warlocks. "You can't have him!"

"I'm okay," Ryan says as he gently presses a hand against the large black wings so he can see again. Kris has obviously followed Skylar's lead and appears next to Justin, cradling the sleeping warlock's head in his lap.

Ryan's eyes lock with Dahlia's for a brief moment across rooms before she spins on her heel and runs towards the table.

"No, the page!" Ryan yells, points at her.

Skylar grabs Ryan's wrist and, between one blink and the next, moves both of them to the table. Ryan has never teleported before, and the maneuver leaves him slightly disoriented. It feels like he's been pulled inside out and flipped around just for a brief moment. It gives Dahlia just enough time to reach for Thomas's spell. Ryan darts a hand out and grips it before she can pull it away. The old sheet of paper tears.

Dahlia shoots Ryan a hateful glare before raising her crystal rod. "Obscure my path," she says.

A cold fog billows from her and fills the room in a matter of seconds. Cries of confusion come from inside the fog, but Ryan uses the distraction to his benefit.

Without looking at the scrap he still has in his grip, Ryan shoves the paper into Skylar's pants pocket. The demon is close enough that they can see only one another through the fog. Her dark eyes widen in surprise. "Skylar, I send you back to the demon realm," Ryan whispers.

Even as the first words pass his lips, Skylar's look of relief turns to one of horror. Her lips form the word "no," but she is sent away before any sound comes.

Once Skylar is gone, Ryan is confused about where he is in the room as the thick fog lingers. He places one hand on the table and waits for the mist to clear. When it does, Dahlia and the other male warlock are gone. The female warlock, whose name Ryan never got, is being restrained by two members of the Order.

"Can someone please tell me what in the world is going on?" The crimson-robed man who issued the "halt" command looks to Ryan as if he's the "someone" who can answer his question.

Ethan runs to Ryan's side, looking him up and down. "Are you okay? Are you hurt?" Alarm is in his eyes as he takes in Ryan's bloodied shirt.

"I was, but I'm okay now," Ryan reassures him.

Kris is still sitting by the open cage with Justin's head in his lap. He doesn't look up from Justin's sleeping face, even as some of the warlocks move to surround him. He just continues to run his fingers through Justin's hair.

"Am I talking to myself?" The man seems to be in charge and doesn't like it when his questions are not being answered.

"I'm sorry," Ryan shakes his head. "I don't know where to begin."

Sunmi steps forward. "Mr. Forrest told us some of the story upstairs."

Ethan nods in confirmation.

"It was a wild tale to begin with," the man says. "We came down here to confirm his accusations."

"I don't know what Ethan told you, sir," Ryan says, offering the man some respect for his position. "Dahlia Jones and Warlock Houghlin are trying to take over the Order with my great-great-grandfather's spells." The explanation feels extremely lacking, but it is the best he can put together on the spot. "Then they were going to take over the world."

"That's expressly prohibited by Order guidelines and rules," the man refutes as if that would somehow make a difference.

"Warlock Garcia," Sunmi says, clearly addressing the speaking man. "I think a thorough investigation by the Council of Elders is in order, but I'm inclined to believe Mr. Forrest and Warlock Smith."

"But what of the demons?" Another voice from the assembled warlocks asks.

"I told you," Ethan sighs. "We didn't know who we could trust, so we got all the help we could get."

"Summoning demons is extremely dangerous business, young man," Warlock Garcia says.

"Desperate times," Ryan sighs.

Without regard for the other warlocks, Ryan walks back to Kris and Justin. Now that the main action is over, the room just feels crowded with bodies. Some are stopping to look at the circled etced on the floor as others clump together to whisper. Only Warlock Garcia seems to be paying Ryan any attention as he crouches beside the sleeping warlocks. He places a hand on Kris's that rests on Justin's chest. "Is he going to be okay?" Ryan asks gently.

Kris nods. "He's just sleeping."

"Can you clean the circle from the floor before I send you back?" Ryan asks the question as quietly as he can. Kris glances past Ryan's shoulder and nods. With a snap of his fingers, the intersecting circles disappear as a cry of dismay comes from the warlocks at Ryan's back. "I'll take it from here," Ryan says with a small, tired smile. He moves his hand to the back of Justin's neck. "I send you back, Kris."

Kris disappears from the mortal realm and only Ryan's hand keeps his head from hitting the concrete.

"Where did the circle go?" Warlock Garcia finally comes over to stand over Ryan. "That would have been proof of your claims."

Ryan sighs, suddenly exhausted from all the activity. "It's also exactly what the Coterie wants," he says, gently putting Justin's head down. He stands to face Warlock Garcia. The man is slightly taller than him and looks to be in his late fifties. "Look, I'm willing to tell you everything I know, but it's not safe to assume that the Coterie ends with just these five warlocks."

The man frowns as he looks down at Warlock Houghlin and nods. "Prudent," he admits. He then turns and gestures to the warlocks standing nearby. "Let's get these three upstairs and to the visitor's quarters. Keep guards on both Warlock Houghlin's and Warlock Kim's rooms." He looks back to Ryan. "I assume you'll be staying with your friend?"

"Both of us will," Ryan says. Without being asked, Ethan comes over and stands at his side. Ryan looks steadily at Warlock Garcia as if daring him to argue.

"A lot of rules have been broken here this evening," Warlock Garcia says, his eyes shifting from Ethan to Ryan. "We're going to have a full discussion of these matters and I can't guarantee there won't be consequences, Warlock Smith."

"I was just trying to keep myself and my friends safe," Ryan practically growls. "I was invited into the Order under nefarious pretenses, and you didn't even notice. But fine, do what you think you must." And apparently that means putting Ryan, Ethan, and Justin in a room as heavily guarded as the perpetrators.

It is a long night. Ryan recovers his bag, phone, and Thomas Andrew Smith's book from the table before he joins Ethan and Justin in one of the upstairs bedrooms. The visitor's room has a bunk bed and Ethan insists Ryan make use of it once he is done being questioned by the Order for the evening. He's done his best to give his account of what happened, but he knows there are going to be more questions in the morning. If only the Order were more open to answering some of his own questions, but they seemed uncertain as to his role in what transpired despite being the one locked up.

He pulls off his soiled shirt before he lies back on the top bunk since Justin is easier to maneuver onto the bottom one. Besides, it would be horrible if the photographer woke up confused and fell off the top. Ryan turns on his phone and in moments gets a flood of alerts. Missed calls and texts from Justin, Ethan, and Skylar. Guilt for making his friends worry hits him unexpectedly in his chest.

"I'm sorry," he says into the quiet of the room.

"For what?" Ethan's voice carries up from where he sits at Justin's bedside.

Ryan takes a deep breath. "For everything? I shouldn't have come here without you and Justin. Hell, I never should have joined the Order in the first place."

"You don't have to apologize for that, Ryan. I'm just glad we got here in time."

"Thank you for saving me," Ryan says instead.

"This was all Warren and Skylar's plan."

"Warren?" Ryan gasps. He rolls over to look down from the top bunk. "Warren helped?"

Ethan looks up at him. "He's how we got into the Order."

"Wow," Ryan says in awe as he lays back down. The man who killed Thomas Andrew Smith had come to save him? Probably not specifically for that. He probably came to stop the Coterie from enacting Thomas's plan.

Ryan takes the next several minutes to go through the voicemails and text messages. Finally, saving it for last, Ryan opens his chat log with Skylar.

Skylar

YOU CANNOT GIVE THE BOOK TO THE ORDER!

TEXT ME ASAP

Ryan, please, please, please look at your phone.

Ryan, let me know you're okay.

I swear, if you're back at home I'm going to kick your ass.

Ryan, please be okay.

We're coming to get you.

Wait for us.

What the fuck was that???

Why did you send me away?

Why aren't you answering your messages still?

Answer me ASAP!

Kris just came back. He tells me you and Justin are okay.

Please text me when you can.

I don't think I'll be able to sleep tonight until I hear from you.

It is nearly two in the morning by the time Ryan finds himself reading through the texts. He sincerely hopes that Skylar is asleep.

Ryan

Sorry for the late reply. I just turned my phone back on.

I had to answer a lot of questions, but I'm okay.

Justin is still sleeping off the spell. Ethan and I are staying with him at the Order for the night.

Skylar

Thank FUCK you're okay.

Why did you send me away like that?

Ryan

I gave you something I wanted to make sure they couldn't take from me.

Demon Skylar

The crumpled piece of paper?

Warlock: Ryan

Yeah. I'm sorry I couldn't explain.

I'm also sorry I couldn't keep our date.

Demon Skylar

Oh? Summoning me over to bone is a date now, is it?

Ryan huffs out a laugh and rolls his eyes. " It doesn't sound like you're sleeping," Ethan calls from below.

"I'm letting Skylar know we're okay," he calls back as he types out his next message.

Ryan

You know it was going to be more than that.

Skylar

I know.

Can we do it tomorrow night?

Ryan

Assuming the Order doesn't keep me locked up for breaking a bunch of rules? I'd like that.

Skylar

I guess we'll have a lot of stuff to talk about.

Ryan

Yeah.

Skylar

Thank you for texting me. You should try to get some sleep.

Ryan

You too. Let Kris know Justin is okay.

And just like that, it is as if the last of Ryan's energy is sapped from him. He falls into a dreamless sleep.

The next morning is full of activity. Ethan and Justin are not allowed to leave the room they'd all slept in, but Ryan is asked to meet the Council of Elders in their official chambers after breakfast. It is a meal of oatmeal and fruit, but to Ryan's relief it is brought to them by Dolores and Sunmi. Ryan has a fondness for the older women. They've always been kind to him, and it turns out they'd helped Ethan convince the Elders that there was a problem to begin with.

"Keep an eye on them?" Ryan asks the two women as the other members of the Order wait to escort him to the meeting.

"They'll be fine," Dolores reassures him.

Ryan nods and looks at Ethan and Justin. They are sitting side by side on the bottom bunk finishing their food. Justin woke up feeling just fine, but curious as to what had happened.

Ryan looks back to Dolores. "There's a book in my bag that you may be interested in," he says with a small smile. Of anyone in the Order, he doesn't mind sharing Thomas's book with these two women.

The last thing he hears before the door shuts behind him is Dolores and Sunmi's delighted gasps. Another small smile comes to his lips, even as he is marched through the halls of the estate to the meeting. He's wearing his own shirt again after a warlock kindly removed the bloodstains from it, but he feels out of place among all the robed warlocks who are gathered when he enters the chambers.

A long, curved table sits at the head of the room, and the rest of the space is filled with other people standing around. Ryan is escorted down an aisle between onlookers to stand before the table. There are eight seats, but one is left empty so Ryan finds himself standing before seven members of the Council of Elders.

"Is Warlock Houghlin not joining us this morning?" Ryan asks, perhaps a little too cocky for the predicament he is in.

Warlock Garcia sits just left of the center of the table. "Warlock Houghlin will not be fulfilling any duties as a member of this Council until the investigation is finished," he says. "Warlock Smith, you are here to face our judgment on your behavior that led to the events of last night."

"My behavior that kept the Coterie from taking over the world? Or my behavior that led to the Order being embarrassed by a couple of non-members?" Even as the words leave his mouth, Ryan knows he isn't doing himself any favors. He feels defensive and cannot understand why *he* should get in trouble. Still, he would rather take the brunt of the Order's anger than have it wash over to Justin and Ethan.

The crowd murmurs and Ryan gets a mix of disdain and approval from the members of Council before him. He stays rooted in place and keeps his hands clasped in front of himself to keep from fidgeting under everyone's gaze. It feels like his skin is crawling with the amount of scrutiny he is undergoing.

When the crowd quiets the hearing continues. "You shared secrets of the Order with non-members," says another warlock. A woman who actually reminds Ryan a lot of his mom: small, but with a commanding authority as she speaks. "You've used magic against other warlocks and have summoned demons without proper instruction or guidance."

Ryan opens his mouth to argue, but he is cut off by Warlock Garcia. "Silence," he says. "Now is the time for listening, not for talking."

Ryan feels rage well up in him, but then he realizes the words aren't solely directed at him. The entire room has begun to whisper again, and Garcia is calling for order once more.

"The Council acknowledges that some of your use of magic has been in self-defense, so we will waive the usual punishment," the woman continues.

"However, this leaves us with you telling outsiders of the Order's secrets and summoning demons without instruction."

Warlock Garcia clears his throat and raises his voice to be heard over the growing whispers of the crowd once more. "Given the circumstances—" he pauses and waits for silence before going on "—the Council acknowledges that in this instance your indiscretion helped prevent a larger crisis. We also acknowledge that Ethan Forrest and Justin Perez have been unfairly discounted from membership due to a faction within the Order working against the Order's best interests."

Ryan listens, but the words are starting to sound too good to be true. Is he going to be off the hook because of the Coterie's influence? He holds his breath, not wanting to hope for too much.

"We have spoken to Warlock Houghlin and Warlock Sousa," says another member of the Council. "They are both tight-lipped about the faction's very existence. However, Warlock Kim has been more forthcoming with information. Their trials will take place when the investigation is done."

Ryan gulps. Was this his trial? Is he seriously on trial for what happened?

"What we have gathered so far is that there is a secret faction within the Order of the Knowing Well that has been quietly influencing policy and actions for at least half a century," Warlock Garcia announces and the crowd gasps. That helps explain to Ryan why so many people are here. It seems what happened last night is a huge wake-up call for the Order. "Because of Warlock Smith's assistance in bringing this to light, he will have a reduced sentence."

"Um, sentence?" Ryan asks, fear churning in his belly.

Warlock Garcia looks at Ryan. "You are being given probationary status. You are not allowed on the estate grounds without an escort until these matters with the faction can be settled. They obviously manipulated the system to get you in, and we have to be cautious of your presence within our ranks because of their actions. Ethan Forrest and Justin Perez will be given prospective membership status again but will not be considered for membership until after we have concluded the investigation."

Ryan lets out a long breath. None of this seems too bad, honestly. He didn't even want to be a member of their stupid Order anyway.

However, it seems like Warlock Garcia isn't quite finished. He folds his hands in front of him. "Then there's the matter of the demons. Warlock Smith, you are forbidden from performing demon summoning magic until you receive the proper training."

Just like that it feels like the rug has been pulled out from beneath Ryan's feet. He is amazed he manages to stay standing. "What does that mean?" he asks, his voice barely a whisper.

"Once you're a full member of the Order again, you will be given proper training and instruction on all magics," says another member sitting at the table. He is a man who wears a permanent scowl on his face. "Until then, if we find you are summoning demons without instruction you will be expelled from the Order."

Ryan wants to tell them to fuck off but he isn't sure what "expulsion" covers, so he bites his tongue for the time being. The thought of not seeing Skylar again, even for a day, is not acceptable to him. Already he knows he'll risk discovery rather than go without seeing the demon, but the council doesn't need to know that.

"Thus concludes our hearing this morning," Warlock Garcia announces.

The room erupts into a cacophony of voices, but Ryan is already being led back out through the crowd. He is escorted back to the room where Justin, Ethan, Sunmi, and Dolores are waiting. Ryan must look as stricken as he feels, because they all look at him with concern as he rejoins them.

"Gather your things and we will escort you from the premises," says one of Ryan's guards before he shuts the door.

Dolores and Sunmi have the book open on a desk in the room and seem to be going over it together while Ethan and Justin are still seated on the bunk bed.

"What happened?" Ethan asks.

Ryan looks at Sunmi and Dolores, who have abandoned the book to face him. "I've been given probationary membership status," he says and watches as recognition forms on their faces. "You know what this means."

"We do," Sunmi says with a nod. "But don't worry about it too much. Dolores and I will always be happy to escort you if you want to come back to the estate."

"Not sure that I do," Ryan mumbles, "but I think I'll have to. They've also forbade me from summoning demons again until I have proper training." That draws a gasp from both Ethan and Justin. Ryan shoots them in the he hopes they keep their thoughts to themselves until they are away from the Order's eyes and ears.

"That's probably for the best," Dolores says with a nod. "It's a miracle that you boys managed it safely so far."

"Ethan and Justin are also going to be reconsidered for membership, but not until the investigation into the Coterie can be done." Ryan feels his shoulders slump. "Who knows when that'll be? Dahlia and that other warlock got away and apparently Houghlin and Sousa aren't talking."

"Chin up," Dolores says. "I'm sure we can get things sorted rather quickly."

"Maybe," Ryan sighs. "For the moment, though, I think we should leave."

No one argues.

Ryan gathers up his book and his bag, thankful that no one tries to stop him from taking his property with him. Then his guards escorts Ryan, Ethan, and Justin through the door and all the way to the front gates.

Looking up and down the road, Ryan doesn't see anything but pavement and trees. "Um, Justin? Where's your car?"

Justin frowns. "I left it parked a little ways down the road. I hope it hasn't been towed."

"Only one way to find out," Ethan announces and the trio begin marching back towards the car.

Luck is on their side and the car is still there. Ryan looks on in confusion as Ethan stomps into the bushes and comes out a moment later with a large crumpled sheet of paper. "I didn't want to leave this behind," he says, catching Ryan's curious stare.

"Good call," Justin nods and opens his trunk to shove the paper inside.

"What is that?" Ryan asks.

Justin sighs as he shuts the trunk once more. "That *was* my summoning circle. I'm going to have to make another since we had to tear it open to let the demons out last night."

Ryan glances over his shoulder to make sure that there isn't anyone from the Order creeping up behind them at that moment. "We should talk about this later," he hisses and ushers everyone into the car. They have a long drive back into the city to go over recent events.

By the time they are pulling up to Ryan's apartment, Justin and Ethan are all caught up. "So, what are you going to do now?" Ethan asks.

"Right now?" Ryan says as he climbs out of the backseat of the car into the bright midday sun. "I'm going to go inside and read through that beginner's magic book you lent me. If this experience has taught me anything, it's that I can't rely on dumb luck anymore. Also, that maybe a magic implement will save me a lot of discomfort in the future."

Ethan frowns at him from the front passenger seat through the window. "What about the Order making you a probationary member?"

"Fuck them," Ryan sighs. "I never really wanted to be a member anyway. The only reason I won't just tell them to shove it is because I don't know what they'll do to me. Besides, I'd hate to ruin your chances of getting in." He gives Ethan a sincere look since he knows that is what the man wants more than anything.

"It won't be worth it if I can't do it with both of you," Ethan replies with a sad smile.

Justin grins from the driver's seat. "I don't care either way, but be careful," he warns. "I don't know if they'll let you off easy again."

"Thanks. Have a good day, you two." Ryan waves as Justin drives away.

Then he trudges into his basement apartment and flops down on his couch. He has all day until he can summon Skylar again. Sure, he wants to do what he told the others he would do, but he needs a little bit of time to recover from the last twenty-four hours. He holds up his hand, staring at the lump of scarred flesh at the center of his palm. It's a reminder that things could have gone so much worse.

24

Nothing but You

FOG FILLS THE BASEMENT room, but Ryan is within her reach. That is all that matters. Relief floods through Skylar that Ryan, bloodied but in one piece, is found. Now they only have to figure out how to get away from the warlocks. Moving Ryan across the basement was easy, but she is less than sure about teleporting a human far distances. Before she can say anything to him, Ryan is shoving something in her pocket and sending her back to the demon realm.

"No!" She calls out as the metaphysical cord holding her to the mortal realm snaps and sends her back home.

She is standing in Warren's living room since that is where Justin had summoned them from. Warren is sitting on his couch sipping an amber-colored liquor from a tumbler. He looks up at Skylar and raises an eyebrow. "How did they manage to send you back?"

"Ryan did it," Skylar growls. She pulls out her phone and starts angrily texting, demanding Ryan explain himself immediately.

"So you found the hidden door?" Warren sits back and sips from his drink again.

"Justin found it." Skylar continues her furious texting while answering.

Warren gives a hum of approval. "Smart boy. Reminds me a bit of myself."

Skylar scoffs at that. Justin is far nicer than Warren has ever been, but maybe that is just the Warren she knows now. Surely a lifetime in the demon realm would change anyone. How has it changed her?

She is about to send another text to Ryan's phone, but Kris reappears at the exact same spot he'd been summoned from. He is kneeling, his head hung low and his hands on his thighs as he takes a ragged breath.

"Kris!" Skylar moves to his side. Warren has enough decency to stay on the couch and out of their way. "Are you okay? What happened?"

Kris looks up at her, tears filling his lash line. "Sky," he says before he breaks into a sob.

She throws her arms around her best friend. "What happened? Are they okay? What's wrong?" She does her best to repeat her questions a bit more calmly than before. She rubs Kris's back in an attempt to soothe him as the sobs rack his body.

"I think so," Kris says through his tears. "But Bunny! He was so helpless."

"Did the other warlocks threaten Justin and Ryan?" Skylar pets the back of Kris's hair.

Kris shakes his head, smearing tears across Skylar's shoulder. "No, I don't think so. I think Ethan got the warlocks to help them."

"Okay," Skylar says and continues to try to comfort her friend while putting her own concerns aside. Despite her efforts, she herself is still tense and wound up inside. What if they had left Ryan and Justin to an even greater threat?

"I don't know what happened," Warren gently breaks into the conversation, "but if warlocks broke up the party, they're probably part of the Order and not the Coterie. Your friends are probably safe. At least for now."

Kris wails again and Skylar shoots Warren a death glare when.

"Shh," Skylar tries to calm her best friend down again. "Warren wasn't even there for that part. He doesn't know what he's talking about."

Warren gets up, knocking back the last of his drink. "I see that my helpfulness has been exhausted. You can see yourselves out, or you can stay in Skylar's old room. Either way, I'm going to retire for the evening." He leaves to disappear into the library, but Skylar doesn't pay him any mind.

Instead, she helps lead Kris to the spare bedroom and gets him settled into the bed. Before she can change herself into sleep clothes Skylar takes out her phone. There are still no messages from Ryan, so she types out a few more to him, letting him know that Kris is back and to text her back when he can.

She then pulls out a piece of crumpled paper from her pocket. It looks like the bottom half of a sheet of notebook paper with a torn, jagged edge. Whatever it was, it is what Ryan was struggling with the warlock in pink for. On the paper is most of a shape made of three intersecting circles. The same shape that had been on the floor where Kris and Skylar fought the warlocks.

There are also a few scribbled words, but nothing Skylar can make out beyond "athame" and "cedar." Whatever was on the top half of this page is gone, taken by the nasty warlock who disappeared into the fog. Hopefully the Order's warlocks caught her before she could get away. Skylar tucks the paper under her phone on the nightstand.

Skylar changes into sleep shorts and a tank top before sitting at the head of the bed, leaning against the headboard with one shoulder to let her wings drape over the side. Kris scoots closer and curls up with his head on Skylar's lap. Slowly, Skylar begins carding her fingers through the hair around the base of Kris's horns. They don't talk, and slowly Kris drifts off to sleep.

Left with her own thoughts, Skylar can only think over the events of the evening. The last she'd seen of Ryan, he was covered in blood and surrounded by warlocks and fog. Skylar is back to helplessly waiting and it exasperates her greatly. Being left to the whim of a warlock to summon her back never felt so frustrating. Even her direct link to Ryan doesn't work if the warlock won't check his phone.

She sits for hours as Kris sleeps in her lap. Exhaustion from the evening is settling in, but her concern for Ryan won't let her sleep. The best Skylar can do is shut her eyes as her thoughts continue to flow back to the warlock.

When the text alerts on her phone finally goes off in rapid succession, she jerks herself nearly right out from under Kris. She takes a breath, trying to calm her heart as she reaches for her phone on the bedside table. Skylar frowns, reading the Ryan's report of the evening. She doesn't like the idea of the three of them staying inside the Order, but Ryan has his phone and is texting her. That has to count for something.

A few more texts and Skylar feels reassured that Ryan is safe. At least for the night. Gently she slips out from under Kris so she can curl up against him. The day caught up to her hours ago. Once she is lying down, sleep overtakes her.

The next morning Skylar wakes up to Kris's horn knocking her in the forehead. "Ow," she groans, still groggy from the late night.

"Sorry," Kris apologizes before leaning down to immediately kiss Skylar's temple. "I rolled over too fast when I woke up."

"Someone should warn Justin what he's getting himself into," Skylar teases which only make's Kris's face fall.

"I wish I knew if Bunny was okay," Kris sighs, collapsing onto his back.

"Ryan texted me last night. He said that Justin was sleeping off the spell. They are safe."

Kris gasps, eyes narrowing in at her. "You should have opened with that!" He dives at her starting a tickle fight. Kris is on the losing end since Skylar's wings don't allow for her to be easily pinned to the bed.

The laughter seems to be what they both needed when they finally break apart to get up and change. It feels strange to Skylar to be back in Warren's house after having left so many years ago, like putting on an old pair of shoes that don't fit the same anymore. She leads Kris to the kitchen where the older demon is sitting in the breakfast nook. He has a bowl in front of him and is sipping from a tea cup when they come in.

"Good morning," Warren says. With a wave of his hand, two more bowls appear at the small table. "I hope you both slept well."

"This one slept like a baby," Skylar teases as she sits down to a bowl. Brunch is two sunny-side up eggs over hash browns. "I didn't really get to sleep until I heard from Ryan."

"Which explains why you're up just before lunch," Warren points out as if he didn't just wake up, too. The man is still in his pajamas.

Kris takes the seat next to her, but his eyes shoot wide open. "That's right!" Food ignored, Kris holds out his hand and his phone appears. He quickly starts tapping through the menu to check his messages. "I don't have anything from Bunny," he whines.

"If he was sleeping off a spell, the effect should wear off soon," Skylar tries to console him.

Warren just hums in agreement. "So, the Order gave Ryan his phone back? That's a good sign."

Skylar nods as she takes another bite of her brunch. The egg yolk breaks over the potatoes, making a tasty mess. "Yeah," she says after she swallows. "I guess they had a lot of questions for him."

"I'm sure they did." Warren finishes the last of his meal. He sets the bowl aside and pulls his cup and saucer closer. "Demons running loose in the Order's secret lair? A cult set on world domination in their own ranks? I imagine the Council of Elders will have a lot of questions and probably more than a few punishments to mete out for the whole debacle."

"But not for Bunny and Ryan, right?" Kris has his fork halfway to his mouth.

Warren shrugs as he sips his tea. "It's been a long while. I don't know what the atmosphere is like at the Order anymore. Probably not Justin, since he's not a member. However, Ryan broke their code of conduct by telling non-members about the Order's business."

"They can't punish Ryan," Skylar declares, slamming her fork down on the table. "If it weren't for Ryan, they never would have found out the Coterie was still in existence."

"And if it weren't for Ryan, the Coterie would never have gotten their hands on Thomas Andrew Smith's copy of that book." Warren levels a look at Skylar. It is his teaching face: he is trying to make her think critically about the situation.

"Ryan might still be in trouble," Skylar says softly.

Warren nods. "Possibly."

It is Skylar's turn to pull her phone back out of her pocket (where she's also stashed the piece of paper) and tries to text Ryan.

Skylar

Hey, did you sleep okay? Are you safe?

As she waits for a response, Skylar considers the piece of paper again. Her first instinct is to show Warren, but a small voice in the back of her head tells her to wait. She remembers watching Warren taunt the warlocks last night with talk of revenge. Was he telling the truth? Would that revenge extend to Ryan? Fear lingers in her chest as she waits for Ryan's response.

"You both are so rude," Warren comments. "Didn't anyone ever teach you not to have your phone out at the table?"

"Nope," Kris and Skylar reply in unison.

"Stop acting like rude demon trainees," Warren mutters under his breath before sipping his tea.

Skylar is ready to be frustrated at the warlock for not telling her everything right away, but as the last text comes up, she feels her cheeks grow warm instead.

"You're both being disgusting," Warren moans, but the smile on his lips belies the jovial nature of the complaint. "Go be gross at your own apartments."

"Not before we finish our meal," Kris says, setting his phone down and scooping a fork full of food into his mouth.

Skylar and Warren laugh as his cheeks puff out with food. Skylar shoots Ryan an "okay" and goes back to her own meal.

That afternoon, Kris goes back to Skylar's apartment with her. When Skylar mentions she has a date with Ryan, her best friend insists on helping her pick an outfit. "Something that says 'you want me, but you can't have me' would be perfect," Kris says as he goes through Skylar's collection of clothes.

"But what if he already has," Skylar says from where she sits on her bedside.

"You harlot!" Kris smirks. "I thought for sure Bunny and I were going to be first. Quick! Details! How was it?"

"Ahem, I thought a gentleperson doesn't kiss and tell?"

Kris pulls two sheer tops out of the closet and turns to glare at her. "How dare you use my words against me!"

Skylar breaks into giggles as Kris holds up the two tops for her to consider. Regardless of how silly it feels to be picking out an outfit like a first date, they still have an ensemble planned by the time that familiar tug pulls in Skylar's belly.

"Have fun," Kris calls as Skylar lets the pull bring her from the demon realm back to the mortal one.

She blinks in surprise when she realizes the magic that is summoning her is familiar, but not the magic she is expecting. Dressed in black jeans and a black sheer top decorated with golden sparkles, Skylar appears inside a paper summoning circle that is laid out in the center of Ryan's living room. The furniture has been pushed to the sides to make room, but Justin is the warlock who stands before her.

"What?" Skylar glances around and finds Ryan standing just to the side. He has also taken the time to dress up in a nice black shirt under a black blazer and actual trousers.

"I'll be on my way," Justin says, a blush highlighting the apples of his cheeks. "Have fun, you two. Don't do anything I wouldn't do."

Ryan rolls his eyes. "Thanks, bye," he says as he reaches over and practically shoves the blushing man towards the door. Justin gives them one last smirk before leaving.

"Why did Justin summon me?" Skylar asks, puzzled.

"Well, strictly speaking, I was told I can't perform summoning magic until I get proper training from the Order," Ryan says, rubbing the back of his neck. "I was going to do it anyway, but Justin showed up before sundown with one of his paper circles and insisted that maybe I'd be pushing my luck if I tried to disobey the Order so quickly after they let me off lightly."

Skylar's jaw drops. "Let *you* off for what? Saving their asses?"

"Well, I kind of broke a few of their rules along the way, but because it kept something worse from happening, I wasn't exiled or whatever. Just made a probationary member," Ryan explains.

Anger erupts in Skylar's chest. "What the fuck! You got used and nearly killed and they punish *you*?"

"I wasn't nearly killed," he argues. He holds out his palm where a mound of hastily healed scar tissue sits. "This is the only damage I took. It looked worse last night than it was."

Skylar gasps. "Is that where all the blood had come from?" She takes a step closer to the edge of the circle to look.

"Yeah." Ryan's eyes are downcast towards the scar. "My magic kind of backfired when I tried to unlock the door of my cell, but I was able to take care of it on the fly."

"You consider that being taken care of?" Skylar is skeptical.

Ryan pulls his hand away and looks offended at her tone. "Hey, for me, this is pretty damn good. I seriously realized I don't know what I'm doing."

"I've been telling you that since day one," Skylar points out. Despite her harsh criticism, Ryan is leaning down to tear the paper and break open the circle.

As soon as she is able, Skylar is kneeling down with Ryan and grabbing his scarred hand. She holds it palm up so she can look more closely at the mangled, pink flesh. "This won't do," she says softly.

Gently, Skylar brings Ryan's hand to her lips so she can press a kiss to the damaged skin. Then she blows softly and the scar resolves into nothingness, disappearing as if it were never there to begin with. She feels Ryan's hand shudder in her grasp.

"Thank you." His voice is deep and breathy.

Skylar looks up to meet those clear eyes swirling with desire. Without a second thought Skylar is launching herself at Ryan. She drops the hand to grip the back of Ryan's neck and pull him close to press her lips to that pouty mouth. Desire zings through her as Ryan kisses her back with equal fervor.

Ryan's hands cup Skylar's face, directing the tilt of her head to deepen the kiss. Skylar allows her hands to roam over Ryan's body, touching him to make sure he is still there and whole. That he isn't hurt anywhere else. That he is solid and real after the nightmare last night had been.

Finally, the kiss breaks so they can both pant for breath with their foreheads pressed together. Skylar's eyes open to find Ryan's are still closed, but color has risen to his cheeks. "I was so worried I wasn't going to see you again," Ryan says softly.

"You were worried?" Skylar huffs a laugh. "I wasn't sure I was even going to make it to you. Don't go somewhere I can't reach you ever again."

Ryan's eyes flutter open to meet her gaze. "I can't promise that," he says. "I want to, but you know I can't."

Skylar frowns. She knows that it is unfair of her to ask. "I know. I just hate that I can't get to you if you're in trouble."

"I'll do my best to avoid getting in trouble," Ryan tries to promise instead.

"I've known you for months now. That seems seriously unlikely," Skylar points out with a teasing smile. "Now, where were we?" She lifts her chin to press her lips to Ryan's once more.

It is a brief kiss before Ryan pulls back. "Wait," he gasps. "I think we have more to talk about before we, you know—"

"Fuck like rabbits?" Skylar jests. Ryan frowns and right away Skylar realizes she's missed the mark with her joke. "Make love?" she asks more seriously.

"You really operate in extremes, don't you?" Ryan sits back on his heels as if trying to create some space, but Skylar sees the smile he's trying to fight off. "But besides that, I have a surprise for you."

Skylar blinks as Ryan stands up and offers her his hand. Skylar's hand is engulfed in the warlock's larger one as Ryan helps her to her feet. Then, interlocking their fingers, Ryan leads her to the kitchen.

The small table is pushed to the center of the room and covered with a white table cloth. Two candles are lit on the table, which holds two plates of steak and vegetables. Glasses filled with red wine are sitting by each plate. Ryan leads her to a chair and lets go of her hand only to pull out her chair.

Speechless for once, Skylar sits in the chair as her eyes roam over the table. When Ryan takes his seat across from her, her words come back. "Is this a date?"

"I mean, I know we can't really go out anywhere, but I wanted to treat you to a nice meal," Ryan says.

Skylar is stunned. She feels a wet knot forming in her throat and it feels like her heart is swelling so large she isn't sure it won't burst open her ribs. She doesn't even realize tears have escaped from her eyes until Ryan is reaching over to wipe them away.

"Did I make a mistake?" Ryan asks, concerned.

"No," Skylar insists. "This is lovely. In fact, it's perfect. I've never been on a real date before."

Ryan's eyes widen. "Never?"

Skylar shakes her head. "Dating in the demon realm is kind of a pretense. We can summon whatever we need or want. No one has ever put this kind of effort into a dinner before." She wipes her tears away, a little embarrassed by her emotional response.

"Then I'm glad to be the first." Ryan smiles at her.

Dinner conversation isn't the pleasant first date kind of conversation, though. They talk over the events of the previous night. Skylar tells Ryan how the demons had worked with the warlocks to go and get him. Ryan tells Skylar about what happened after all the demons had been sent back.

"Maybe it's a good thing I wasn't there anymore," Skylar mumbles. "I'd have told that council exactly where they could shove their rules and punishments."

Ryan chuckles as he sets his fork and knife down. They'd finished their delicious meal as they talked. The man may not know much about magic, but Skyler is delighted to learn he can cook. "I appreciate that, but I don't think it's over yet."

Skylar's lips turn down in a frown as she rests her elbows on the table and props her chin on her hands. "Yeah, some of those warlocks that tried to trap you got away."

"And who knows how many others in the Coterie are still hiding among the members of the Order," Ryan points out. "But at least they didn't get away with Thomas's spell sheet."

"Right!" Skylar drops her hands to reach into her pocket to pull out the piece of paper. "I still have this."

"No," Ryan says immediately and shakes his head. "You should keep it. As long as it's on this plane of existence, the Coterie might get it back. Keep it in the demon realm."

Skylar nods, eyes wide. She tucks the paper back into her pocket. "I understand," she says solemnly. "Looks like you managed to get the half of the paper with the majority of the circle and a few needed materials."

"Hopefully it's enough to stop them. Or at least slow them down until they can be caught," Ryan sighs.

Silence falls between them on that last thought. "Dinner was delicious," Skylar finally says to bring them back to something less dour. "Will there be dessert?"

A wicked smile spreads on Ryan's lips. "I was hoping you'd be willing to be the final course."

Heat flushes through Skylar as if a switch has been flipped. The heavy topic is wiped from her mind. "Yes, please," she practically moans. Suddenly the distance across the table is too far.

Skylar snaps her fingers and immediately several things happen. The table is cleared, the dishes cleaned and stacked by the sink beside the extinguished candles. Simultaneously, Skylar is seated on the table with her legs on either side of Ryan. Her wings spread wide so they drape off either side of the table. All Skylar has to do is reach out and cup Ryan's face to tilt his head so they can kiss.

Ryan recovers quickly if he was startled. His hands come up to cover Skylar's knees before sliding up the tops of her thighs and grasping at the meat of her legs. A moan is pulled from Skylar's throat through the kiss. Ryan's large hands knead her thighs as they continue to kiss as if they could devour one another that way.

After a sweet eternity of kissing, Ryan moans. He slides his own seat back from the table before reaching forward and gripping Skylar's hips to pull her from the table into his lap. Immediately, the warlock's arms lock around her waist to keep her firmly seated.

Skylar gasps in surprise but feels electricity zip through her as she feels Ryan's hardness pressing against the confines of his pants.

"You're so beautiful," Ryan sighs into the crook of her neck before planting a kiss where his words brushed against her skin. He then sits back to look up at her. "You're like a dark angel, but I can't tell if you're here to tempt me or save me."

Skylar cards her fingers through Ryan's hair as she gazes into those shining eyes. "Can't it be both?"

"Please," Ryan groans before leaning forward to capture her lips in a kiss once more.

Perched atop the warlock, Skylar continues to grind and writhe in his lap to work them both into an irresistible ardor. Ryan's lips travel down Skylar's jaw to her neck, sucking harsh bruises in his wake. Skylar grips his hair harder but doesn't stop him. Instead, Skylar is left gasping, her heart racing under Ryan's attention.

"Ryan," she says. "Tell me what you want."

Ryan pulls back to look up at her. "You. I just want you."

Again Skylar's heart swells as if it could possibly burst. "You have me."

Ryan smiles, leaning forward to press a quick kiss to her chin. "Then nothing. I have everything I need if you're here with me."

A sadness lances through the euphoria Skylar has been floating in. "I can't always be here," she whispers.

"We'll figure this out," Ryan says, pressing kisses to the skin over Skylar's exposed collarbones. "But if you ask me what I want, all I want is you."

Skylar cups Ryan's face to make sure she can look him in the eyes. She searches there and finds only the truth staring back at her. For the first time ever, since finding herself in the demon realm, Skylar has someone who wants her. Not for what she can do for him, but for Skylar herself. This powerful but hapless man who doesn't feel entitled to anything he didn't earn. Who is handsome of face and beautiful of soul. And of everything in the world he could ask for, he asks only for Skylar. "I want you, too," she replies as the truth of the words shake her to her core.

And with that, their wish to one another is sealed with a kiss.

25

A Future to Plan For

Skylar's soft lips move against Ryan's as he holds the demon firmly in his lap. His heart is soaring with his confession. Hearing Skylar say she wants him too only solidifies the swirling emotions in his chest, as if the words were an incantation. He licks into Skylar's mouth, deepening the kiss as he tries to relay all that he is feeling.

Skylar pulls back. "Can we take this elsewhere?" The demon's cheeks are flushed and Ryan wants to give her anything she asks.

"Yeah," he sighs.

A wicked smile appears on Skylar's lips as she slips from Ryan's lap and leads him through the apartment back to the bedroom. It is a short trip, but one that feels too long until Skylar is back in Ryan's arms. His hands reach for Skylar's hips as the demon turns back to face him, their lips drawn together like two powerful magnets. Skylar's hands make quick and nimble work of Ryan's shirt, and she shucks it to the floor faster than Ryan could have done himself. Tongue tangling with Skylar's, Ryan tries to do the same, but the buttons on the sheer top are far too slippery for his taste. Frustrated at their lack of cooperation, he fists both sides of the shirt and pulls. A satisfying *pop, pop, pop* follows as the buttons disappear into the carpet at their feet.

Surprised by his own aggression, Ryan pulls back to stare at the black bra left behind as the button-less shirt falls away. "I've never done that before," he admits in awe.

"You're lucky you're cute," Skylar huffs. "And that I can fix it, because that is my favorite top." The smile on her lips doesn't match the stern scolding and Ryan can't help but smile back.

"Can I eat you out properly this time?" Ryan dares to ask.

He doesn't miss the way Skylar's eyes drop to his lips as the demon nods. "Yes, please," she sighs.

Immediately Skylar is taking her belt off as Ryan undoes the fly of the pants. Together they peel Skylar out of the tight jeans before the demon crawls onto the bed, her ass up and tempting Ryan to come have a taste. Ryan can't wait to sink his fingers into her full, plush cheeks. Skylar glances over her shoulder, her wings draping down her sides and over the bed to get a view of Ryan and chuckles. "What are you waiting for?"

Her words pull Ryan out of the stupor he'd gone into. "Right." He kicks off his shoes and crawls onto the mattress before leading Skylar to the head of the bed, guiding her hands to the headboard. Ryan wants to take his time. He lays on his back and guides Skylar to straddle his face, planting gentle kisses to the insides of her thighs.

Ryan's hands slide up the back of Skylar's legs to palm the full curve of her ass. He stretches his fingers wide to touch as much as his handspan can reach. Pressing his fingertips into her skin, he guides her to settle over his mouth. With the flat of his tongue Ryan licks between her delicate folds, her taste bursting in his mouth and making him lightheaded with arousal. He continues to lick and suckle her sex, and Skylar's soft panting grows heavier as her hips start to grind against his face. Her wings flutter and brush against his legs and torso as he drinks deep of her.

Skylar moans and swivels her hips, coaxing Ryan to do more, go faster, but he won't be persuaded. He keeps up his pace, alternating between long flat licks, suckling kisses, and flicking his tongue back and forth over her. His hands roam over her ass and thighs. Only when he's ready does he point his tongue and press into her core.

"Fuck, Ryan," he hears her cry, breaking up the soft moans from before.

Ryan can't stop his lips from spreading into a smile even as he fucks his tongue shallowly into and out of Skylar. His chin is dripping with saliva and her pleasure as he continues to work her over. His own cock is straining in his slacks as slips one finger into her, curving it to stroke along her walls in a come hither motion as he seals his lips around her bud. He continues to suckle and tease as he adds another finger to fuck into her, ignoring his own hard-on in favor of making sure Skylar feels good.

The longer Ryan pleasures her, the less control Skylar seems to have over her wings. Occasionally they would brush against him, or not touch him at all. Other times they nearly flapped, causing a strong gust of wind in their wake. And throughout it all, Skylar's moans continue to climb.

Just as Ryan is getting ready to add a third finger, Skylar reaches behind her and grabs his wrist. "No, wait," she pants. "I need you, now."

"Are you sure?" Ryan asks. "I can wait until you've come."

"I'm sure," Skylar gives a harsh laugh. She lifts her leg and shuffles off of Ryan. She's breathtaking when Ryan can see her fully again. Her already sun-kissed skin is flushed deeper across her cheeks, down her neck, and across her chest. "I want you inside me, please."

Skylar's desperation does something feral to Ryan. His stomach clenches as he sits up, reaching for the box of condoms Skylar pilfered their first time together in his bedside drawer. He grabs one before making quick work of his pants and boxers, shucking them off and kneeling on the bed. Skylar smirks at him and gets on her hands and knees before him. He'd love to get her on her back, but her wings make that difficult. So instead, he enters her from behind. His cock slides into Skylar's hot, tight heat as the demon's wings flutter out at her sides. Ryan's hands caress over her hips as he sinks all the way to the root, feeling her stretch and accommodate to his length.

"You feel so good," Ryan groans. One hand slides up over the soft, warm skin that forms the junction between her wings.

When she's ready, Skylar starts gyrating her hips again. Ryan moans and starts building up a steady pace thrusting into her. Skylar has gripped one of his pillows and is pressing her cheek into it, her mouth hanging open as she pants with pleasure. Her eyes flutter shut and squeeze tight at the same time her walls pulse around him. Too quickly Ryan fears he'll reach his height before her if she keeps this up.

His heart swells at the sight of this beautiful, strong woman. This woman who has been dealt a raw deal so early in her life and still has compassion for those around her. Who has helped save Ryan from his own stubbornness and willful ignorance.

"Fuck, Skylar, ah, ah, I-" Ryan is trying to say as the heat swirls lower and faster in his belly.

Instead, he moves his hand from Skylar's back to reach down between her legs. She's still so wet and he can feel himself moving in and out of her as he presses his fingers to her clit. He rubs circles around the sensitive bud with renewed vigor.

"Ah, ah, ah," Skylar is panting as her body stiffens beneath him. Then she's coming, her walls spasm around Ryan's member as he fucks into her faster, chasing his own high. She clenches down on him tightly, creating a cascading effect that has Ryan spiraling over the edge and twitching his own release into the condom.

Ryan can't stop the swelling of emotions that wells up in him as the waves of pleasure wash through him. How is it this amazing woman has chosen him? He drops down to press kisses over Skylar's shoulders. "You're amazing," he sighs.

Skylar hums, slipping away from Ryan so she can turn and face him, kneeling on the bed with him. "Right back at you," Skylar chuckles and ducks in to press her lips to his in a much calmer but not less heated kiss. He fumbles to keep hold of the condom over his softening cock as they kiss, but she just laughs at him. With a snap her fingers and, just as before, the condom and mess are cleaned away. As if fresh from a long, relaxing bath, she pulls him down to the bed to slot their bodies together. Ryan lies on his back as she curls up against his side, her wings draping over the edge of the bed once more. They lazily kiss as the cadence of Ryan's pounding heart comes back to something close to normal.

Ryan holds Skylar and strokes her back, even over her wings. Sleep is tugging at the edges of his consciousness, but this is the only time he has with her, and he doesn't want to miss a moment of it.

"What would have happened if the Coterie had managed to get their spell off?" he wonders idly.

Skylar smirks. "This is some really sexy pillow talk."

"Sorry," Ryan says bashfully. "It's where my thoughts drifted."

She shrugs her shoulders. "Not sure," she admits before pressing a kiss to Ryan's chest. "Warren said it was supposed to eliminate the demon realm and put all demons under the warlock's control who cast it. There's no telling if it would actually work or not."

"Hmm," Ryan frowns as the gears start to turn in his mind. "What if it could?"

"Then hundreds of demons would exist to serve at the whim of one person who is ambitious enough to pull it off," Skylar tilts her head up to look at him. "And I wouldn't trust any single person with that much power."

"I don't disagree." Ryan threads his fingers through the back of Skylar's hair. "But what if we could make just part of that spell work?"

"Which part?" Skylar asks cautiously.

Ryan looks up as his gaze wanders over the blank ceiling of his dark room. "What if demons didn't *have* to go back to the demon realm?"

Skylar sits up to stare down at him. "You're talking about getting rid of the demon realm," she says softly. Her eyes are wide and Ryan wonders if it's hope there and not fear.

"Maybe?" Ryan runs his hand up and down Skylar's arm. "What if you could stay here with me? All the time?"

Skylar bites her bottom lip and stares at Ryan as if considering his words. "I think that's a very complicated question," she finally says. "I want to be able to be here and spend time with you, but then what? It's not like I can just walk around in the mortal realm. I wouldn't be able to pop down to the corner store, or go on coffee shop dates." She flutters her wings as if making a point. "Not everyone knows about magic. And those who do would be scared of me wandering around outside a protection circle."

"Can't you just glamour it away?" Even as he asks, Ryan runs his fingers over the feathery soft wings.

Skylar frowns, dropper her gaze. "No. It's the one thing we can't do: hide our animal traits."

"Oh." Ryan gently tugs her back into bed and pressies his forehead to the top of her head, quietly breathing her in. She smells of vanilla and some sort of spice.

Quietly, Skylar adds, "and not all demons deserve to be free. There are some who are there because they need to be. They killed people."

Ryan's heart clenches at Skylar's words. "But what about demons like you and Kris? You didn't do anything wrong. You don't deserve to be trapped there."

"Don't give me false hope, Ryan Smith," Skylar says, her voice wavering. Tears fill her lash line.

Ryan feels his heart sink. He reaches out and cups Skylar's face so he can wipe away the stray tear that has fallen. "I'm sorry. We don't have to talk about it right now. I was just thinking out loud. I'm sorry."

Even as he says it, he knows the idea is too deep inside him to let it go for long. If Thomas Andrew Smith could figure out how to break all the demons out, why couldn't Ryan figure out how to just realm-break some of them? He wouldn't have to tell Skylar about it until he has something more solid to offer.

Skylar places her hand over Ryan's and gives him a sad smile. "I know you're coming from a good place, but you know what they say: the road to Hell is paved with good intentions."

"I thought we already determined Hell isn't a real place." Ryan gives a soft laugh, trying to lighten the mood.

"It can be, for people," Skylar insists. "But I think that's enough heavy talk for tonight. I want to enjoy my time with you. At least for now. We can take on the big problems tomorrow. Or the day after. Deal?"

Ryan leans forward and presses a quick kiss to Skylar's lips. "Deal."

They settle into the bed and, while he may not sleep, Ryan enjoys holding Skylar for the rest of the night. When the morning comes, he dutifully sends her home before Skylar can be cruelly ripped away from him.

"Thank you for everything," Ryan whispers against Skylar's temple as her head rests on his chest. Skylar gives his hand a small squeeze. A silent permission. "Skylar, I send you back to the demon realm."

The demon vanishes, taking all her belongings and Ryan is left with only the warmth of her body. Sleep slowly takes him under, even as the sun rises through the tiny window in his bedroom.

It is several hours later when Ryan awakes to a sudden crashing noise. He jolts from his bed, disoriented and groggy. The clock on his nightstand reads one in the afternoon. He sits and listens for a long moment, trying to figure out what pulled him from his slumber. There was the sound of passing cars on the street. Neighbors moving around upstairs. A car horn honking in the distance. Daytime noises in the city.

Shrugging, Ryan gets out of bed and takes a long shower. The events of the last few days feel surreal in the light of day. He makes himself some lunch before forcing himself to head out to the bookstore. He wants a sense of normalcy and work will bring that.

He checks his phone as he packs his bag to leave.

Nadia

Hey Ryan. This is Nadia, from the bookstore. Here's my schedule for the next week. Pick an evening and place and we can have that talk. My treat.

She then sends him a list of open nights.

Nadia

I look forward to picking your brain.

Ryan

I'm free whenever. Lots of free time, I suspect. Whatever works best for you, just let me know.

He smirks, already plotting how to get the bookseller and her clueless boss at the same place. Then he shoots off another text to Skylar.

Ryan

I hope you slept well. I'll talk to you soon.

Not sure if the demon is awake or not, Ryan tucks his phone into his pocket and grabs the bag. After tying up his bootlaces, he leaves the basement apartment to make his way into the real world. However, when he turns to lock the door, he finds that the keyhole of his deadbolt is mangled. It looks partially melted and he can't even attempt to fit his key in. The handle is crushed and discolored, but functioning as he shuts the door.

"What the fuck," Ryan mumbles as he inspects the damage to his door.

The deadbolt is useless, but he doesn't even need a lock on his door anymore. Never has he been more thankful for the wards he put up in his house. He turns to head up the short set of stairs that lead to the alley. The hair on the back of his neck feels like it is standing on end as he rushes to make it out to the sidewalk. As if the sunlight and the people will protect him from whatever might have came at his door.

Ryan doesn't notice the car parked across the street that has been there since just before sunrise. The woman wears a headscarf and a large pair of sunglasses as she watches Ryan make his way around the corner and onto the busier thoroughfare.

Her gaze shifts back to the alley. She hadn't expected the warlock to know how to make wards, let alone have them in his place. Ryan Smith is full of surprises and Dahlia Jones finds she is not fond of that.

Not one bit.

The summoning continues with

TO WANT FOR SOMETHING

Book Two of the Urban Warlocks

Want to know when the next book will be released?
Join the Order, M.B. Kelly's monthly newsletter: subscribepage.io/ndgaCZ

About the author

M.B. Kelly is extremely susceptible to peer pressure, which is how you've managed to read this book. After decades of sharing her stories with her friends, they finally told her to publish something and leave them alone. It took a degree in Creative Writing and a decade of supporting other authors in their writer's journeys, but finally M.B. Kelly amassed enough general knowledge about publishing to accomplish this feat.

When she's not working or writing, she's immersing herself in all forms of storytelling. She loves movies, television, videogames, music, boardgames, etc.